Nailer

Nailer

Tom Phelan

GLANVIL

Printed in the United States of America.

Material in this book is quoted from "The Lady of Shallot" by Alfred Lord Tennyson; "She Dwelt Among the Untrodden Ways" by William Wordsworth; "Leda and the Swan" by W. B. Yeats; "Ode to the West Wind" by Percy Bysshe Shelley; Ulysses by James Joyce.

Copyright ©2011 by Glanvil Enterprises, Ltd., Freeport, New York.
All rights reserved
Published by Glanvil Enterprises, Ltd.

ISBN: 061543441X
ISBN-13: 9780615434414
Library of Congress Control Number: 2010943515

As ever,

to Patricia and Joseph and Michael

with love

The true history of the thirties, forties and fifties in this country has yet to be written. When it does, I believe it will be shown to have been a very dark time indeed, in which an insular Church colluded with an insecure State to bring about a society that was often bigoted, intolerant, cowardly, philistine and spiritually crippled.

— JOHN MCGAHERN

Author's Note

The action in *Nailer* takes place in Ireland's midlands, and the story provides a sampling of the area's dialect. For readers unfamiliar with these local words and expressions, a glossary is included beginning on page 417.

Nailer

✝

THURSDAY
NOVEMBER 9, 2007

1.

In the gloom, in a battered armchair the old man slept, sprawled. On his stubbled chin, drool glistened and stretched toward his swollen, heaving belly. Nostril hairs wisped out of the red and bulbous nose. His fat ears, corpselike in their pallor, were as finely haired as a pig's twisted tail. Sparse strands of silver hair meandered across his pink, scabbed head.

The open-necked, white shirt was grey with grime and age, and the underlying pattern of the greasy jacket was reminiscent of tartan. The top button of the jacket kept the flaps together over the bulging belly, the collar turned up as if the old man had been cold or careless. The turf fire had been reduced to dead ashes hours ago. Like two ponds streaked with the glow of two distant moons, the greasy thighs of the black trousers were lined with reflections of the kitchen light. Each big toe, with yellow, unpared, dirt-lined nails, protruded through holes in the ancient, faded green slippers.

An unpleasant smell, mindful of sour milk, wafted off the old man. On the floor beside the broken-armed chair sat a large glass ashtray. An empty pint bottle, WHISKEY handwritten on its misaligned label, stood in the ashtray among the butts.

The kitchen on the far side of a four-foot divider reflected the occupant's personal uncleanliness: sticky floor, sink piled high with crockery and saucepans, countertop littered with the crumbs of many meals. Bits of flung leftovers and water-soaked cigarette butts were scattered on the floor near the rubbish can. The can itself was pockmarked with dried splatters of color—red of tomato, brown of tea bags, blue of something, green of something. Black beetles, which had set up a colony under the sink, were sniffing at the rubbish with flicking antennae.

The pull-down shades on the two kitchen windows were smoke-browned and cracked along the sides. Both shades had been yanked down carelessly and their shredded bottom edges bore the prints of filthy fingers. Four stacks of newspapers, each four feet high, stood against the end of the counter. The shade of the twenty-watt bulb hanging from the ceiling was coated in years of grease and dead flies.

It was nighttime.

The old man stirred. Without opening his eyes, he brought a hand up and rubbed the drool off his chin. He closed his mouth and sucked in his cheeks as if he had bit into a sloe. He grabbed the loose arms of his chair and levered his body out of its various pains. Then, like a cat using the back of its paw for the same purpose, he poked at the corners of his eyes with his knuckles. He opened his eyes, and dropping his right hand to the floor, he gingerly fingered his way to the whiskey bottle. He held it up to the light.

"Scutter," he muttered. He put the bottle to his mouth and waited for the trickle to reach his wet, red lower lip. Like an unsatisfied calf searching for more when its feeding bucket is empty, the old man flicked his tongue into and around the neck before letting the bottle fall out of his hand and onto the floor. He sighed and grasped the chair arms as he prepared to stand.

It was then he saw the two greenish things.

They were on the floor in front of the wooden chair that he used as a hassock whenever he felt sleep coming on. He narrowed his eyes and peered as if trying to remember. After some thought, he decided they were paper galoshes used in sterile rooms or operating theaters.

Beside the galoshes was the cardboard box filled with the food and whiskey and newspapers and cigarettes that Frank brought once a week—brought and left outside in the bushes in the dark, Frank ashamed to knock, ashamed to look at his own brother. A flash of alcoholic relief spread across the old man's face, then vanished almost immediately.

"I didn't bring the box in," he muttered. His eyes had now adjusted to the weak light and he saw the shape of a man sitting on the wooden chair, saw that the paper galoshes belonged to him.

"Frank," he whispered, afraid it might indeed be his brother. The intruder did not answer. "Is that you, Frank?" the old man said. But still the man on the straight-backed chair was silent.

Then the old man knew he was going to be robbed. There had been many rural robberies in *The Telegraph* lately. But he wasn't afraid. It was simply his turn and he wasn't going to put up a fight. As well as that, he wasn't afraid of losing his money, because he had none, and he would have none until the next payment of the old age pension. "You can look all you like. I have nothing," he said.

The man in the shadows didn't speak, didn't move.

The old man peered at the face but the intruder might as well have been wearing a mask made of the dark. "Who are you?" the old man asked. "How did you get in here?"

The intruder said nothing and the old man moved forward on his chair, prepared to push himself up.

"Don't get up," the intruder said. His voice was flat, commanding.

"Go to hell," the older man said, and as he struggled to raise himself onto his feet he felt a severe, breathtaking pain in his chest. He remembered an electric fence beside the Barrow River he had accidentally touched in the dark. His body collapsed back into the chair with such dead weight that the chair moved several inches on the floor. "My heart," he whispered. "My heart..." His fingers, their tips demarcated on the faded shirt by the lines of dirt beneath the nails, bunched the shirt, squeezed the pain. "Heart attack...I'm having a heart attack," he gasped, and he pleaded with his eyes into the gloom.

"You're not having a heart attack. I hit you." The visitor's voice was devoid of emotion, devoid of the breathiness that should have accompanied a physical attack.

Fear seeped into the old man's eyes. The old lips moved, got into gear to say something. He continued to bunch the shirt in his squeezing fingers. He stared into the place where the man's head should be, and the fear leaked out of his eyes into the rest of his face. Finally he squeaked, "Who are you?"

There was no reply for several minutes. Then "What's your name?" came calmly back to the old man.

The fleshy lips pushed each other around before the words came. "Dan...Daniel Geoghan," he said.

"You had another name."

The old eyes narrowed. "My name is Daniel Geoghan," he said, and as he spoke his left foot erupted in pain that surged up his spine to the top of his skull. His scream was the sound a dog makes when its belly is in the teeth of a bigger dog and the bigger dog shakes its head. Bending forward, Daniel Geoghan squeezed his shin with two hands, desperately tried to cut off the alarming messages flashing to his brain. "Oh, Jesus. Oh, Jesus," he prayed, or cursed. He moaned. Then he saw his smashed big toe, saw the shards of bone in the mashed flesh, saw the gathering purple, saw the bloody nail on the floor. Pain sloshed through Geoghan's body like rancid watery muck slopping around in a ship's bilge in a storm. "Oh, Jesus,

Mary and Joseph," he whispered. And then he screamed, "What did you do to me?"

It was a long time before the intruder spoke. "You had another name," he said.

The old man was on the verge of passing out. He sat up, brought his hands to his face. He rocked back and forth. "Boniface. Bro...Brother Boniface," he said.

THURSDAY
NOVEMBER 21, 2007

2.

At last, at long last, Brian Deegan was having his lucky break. Not only was he on his way to Garryhinch in the dark of morning, but he was on the high road to a new job—and glory. Bink was lying on a sack in the backseat under a blanket, the rear window on the passenger side slightly open to vent the dog's breathtaking farts. Deegan, wearing leather gloves, had pulled the hood of his jacket over his paddycap; he would rather be cold than have to listen to snide remarks from the gardai about smelling like a dog.

"Luck!" Deegan said, slapping the steering wheel with his open hand. He had the habit of speaking his thoughts aloud when he was alone. "The old cratur's bad luck is my good luck. Sorry, but that's the way it is, Missus Daly."

The Civil Defense dog in Cavan town had a sore foot, had stepped on glass in a plowed field. If all went well this morning, from now on the whole southern part of the country would be Deegan's. All Bink had to do was show he was as good as the Cavan dog, or better.

Four days earlier the old woman with Alzheimer's had wandered away from her home in Garryhinch. As neighbors searched the bog and the farms and a nearby forestry plantation, Brian Deegan, working in Cappancur twenty miles away, had been biting his nails, afraid Missus Daly would be found—and praying she wouldn't.

Yesterday, as he'd walked back along the scaffolding to begin laying another course of blocks, he'd brought the small radio with him along with his trowel and level. Midlands Radio in Tullamore was keeping its listeners tuned in with promises of breaking news from the searchers. Extra gardai had been brought in from surrounding towns and it had been newsworthy that they were all wearing wellingtons.

"Wellingtons! Christ almighty!" he said to no one. "Who gives a shag about wellingtons? Everyone in County Offaly wears wellingtons, gets married in them, buried too."

The latest bulletin had said that the missing woman was the great-grandmother of an Offaly football player. "But is she dead?" Deegan growled, and he swung the edge of his trowel into a block. Sparks flew.

Deegan at forty-seven was six feet tall, had crow-black hair. His neck, his face and his arms to his elbows were brown, but glimpses of skin on the edges of the brownness were as white as the belly of a fish. He weighed what he had weighed at twenty-two, still fitted into the duds he had worn twenty years ago, and those few garments were still in the bedroom wardrobe waiting for the day when they would be fashionable again. Brian Deegan had been born poor enough to make the discarding of good clothes impossible.

All day long Deegan picked up cinderblocks in his left hand and placed them in their bed of fresh cement on the wall he was building. Except during tea breaks, his trowel flashed nonstop.

Over the years a succession of helpers had complained that Deegan overworked them. "He never stops! He's like a fooken shark. You'd get deh scabs offim deh way he's always bein' nervous."

Deegan was a self-contained blockie: he owned his own cement mixer and he used a tent-like structure of his own design and making that allowed him to work in the rain. His helper was on the job every day before Deegan arrived, already had the tent raised, the cement and blocks at the ready. Under threat of an angry snarl, the

assistant kept his employer supplied all day long. When
Deegan stopped working at five o'clock, the helper stayed
behind to clean the tools. Even though Deegan paid his
navvies half as much again as most builders did, only one
had lasted two years.

At six o'clock Missus Daly had still not been found and
Deegan was at home in Edenderry, still fretting. Like a
disinterested child, he pushed his cabbage and potatoes
around on his plate. "Shag!" he said.

"What's wrong, Brian?" his wife asked.

"Nothing. I just wish the shaggers would call me and
get it over with. That detective Breen asked me yesterday
to be on standby, but how long can a fellow be on standby
without going half daft? Shagging guards! By the time
they call me, the Cavan dog will be better. They *know* doul
wan's dead."

"You're *hoping* she's dead, Brian. That's not right.
You'll have bad luck."

"I just want them to see how good Bink is."

"But not at the expense of that poor old Missus Daly
who could be your granny."

"It has to be at someone's expense, and she's only an
oul wan with Alzheimer's."

"Oh, Brian. Listen to yourself. Stop it! And you haven't
even asked about the lads."

"God! You're right, Peg. How did Peter manage with
Professor McGetterick today?"

Brian's mobile rang. He looked at the screen. "It's
them!" he said, and he stood up, a piece of pork stuck in
his front teeth, the bentwood chair falling on its back on
the kitchen floor with a clatter.

He took a deep breath to calm himself. "Deegan
Human Remains Detection, Limited," he said. His wife
raised her eyes to the ceiling—anyone would think he
had a pack of dogs and a fleet of small lorries for trans-
porting them.

When he snapped the phone shut he laughed aloud. He slapped his thigh. "That was Detective Breen," he said. "One hundred and eighty-five euros an hour plus mileage, and I never even mentioned money. Now they'll know there's more than one carrion dog in Ireland. Thank God." Deegan clenched his fists near his shoulders and sought out God in the space between the kitchen clothesline and the ceiling. "I'm to be at Garryhinch Cross at half six in the morning. God! This is what I've been waiting for." Deegan sat down and dug into his dinner.

"Brian," Peg said, a touch of excitement in her voice. She put her hand on his shoulder. "I'm glad it's finally paying off after all your work. A hundred and eighty-five euros an hour! That's better than a vet."

Brian Deegan was beaming like an early summer rising sun.

†

FRIDAY

NOVEMBER 22, 2007

3.

At half-past five, Brian Deegan and Bink were speeding in the dark along the narrow road between Edenderry and Daingean. He would be early, but that was part of his plan; he had to impress on the gardai that he was dependable: *If Brian Deegan says he'll be there with his dog, then he'll be there.* That was the best advertisement—one hundred percent dependability, like in bricklaying. He turned on the interior light and glanced around at Bink on the backseat. The dog was awake, head on paws. He turned his eyes to the sound of his master moving.

"Good dog, good dog," Deegan said, and Bink thumped his tail under the blanket. Brian wished again that the Dutch trainers hadn't called him Bink—it sounded too much like a woman's word for a fart.

In the headlights, the low bog heather growing at the edges of the road fled past in a black blur. Lonely stunted sallies and whitethorns and furze loomed and flamed in the lights like rushing ghosts, then disappeared again into the darkness. But Brian Deegan was paying no attention to the flora. His mind was on the upcoming search. He desperately hoped, prayed, that Bink would take off like a squart from a duck and discover the dead body immediately. But that was fantasy—no dog could ever find a corpse that quickly. Still, everything had to go right this first time: the gestures, the commands, the tone of voice. All the things Deegan had learned during that fortnight in the Netherlands flooded his mind until he consciously ejected them—told himself that he knew his stuff, he knew his dog, the dog knew his stuff, and

they knew each other. All he was asking of God was that
Bink would be the talk of the country after the six o'clock
news tonight. He and Bink would be on the front page
of *The Telegraph*; that's what he had been fantasizing ever
since he saw the carrion dogs on television after September 11 in New York. The Irish Civil Defense got their idea
at the same time, and they got their dog first because they
had the government behind them. After today, Deegan
would have his own carrion dog business. Soon he'd be
doing what he always wanted to do—training dogs. He
would outdo the search-and-rescue trainers in Rijen, and
in a few years, police departments from all over the world
would come to him for their dogs.

"This is the six o'clock news. Rescuers using Deegan
Dogs found four more bodies in the aftermath of the ter-
rorist attack in London's Underground this morning."
Everything was going to move very fast after Bink found
this oul biddy today. "God bless you, Missus! Half the
country will be mine."

The red eyes of a crossing fox in the headlights
yanked Deegan out of his reverie. He looked for mark-
ers that would tell him where he was on this long, lonely,
ghosty road. A shiver ran down his back when he saw
the twin blackthorn bushes marking the corner of what
had once been the Dunnes' garden. Back in the days
before cars, a house had stood off out here in the bog,
five miles from the nearest town. Nine Dunnes had died
here in a fire one night, but it wasn't till a woman in
an ass-and-cart jogged by in the middle of the next day
that the house was missed, the ashes found. All that was
left now was the vague outline where the mud walls had
stood. Brian Deegan hated passing Burnt House. He
crossed himself as he passed, muttered, "God between
us and all harm." Then he wondered would Bink have
been able to sniff out the burned bodies beneath the pile
of ashes?

"I hope he behaves and goes to work the minute I tell him, not run around in rings barking like an eegit. I'd better stop being anxious—first thing Bink will pick up on is me being nervous and then he'll get nervous, too."

Deegan began to sing "Kevin Barry," thinking it might relax his dog. But he had just reached "Mountjoy jail one Monday morning" when Bink suddenly yelped and began to scamper and claw around on the backseat. Burnt House was still sufficiently in Deegan's mind to connect the dreadful noise he was hearing with the screams of the burning family. On his neck and arms the hairs stood up, and he brought the car to a wobbly stop in the middle of the road.

"He's having a fucking fit!"

The dog was still whining when Deegan twisted around. Bink had his nose in the opening in the window, his head turned flat, the nails of his back feet seeking purchase on the smooth vinyl seat.

Deegan fumbled his seatbelt out of its buckle. When he opened the door he toppled out of the car, landed on his hands and knees, but he didn't feel the coldness of the road nor the sharp-edged, winter night breeze. He jumped up. "Bink!" he roared, and he ran around the front of the car. He pulled the handle and Bink pushed the door open. Deegan stumbled back and swung up his arm for balance; Bink, interpreting the swinging arm as the command to search, scampered into the darkness behind the car.

"Christ almighty!"

In the Netherlands, Deegan had once witnessed the smell of a bitch in heat overcoming the smell of a cadaver. Now his fantasies rattled like a loose pane of glass on a windy day.

"Where did you go, you bollicks?" he shouted into the blackness. "You scuttering eegit!" Then, running around through the headlights again, he bent into the car for his big flashlamp. He yanked it out without thinking to unplug it from the lighter portal. "Shite!"

He ran back into the darkness, the fierce beam of the lamp jerking all over, the tops of his triple-socked wellingtons smacking at his legs. The vague outline of a lane appeared on his right and Deegan ran onto it. He heard the dog barking the way he was supposed to bark when he found a corpse. Deegan stopped to listen. Sweat trickled down his spine, but that one bark had lowered his anxiety a notch. Sweeping the light around in a semicircle he looked for Bink with the tip of the beam. Quickly, he came to a narrower pathway bearing to the right again, no wheel tracks in it. He pointed the beam down through a tunnel of overhanging bushes. To his surprise, he saw a house at the end. Another bark came from Bink, and Deegan believed he had pinpointed the source.

The torch's jerking beam flashed across the house, hitting it in different places. As he ran, Deegan put the lit-up pieces together in his head and a small three-roomer took shape: door, three windows, dark slates. Deegan stopped when he smelled the smell of rotting meat.

"Christ! That's strong. But the old biddy couldn't be here. Garryhinch is fifteen miles."

Standing in the waft of putrescence, he became fearfully aware that he was alone on a dark track off a dark lane off a dark and lonely stretch of bog road. He spun the beam around quickly to make sure no childhood monsters were lurking. The burned house was only a quarter of a mile away.

"Christ almighty!"

The dog barked from the back of the house.

Carefully, Deegan eased his way through the dead, white-frosted, crackling, thigh-high weeds at the side of the house, the hand holding the flashlamp held high to avoid the lurking sting of dead nettles.

"That's a terrible shagging smell!" With the flashlamp under one elbow, Deegan fumbled a plastic bag out of his coat pocket, removed a Vick's-coated mask and raised both arms over his head to put it on. He knocked off his paddycap. The flashlamp fell silently into the weeds but its beam stayed steady. "Scutter!"

Slowly, he stepped around the back corner of the house, and there, lying on the ground the way he was supposed to when he'd found a body, was Bink. He looked expectantly at his master.

"Stay!" Deegan commanded.

In Rijen, Deegan had been trained to approach a "find" cautiously and not let the dog scurry all over the place and upset the scene of a crime, if one had been committed. Now Deegan took careful steps toward Bink, and the stink seeped through his mask. He reached the dog. "Heel," he said. Bink moved back and Deegan swept the ground with his light but saw nothing. Then he turned and saw the window, saw the four-inch opening at the top.

"That's where it's coming from."

Deegan placed the lens of the flashlamp against the glass and peered in. At first he saw nothing except the far wall of the room, wallpapered. He pointed the beam onto the floor. He was looking at what he was looking at for several seconds before he saw what he was seeing. It took an enormous effort to pull his eyes away. Then he spun away from the window and pushed the length of his body, from his heels to the back of his head, against the wall of the house. "Oh, good scutter," he gasped.

Because he was the type of man who knew the exact contents of each of his pockets, he did not have to search for his mobile.

4.

Even though the ringing phone was part of the dream in Tom Breen's sleeping brain, his hand went under the pillow. He woke up, flipped the cover and looked at the screen: STATION 5:56 A.M.

"Yes?" He sat up in the bed, swung his legs over the side.

"Nolan, sir—duty officer."

"Yes, Tim?"

"Supe on way in. Body in house on Edenderry/Daingean Road on Daingean side of Burnt House."

"Tell me everything."

"Caller calm, sir. Name is Deegan from Edenderry. On way to Garryhinch with search dog to look for Missus Daly."

"Yes, I spoke to him last night."

"Driving along, dog got agitated in backseat. Stopped car to look after dog. Dog jumped out and took off." Tim Nolan knew that Detective Breen liked undressed language in oral reports, and most times Nolan was as annoying as hell with his shortcuts. "Followed dog to small house and saw body though window with frashla...flashlamp. Body rotten. Nails hammered into body. Something odd about crotch, like the prick...penis, but there was something. Saw the bollicks...balls...bag. That's how he knew it was a man. Didn't investigate further. Thought might be crime scene. Sergeant Hickey was over in Clonbullogue in the prowl. I told him to get over to Deegan right away."

"Good, Tim. Did the supe tell you to do anything?"

"Call you, sir."

"Hold on a minute till I think." Breen put his forehead in his free hand and closed his eyes. He returned to the phone. "Tim, tell me again what your man Deegan said about nails."

"There were nails hammered into the body, sir."

"Like it was crucified?"

"Didn't say like Jesus on the cross."

"Hold on, Tim." Again Breen reassumed his thinking position. "Tim, has Bill Hickey a mobile?"

"Yes."

"Good. Don't use the radio. Call him on his phone. If he has the lights flashing tell him to switch them off, but to get to Burnt House as quick as he can. Do you have Deegan's number?"

"On the monitor, sir."

"Tell Deegan not to call anyone about the body or anything else either. Tim, make those two calls right away and get back to me. Call Deegan first."

"Yes, sir."

Tom Breen placed the phone on the night table beside the lamp. After switching off the alarm clock he padded into the sitting room in the dark, crossed to the kitchen and turned on the light over the cooker. He switched on the electric kettle into which he'd measured a mug of water the night before. Like a scrupulous priest following a book of rubrics, he opened the cabinet door in front of his face; took out a mug; closed the cabinet door, held it until it silently touched its stopper; removed the lid of the largest of five canisters on the counter; separated two Barry's teabags and put one in the mug; returned the remaining teabag to the canister; and replaced the canister lid. As he headed back to the bedroom he began pulling off the T-shirt he used as a pajama top. The phone rang. He switched on the overhead light in the bedroom.

Breen was wearing black underpants. Like a yellowing Greek warrior on a black krater, Breen had thighs that showed signs of hard exercise. At six feet two inches tall, he knew that his co-workers referred to him behind his back as Tom Thumb, only most of them said, "Tom Tum," because this was the midlands.

"Nolan, sir. Made the calls. Deegan hasn't phoned anyone besides us."

"Sounds like a reliable fellow. Tim, call Sergeant Hickey again. When he gets to the house he should tell Deegan to go on to meet the lads at Garryhinch with his dog; tell Deegan we'll catch up with him later for a statement. And Tim, tell Sergeant Hickey to pull his car in off the road so as not to draw attention. The supe and I will be over there in a while. And Tim—" Breen paused to get Nolan's attention.

"Yes, sir?"

"Keep this one under your hat till the supe and I have a look."

"Yes, sir."

Tom Breen went back to the kitchen. He watched the flowing stream of boiling water bubbling into the mug and felt the chill in the house. He moved his bare feet on the floor. While the tea steeped, he took his usual quick shower. Even though he never went to work without showering he was impatient with the time it took, especially the drying. Over the years, while toweling, he had invented several robotic ways for drying the showered body. They all involved gently flailing towels and strong jets of warm air. There was a hot-air jet in the floor for between the legs. Sometimes his invention included a nubile nymph with eager fingers and lips.

Every day, Breen donned a freshly laundered blue denim shirt and a red tie. His two dozen pairs of dove-grey socks were identical, no matching necessary. His three pairs of black shoes were identical, except that two of the pairs had been resoled. His five suits were dark blue, and he wore a different one every day, rotating them from left to right on the wardrobe pole. Once a month he brought the suits to Mike and Maggie's Dry Cleaning in Tullamore.

When he finished dressing, Breen filled the kettle again, and while it boiled he toasted two slices of bread, plastered them with butter and marmalade and ate at the kitchen table with yesterday's *Telegraph* propped up against the milk carton. Even two years after the Ferns Report had been published, Catholic priests and their meddlesome peckers and fingers were still making headlines. His eyes were drawn to the article even though he knew it would be just one more depressing story about a Catholic priest caught sexually abusing a minor. Breen would have enough dealings with pedophilia today without having to read sordid details in the paper. He knew that the body nailed to the floor in the cottage near Burnt House was that of a pedophile who had once been a religious brother. Exactly two weeks earlier he had spoken to Brother Boniface.

Breen made a lot of noise with the newspaper as he flipped away from the latest priestly pederast who, undoubtedly, would magically disappear into the deep, obscuring folds of the church.

The kettle boiled again. Breen put two tea bags in the flask and filled it to the top. He made a sandwich of bread, butter and marmalade and wrapped it in tinfoil. He removed the tea bags from the flask with the handle of a fork, poured out some of the tea, put in four spoons of sugar, and poured milk into the flask until it was full. Then he placed tea, mug and sandwich in a much recycled plastic bag.

Before he left the house Breen washed and dried the plate, mug, two spoons and the knife and the fork. He returned everything to its place, wiped the counter and tabletop with a damp sponge, rinsed the sponge, squeezed it and returned it to its container beside the sink. He measured a mug of water into the electric kettle in preparation for the evening boiling.

Detective Sergeant Tom Breen removed a scarf from the rack inside the front door. As carefully as if he were knotting his tie, he placed the scarf around his neck. He slipped into his lined, black gabardine overcoat and, using both hands to put his paddycap on his head, pulled the peak and the back at the same time. Then he picked up the food bag and went out to his car.

The detective shivered in the chilled November air. It was still dark and early enough for the Killeigh/Tulla-more road to be traffic-free. The car's clock read 6:46 a.m.

To those who worked with him, Tom Breen was either a confirmed bachelor or a celibate gay or a celibate het-erosexual or he was asexual or a secret womanizer who made secret trips to secret places in Dublin. Some of his fellow workers knew he was a serious fisherman. His part-ner, Jimmy Gorman, knew Breen was a reader of heavy tomes, listened to recordings of Broadway shows and had a fitness machine in his house.

When he pulled into the flood-lit car park at the garda station, Breen saw Superintendent Donovan casting admiring glances at his new, light blue Citron C3, which he had just parked. Breen rolled down his window. "I saw a scrape on your passenger door yesterday," he called.

"Hah! She's still perfect, Tom. You're jealous."

Christy Donovan was six feet one inch tall and pink complexioned. His hair was so black that stationhouse rumor said the color came out of a bottle, but it didn't. His eyes imparted a perpetual air of expectancy, as if Donovan knew a departmental missile had been launched somewhere and would whack him in the back at the most unsuspecting moment. He had the nose of a conquista-dor.

Once, in his early days on the force, Donovan had grabbed an obstreperous and abusive drunk by the testicles and reduced him to lambish gentleness. The drunk, walking on tiptoes and making short, sharp whistling sounds, followed the guard out of his own house and into the patrol car. Thereafter Donovan was called B.G., for Ball Grabber, a nickname that had faded away once he'd been promoted to superintendent.

Despite his wife's newly honed culinary talents, Donovan did not have an ounce of excessive meat on him. After the children had flown the nest, Liz Donovan had discovered Ireland's Culinary School in Athlone and had become a gourmet cook. She now served wine every night with dinner, but despite Donovan's most sincere efforts he still had trouble distinguishing Beaujolais from Bulmer's Sedona.

The superintendent was wrapped against the early morning icy breeze, only his mouth, nose and eyes exposed. He waited for Breen to join him. Breen, with lunch bag in hand, opened the boot of his car and took out a second bag, MARTIN's on it in red letters. While he locked his car he asked, "Did Tim Nolan give you any details, sir?"

"Told me Deegan-with-the-dog found a body. I told him to give me the details when I got in." Donovan tugged at his overcoat collar and yanked at his scarf.

"Before we go in you might want to know the victim is a former religious brother. He's nailed to the floor—"

"Fecking shite, Tom! Another!" the superintendent spluttered.

"He's nailed to the floor in a house on the Daingean Road near Burnt House. Pedophile, dead for some time. Geoghan is the name."

"This is the same as your man in Carrowreagh? What was *his* name?"

"Brother John the Baptist."

"Did we warn this fellow Geoghan when John the Baptist was found?"

"We did." Breen slipped the handles of the plastic bags up his left arm, took out his notebook and flipped back through several written pages. He moved into the light of one of the car park lamps. "Jimmy Gorman and I warned him a fortnight ago, same day the story was in *The Telegraph*—"

"Thank you, Jesus," Donovan interrupted. "My arse is covered."

"Geoghan worked in Dachadoo under the name Brother Boniface." Breen looked at Donovan.

"Shite! There *is* some fucker out there with a list. A maniac. When was your man in Carrowreagh killed…Jack the Baptist?"

Breen checked back through his notes. "Killed on October the twenty-fifth, found eleven days later on the fifth of November."

"Today is the twenty-first. Thirty-one days in October. Six and twenty-one? Twenty-seven days since Jack the Bap was killed. I wonder when this lad Boniface got his."

"According to your man Deegan, the body is rotten, so he could be dead a week or more," Breen said.

"And you told Boniface about Jack the Bap when?"

"Two weeks ago—on November the sixth, a Monday."

"So he got it sometime in the last two weeks," Donovan said. "If he's putrid already he might have been killed just after he was warned. How the hell did Deegan find him?"

"He was on his way to Garryhinch to look for that old woman Missus Daly."

"What? Did he stop to let the dog piss or something?" Donovan asked.

"No. The car window was open. A window in the house was open. When Deegan was driving by, the dog began jumping around."

"Jesus! Must be a hell of a dog. I hope Deegan didn't upset anything, plough around in his big boots through the scene."

"I don't think so," Breen said. "He knows what to do if his dog sniffs out a crime scene. He didn't go into the house, only looked through a window at the back. He could see the body was naked and he saw some nails."

"Like Christ on the cross?"

"Deegan wasn't specific."

"I suppose the shite was frightened out of him—Deegan, I mean. Would be out of me. The Portlaoise lads didn't give many details when they posted the Carrowreagh killing—Jack the Bap—on Pulse," Donovan said, referring to the national crime-alert computer system. "*The Telegraph* had more details than Pulse, wherever the hell they got them. That's one thing that's not going to happen here. We'll keep this as tight as a bull's hole in August."

"I told Tim Nolan on the desk not to talk to anyone till you got here. Deegan won't tell anyone what he found. Bill Hickey's at the scene and you know Bill—a rock."

"Two religious brothers killed within three weeks! Every newspaper raker will descend on this like flies to a fresh cow shite. You sign out the car and I'll print out the Pulse report for...what date was Jack the Bap killed again?"

"Twenty-fifth of October, found fifth of November—a Sunday," Breen said.

"So he'll be on the sixth of November Pulse. I'll call Portlaoise, too; have them fax the details they kept off the computer. Their fax might be our checklist when we look at Brother Boniface."

"Besides Brother Boniface, two other religious brothers out on Croghan Hill were warned, sir. Do you think someone should be sent right now to warn them again—and at the same time cover our arses with Dublin?"

"Good thinking, Tom. Will you take care of that? Whoever you send, tell him to call us the minute he finds out

if the reverend brothers are alive or dead. And wait…
wasn't there another one?"

"Yes, Brother Beatus. He's in Saint Fintan's in Portlaoise. He's safe. Maybe you could be officious with Tim
Nolan about not talking here at the station or when he
goes home."

"I'll do that, Tom."

They walked toward the back door of the station and
into the warmth.

5.

Pauline Byron looked at the clock; there were twenty minutes until the quarter-to-seven alarm. She pushed her hand out of the warm clothes, and before her fingers touched the off button, the happenings of the last few days flowed quietly into her brain, followed by a seeping of well-being down into her stomach. She was reminded of the pleasantness of birthdays when she was a young girl; lemonade and biscuits in the parlor and the present from Aunt Teresa.

Without disturbing Raymond, she slipped out of the bed, crossed the room silently. But as she was closing the door, her husband said, "Look out for men on motorbikes at traffic lights."

"There's no traffic lights in Emo, and I'm not as dumb as Veronica," Pauline replied. Pauline would never publicly say that Veronica Guerin had been dumb to end up bleeding in her little red car at a traffic light while her druggie killers disappeared in a haze of motorbike exhaust, and while her dismissed bodyguards were fulfilling other garda duties. Because the myth of Veronica's martyrdom had been assembled by self-serving newspaper people, Pauline, as a member of the fourth estate, felt she had to be seen as an admirer of the late reporter.

She went downstairs, through the kitchen and the laundry room. As she passed the back door she touched a button and a computerized voice quacked after her, *Good morning, the indoor temperature is fourteen point five degrees Celsius; the outdoor temperature is five degrees Celsius.* After using the loo, she splashed cold water on her face and

patted herself dry. She touched her hair into shape with
her fingers and glanced at herself in the mirror. Pauline
Byron was contented with the state of her forty-four-year-
old, five-foot-five body. Almost-daily jogging and the avoid-
ance of desserts and all other confections were keeping
her various bits in proportion to each other.

Back in the laundry room she removed her knee-
length illustrated T-shirt. It was an old present from her
boss at *The Telegraph*, Jack Rafferty, showing the late Irish
prime minister Charles Haughey with *Thief in Chief* in the
shape of a halo around his head. Haughey's hands were
prayerfully joined at his chest, his eyes looking upward
at a heavenly cash account. Pauline pulled the cups of
a black jogging bra over her breasts, and from the shelf
above the dryer she selected a pair of red sweat pants and
a matching top.

"Five degrees," she muttered, and decided to wear her
blue-and-white County Laois football jersey.

She stretched out her jogging muscles. Pauline
believed body-stretching for women, like scrotum-scratch-
ing for men, should be done in private. She took a pair of
gloves off the shelf.

Tiny flashlamp in hand, she walked across the damp
grass in the barely gloaming back garden. She stepped
over the stile into Joe Scully's field and jogged along the
cow-path to the stile in the cemetery wall. The narrow,
clayey track through the short grass was a black snake
through the hoar-covered pasture. Pauline switched
off her flashlamp and Veronica Guerin came back into
her head. She had just told Raymond that she wasn't as
dumb as Guerin, yet here she was taking her usual jogging route. Even though the final article of her latest
investigation had been published in yesterday's *Telegraph*,
the disgraced minister Francis X. Culliton and his henchmen had known for months that she was digging and they
knew what the results of her digging would be. Her daily

routine could easily have been noted months ago; yet, no matter how improbable it was, it was still possible that the fallen minister had an underling as sycophantic as the knights who galloped off to Canterbury to whack Beckett when Henry whined. Pauline thought it unlikely that any politician or his henchmen would stoop to the level of Veronica's drug dealers, yet she decided she would take a new path once she got into Emo Park.

She climbed over the stile into the cemetery and ran along the pebbled paths between the headstones.

On the first morning after his arrival in the parish, Father Maher had met the jogging Pauline at the church gates as he was going in to say mass. "Do you not think it unbecoming to jog through a cemetery?" he had asked her. Pauline replied, "No," and jogged on. The second morning Maher said, "Jogging in the cemetery is forbidden." "It's not your cemetery," Pauline said. On the third morning the priest said, "I forbid you to jog through the cemetery," and he closed the gate as she approached. But Pauline easily pushed the man aside and opened the gate. "You're an arsehole," she said. She hadn't seen him since.

Now she jogged through the church gates and crossed the Emo-Mountmellick road. She turned right on the footpath, and almost immediately went left into the approach to the main entrance of Emo Park. When she passed through the high iron gates she stretched her arms above her head and took deep breaths. The air was brisk and as clear as bubbling well-water in a faraway field. She loved this—the air, the weak autumnal light drifting down from the thinning canopy of the mighty beech trees; she loved the sound of disturbed animals in the woods, loved the loud, defiant caws of the rooks and crows and jackdaws, loved being alone for these forty minutes with her heart in top gear, her veins throbbing with spating blood.

And then, to anyone who might have been watching but who'd blinked, she disappeared off her usual route.

One moment she was on the main avenue, the next she was on a narrow, mulch-carpeted track among bushes and trees. She settled into her pace, and Francis X. Culliton came back into her head. She knew she had a right to savor her success. But the job was finished; the investigation was published, the hubristic Culliton was "in seclusion" for the moment, sweating in anticipation of humiliating court appearances and inevitable jail time. Except for a few television and radio interviews in the works, the case was over for Pauline. The first thing she had to do when she got home was send chocolates and flowers to Melissa and the rest of the Diggers at *The Telegraph*.

But before she finally dismissed Francis X. Culliton from her thoughts, she allowed herself a final loud whoop of delight at having got this particular bastard, this greedy pig with his snout so deep in the public trough that he had grown into a fat, fatuous fainéant who didn't even know how corrupt he had become. Culliton had been as greedy as the lately deceased Haughey but he was not nearly as clever.

And with her ringing whoop, Pauline dismissed Francis X. It wasn't so difficult to get rid of him because a new investigation was already percolating in her brain, had been sitting in there since Guy Fawkes Day.

Carrowreagh.

Sixteen days ago, when she was too busy with Francis X. to be sidetracked, she had read about a dead body in Carrowreagh in south County Laois. Her own paper, *The Telegraph*, got the scoop and had quoted an unidentified source. The murdered man had once been a religious brother, he had been nailed to the floor of the shed behind his house and he had been dead for two weeks before being discovered. The Portlaoise guards would not comment on the case. The story had run on the front page under the two-column headline, "Religious Brother Savagely Slain."

The rumor floating around the offices of *The Telegraph* was that the dead man had been a pedophile. Religion, sex, murder and police silence—Pauline knew that these were the makings of a good story. But she still had to submit her idea to Jack Rafferty.

But...

During this past summer Pauline had promised her husband, the very patient Raymond, that within a week of the publication of the Culliton story she would take a break and they would go to New Zealand for a month. Raymond had already studied the history and geography of New Zealand; he had poured over street maps of Auckland and Wellington; he had chosen the places they would visit on the coast road between the two cities. He even had the schedule for the ferries between Wellington and Picton. But the Culliton investigation had taken longer than expected and now the year had shrunk to the end of November. They had agreed it was too late to go antipodal if they wanted to be in Ireland for Christmas. Now they would go on December 29, and the girls would get themselves back to Galway for the new term. In a little over a month she and Raymond should be on their way.

So many revelations of physical and sexual abuse within the ranks of the professionals of the Catholic Church had surfaced in the last few years, that Pauline suspected the gristly murder of a religious brother was unlikely to be a run-of-the-mill crime. But she was concerned that if she even gave Carrowreagh a quick look the story might mushroom into a full-blown investigation that would last several months. If it did, would she be able to walk away in mid-course to keep her promise to Raymond? And how about Raymond's department head? Already he'd shuffled and reshuffled on Raymond's behalf.

Through the bushes on her right she saw the great verdigris dome of Emo Court rising over a small hill. She stayed on her carpeted path for another half mile and then reemerged back onto the main drive within a hundred yards of the mansion.

The pillared neoclassical house loomed before her, and the two groups of playing rooks were there, fighting it out for possession of the high dome. Pauline liked to believe that the jousting, long-trousered birds of Emo Park were her secret, and during her weekend runs she often sat watching them, one flock erupting out of a nearby tree and swooping swiftly toward the dome from whence the present kings of the hill soared up in defense, the air rent with battle-squawks. But Pauline had never figured out if the two groups simply flew through each other or whether the attackers were successful or repelled.

In the noisy, loose pebbles, she jogged across the front of the empty building. She raised her hand to the two weathered and emaciated lions guarding the steps of the front entrance and ran to the far end of the house to turn left. She glided down the steps and into the formal gardens like a nocturnal sprite fleeing to the shading bushes in Mad Margaret's Walk. Along the reeded lake with its distant swans and wild ducks she ran, and there was helium in her legs, in her lungs, in her head; in her mind she soared over the treetops, turned and spun, wheeled and twisted.

Away from the lake, the smaller birds, warming themselves in the weak solar heat, chattered anxiously at winter's airborne nip. In the unshaded places on the path the rising sun cast the jogger's elongated shadow before her.

Before she came to a stop at her laundry room door Pauline knew that she had run her body too fast. She was winded. Bending over, she put her hands on her knees. Her short, wheaten hair hung down like a mop left out to dry. The laundry door opened and Raymond, dressed for work, was standing there holding out her ringing mobile phone. "It's Rafferty. He's been calling nonstop."

Pauline took the phone and flipped it open. "Yes?" she panted.

"Pauline. It's a quarter to eight. Where the hell were you? I'm calling you all morning."

"And good morning to you, too, Jack." Big-bellied, big-shouldered, big-chested, big-browed, big-haired, thick-spectacled: this was what Pauline saw when she heard Jack Rafferty's voice.

"Why are you breathing like that?"

"I was out jogging...just got home."

"All joggers are mentally ill. How far are you from Daingean in Offaly?" Rafferty was breathless too, and Pauline knew he was bursting at the seams—like a two-pound bag stuffed with five pounds of shite. She also knew that in her discourse with Jack Rafferty, she had to become as rude as he in order to defend herself against his steamroller personality.

"Daingean? That's cross-country from here. Through Portarlington and maybe left in Cushina...about twenty miles to the Daingean road...about three quarters of an hour, if there are no cows or slurry spreaders on the road. What's going on?"

"Did you ever hear of Carrowreagh?"

"Vaguely."

"Well, our mysterious source has called again. There's another—" Jack was a little boy wanting to tell his mother he had whistled with his lips for the first time.

"Wait, Jack. Stop rushing like that. What mysterious source?" Pauline liked reining in Jack out of his gallop.

"Our *unidentified* source. When Brother John the Baptist was discovered in Carrowreagh we got a call from a man who knew things. That's where we got the details about the nails and—"

"Was the brother crucified?"

"That wasn't clear. The caller said the victim was nailed to the floor, that he was rotten and that he'd once belonged to a religious order."

"And?"

"And what?"

"Who did you send down there?"

"Dandelion Head—Mick McGovern—but the guards wouldn't let him within a mile of the place and they wouldn't tell him anything. About fifteen—"

"And that was the end of it?"

"I was waiting for you to finish with fat Frankie X. I was afraid you'd be distracted so I didn't talk to you about it. Let me tell—"

"How did everyone in the office know the man in Carrowreagh was a pedophile?"

"That was an aperitif. I left that out of the paper but let it float around the office to whet your appetite."

"And you knew Raymond and I had already put off our trip to New Zealand once, and you know we're going in late December." Pauline knew from experience that she had to bargain with Jack. "You're a conniving bastard, Jack. You know if this story develops legs, it won't be finished by then and we'll have to cancel again."

"Pauline, if you'd only let me tell you what I'm going to tell you, you'll be jumping up and down to get at the story. About fifteen minutes—"

"Before you tell me anything, Jack, I want a guarantee that if this turns into an investigation, I will have all the support I need to finish it before December 20, no questions asked, no overtime questioned."

"One hundred percent, no holes barred. Guaranteed."

"It means I can plug into your personal computer to read exactly what you have?"

"Yes, yes. 'Asparagus,' as in the vegetable, will let you into the file. Now let me tell you what I know before I wet the floor."

"I wouldn't want you to flood the building, Jack."

"The mysterious caller phoned about thirty minutes ago and said there's been another blood-and-guts event—

an exact replica of Carrowreagh. Body nailed to floor, body rotten, victim a religious brother, pedophile; in a house somewhere between Daingean and Edenderry."

"Shit, Jack, the caller is the killer," Pauline said, and she knew she was pulling the cork out of Rafferty's bottled effervescence.

"And he's ours, Pauline," he spurted. "He's fucking ours. A fucking serial killer and the guards know it too. He's ours. We own this story, Pauline. This is the stuff that brings advertisers flocking with cap in one hand and euros in the other."

"You sound happy, Jack." Sometimes, Rafferty's acidic cynicism got under Pauline's own cynical skin.

"A-fucking-one I'm happy and don't try to pretend you aren't excited too. At last the country has its own serial killer. *The Telegraph* will be quoted around the world, to say nothing of your byline. The guards are hiding their cars in the bushes around the victim's house. The caller talked about a man with a bloodhound passing the house around five this morning and finding this thing in the house."

"The thing could be your own brother, Jack," Pauline said, then bit her tongue.

"But it's not. Con's bits and pieces are splattered on the walls in fucking Baghdad."

"I'm sorry, Jack. I—"

"Doesn't matter. We all die. The corpse is in the house. The body's rotten, stinking as a matter of fact. Bring a jar of Vicks with you."

"Jack, you should hear yourself. You don't know how cynical and cruel you sound."

"Yes, I do. The only way you can survive in this fucking life is to laugh at everything, even a missing wanker as long as it's not your own. Get out—"

"Who's missing his wanker?"

"The victim's wanker is gone, snipped off. I think the caller told me that to get our full attention, to encourage us to get past the guards on this one. Maybe the killer takes the wankers home and fries them like your man— the Milwaukee cannibal—remember he kept the edible bits in his refrigerator? America has the best serial killers. Get out there and don't even hint that we know what we know. If you happen to discover the name of the killer in the first three minutes, don't tell the guards. It's better for us if he gets a chance to knacker another few before he's caught."

"Jack...I think you need—"

When Pauline heard Jack hanging up she yelled into the phone, "Take a long holiday, maybe a retreat in a Buddhist monastery on the slopes of Nepal for ten years. Get your distorted fucking brain back into working order. You might be a brilliant editor but you're one fucking awful human being."

Raymond opened the door and stuck out his head. "Are you alright? Jeese, I thought there was a bull after you."

"There was, and his name is Jack Rafferty; that man is getting sicker and sicker."

Raymond stepped out onto the gravel. One inch short of six feet, his jowls were shining from the recent passage of a razor blade. His mop of recently washed, damp black hair was still stuck to his skull, but by the time he arrived in his classroom in Newbridge College his mane would have recovered its springiness. "Is he trying to intimidate you into another long investigation already and the ink not even dry on Culliton's miserable arse? Remember New Zealand."

"He just wants me to go over to Daingean to sniff around. There's been a murder, and I happen to be closest to it. It's just the way he talks...his cynicism, sarcasm... The man's got worse since his brother died in Baghdad."

Raymond clunked across the rattling pebbles and surrounded his sweating wife with his arms, pulled her into himself and nudged her with his pelvis. "I could wrestle you onto a mattress when you're all sweaty and fighty like this. When you come back from your run tomorrow morning, have a row with Rafferty and then jog straight up the stairs."

"It's better if you come down the stairs and drag me up by the hair." Pauline raised her face and kissed her man goodbye. As they separated, Raymond's hand slid down her right breast. "Sorry," he said.

"Raymond, you're so smooth. If you don't mind being late for—"

"Only Protestants screw this early on Friday mornings," Raymond said. Then he went around to the back of the house to his car. In twenty-four years he had never been late for school.

As Pauline undressed and flung her clothes into the basket in the laundry room, she felt a new sensation coursing through her body—the rush a Neanderthal woman with a hungry family felt when she'd spied a mastodon aimlessly wandering over the horizon in her direction. She got into the shower, and as the lukewarm water cooled her, she thought about Jack Rafferty—about how the more cynical, the more adolescently he behaved, the more excited he was about a story. But she had accepted a long time ago that the world runs on individuals' obsessions, insane as some of them might be.

She scrubbed the shampoo into her scalp with her fingernails and thought of Raymond. She hadn't been exactly truthful with him.

6.

The same autumnal sun that had been shining on Pauline Byron outside her laundry room in Emo was blinding Detective Sergeant Tom Breen. As he drove out of the police station car park into the morning quiet of Tullamore he slipped on his dark glasses. Beside him, Superintendent Donovan, with one hand shading his eyes, was flipping through the pages of a three-ringed binder on his knees.

"Shite, Tom, we don't have any Vicks." Donovan spoke so urgently that Breen's foot came off the accelerator and hovered over the brake.

"I have a jar and a handful of masks, sir," Breen said, and he returned his foot to the pedal.

"Oh, thank God," Donovan said.

"It's me you should be thanking, sir, not God. I don't see what God had to do with the Vicks."

"You know what I mean, Tom, you bloody atheist. I hate the smell of a dead body."

"Who doesn't?"

"Brian Deegan's dog doesn't," the superintendent said. "How do they train dogs to like the smell of rotting corpses?"

"They don't necessarily *like* the smell…and it's not just dogs that can be trained. Food companies train people to be smellers and tasters. A person can learn to identify all the ingredients in a wine."

"I should get myself trained to keep the wife happy."

"If she's going to buy wine you might as well learn how to enjoy it."

"Even if I could tell the different ingredients, wouldn't it still taste like musty fruit juice without sugar? And can you imagine what the lads would say if they knew I was going to wine classes?"

"Who deh fuck does he tink he is—Monshure Rots Child?" Breen said.

On either side of the road in the low-angled sun, the heathered bog stretched out to the horizon like a purple desert, a few stunted and leaf-bare birches breaking the monotony. Donovan noisily turned the pages in the binder, but his mind was elsewhere. "When the first fellow, Jack the Bap, was found in Carrowreagh," he said, "the bosses in Dublin showed more than casual interest in the case."

"Since the Ferns Report, anything with a whiff of pedophilia sets the bells off, especially if it's ecclesiastical."

"Yes, and the minute Jack the Bap showed up on the Pulse, Dublin sent out word to move quickly, warn the other religious pedophiles hiding out. Dublin's as interested in covering their arses as they are in warning the bastards who might be in danger."

"Warning this one at Burnt House—Brother Boniface—was one of those policing jobs that went against my nature, sir," Breen said. "When he came to the door looking like he hadn't washed in a year, and his breath smelling like the back end of a sick cat, I wanted to give him a few whacks."

"Who could blame you, Tom, with all that shite still floating in the air in Ferns? And your man in the north— what was his name?—got murdered in prison."

"Smyth...Brendan."

"Him, and that sick fuck in Ferns, the Reverend Father Sean Fortune and his mishandler, Comiskey-the-bishop. I know you don't like talking religion, Tom, but there's a bit in the Gospel where Christ was anything but forgiving: he said, 'Whoever gives scandal to one of these, the least of my brethren'—meaning children—'a millstone should be tied around his neck and he should be drowned in the depths of the sea.' Not just in the sea—but in the *depths* of the sea, just to make sure the bastard really drowns."

"He did sound fairly angry about it."

"More than *fairly*, Tom. I think as the millstone rolled toward the cliff with your man attached, Christ would have been running alongside kicking the shite out of him."

Breen took back the conversation. "Just to annoy Geoghan, I kept calling him Brother Boniface. In the end he told me to fuck off. I lost it and shouted at him about being a fucker of little boys. Jimmy Gorman pulled me away."

Donovan didn't respond for a while. Then he said, "I lost it once, too, a long time ago. It involved a tortured child. I nearly killed the father, bet the living shite out of him so badly he had to tell the hospital a cow fell on him."

A breeze stirred the heather on each side of the narrow road, rolling it like a field of barley in July.

Donovan surfaced out of the past with a loud sigh and said, "Before we even look at the file from Portlaoise, we already know that Jack the Bap in Carrowreagh and this one, Boniface, have some things in common: both belonged to the Order of Saint Kieran; both were pedophiles; both had been thrown out of their order after the public got wind of their carrying-on; both were nailed to the floor."

"The man in Carrowreagh, Jack the Bap—what was his real name?" Breen asked. He waved at the three-ring folder on Donovan's knees.

Donovan looked down at his files. "O'Brien, Joe O'Brien. And another connection—O'Brien worked in Dachadoo Industrial School like this lad." Donovan turned a page. "Look at this: *O'Brien's crotch was slathered with butter that was very hot when applied. Dairygold, unsalted.* Good fuck! Imagine getting your stem and berries splashed with boiling butter. Jee-zus. I'll bet the irrever-ent Dublin lads had some fun with that—called him But-terballs...Butterballs O'Brien."

"Why scald his crotch with hot butter?"

"Hold on, Tom. Listen to this: *The victim was found on the floor of the shed behind his house. The body was naked, nailed to the floor with eleven ten-penny nails; one in each wrist, one in each instep; one nail in each ear; one nail through the outside of each thigh, one nail in the skin of each calf.*"

"Holy Jesus."

"*The eleventh nail was through the cheeks—in through the right side of the face and out through the left. Both kneecaps were smashed, probably with a hammer.*"

"Holy Christ!"

"*The victim's penis was tied off near the body with blue baler twine, and the remainder of the penis removed with a sharp instrument. The severed part of the penis was in the mouth, and the lips were sewn together with black thread. The piece of penis in the mouth had been cooked in Dairygold unsalted butter.*"

"Oh, for fuck's sake!" Breen jammed on the brakes and before the car stopped he had the door open. The engine cut out. He vomited into the heather at the side of the road, then stepped back and went down on all fours. He didn't notice the keen-edged winter cold, the cold-ness of the tarmacadam.

The fine hiss of the wind in the heather was the only sound to be heard as Superintendent Donovan, a wry smile at his lips, gazed through the open car door at Breen's rear end, the split in his gabardine exposing his trousered cheeks. Breen, his head dropped between his shoulders, looked like a broken-winded horse, sounded like one too.

"You must have et a bad egg for breakfast," Donovan said, and he smiled to himself.

Breen stood up, took out a handkerchief and cleaned his face. With his back still to the car, he took deep breaths.

"Maybe the milk in your cuppa was sour," Donovan said, his self-satisfied smile growing.

Still keeping his face averted, Breen moved away from his own mess.

"Maybe you're getting the great Offaly vomiting bug," Donovan said, and Breen heard the low "heh-heh."

Breen put his hands on his hips and drew in deep draughts of fresh, heathered air. The air was like sharp knives in his lungs.

"I know!" Donovan said. "Maybe you heard a story about a man with his own fried dick in his mouth with his lips sewn together, and your delicate insides had a bad reaction."

Again Breen heard the superintendent's chuckles. He came back across the road, put his hand on the roof of the car and bent down. "Did anyone ever tell you that you have a lousy sense of humor?" he asked.

7.

Tom Breen sat into the car, closed the door and put his hands on the steering wheel. "Hearing about that stuff is worse than looking at it. My imagination plays hell on me. When you said his schlong was in his mouth I could only think of the poor bastard gagging."

He started the car and drove off.

For a few moments the men were silent. Then Donovan spoke. "Under 'Speculation,' it says, *The detailed planning that went into the killing would seem to rule out passion as the motive, despite the intense brutality of the crime. The broken kneecaps and the strategic use of the nails suggest an effort on the part of the killer to inflict the maximum pain for the longest time before the victim died.*"

"Any surmising about the butter and the penis?" Breen asked.

"Nothing. But it's a wonder they didn't come up with something just to show how clever they are. *The nail in the cheeks, like the thread sewing the lips, may have been utilitarian; the nail may have kept the victim from swallowing the penis and choking him, thereby causing him to die quickly; the lips sewn to keep him from spitting out the penis.*"

"Holy shit!" Breen brought his hand to his mouth.

"Don't, Tom," Donovan said.

Breen emitted a loud belch.

"Better than puke," Donovan said. He lowered his window and spat. "Sweet Jesus! The thought of it—the cooked willie—puts a bad taste in my mouth," he said. The car filled up with cleansed air. As he closed the window, he said, "If Geoghan's—Boniface's—wanker is in his mouth,

that will give us six things in common with Carrowreagh."
He flipped over a page. "The autopsy: *The bruise on the fore-head was possibly made by a heavy stick, the injury sufficient to render the victim unconscious but not sufficient to kill him*" He flipped back to the last page he'd been reading. "Under 'Speculation,' it says, *The mark on the forehead might suggest that the killer needed his victim unconscious while the penis was removed, the lips sewn and the nails hammered.* From what Deegan-the-dogman called in, I think we're going to walk in on the same scene here, Tom."

"And if we do, we won't be dealing with a copycat. Portlaoise kept a lot of stuff off the Pulse."

"Yes, Tom, but even so, *The Telegraph* was able to report that the murdered man had once been a religious brother, he had been nailed to the floor of the shed behind his house and had been dead for two weeks before he was discovered. There's a copy of *The Telegraph* story in here. Wait a minute…Jack the Bap was discovered when?"

"November the fifth."

"And here it is: *The Telegraph* had the story on the front page the next day: Religious Brother Savagely Slain. Someone involved in the investigation—some hure—*had* to be their source. I hope Deegan doesn't brag about what his dog found this morning."

"I think Deegan is too interested in the success of his dog to put himself into anyone's bad books."

"I hope so."

For a while the only sound in the car was the singing of the tyres. The two gardai drove through the still-sleeping village of Daingean. The only person they saw was the owner of Tess Westman's Tea Rooms standing on the step unlocking her premises. She looked up, blew a wandering tress off her face and squinted at the passing car.

When the guards emerged again onto the plain of heathered bog, Breen asked, "Did the Brain Trust find nothing at all in Carrowreagh?"

"Nothing!" Donovan opened the file again. "Besides the thread in the lips, the twine on the willie, and the nails in the skin, and the butter, not one thing was found. *The twine tying off the penis was blue baler twine that could have been picked out of a hedge near any farm; the thread could have come from any one of thousands of spools; the nails are sold loose by the pound in hardware shops; butter is in every grocery shop.* It looks like the Brains put everything through every ringer and hopper they have and came up with nothing. What does that tell you?" Donovan asked.

"The killer knows something about not leaving evidence."

"And that he prepared for the job," Donovan said. "It says here, too, *Faint traces of ammonia were found in the mucus membrane of the upper nostrils and in the lungs, suggesting that smelling salts were used to revive the victim at some point.* The killer probably brought the poor fucker around to let him enjoy the last few painful hours of his life. *Cause of death was renal failure. Victim may have lived forty-eight hours after the assault.* He'd have died roaring, as they used to say, only it's hard to roar with your dick in your mouth."

Breen waved his right hand at the three-ringed binder. "If they are right about the killer wanting to inflict the most pain and wanting it to last as long as possible, the killer must... the pain he inflicted must reflect pain dished out to him by Jack the Bap."

The two detectives lapsed into silence as if contemplating a body writhing on the floor like a worm on a fishhook.

"It almost makes you feel sorry for the bastard," Donovan finally said, "if you could forget what he did to small boys. If the same person killed these two religious brothers, then I wonder is he working off a list and to a timetable. And if he is getting revenge, why has he waited till now?"

"Who found Jack the Bap in Carrowreagh?" Breen asked.

Donovan flipped more pages. "Two Sunday hunters went into his shed out of a spill of rain—November the fifth, around half-past two. Autopsy estimates he died October twenty-fifth."

"Didn't anyone miss him? Surely he had to shop for his—"

"Tom, you know how people deal with pedophiles— lepers—and religious ones are treated like atomic waste. Nobody wants anything to do with them."

"But the family. Surely there—" Breen said.

"Families, especially, want nothing to do with them."

"But even pedophiles have to eat, get food. Why didn't someone miss Jack the Bap or Geoghan?"

"That's something we can check on here—where Geoghan got his food. Listen to this: *Brother John the Baptist received a weekly delivery of food from Mister Paud Hughes, a small-time grocer in Carrowreagh. On the morning of October the twenty-sixth, Mister Hughes found a note had been put under the shop door during the night canceling the weekly order. Mister Hughes discarded the piece of paper, a torn-off piece of a brown bag.*"

The angle of the sun had brought out the purple of the heather and it rippled toward them on one side and away on the other.

"So we have a serial—" Breen began, but Donovan cut him off.

"Don't even *think* that word, Tom, because it'll become too easy to say. You know how reporters love to frighten everyone with a serial killer—sells a lot of papers. Doesn't matter if the killer's in Youghal or Yorkshire or Ypsilanti. Some people get frightened to hell, and some smack their lips and wait for the next victim to pop up. In their own way they're cheering on the serial killer, hoping he won't get caught."

"Where's Ypsilanti, sir?" Breen asked.

"Buggered if I know, Tom."

Breen pointed. "There's Burnt House. That clump of bushes in on the right? That's Geoghan's...Brother Boniface's house."

The silver, unmarked Toyota bumped in off the main road.

8.

It wasn't until they turned into the short lane to the house that they saw the police car and Sergeant Bill Hickey standing beside it.

Breen spoke through his open window. "Hello, Bill. Any action?"

"Not a stir, Tom—just the smell." Hickey smiled a twisted smile. His face was mindful of a crag shaped by wind and weather in a child's adventure story. His brown hair was perfectly sculpted in an effort to draw gawking eyes off the unfortunate visage. How Hickey had won the hand of a beautiful woman was the perennial question in the station.

When the two men got out of the car, Hickey addressed the superintendent. "Good morning, sir."

"Hello, Bill. Did you look around?"

"I didn't go in, just looked in through the window at the back—it's like your man with the dog said, nailed to the floor, naked, rotten. There's a bit of blue tarp over there with a stone on it, the only sign of life I could see on the outside."

A breeze blew. "Oh, God, what a stink!" Donovan said, his nose and lips scrunching against the wafting stench. "Maybe Deegan's dog isn't so great after all. My granny could have smelled this one ten miles away."

"I didn't know your granny was alive, sir," Breen said.

"She's not. But when she died at ninety-six she was still sucking eggs."

Breen knew the nervous chatter was just something to keep their minds off what they were there for.

Breen held out a plastic bag to Sergeant Hickey. "There's tea and a bachelor-made sandwich for you, Bill, if you can eat it. Why don't you walk out to the end of the lane here, get away from the corpse, take a break? Keep out of sight of the main road."

"Thanks, Tom," Hickey said. His eyes met the superintendent's for a moment. Both men raised their eyebrows, and somewhere in that gesture was an acknowledgment that Tom Breen was a better human being than most. Even if he was an atheist.

"Open the booth before you go, Bill, just in case we need anything," Donovan said.

Breen looked at his watch, took out his notebook and wrote, "7:22 a.m. supe at Geoghan. Bill H." When he put his pen away he opened the second plastic bag, drew out a surgical mask and gave it to Donovan. The superintendent laid the Vicks on thickly.

"If the stink of the corpse doesn't kill you, sir, the Vicks will," Breen said. "Go easy on that stuff and leave some for me."

"There's nothing worse than smelling rotting meat," the superintendent said.

"There is—having your own peter cut off and sewed into your mouth," Breen said.

"At least it was cooked."

They tied on the masks.

Through the frosted, lifeless, high weeds and long grass Donovan walked along the gable end of the house. He stopped at the back corner. Breen followed.

Twenty feet to their left, leafless, entwined briars, ivy, whitethorn, and dead elms created a thick and out-of-control hedge. Except for the entrance into the front yard, the hedge formed an all-encircling, impenetrable barrier around the house. Looking to his right, Donovan noted indentations in the weeds and grass where Bill Hickey and Brian Deegan and the dog had walked, saw

where the men had stood as they'd peered through the
window while it was still dark.

"I wonder what Deegan's pulse was doing here in the
dark," Donovan said. He stepped over to the window and
examined the bent grass before peering in through the
glass. With his hands at his face to block the reflection he
was a submarine captain at the periscope looking for prey
in a Second World War picture. After a few moments he
stepped away, glanced up at the four-inch gap at the top of
the window, and beckoned to Breen. "Take a gawk, Tom."

The detective cupped his hands around his eyes and
peered in for a long time. Behind him, Donovan said,
"From here it looks very like the Reverend Brother John
the Baptist's scenario in Carrowreagh. I get perverse satisfaction referring to these fuckers by their religious titles:
Most Reverend Bishop Brendan Comiskey, *Most* Reverend
Bishop Eamonn Casey."

Breen straightened up and while he jotted in his notebook, he said, "The bigger they are, the harder they fall."

"Did you just make that up, Tom"?

The two policemen walked around the house checking the other windows. The front door was locked, but
one well-aimed whack from the emergency sledgeham-
mer splintered the jamb holding the bolt. As the door
swung in, the putrid smell gushed out and pierced the
men's masks.

"Fuck and a half!" Donovan spluttered.

They stood in the doorway. A narrow hallway ran from
the front to the back of the house; halfway down was a
pair of ill-kept leather boots, their uppers collapsed and
wrinkled, their laces like dead black worms; a broom was
leaning against the wall within arm's length of Donovan.
Whoever had swept the floor last had left the sweepings in
a pile behind the broom's head.

Breen jotted in his notebook.

"Ready?" the superintendent asked, his hand over his mask as if that would reinforce the Vicks. He led the way to the end of the short hall, and the two men looked through the door on their left. From this angle only the lower legs of the victim were visible. Heads of nails were driven deep into each instep and one nail was sunk half-way into the side of each calf.

"How's your guts, Tom?" Donovan asked.

"Fine. Not a stir."

The window the men had peered through from the outside was on their right. Ahead of them, along the end wall of the house was an unmade bed. When Donovan switched on the overhead light he saw that the once-white sheets were grey. A jacket, trousers, shirt and under-clothes were thrown roughly on the foot of the bed. Red long-johns, lying arse-up, were caked with dried shite.

"The big toes...look, sir," Breen said. "The two of them...he couldn't—"

"Remember Jack the Bap's kneecaps? Looks like tor-ture to me." The remaining toenails were long and dirty, reminding Breen of the hoofs of an uncared-for donkey. Bracing himself with a loud inhalation, Donovan moved into the room. Breen followed.

"It's Geoghan alright," Breen said, as he dragged his eyes away from the collapsed face.

The naked corpse was well on its way to corruption. The blue twine around the remaining piece of shriveled penis looked like the string at the end of a dried-up sau-sage. Grease glistened at the crotch. The lips were sewn together, but some of the stitches had pulled through the decaying flesh. Breen had just noticed the nails in the ears when Donovan said, "Eleven nails and a mark on the forehead similar to Jack the Bap's."

"Did you count the nails in the ears?"

"I did."

"I'll count again for the report." Breen bent over the body.

"Hold on, Tom," Donovan said. "Don't move." He made a sweeping motion with his hand. "Look at that—the floor all around the body has been cleaned—and the clean area goes out through the door and up the hallway toward the front door. What do you make of that?"

They took giant steps out of the broom-swept area. "I hope we haven't given the Brains something else to do—eliminate us," Breen said. Then he answered Donovan's question. "The fellow who did this…all he had to do was sweep up the footprints, the floor is so dirty." He began again to count the nails.

Donovan stepped aside. Even though nails had been driven through the wrists, the body was not arranged in the classical configuration of a crucifixion. The right hand was above the head and out to the side, while the left one was positioned close to the hip. The nails through the insteps and wrists were hammered down to their heads. The rest of the nails had been driven only a few inches into the floor.

"Eleven, sir," Breen said, when he'd finished counting. He scribbled in his notebook.

"What jumps out at you, Tom?"

"Blood; there's so little. This fellow could have stayed alive for a long time after he was nailed."

"The same as the late Jack the Bap, Joe O'Brien," Donovan said.

"And it looks very personal, sir, not rushed. This was well planned. And it took time, a lot of time—not just the planning, but the execution, too."

"Good word—execution. But I'd say the planning took longer than the execution. How long is he dead, do you think?"

Each man stood with one arm across his belly, an elbow in one hand and the chin in the other. They were two visitors in a museum searching for an artful response to a piece of modern sculpture that looked like a greyhound's turd.

"I'd say close to two weeks," Breen said. "The jowls are slipping off the face, and the eyes are almost in the skull...Do you think the position of the body is supposed to mean anything?"

"No. I think he was just nailed where he landed. This poor fucker suffered before he died," Donovan said. "Imagine slowly waking up. All he would have seen was the ceiling above his face. His eyes were the only part of his body he could move. Did he ever figure out what had happened to him? Would he even have known that his pizzle was in his mouth, that his lips were stitched closed? Maybe he thought he'd had a stroke. Maybe all his attention was focused on the terror of choking on the sausage in his mouth until he felt the swelling pain in his bladder and kidneys. He probably died in terror, maybe mad, but I doubt that he knew he was nailed to the floor."

In silence the two men contemplated the body for a long time.

Finally, Superintendent Donovan broke the spell. "Alright, Detective Sergeant Breen," he said. He shuddered away and broke the emotional connection to the victim on the floor. "Whoever did this might...must have... This is exactly like Jack the Bap; this fellow must have done rotten things with his dick, too, put it into someone's mouth."

"This isn't necessarily payback for fellatio, sir, just because the whanger is in the mouth. It's easier to put a flaccid dick into the mouth than push it up the arse."

"Jesus Christ, Tom!" Donovan said. "Come on, we'll look at the rest of the house. Maybe the action only ended up in here."

Because the kitchen-cum-sitting-room was so filthy, it was the clean track on the floor that drew the eyes. From the cooker, through the space between a broken armchair and a straight-backed chair, the clean trail came toward them and continued out through the door. Beside the broken armchair sat a brown glass ashtray with an empty pint bottle lying among the cigarette butts. On the label was the handwritten word WHISKEY.

Both men pulled on latex gloves, then tiptoed like cats walking through a carpet of chicken shit. The two dark marks directly in front of the armchair could have been blood. A pair of worn slippers had been carelessly discarded under the chair. On one of the cooker's hotplates Donovan found a small cast-iron frying pan covered in a scum of grey grease with insect tracks like bird-feet in fresh snow.

"Looks like this lad's sausage might have been cooked, too," the superintendent said over his shoulder. As they left the kitchen, Donovan glanced back from the door. An old-timer had once told him, "Always look back when you're leaving a scene, and most times you'll see something." Now Donovan's eyes were drawn to a cardboard box on the bare concrete floor beside the straight chair. He stepped back in. "Tom," he called.

9.

Tom Breen went down on his hunkers. Stenciled letters on the box indicated that it had originally held twenty-four tins of baby formula. The words "dan demp" were scrawled on one side with a wide-tipped felt pen. Breen opened the flaps. Seven copies of *The Telegraph*, folded in half, lay inside. He took them out and handed them up to his boss. The papers had been resting on two layers of packaged and tinned groceries: tea, salmon, sardines, corned beef, soup, marrowfat peas, mayonnaise, sugar, two loaves, butter, Bovril, marmalade, oats, cigarettes, a full pint bottle with WHISKEY written on the label. The only fresh food was the carton of eggs and the two-liter container of milk. No bill or receipt was in the box.

"I think we can figure out the time of death, give a day or two," Donovan said.

Breen stood up. He looked at the bundle of papers in his boss's hand. "Those papers were read before—look at the way they're folded—unless Geoghan read...But he'd never...Are they in order of date of issue, sir?"

"A whole week's worth from Thursday to Wednesday. Wednesday, November the eighth, is the last one."

"Jimmy Gorman and I were here two days before... Monday the sixth."

"Where did he get the box? And why didn't he open it when he got home with it?"

"Especially with a full bottle of whiskey in it and an empty one there on the floor." Breen pointed. "What do you think of 'dan demp'?"

"'Dan' might be a name, but I never heard of 'demp' as a name, unless it's short for Dempsey...Dan Dempsey?"

"Good one, sir. Dempsey the grocer in 'dan' for Daingean. 'Dan demp'—a vanman's shorthand."

"This is a good find, Tom, but I have to go outside," the superintendent said quickly. "The stink's making me nauseous. We'll leave the rest to the Brains, unless you want to poke around in the front rooms."

As Donovan stepped out through the front door, a black jeep drove into the small, overgrown yard and stopped beside the police car. Sergeant Bill Hickey was trotting in from the lane, but before he could get around to the driver's side a woman stepped out of the jeep. She was wearing Gore-Tex walking boots with green and black laces, black-belted black jeans, a black turtleneck and an unzipped jacket the color of hips on a winter dog-rose.

Sergeant Hickey glanced at the black-clad breasts. "Ma'am!" he said. "This is a restricted area. You'll have to…"

"Your superintendent knows me, Guard," the woman said. She turned to the cottage door. "Hello, Superintendent Donovan. It's been a long time since we saw each other."

Donovan stopped in his tracks. "What the fuck?" dripped over his lips

He pulled off his mask and said, "Good morning, Ms. Byron." He wasn't smiling.

Hickey looked over at the superintendent and relaxed. This woman was Donovan's problem.

10.

Superintendent Donovan stepped away from Daniel Geoghan's front door and walked toward Pauline Byron. Pauline had already smelled the smell of death and was pulling a folded, man-sized handkerchief out of the right pocket of her jacket. "I don't suppose you have any Vicks for me, Superintendent Donovan?" she asked, as she removed a jar of Vicks from a side pocket.

"I see you came prepared, Ms. Byron."

"Yes. I learned a lot in the Girl Guides." With her finger, she spread the eucalyptus paste on her handkerchief, folded it and put it over her mouth and nose.

Donovan's eyes caressed Pauline's breasts, and he knew she had seen his glance. Sometimes when he was chatting with a woman and looking into her eyes, Donovan would imagine himself naked between her legs, his brain drained of blood. But he knew that when dealing with a woman like Pauline Byron, this mixing of business with pleasure could result in the detriment of the business. But still, for a moment the demands of his testosterone betrayed him.

Even though it was a year since he had been interviewed—interrogated—by Pauline Byron, this harridan, this fearless Amazon still inhabited a boudoir in his brain, a chamber which he frequently visited when drifting off to sleep with his arm around his wife. Now, as he looked at her, he renewed her boudoir image like a restorer bringing out the colors in a faded masterpiece. With her face half-covered by the handkerchief, her intense eyes peered into his with the directness of an exotic belly dancer, jewelry hanging down her forehead and out of her navel. The short wheaten hair, the unzipped and open jacket, her very boots…if she only knew of his nocturnal fantasies.

But in real life, Superintendent Donovan was intimidated by Pauline Byron, and now in Brother Boniface's yard, he attempted to keep Pauline at bay until he collected his wits—or until Tom Breen came out of the house and rescued him.

"That was a nice job you did on Francis Xavier Culliton. Where were your likes when Charlie Haughey was robbing the country blind?" Donovan said.

"Thanks for the compliment, Superintendent, if that's what it was. Francis X. Culliton was the one who did the job on himself; I just wrote about it." Pauline leaned back against the side of her jeep, gave the impression she was here to stay. She pushed her free hand into the pocket of her jeans, and Superintendent Donovan wished he was her hand. "As for Haughey, *The Telegraph* now has an aggressive editor who is not intimidated by the establishment. And, may I modestly say, the editor had the good sense to hire me."

"You're not saying the papers knew what Haughey was up to, are you, Ms. Byron? Knew and didn't do anything?" The superintendent stepped over to the jeep and leaned against the metal above the front wheel well. From this position he wouldn't have to worry about where to put his eyes. He felt the heat of the engine on his back.

"And surely you're not saying, Superintendent, that you are one of the twelve people in the country who don't know Haughey's corruption infected others to build walls and moats around the great leader. But I think you're trying to redirect my focus."

"Your focus, Ms. Byron? I don't know what you're focused on, so how could I be trying to redirect it? I thought you were just passing by and stopped to say hello when you saw me."

"You're right, Superintendent. I drive from Emo to Daingean every morning with a jar of Vicks to take in the heathered bog air. It does wonders for asthma."

"I didn't know you suffered from asthma, Ms. Byron. I'm sorry to hear that."

"I don't suffer from asthma any more than you excel at poker, Superintendent. But even if you did have a good poker face, you know you have nothing to bluff with here." Pauline raised her chin and took in the house and surrounds with the tiny gesture. "No one could bluff his way out of this stink of rotting flesh."

"Ms. Byron—"

"You may call me Pauline. May I call you Christy?"

"No, and I will call you Ms. Byron. That way we will both be reminded that we don't work the same jobs, that as a press person you have the capacity to interfere in a... interfere in police procedures."

"Were you just about to say, 'interfere in a murder investigation'?"

Donovan knew he was losing ground. "I *said* police procedures," he began, and then stumbled into official-dom. "Like Sergeant Hickey just told you, Ms. Byron, this immediate area is restricted."

Pauline Byron cast her eyes over the secluded house. She looked around the unkempt yard. "You know what this reminds me of, Superintendent Donovan?"

"No, I don't, Ms. Byron. Maybe something by Constable?" He looked straight into her eyes.

"You remember that shed down in Carrowreagh in County Laois where that man was found about sixteen days ago? His house was as isolated as this one," Pauline bluffed, as she swept her hand across the surrounding bog. "No neighbors within hearing or seeing distance."

"Ms. Byron," Donovan said abruptly, "get into your vehicle and leave the area."

"How long has this fellow been dead?" She waved her hand at the house behind Donovan.

Donovan looked over to Bill Hickey. "Sergeant Hickey," he called, as he pulled his sleeve off his wristwatch. "If this woman is not reversing her car in five seconds, you are to arrest her for trespassing, for interfering with police procedures and for obstructing a restricted area with her vehicle. One...two..."

Bill Hickey came around the front of the jeep in a hurry. Pauline Byron got behind the wheel and started the engine. When she closed the door, she lowered the window.

"Just tell me one thing, Superintendent Donovan. Was this one—?"

"Sergeant Hickey, hitch your towing rope and drag this vehicle out of here."

Hickey turned to go for the tow rope, but the jeep moved away slowly. As she backed out of the yard Pauline Byron called, "Is there a serial killer on the loose, Superintendent?"

Donovan had turned around and was heading back to the cottage, leaning forward like a man walking into a strong breeze. In his backward glance, he could see Pauline was taking her time reversing onto the lane and he was forced to go in through the front door to keep up his pretense. He slapped his mask to his face and held it there with his hand.

"That fucking woman!" Donovan muttered to Tom Breen, who was coming out of the tiny front room on the left of the hallway. "How the hell did Pauline Byron find out so much so quick? Serial killer! The hures! When I find the fucker who called her, I'll cut off his balls with a blunt beet knife."

"Jakers! That would hurt," Breen said.

"It sure would," Donovan said. "I'll bet she's just around the corner behind the trees waiting to ambush me." Donovan yanked open the front door. "Bill," he called to Sergeant Hickey, "go out on the lane, and if that woman's parked there tell her to move on. And tell her if she parks her car within a mile of here it's going to be towed away and impounded."

Donovan turned back to Breen. "Who the fuck could have told her so soon? If it was that fucker Deegan I'll kick him and his fucking dog back into the bogholes of Edenderry."

"If she's still around when we leave, would you like me to handle her, sir?"

"Please do, Tom. She always makes me feel...inadequate, and she knows it. Did you find anything new in here?"

"Nothing. Did the Portlaoise report mention anything about the floors of the house in Carrowreagh, sir?"

"I don't think so. Why?"

"It would be interesting to know if the floors were all concrete. The floors here are concrete except in the bedroom. Maybe that's why John the Baptist O'Brien was killed in the shed; maybe all the floors in his house were concrete."

"I'll check that, Tom."

When Breen and Donovan came out of the house, they stood out of earshot of the squad car.

"Here's what we'll do, Tom." Donovan took out his notebook and wrote in scribbles that only he could read. "You wait here with Bill till Jimmy Gorman gets here—if Pauline Byron comes back she might unnerve Bill with a titillation of tits. You and Jimmy check out Dempsey the grocer in Daingean about the food box and the papers. I'll get the Brains and T-Bone down here; I'll check with Portlaoise about the floors in Carrowreagh; and I'll organize a gang of the lads to do the usual legwork. How many do we need, do you think?"

"Well, for a start," Breen said, "we'll have to find out who travels the road between Edenderry and Daingean over the course of a week, day and night—maybe someone saw something. That'll take two lads each shift for a roadblock; two working together should be enough if they set up the block at the road leading into Dachadoo. It's the only side road between Daingean and Edenderry. There are no front doors around here to knock on. I don't think we're going to find anything, but we should get the Slashhook Brigade out to examine the area around the house. I'd say eighteen lads to begin with."

"I'll send out two traffic lads when I get into the station. I'll come back with the Slashhooks and organize that. Anything else?"

"Maybe you should get the Brain Trust to move fast comparing the nails and twine and thread with the stuff from Carrowreagh."

"Good one. We'd better be absolutely certain it's the same killer—leave no loose balls hanging around for the politicians to kick. Maybe check out the grease at the crotch, too."

"Maybe there's a message in the specific grease used," Breen said. "By the way, tell Jimmy Gorman to bring out the Vauxhall, sir. It might be a bit battered but it has more room than that yoke." With a tilt of his head, Breen indicated the unmarked Toyota Corolla.

As Superintendent Donovan sat into the Toyota, he said, "The sight of your man inside will render Gorman speechless."

"I don't think so, sir. Jimmy could squeeze humor out of a squashed frog on a tarred road."

Donovan's mobile rang. He said hello and yes, listened, said, "Hold on." Then to Tom Breen he said, "The other two pedophiles up on Croghan Hill are alive and well. What do you think, Tom? Should we get them to move?"

"Who's going to take them in, sir? Unless you want to take them home with you."

"Feck off, Tom. We'll have to put a watch on their house and have more frigging overtime to justify to Dublin, but as long as it's an arse-covering exercise they won't mind. At least the two buggers live in the same place."

"It could be useful to talk to those two lads, sir. Maybe Jimmy and myself should see them when we finish in Daingean with Dempsey."

"Good idea, Tom. Make that part of the plan for now. We can change it later if we have to." Into the phone he said, "Joe, are you there?...Call the station and set up a twenty-four-hour watch on those two right away, till we get more organized. No...Have the two lads dropped off immediately; you can work out the food and schedules later. Make sure they keep out of *everyone's* sight...Good man, Joe. I know I can depend on you to set it up." He hung up. "Do we have everything covered, Tom?"

"I think so. But let's have a look at that tarp Bill found out here."

"Right." Donovan got out of the car. "Bill," he called "you said you found a piece of tarp?"

"Yes, sir. Over here." Bill Hickey pointed and walked over to the hedge near the entrance to the yard. A piece of carelessly thrown blue tarp, with a fist-sized stone weighing it down, lay on a bare patch in the dead weeds. The tarp, about five feet square, was so splashed with guano that it might have been lying out in the open for several years.

"I wonder what that's about," Donovan said. No one offered an explanation. "They can get fingerprints off stuff like that. Make sure no one touches it, Bill. The Brains will bag it."

"Right, sir."

As Donovan drove out of the weedy yard, he called out, "Sergeant Hickey...Bill...don't repeat what that woman said about a serial killer."

Hickey waved in acknowledgment.

11.

Two minutes after Donovan had driven away, Pauline Byron drove back into the yard. But before she emerged from her jeep, Tom Breen was at the driver's door blocking her. She lowered the window.

"My name is—"

But Breen lowered his mask and cut her off. "You know I know who you are, Ms. Byron, and I know, too, that Superintendent Donovan told you this is a restricted area."

"Are you going to arrest me, Guard?" Pauline brought her homemade mask to her face.

"Detective Sergeant, actually. And I *will* have you arrested if you get out of your car."

"You won't arrest me yourself? Put the cuffs on me? Search me for weapons?"

Breen bluntly deflected Pauline's attempt at sexual befoggery. "How did you know we were here—the guards?" He threw his hand over his shoulder at the cottage.

"Birds sing," Byron said. Then she gave an unmusical whistle through puckered lips.

"The birds must get up early where you live."

"Actually, the bird sang to my editor in Dublin and then the editor sang into my ear in Emo by way of the phone."

"I didn't know phones had reached Emo already."

"Oh, yes. Everything's up to date in Emo city."

"Have they gone about as far as they can go?"

"You listen to old music, Detective."

"So do you. What time did the bird call you...your paper?"

Pauline Byron put her elbow on the open window and appeared to move closer to the detective sergeant. "What's your name, Detective?" she asked.

"Detective Sergeant Breen."

"That's your rank and last name."

"It's my name when I'm working."

"What's your name when you're off duty?"

"I would have to be off duty to tell you that."

"Well, Detective Sergeant Breen, how about we do some swapping of information?"

"I'm afraid I have nothing to swap," Breen said, "and I doubt you have either. The call to your editor was probably anonymous."

"Not bad for a policeman," Pauline said, but her smile took all insult out of it. "But you would be surprised to hear what I know already, Detective Sergeant. The bird that sang, sang a long song with enough notes to connect this to Carrowreagh."

"You will have to leave, Ms. Byron."

"You may call me Pauline," she said.

"I wouldn't be comfortable using your first name; you're too important," Breen said.

She knew he was mocking her. "What's your first name, Detective?"

"You will have to leave now, Ms. Byron, or I'll have to let the dogs out."

"Just tell me one thing, Detective—"

"Sergeant Hickey!" Breen called, not loud enough for Hickey to hear.

"What's this one's name?" She waved her arm at the cottage.

"A statement will be issued later," Breen said. "Sergeant Hickey!" he called again. But Hickey could not hear him.

Almost in a whisper Pauline said, "Give me your home phone number and no one will know." She handed her card to Breen.

"Sergeant Hickey!" Breen called loudly, as he put the card in his pocket. "Arrest this woman for trespassing and attempted bribery of a police officer." Hickey came around the front of the jeep.

"What bribe did I offer you, Detective Sergeant Breen?" Pauline asked.

"P.T.A. and your home phone number," Breen said.

"P.T.A.? What's that?"

"You're clever, Ms. Byron. Figure it out."

Bill Hickey arrived at the front of the jeep. Pauline started the engine and put the vehicle in reverse. She called, "We'll have to stop meeting this way, Sergeant Hickey—through the window of my jalopy and with you under orders to arrest me. Maybe we could meet in Tess Westman's in Daingean when you come off duty."

"Goodbye, Miss," Hickey said.

"I'll be in touch, Detective Sergeant Breen," Pauline said, as she rolled up her window. She reversed out of Brother Boniface's yard.

"Is she somebody famous, Tom?" Hickey asked the detective. The radio in the patrol car began to squawk, and both men cocked an ear. Someone was calling in from the search party in Garryhinch. Brian Deegan's dog had found Missus Daly's body in a two-foot grave.

"It doesn't rain but it pours," Breen said. "If she was buried she was murdered."

12.

When Detective Sergeant Jimmy Gorman joined the Garda Síochána as a cadet in Templemore he was nicknamed Six Month Jimmy.

Gorman had spent eleven of the best years of his life training to be a Catholic priest. But after six months on loan to a parish in London following his ordination, he had discovered a side to the priesthood he had never been told about, never even suspected. After one half year of living with three uncommunicative, mole-like clergymen who ignored him as if he were a contagious disease, he packed his bags and simply left without telling anyone. Gorman flew home to Shannon, visited his family in Ballysteen in County Limerick, and the following week, with an inch of height to spare, was accepted as a garda cadet. Nine months later his family received a letter from his home diocese of Limerick inquiring into his whereabouts. Jimmy didn't answer the letter, but he framed it and hung it inside his front door. Like a devout Jew caressing the mezuzah on the way into the house, Gorman touched the parchment every morning on his way out. Doing so reminded him to show courtesy and respect to every person he would encounter.

Dressed every day in grey trousers, blue blazer, white shirt and grey tie, Detective Sergeant Jimmy Gorman was six inches shorter than Detective Sergeant Tom Breen. His curly black hair always had a sheen to it. "One raw egg a day gives it the shine, lads, but you don't rub the egg into your hair, and you don't stick it up your arse either."

During his years in Saint Patrick's Seminary in Carlow, Jimmy had been a scrappy hurler who never shirked from taking on the heavyweights. A fellow seminarian, looking at Gorman in a tornado of dust, pointy elbows, knobby knees and flailing hurling sticks, remarked, "Jimmy Gorman has that graceful style of a mechanical potato digger."

Gorman's face was permanently set to break out in a grin. Some of his fellow policemen thought his sense of humor too macabre, and they sometimes didn't know whether to laugh at his jokes or turn away to hide their sickly pallor. His oft-used expression, forged in the dungeons of the dark and humorless rectory in London—"It's great to have an oul laugh, lads"—had become a byword in the Tullamore Garda Station.

Except for intermittent revelations to Tom Breen, with whom he had been paired for the last five years, Jimmy Gorman did not elaborate on his adventures in the priesthood. At forty-nine years of age, and more than two decades after drop-kicking his clerical collar into the Thames, he was still embarrassed by the depths of his youthful naiveté.

Gorman's wife, Beatrice, recently appointed head of the Tourism and Hospitality Department in the Athlone Institute of Technology, had borne three daughters who were now adolescents. Periodically, the Gormans invited Tom Breen and his widowed father to their house for one of Beatrice's culinary presentations. In their turn, the Breens brought the Gormans to Dooly's Hotel in Birr. The Gorman girls used these occasions to discard their drab school uniforms and spend hours preening. Whenever the two policemen's erratic schedules allowed, Breen joined the Gorman family to support the County Offaly football team. The three Gorman girls were in love with Tom Breen, wondered aloud in the presence of Jimmy Gorman why Breen was so brilliant and their father such a turkey. Gorman was confident that his once adoring daughters would return to him when they emerged from their hormonally unsettled selves into young adulthood. In the meantime he tried to have an oul laugh, lads, instead of trying to reason with their maddening, unpredictable, illogical selves.

"At their age, I was probably a bigger prick than the three of them put together," Gorman had once told Breen.

"There's no 'probably' about that, Jimmy," Breen had replied.

When Gorman arrived in Brother Boniface's front yard he began talking before he got out of the car. "Missus Daly was found in a shallow—"

"We have radios, too, Jimmy," Breen said, always on the alert to give Gorman a poke.

"You mean 'Shut up, Gorman'…Jesus Christ! What's that smell? Did someone die a month ago or did you fart, Tom?"

"You're quicker than usual today, Jimmy."

Hoping Gorman would notice something new, Breen gave him an unrushed tour of the cottage, pointing out the similarities to the Carrowreagh murder. "What jumps out at you?" Breen asked, as Gorman looked at Brother Boniface's body.

"He died giving himself a blow job, and now that I've got that out of the way…what jumps out at me, Tom, is the lack of blood and the lack of evidence; the care that's been taken; the planning that went into this. Someone who knows the business did this."

"What business?" Tom Breen asked.

"Our business."

"The same thought crossed my mind earlier—one of ours," Breen said. "I didn't mention it to the supe; maybe I don't want to even *think* it could be one of ours."

"If one of ours is suspected, the whole district would be ripped apart."

"It doesn't necessarily have to be someone in our district. John the Baptist was murdered in the Portlaoise District. But we can't ignore our own separate first impressions, Jimmy. Let's keep them to ourselves. The Brain Trust lads will probably think what we're thinking, and they can bring their suspicions to Internal Investigation."

"You're right. I'd rather be a suspect than an investigator if suspicion falls on a guard."

"And you know how much collateral shite floats to the top in any investigation. I wouldn't want to know the secrets of the people I work with. If a guard is suspected then we'll be suspects, too."

"I'd have to tell them that I pulled you off this here Boniface two weeks ago, that you called him a child-fucker—"

"You're right, and I'd have to tell them how often you've said you'd love to be a serial killer." They went out into the hallway.

"A *successful* serial killer, Tom," Gorman said. "Suddenly begin and suddenly stop like Jack the Ripper. You'd have to tell that to Internal Investigation."

"There are many things I could tell Internal Investigation about you, Gorman. I only keep my mouth shut because you have a family to support."

"I love you, too, Tom."

"And talking about serial killers—they can't stop," Breen said.

"How about Jack the Ripper?"

"Maybe he died, caught a disease when he was slicing up his victims. He didn't know about blood-borne pathogens, didn't wear latex gloves and a mask."

Breen pointed out the box on the floor, told Gorman what it contained and gave him time to take in the kitchen scene. When they emerged into the fresh air, Tom Breen went over to Sergeant Hickey.

"You should be going home soon, Bill," he said. "Tell your relief that a crowd of Hands and Knees will be here soon, and the lads from Dublin should be here before twelve." He handed Hickey a couple of masks and the jar of Vicks.

"Thanks for the sandwich and tea, Tom," Hickey said, as he handed the empty flask to Breen.

13.

With Gorman driving, the two detectives left Geoghan's house and headed into Daingean in the Vauxhall. Immediately, Gorman jumped into the long grass of speculation like a dog who's found the fresh scent of a rabbit. Breen liked Gorman's imaginative detection skills and he appreciated, too, his whacky sense of humor. The humor helped make police work tolerable at those times when the work exposed the guardians of the peace to the vilest aspects of human depravity. Breen believed, too, that when they were dealing with something particularly gruesome, Gorman himself needed to escape now and then for a breather.

"The stitching of the lips, Tom...was it a backstitch or just plain tacking?"

Breen looked at him. "Jakers, Jimmy. Why didn't I think of that? Round up all the tailors in Offaly, make them all give a sample of their backstitch."

"Or all the nuns in Limerick, Tom. My sister used to imitate a Sister Agnes who taught her how to sew: *There's tacking rhyming with smacking; running rhyming with cunning; backstitch rhyming with back-itch; hemming rhyming with hawing, only it doesn't; and buttonhole to save your soul.* Before she became a nun, Sister Agnes was Maggie Murphy and she hailed from Gortnahurragh near Ennistymon."

"Maggie Murphy from Gortnahurragh!"

"She screamed that from the top of a student's desk when she was madder than usual. I remember more of the stuff my sister learned at school than I was taught in my own classroom. She was always memorizing something

out loud; catechism or multiplication tables or poems or
rivers in China or provinces in Canada. Saskatchewan. I'd
swear it took her five years to learn 'The Lady of Shallot.'
I always thought Tennyson was sitting in the hedge in our
Big Field when he wrote that."

"Maybe he was," Breen said. "Maybe he was a starving
artist with a day job cutting hedges in Limerick with a
billhook."

The heathered bog sped by. Then Breen asked, "The
stitching in the lips, Jimmy…was that supposed to be a
joke?"

"At first it was, but maybe it's not. O'Brien and
Geoghan—the Reverend Brother Pedophiles—both
worked in Dachadoo. Trades and skills were taught
in industrial schools, or at least they were supposed to
be. Maybe this lad, the killer…What are we going to call
him…? How about 'Nailer'? Maybe he was taught the tai-
lor's trade. So, throw the following ingredients into the
bowl: sexual abusers, snipped mickeys in mouths, lips
sewn, very painful deaths. Mix the ingredients and what
do you get?"

"You might get a former inmate of Dachadoo Industrial School who was taught tailoring, who was abused by
Boniface and Jack the Bap, as the supe calls him. Or he
could have been taught carpentry, because he uses nails
and a hammer. Or maybe he learned horse-shoeing."

"My name is Holmes," Gorman said. "All we have to
do is go through Dachadoo's records, do a little bit of
adding and subtraction and we have him."

"Congratulations, Sherlock," Breen said. "But you
do know that getting our hands on any of those records
won't happen."

"We're the cops, the good guys. They'll have to give
them to us."

"The Department of Education tried for years to get
the industrial schools to open their books. The religious

orders more or less said go fuck yourselves—in liturgical language, of course."

"But surely with all those schools closed down, and this being a criminal investigation—"

"Let's get to that bridge when we cross it, as George Bush would say," Breen said. "Get back to the danglers... forced fellatio on a child would be a good reason for Nailer to put the reverends' members in their own mouths. But we can't rule out rape."

"You're right," Gorman said. He paused, then made the same observation that Breen had made to Superintendent Donovan. "The pain the brothers were forced to endure might be a statement about the pain suffered by Nailer at their hands."

"The number of nails used might be symbolic to Nailer," Breen said.

"I agree. I think everything about the way the bodies were dealt with is significant—the size of the nails as well as the number. Ten-penny nails are big; they're not used that often. If you ask a carpenter for a ten-penny nail out of his apron he wouldn't have one. So why use that particular size unless it means something?"

"We should keep that in mind if we have to canvass the local hardware shops. But these two killings were so well planned that the nails were probably bought years ago. And Nailer could have bought them just as easily in Lanzarote as Lisdoonvarna."

"But why wait till now?" Gorman asked. "If Nailer is as angry as he seems to be, why didn't he kill these fellows a long time ago? What was he waiting for? What set him off?"

"Maybe the dates of the killings are significant." Tom Breen took out his notebook and flipped pages. "Jack the Bap in Carrowreagh was killed on the twenty-fifth of October. Does that mean anything to you?"

"It's two months before Christmas Day."

"Jakers, Jimmy, that's brilliant."

"It's the only answer I have. Do you have a better one?"

"It's seven months after the twenty-fifth of March."

"And?"

"That's seven months after the angel did it to Mary."

"And?"

"There's no and. That's *my* best answer."

"You're developing a sense of humor, Tom. You'd better be careful."

Breen put away his notebook and sat back in his seat, consciously allowed himself to relax. He took deep breaths and, beginning with his toes, he eased his muscles up to his forehead.

"Does the angel doing it to Mary remind you of anything?" Gorman asked.

"A goose having sex with a woman—the wings. I know you're bursting to tell me what it reminds you of."

"Bursting? A poem by Yeats. 'Leda and the Swan.' Leda's lying naked and Zeus, pretending to be a swan, waddles up all horny and more or less rapes her. Leda is too terrified *to push the feathered glory from her loosening thighs*. And when the swan spews his sperm into Leda he plants the seed that will eventually blossom into the Trojan War."

There was silence for a while in the car. Then Breen said, "Leda has a casual fuck with a bird and it leads to Troy, the Trojan War."

"Yes. Helen of Troy was born of the casual swan-fuck and the rest is history, as the man said."

"I wonder was Helen in an eggshell when she dropped out of Leda."

"I wonder did Leda cackle," Gorman said. "We should start talking like Yeats, Tom; he's able to describe in detail how a swan screws a woman and not once uses the word 'fuck.' He describes the orgasm as a shuddering of the loins."

They motored along in silence for a mile until Tom Breen spoke. "If the shuddering loins belonged to a religious brother and the loosened thighs belonged to a child, then what's engendered?"

Gorman was rendered silent for half a mile. "I was doing my best to get away from the pederasts for a few minutes. I thought we'd dwell on Leda's loosening thighs for a while, but you've gone and ruined the image forever by...Shite!"

14.

It was half-past ten when Jimmy Gorman drove the yellow Vauxhall into Daingean. He turned left, crossed the Grand Canal at Molesworth Bridge. Immediately on the left was a two-storied house with DEMPSEY'S GROCERY AND BAR in gold lettering on the varnished black fascia. The glass in the two large windows and the double black doors was etched with sheaves of barley.

Detectives Breen and Gorman walked in, stood for a second to get the lay of the land. It was an old-time grocery shop, with shelves of boxed, bottled and tinned food behind the counter. A heavy, carpentered door in the wall on their right led into the bar.

"Good morning," Tom Breen said to the man behind the counter. The shopkeeper was about fifty, his hair was the same red as an Irish terrier's. An apron with narrow white and blue vertical lines hung from his neck. He had a kindly face, one that might consider a request for an extension of credit in hard times.

Breen opened his wallet and showed his I.D. card. "I'm Detective Breen from Tullamore and this is Detective Jimmy Gorman. Are you the owner?"

"I am. Andy Dempsey." Anxiety swept across his face. "What's wrong?"

"Nothing, at least nothing you have to worry about. We're making enquiries and maybe you can help us. Can we talk someplace where we won't be interrupted?"

"In the snug." Dempsey inclined his head to his left and then opened a door behind him. "Mary," he called, "I need your help for a minute."

Wearing a wrap-around apron, Mary Dempsey came through the door wiping her hands on a red towel. She was at an age when she would soon have to decide whether to go grey gracefully or reach for the bottle. She was very slim and stood three inches taller than Andy. Breen was reminded of the Howdos, a couple he had often seen on the streets in Clara, who looked like the pairing of a wolf-hound and a chihuahua. The husband was so big and the wife so tiny, they got their nickname from the question posed by the cornerboys: "How do they do it?"

"I'm going in the snug," Andy Dempsey said to his wife. "Guards making enquiries, nothing to worry about." He came around from the back of the counter and with a nod told Breen and Gorman to follow.

The moment he stepped into the snug, Breen, a teetotaler, was assailed with the stink of old porter. If a smell could cause depression in the human soul, Breen thought, this was it. He could almost hear the echoes of inebriated, slobbering talk floating among the imitation rafters.

The three men went to a round table with four stools in attendance. As they were seating themselves, Andy Dempsey said, "You're guards. You know there's an arrest for that woman in Garryhinch?"

"No, we didn't hear that," Gorman lied, luring Dempsey into thinking he had the guards at a disadvantage. "Was it on the radio?"

"No. Kearneys' bread van just left—the driver heard it in the shop in Garryhinch. The son-in-law couldn't wait for the old woman to die. Had the price of a new tractor in the bank. Terrible way to get a new one."

"Desperation can drive people into great stupidity," Breen said. He wondered if Andy Dempsey had developed his shorthand style of talking from years of warding off logorrhoeic customers, getting rid of them so he could serve the next one.

"We're here to find out something about one of your customers," Gorman said. "A man by the name of Geoghan."

"Frank Geoghan...Frank can't be in trouble."

"Any other Geoghans shop here?"

"No, just Frank."

"Where does he live?"

"Ballyglass, just beyond the Philipstown River Bridge. Third house on the right. Red door. Reed thatching. Big hay sheds."

"How often does he come to do his shopping?" Gorman asked.

"Once a week. Every Thursday at half-past seven—just when I'm closing up."

"Does he buy a lot of food?"

"Shops for a neighbor as well as himself. Doesn't do it like most people, though."

"What do you mean?" Breen asked.

"People shopping for a neighbor keep everything separate. Separate bags. Separate money. Frank makes one payment. Everything goes in the one box."

"What makes you think he buys for a neighbor?"

"There's just himself and his missus. He buys too much for two people; two of everything, nearly. Frank and the missus are teetotalers...Pioneers. But Frank buys a bottle of whiskey every second Thursday. Cheapest stuff."

"The box he puts his messages in...do you give him that?"

"I do."

"Does his wife come in with him?"

"No. Bent in two. Dowager's hump."

"So she sends Frank to shop with his list?" Breen asked.

"No list. It's the same every week. I have it ready when he comes."

"Did he buy his usual stuff last Thursday?"

"Every Thursday for some years now."

"You're sure about last Thursday?"

Dempsey thought for a second. "Yes. I asked him if he'd all the cattle in for the winter."

"Frank Geoghan has not done anything wrong, Mister Dempsey," Breen said. "I realize from the way you answered our questions you don't gossip about your customers—that you know how stories get changed every time they're retold. I know you won't talk about this enquiry." The two detectives stood up. "You have been very helpful. Thank you for your time."

"I'll let you out the back door. If anyone sees you leaving I'll be asked questions." Andy Dempsey led them in through his kitchen and out into a narrow hallway. Breen and Gorman stepped out into a tiny backyard with two outdoor tables and several aluminum beer barrels.

"That lad talks like a machine gun," Gorman said as they walked back onto the main road. "He'd give me the pip if I had to listen to him for long."

15.

Back behind the wheel of the Vauxhall, Gorman said, "Out to Frank Geoghan in Ballyglass, I suppose?" Without waiting for an answer he turned the car and drove back over the canal bridge and took the Ballingar road. "Was he taking care of Frank Geoghan or himself by letting us out the back? Cagey shopkeeper—he didn't want to be seen cooperating with the guards—he'd be an informer." Gorman said "informer" the way he'd say "Drac-ul-a" to frighten a child.

"Dempsey doesn't seem to know anything about Brother Boniface," Breen said. "So, what did we find out from him?"

"I agree. Even though the box in the cottage has Dempsey's name on it, Andy Dempsey knows nothing about Boniface," Gorman said. "Frank Geoghan buys extra food in Dempsey's shop every week along with a bottle of the *cheapest* whiskey every *two* weeks. It could be concluded that Boniface has a brother named Frank; that Frank shopped for Boniface every week; that Frank doled out the cheap whiskey instead of giving Boniface a full bottle; that Frank doesn't know his brother is dead. Or maybe Frank murdered his brother but had to keep the food charade going to keep anyone from suspecting."

"Frank didn't kill Boniface unless he killed O'Brien in Carrowreagh...Jack the Bap. But how could Frank not know his brother is dead? If Frank buys—bought—his brother's food, he had to give it to him somehow."

"So if Frank went to his brother's house yesterday, he must know his brother is dead."

The two men drifted into their own thoughts. Breen stared through his window, and in his unfocused eyes the wind-waved heather was the rippling purple clothing of a king in the pictures.

"Why was Frank Geoghan so cagey, trying to hide from Dempsey that he was buying extra food?" Jimmy Gorman asked.

"Because no one goes around telling the world his brother is a pedophile."

"But Frank wouldn't have said, 'I'm buying food for my pedophile brother.' "

"When the industrial school scandals erupted a few years ago, the religious orders got rid of their pedophiles as quick as they could, threw the shite out of the listing ship. Dachadoo had its share of pedophiles who slithered out into Laois and Offaly and went to ground. If Frank had told Andy Dempsey the extra food and whiskey were for his brother, then Andy might have wondered where this brother suddenly came from and then discovered Frank had a pedophile sibling."

"God! I hadn't thought about it before—how do you deal with a pedophile in your family?" Gorman asked.

"You don't," Breen said.

They drove across a narrow river bridge, the rounded coping stones on the parapets reminders of the long colonial presence. Gorman pointed. "Third house on the right, thatched with reeds, red door, hay sheds."

"You're showing off, Jimmy."

"You know I'm a walking memory bank."

"Do you remember the day you were born?" Breen asked.

"Of course. Doesn't everyone? I was wrapped in swaddling clothes and laid in the turf basket near the fire."

"Are you sure you weren't laid in a manger?"

"No, never in a manger, but twice in a hay shed."

"You wish, Gorman…There's the red door."

"And maybe that's Frank Geoghan going around the side of the house to the farmyard," Gorman said. "Good, we'll be able to keep his missus out of this."

"That would be a break—fewer emotions to deal with."

Gorman drove past the house and parked the car in a field gateway. The two guards closed the doors quietly, and without speaking they walked into the paved driveway and followed the route the farmer had taken. They heard the distant bawling of the winter cattle in their outdoor pens. The hay shed was vast; three individual sheds, each ninety feet long, were attached side by side. A sixty-foot-wide lean-to, which ran across the end of the main structure, was divided into four spaces for the cattle. The bales of summer hay and straw were piled to the tops of the sheds, stored with aforethought for the one-man foddering and bedding. Except for the lean-to, which had three skylights, the shed was dusky, and even the light coming through the skylights was filtered through a coat of dirt.

Breen glanced up at the blue plaques with white lettering attached to each shed: KELLY'S OF PORTLAOISE. "Kelly's must have erected every hay shed in the country," he said.

"I love the smell of a hay shed," Gorman said.

When they came to the shed door the two detectives saw the farmer holding a piece of board against the manger that ran along the top of the low wall separating the lean-to from the sheds. He was marking the wood with a pencil.

Breen tapped on the open galvanized door and waited for the man to turn around. "Hello," Gorman called. "We're looking for Mister Geoghan...Frank Geoghan."

"I'm your man if you're not excise men or buggers from Brussels," Geoghan said. He was wearing a battered dark fedora with a dark rim.

"We're neither," Gorman said, "but we *are* detectives from Tullamore."

Geoghan placed the board he had marked across the top of the barrel he was using as a work bench. Beside the barrel, a rip saw lay on its side on a backless kitchen chair along with a jam jar half full of nails and a hammer with a steel handle.

A dozen hens were scratching or snuggling in the deep, dry molderings of years of hay, and they fluttered out of Geoghan's way as he walked up into the brightness of the doorway.

He was a large man, probably in his late sixties, and his most striking feature was his ears; they were too large and too acutely angled away from the sides of his head. The fine hairs rimming the ears were highlighted by the November light. His weathered face was furrowed from years of facing into wind and sun and blowing rain, and his white eyebrows stood out against the redness of his complexion. The dark eyes had done more peering than gazing in their lifetime and the skin around them was now as wrinkled as the udder of a dry cow. Geoghan hadn't shaved since the previous Saturday night, and the stubble on his chin was as white as his brows.

Frank Geoghan belonged to that generation of farmers who worked in the suits that had once been their Sunday best. He was even wearing a waistcoat buttoned from top to bottom. His ankle-high, leather lace-up boots were not acquainted with polish. The man's daily grind could be deduced from the assembly of stains on his suit and the once-white shirt.

"I'm Detective Breen and this is Detective Gorman," Breen said. He put his garda I.D. card into Geoghan's broken-nailed and welted hand.

Geoghan stood in the doorway and narrowed his eyes. "Glasses," he said. "Never have them when I need them... but this looks impressive." He squinted again. "Detective Sergeant Breen," he said, as he handed the card back. "And you, sir?" he asked, turning to Gorman. Jimmy rummaged in his wallet and handed over his I.D. After more squinting, Geoghan said, "Detective Sergeant Gorman. Are you related to the Gormans in Geashill?"

"No, sir."

"Thought not. You're a bit on the short side."

"Sure they lowered the height limit for guards years ago, Mister Geoghan. That's how Detective Gorman got in."

Gorman speared Breen with his eyes.

"They'll be letting dwarfs in next," Geoghan said.

"We're here on what may be a matter of some delicacy," Breen said.

"I'm not in trouble, am I? Here, sit down." Geoghan pointed at a cluster of square bales of hay. They all sat, the two guards with their backs to the door, Geoghan facing them in the weak light.

"Fire away," Geoghan said.

"Do you have a brother named Daniel?" Breen asked.

So suddenly did Frank Geoghan stand up that he startled the two detectives. He strode quickly back into the darkness of the hay shed, squawking hens fluttering out of the way of his determined boots. Breen and Gorman looked at each other and stood up.

"Frank, besides us, no one knows about him," Gorman called after Geoghan.

While the two policemen waited, red hens resumed scratching and bathing in the dusty chaff. On stiff legs and with tail erect, a black cat approached the doorway and sinuously writhed against the jamb, tail in the air. Eventually, Geoghan's shape materialized against the wall of golden straw behind him.

"Frank, Daniel is dead," Tom Breen said.

Hands at his sides, thumbs in his trousers pockets, Jimmy Gorman sauntered down in Geoghan's direction and stopped when he was close enough to make out Frank's features. "Frank," he said, "Sergeant Breen and myself believe we may have some idea about the situation you're in...you're probably embarrassed, maybe ashamed."

Breen had followed Gorman. "Frank, we wouldn't be here only your brother is dead," he said.

Geoghan held his ground, stayed in the shadows.

"Did you bring food to your brother's house last Thursday?"

"Who knows?" Geoghan asked froggily. He cleared his throat.

"Who knows what, Frank?" Breen asked.

"About him...about what he is."

"Us—the two of us—and three other guards," Breen said.

"Then it's too late."

"Too late for what?"

"To keep everyone from...Who found him?" Geoghan asked.

"Someone passing by."

"How was that?" Geoghan asked.

"What do you mean?" Gorman asked.

"He never came out of the house in the day."

"Were you out there with food yesterday?" Breen asked.

"I was."

"Did you talk to him?"

"No. I haven't talked to him since..." He became silent.

"Did you see him?" Breen asked.

"No. I haven't seen him since he..."

"What was the arrangement about the food, Frank?" Gorman asked.

"Every Thursday I leave the food and the newspapers in a box behind the bushes in the yard around eight; there's a piece of blue tarp to cover it. Sometimes he leaves out last week's empty box and sometimes he doesn't."

"Have you ever missed a delivery?" Gorman asked.

"No."

"You haven't asked how he died, Frank," Breen said.

"Liver or lungs, I suppose. Whiskey and cigarettes. It doesn't matter."

"You don't seem to care much."

"I wouldn't have brought the food only for a promise I made."

"To your father? To your mother?" Gorman asked. Frank didn't answer.

"Missus Geoghan...your wife," Breen said, "does she know about Daniel?"

"No. She thinks he was sent to Australia by the Order... This is going to be all over the papers, isn't it?"

"Only because of the way he died, Frank," Gorman said.

"Alright! How did he die? You're going to tell me one way or the other."

"He was murdered about two weeks ago," Breen said.

"Two weeks ago?" There was a long silence. Then Geoghan said, "I brought the food out last night. I never missed a Thursday. If he died two weeks ago then I would have seen last Thursday's full box still out under the tarp."

"Last Thursday's box is in the house, but last night's isn't. We're trying to find out what happened to it."

"Well, I put it there."

"Do you want to know how he was murdered?" Gorman asked.

Directly in front of the two detectives a red hen flapped and clawed herself down into the dry chaff. A cloud of dust rose up around her.

"He was my little brother once," Geoghan said. "We looked for birds' nests together." Then as he remembered two small boys, one on the other's shoulders pulling the young spring leaves apart to look at the colored eggs, Frank gave a single strangulated cry. "I don't want to know how he was killed."

"It might be better hearing it from us, Frank," Gorman said.

"I don't want to know."

"The papers, Frank."

"Can it be kept out of the papers?...I suppose it's too late for that. Three other guards know already."

"There was a reporter sniffing around just after we got there this morning," Breen said.

Geoghan covered his face with his hands. "The shame," he said, "the shame of it all. How will we live it down, me and the missus when she finds out? She'll be cross as hell at me for not telling her...The shame, the shame." Geoghan dragged his hands down along his face, the pulled-down bottom eyelids glistening red.

"Frank, maybe we can help with the papers," Gorman said. "We can't promise anything, but we will try to keep the Geoghan name out of it. We'll refer to your brother by his religious name instead."

Frank shot out a defensive hand. "Don't say his religious name to me. I can't bear to hear it." Geoghan put his big maulers over his face for a moment. "I would appreciate it very much if you could keep the family name a secret...not let reporters...I would thank you very much if that could be done."

"We will do our best, Frank," Breen said. "And you must do your best to answer all our questions. Come on back to the bales."

As he walked by the backless kitchen chair, Gorman picked up the jam jar with the nails, held it up near his eyes. "Are these ten-penny nails, Frank?" he asked.

It took a moment for Frank Geoghan to change his cerebral gears. He stopped and looked at the jam jar as if he had never seen it before. Then he said, "Ten-penny?... No, eight-penny nails."

For a long while Frank Geoghan stayed in the dark. While they waited, the detectives pretended to look at old farming tools hanging from the wooden crossbars between the steel pillars: the wide-rimmed, wooden wheel of a bog barrow; a four-grain dung fork, one grain snapped off near the head; a black-handled slane; the wing of a horse-drawn plough; a T-shaped hay knife; a hand-woven basket full of small rolls of blue twine that had been cut off the bales and wound up around the hand. The two men kept their backs to Geoghan until Gorman saw him pulling up the knees of his trousers preparatory to sitting on the bale. When Gorman and Breen took their seats facing him on the warm hay, Breen took out his mobile and called Superintendent Donovan. "It's Tom, sir. I have a request. Can we avoid using Daniel Geoghan's name— refer to him only by his religious name? He has living family members. We'd like to spare them the publicity."

The three men heard the superintendent's reply. "Tell him we'll do our level best, Tom. Call me back when you can."

Breen put his phone away and took a card from the top pocket in his jacket. "Give me the loan of your phone, Jimmy," he said and held out his hand. He dialed a number. "Ms. Byron? This is Detective Sergeant Breen. We met this morning." He stood up and stepped over the bale away from the others when he heard the beginning of her reply.

"I worked out what the P.T.A. bribe was, Detective Sergeant Breen; crude but clever. I always thought it stood for Parent Teacher Asso—"

Breen interrupted. "I want you to do something for me as a fellow human being and for no other reason... Alright. If you do uncover the name of the man who was found murdered in the house on the Daingean Road, please do not put it in your paper. No...No, not now...Am I not calling you now? I will...alright, by four o'clock."

Gorman gave his boss a curious look as Breen returned the phone. "I'll explain later," Breen said.

Not once, the detectives later noted, did Frank
Geoghan look either of them in the eye while he described
the routines he had followed to feed his brother and keep
his existence a secret.

The only thing of consequence he revealed was that
a key to his brother's front door was hidden under a flat
stone three feet out from the front step.

16.

At half-past nine, Pauline Byron had asked Tess Westman why a woman living in Daingean in County Offaly spoke in a Cork accent, and at twenty to ten the answer was still being delivered in a Gatling-gun style that bode no interruption. Tess was standing at the edge of Pauline's table, folded arms supporting her old bosoms. Her hair had once been red, and stray rusty strands had escaped from her hairnet. A strand at her mouth was puffed away with upward jets blown through lips funnel-shaped briefly for the purpose.

The reporter sliced her scone in half, plastered it with clotted cream and strawberry preserves as she listened. Pauline was the only patron in the Tea Rooms.

Finally, thirteen minutes after she had started, Tess drew in a deep breath. "And that's how I ended up in Daingean forty-one years ago and I'm still a blow-in, an outsider, and every time there's a bit of gossip the locals whisper in case I hear it. And every time a stranger like you comes in here they ask me the same question. And you're a commercial traveler yourself, are you?"

The quick question caught Pauline with her mouth full of scone, jam and cream. She waved a hand and pointed to her face.

"Take it easy. You won't choke on us now, will you?" Tess said.

Pauline swallowed. "I'm a newspaper reporter."

"Be janey! Now I know who you are. I thought there was something about you. You were on television…There was never a reporter in here before. What are you reporting in a place like Daingean? Did a cow die?"

"I've been in here a few times before when I've passed through. I tell everyone how good your scones are."

"Well, that's very good of you, isn't it?" Tess said.

"Would you mind if I stayed for a while, Missus West-man?" Pauline asked. "I have some phone calls to make and a few things to look up on my laptop."

"Sure, everyone calls me Tess, and you can of course."

The ancient bell attached to the spring above the door rattled and a man pushed a shy child into the shop. Tess said, "Pete, you're looking grand, aren't you? And Maura is getting so tall, isn't she?" The little girl turned and buried her face in her father's thigh, wrapped her arms around his leg.

Pauline pushed her plate to the end of the table. She looked around, then dipped her sticky fingers into her teacup and dried them in her handkerchief. While she waited for her laptop to boot up, Pauline flipped open her phone. It rang in her hand. She glanced at the screen but she didn't recognize the number. Her eyebrows arched when she heard, "Ms. Byron?"

"Yes?"

"This is Detective Sergeant Breen. We met this morning."

Pauline began to tell Breen she had figured out the P.T.A. bribe, but Breen cut her off and asked her "as a fellow human being" not to publish the name of the victim near Burnt House if she discovered it. Pauline agreed, and although neither Breen nor she mentioned the words *quid pro quo*, Breen promised to call her again before four o'clock. Pauline felt she had got the better end of the deal because as well as the promised call, she now had Breen's mobile number.

She put the phone aside and brought up the homepage of the Garda Síochána on her laptop. There was a bare-bones history of Detective Sergeant Thomas Breen's career within the department, but nothing

personal at all, not even his age. Detective Breen had
spent his career in the Tullamore Garda District. While
stationed in Clara he had saved a child from drowning
by jumping into the flooding Brosna River. For the rescue, he had been awarded the Scott Medal for Bravery.
Pauline Googled the Scott Medal. As she read the blovi-
ated requirements for the winning of the award she face-
tiously decided that within a fraction of a second Thomas
Breen had shown he was personally brave, that he had
behaved intelligently while risking his life, and had not
won the medal because of someone else's act of bravery.
Pauline wondered whether a person who plunged into
a frigid, flooding river to save a child was acting instinctively or intelligently. She wondered, too, how Breen felt
about the citation. Maybe she'd ask him.

Next Pauline dipped into *The Telegraph* computer
files and clicked her way through several links before
she entered the Asparagus file. When it opened, the first
thing she saw was the word "Cayenne" in a large font, in
red, in boldface, in italics and underlined. She assumed
that Cayenne was Jack Rafferty's not-too-obtuse codeword
for "red hot."

Besides the details that Jack Rafferty had passed on
to her, there was nothing except some notes from Mick
McGovern's Carrowreagh report dated two weeks previ-
ously. From McGovern's notes, Pauline inferred that the
crime reporter had gone to Carrowreagh on November
sixth, the day after the discovery of Brother Boniface's
body. When McGovern finally located the dead man's isolated abode, a garda patrol car was blocking a gate on the
lane to the hill on which some lunatic of yore had built
the house. McGovern had been told that the house was a
crime scene and that it would belong to the authorities
until the case was closed. The reporter then had driven
back into the Carrowreagh village to make inquiries. The
only person he spoke to was a Mister Paud Hughes, and

Mick McGovern suspected that Hughes had stonewalled him: *The sole shopkeeper in Carrowreagh knew nothing, not even that the isolated house existed, not even that a man had been murdered in it. His not knowing anything made me suspect the gardai had told him not to speak to reporters.* McGovern had knocked on four doors in the village but no one answered. *The smell of animal waste—steenk de slurry—pervaded the entire place,* McGovern had gratuitously concluded.

A later entry in the file, initialed by Jack Rafferty, stated that one of *The Telegraph's* garda moles had sent in the Pulse bare-bones posting on the case. That posting had concluded, *For operational purposes, no further details available.*

Pauline put her chin in the heel of her hand and stared at the screen. It was no wonder Jack Rafferty had been excited on the phone this morning. For two weeks he'd had a cayenne pepper up his fundament and this morning he'd been given another red-hot tip by the anonymous caller.

Pauline shook herself back into Tess Westman's Tea Rooms and set her fingers to dancing around her laptop's keyboard:

KNOWN
- *Both bodies phoned to The Telegraph.*
- *Both victims male; both former religious; both nailed to floor.*
- *Both bodies rotting.*
- *Both houses isolated.*
- *In both cases guards tightlipped.*

POSSIBLES
- *Phone-caller is killer.*
- *Same killer in both cases.*
- *Detail of missing penis at Burnt House given to whet our interest.*

TO DO
- *Names of the victims.*
- *Check background of both.*
- *Was Carrowreagh penis removed?*

Pauline shifted her position on the hard, wooden chair, and her eyes went back to the Pulse report: *a body was found.*

"Stupid," she said softly. "*Who* found the body at Carrowreagh?" She added the question to her to-do list. And what had Jack Rafferty said about...? She picked up the phone and within four seconds Rafferty's voice was in her ear.

"Jack, it's Pauline..."

"Tell me what you have, girl."

Rafferty's paternalism was a nail scraping on Pauline's mental blackboard.

"Not yet, Jack. Who found the body this morning?"

"A man with a bloodhound on his way to Garryhinch to look for that old woman."

"The dog owner, Jack...do you know his name?"

"Brian Deegan—his name has been all over the radio this morning. He called the guards in Tullamore about the Daingean road body. Don't you ever—?"

"If Brian Deegan called the guards then he must have seen the body. What do—?"

"Deegan is still in Garryhinch with his dog waiting for RTE to arrive with the cameras. McGovern's on his way there, should arrive soon."

"Jack, ask McGovern to talk to Deegan, find out what he can about what Deegan saw...the state of the body, the crucifixion, anything...the name of the dead man, anything."

"Pauline, you call McGovern your—"

"Jack, you have forgotten the frigging guarantee you gave me a few frigging hours ago. I'm already on my way to Carrowreagh. I'm going to find out who found the body there. Tell McGovern to call me after he talks to Deegan." She hung up, mentally stuck her tongue out at Rafferty, and went to the counter.

"It's yourself, is it, Pauline?" Tess answered and asked. "You're leaving us, are you?"

"I have to run, Tess. Could I have a tuna sandwich to take with me? Go light with the mayonnaise and heavy with the salt and put a thick slice of tomato on it. And a cup of tea, no sugar, too."

"Eating on the run, are you, Pauline?"

"Right, Tess."

Pauline went back to her laptop and brought up AA Roadwatch. It would take over an hour to get to Durrow and another twenty minutes after that to reach Carrowreagh. Forty-two miles. She went back to her list of Knowns and entered *Brothers live about fifty miles apart.*

17.

It was almost one o'clock when Pauline drove into Carrowreagh. On the way down she decided that Paud Hughes's shop would be the best place to start even though Mick McGovern got nowhere with the owner.

The shop stood out in the middle of the short row of attached houses that made up the village, HUGHES GROCERY painted in white on the red fascia above the entrance. As she was parking the jeep, her mobile rang. It was McGovern in Garryhinch: six feet six inches tall and as skinny as a twig; wire-rimmed glasses; early forties with a shock of prematurely grey hair as startled as a dandelion gone to seed; looking as if he'd just hatched out of an egg, but with instincts as sharp as a dog-rose thorn.

"Pauline, Mick. Only thing Brian Deegan would say is that his dog discovered a body on the Daingean road. I felt he was watching his Ps and Qs in the interests of his canine business."

"Alright, Mick. Thanks for trying."

The small grocery shop was empty except for the little round man behind the counter dividing a handful of receipts into four piles as if he were dealing cards for a game of whist. A white apron hung from his waist, and the sleeves of his blue shirt were rolled up to the elbows. His hairy arms were short and pudgy. He was bald on top with silver hair on the sides.

"Doing the paperwork?" Pauline said from the door, breaking his concentration.

Paud Hughes looked up and smiled. "The worst part of having your own shop is the paperwork. I hate it so much that I try to stay ahead of it, like your man jumping off a building to get rid of his fear of heights. And I never thought the selling of a few postage stamps would involve so many forms to fill in. I'm sorry I started it."

The man's volubility was promising.

"You're not from these parts, Missus?"

"I'm not. I live in Emo."

"Emo!" the shopkeeper said. "If I've asked one person I've asked a thousand, what kind of name is Emo? It doesn't sound Irish—or English. Do you know what it means?"

"In Irish, Emo is *Iomagh. Magh* means—"

"Plain," the man interrupted, like a schoolboy not able to contain himself, and he clapped his hands.

"And *Iomagh* means the edge of the plain. And Emo is on the edge of a fertile plain."

"After all this time...the edge of the plain. It's a poor day when a man doesn't learn something new. Now... what can I do for you?"

"First, I'd like a bar of Bourneville, and then I hope you can give me some information."

Before he had turned to the shelf behind him, Paud Hughes's hand grasped the chocolate. Pauline paid him.

"Alright, Missus, fire away."

"My name is—"

The man clapped his hands again. "Byron, Pauline. I knew you the minute you walked in but I couldn't place you. TV...and I read the last of your report on F. X. Culliton in *The Telegraph* yesterday."

"I should wear a paper bag over my head. And are you Mister Hughes?"

"Call me Paud." He stretched his small fat hand across the counter and they shook hands. "You sure gave it to that bugger F. X. All corrupt politicians should be shot. I hate the feckers when they go bad. How does a reporter find out all that stuff?"

"I work with very talented researchers. They point me toward the people with the information."

"I never thought I'd see someone like you in this neck of the bog, Ms. Byron. What have we done to attract your attention?"

"Flattery will get you nowhere, Paud. I want to ask you some questions in confidence, and if you can give me answers I will keep the source a secret, too."

"That sounds fair, but let me hear some of the questions first. I had another reporter in here a few weeks ago sniffing around; he looked like a blown-out dandelion."

"A man was found dead in a shed near here on the fifth of November."

Hughes held up a hand to fend off the question. "The guards told me not to talk to anyone about that, Missus."

"I understand, Paud. It's sometimes necessary for the guards not to give out details about a crime because that information might help the killer or a copycat might try to get into the limelight. At the moment I'm not writing about this murder. I'm gathering the background for a long report that won't be in *The Telegraph* till after Christmas, and by that time the murderer will have been found."

Pauline waited for Paud Hughes to say something. But he didn't say a word, and worse still, he folded his arms across his chest.

"I can see the situation you're in, Paud. The guards asked you not to discuss the murder. Now I'm asking you to talk about it, but I promise you I will not use what you tell me in any way that will interfere with the guards' investigation. Nor will the guards know you ever spoke to me. Hopefully, the information I'm looking for will fit into a much larger picture. It would be unethical for me to tell you what that larger picture is."

"Wouldn't it be as unethical for me to tell you what I know?" Paud asked.

"I don't think so, because whatever you tell me will be old news by the time I write about it."

Mister Hughes took his eyes off Pauline and locked them onto something behind her. He pursed his lips. He lowered his arms. He put his hands on the counter and said, "If anyone comes in while I'm talking, you will pick up the paper there"—he pointed to a small pile of *The Leinster Express*—"and open it like you're looking for something. I'll tell you all I know, with the above conditions attached, as they say in the small print."

Without hesitation, Pauline lunged. "Do you know the name of the man who was murdered?"

18.

Paud Hughes was as eager to talk as a scrupulous penitent. "Yes, I know the dead man's name. Joe O'Brien. I
delivered his groceries every week. Four point six miles
exactly back and forth and two gates each way. I charged
him for mileage. I should have charged him for the time
it took to negotiate the gates, too. I counted one time—
eighteen different moves to get through each gate, and
it raining cats and dogs most times and the fecking goats
always trying to get out."

"Did you know Joe O'Brien well?" Pauline moved over
to the stack of *The Leinster Express* on the counter.

"Not at all. I wouldn't have known him if I met him on
the road. Aren't you going to take notes? I always thought
reporters scribbled in little notebooks."

"Like I said, this is all background for a larger story.
I'm trying to get a picture more than facts," Pauline said,
as she began to mine all the facts that Paud Hughes had in
his head. "What was the arrangement with the food? How
did O'Brien pay you? How did he order what he wanted?"

"About four years ago I found a folded piece of paper
pushed in under the door there." Paud gestured across
the shop. "It was a list of items and a request for me to
deliver them to the shed at the back of his house every
Wednesday; there would be money in a tin box on the
bench inside the door and I was to leave the change in
it. The list would be the same every week unless there
was a note left on the bench. The paper was signed Joe
O'Brien. I was a bit wary that someone was trying to cod

me, but I went out to his house anyway, and there was the
money in the tin box."

"And you never saw the man? Not once in four years?"

"Not once. Of course I wondered about who he was.
For a while I thought he might be a hermit—a religious
hermit. In the end I decided he was hiding a disfigure-
ment."

"Did many people know about him?"

"I'd say everyone in Carrowreagh knew someone was
living in the house, but I doubt if anyone knew anymore
than myself."

"You thought he was disfigured? Were there any other
speculations?"

"Everyone did their own speculating, and some of
them were downright vicious, depending on the nature
of the speculator."

"Who found him dead?"

"Two of the local lads out Sunday-hunting, getting in
out of a heavy shower, Joe and Mike Conran, Irish twins
and almost identical. They've been codding me for years.
Real nice lads."

"Did either of them tell you anything about the body?
Were there signs of violence?"

"Sure, I saw the body myself, Missus. Mike called me
on my mobile and asked me to go to O'Brien's house
because something had happened. He didn't say O'Brien
was dead, but I could hear Mike shaking with the fright
on the phone."

"Why did they call you?"

"I asked them the same thing; because I was the only
one who ever went to the house, they said. They never
thought of calling the guards."

"So you saw the body?"

"I did." Hughes opened and retied his apron strings.

"And?"

"When I got there, Joe and Mike were standing at the gate in the garden wall, well away from the house and the shed. I asked them what was going on and they pointed and never said a word. The stink stopped me in my tracks and I looked back at the boys just to make sure they were still there. I thought there might be a dead animal in the shed, but when I walked in, there was this naked body nailed to the floor, all blackish and the flesh falling off it. It was like a prop in a picture to frighten children—and adults, too." Paud Hughes's apron flapped up and covered his face, the small hands pressing the cloth into his eyes. After several deep breaths he lowered his hands and let the apron fall down.

"I want to make sure you understand this, Missus Byron: I only looked at the body for as long as it took the image to get to my brain and for my brain to send a signal to my eyes to look away. I'm telling you this because I only have an impression in my mind. There were a lot of nails in the body, there was something about the terrible lips, and he was castrated, if you'll excuse me."

"Feck!" Pauline couldn't help herself.

"Feck is right, Missus Byron. I keep seeing it."

"Was he nailed like Christ on the cross?"

"I couldn't tell you that…don't remember."

Neither of them spoke for a few moments. Then Pauline said quietly, "I imagine it was a dreadful sight, Paud, all the more so because you stumbled onto it."

"I think it was worse for the Conran lads. They ran into the shed out of the rain, hadn't even time to get the smell first. O'Brien had to be dead a few weeks at least. I wish I could get the image out of my head. When I wake up in the night the rotting corpse with the nails and the… the crotch. Somebody had to hate that man to do such a thing to him."

"How are the Conrans doing? Have you seen them since?"

"Only once did I see Mike, though they used to be in and out of here the whole time. When Mike came in, he didn't bring up the subject and he kept not looking at me, as if I'd caught him doing something embarrassing."

"They probably need to talk to someone about it. How old are they?"

"Nineteen, but ten months apart."

"I don't suppose it matters how old you are when you see something like that; it gets fixed in the brain."

"It does."

"The last time you delivered—"

Hughes interrupted Pauline. "I made the last delivery on Wednesday, the..." He turned around and took a calendar off the wall, placed it on the counter and flipped back to October. He put his finger on a date highlighted in yellow. "October the seventeenth. That's the last time I brought out the food."

"So if he was dead a few weeks when you found him on November the fifth, that would—"

"That's only a guess, Missus. I've never seen an old corpse before. And the morning after my last delivery on October the seventeenth I found a note under the door there, written on a torn-off piece of brown bag. It said something like, 'Going away. I don't need any more food delivered,' and it was signed 'Joe O'Brien.'"

"Did the guards ask you for the note?"

"They did, but I had thrown it out. Why would I have kept it?"

"Why indeed, Paud? Do you know who owns the house where Joe O'Brien lived?"

"I don't. The last owner was Paddy Larkin. The wife died young and he was very old when he died. Paddy had a son who went to Australia about twenty years ago and never came back, not even for the father's funeral. There was a falling-out. The house stayed empty for about four years before O'Brien moved in. It must have been as damp as hell. Maybe he bought it or maybe he rented it."

"You never heard of O'Brien having any relatives?"

"Like I said, all I knew was his name and for all I know that wasn't his name at all."

"Who's the local auctioneer?"

"Danny Dowling from Abbeyleix does most of the auctioneering around here—hay and straw and land to let, houses to set or sell. You're right—he might know if O'Brien bought or rented."

Pauline took the bar of Bourneville out of her jacket pocket. She pushed the wrapping aside, snapped the chocolate squares and held one out to Hughes.

"No, thanks, Missus Byron. If I start eating chocolate I'll eat myself out of the shop and out of my clothes."

Pauline slipped a square into her mouth and rewrapped the rest.

"I know what you're talking about, Paud. This bar has eight squares. It will last me eight days. Can you think of anything else about Joe O'Brien or the way he died?"

"I can't. I told the guards that I was kind of glad I'd finished dealing with him. Did you ever notice how you hear something about someone and even though you don't know whether it's true or not it affects the way you see that person ever after? Remember you were talking about people speculating? Everyone knew that a police car drove out to Joe O'Brien's house every couple of months, and someone speculated that O'Brien was on the guards' list of pedophiles and that he was being checked. After that I felt...sort of...I felt like I would have felt when I was a child going into a haunted house. I was afraid I'd see him."

"I know the feeling, Paud. I would be very uncomfortable talking to a person I knew was a pedophile. But for all you know, the guards could have been just checking every highway and byway in the district several times a year the way they do."

"You're right, Missus. When I'd be going out to the house I used to wish I hadn't heard that speculation at all."

"Well, Paud, thanks for all you've told me. I appreciate it and I'd appreciate it if you didn't tell anyone about—"

Paud waved a dismissive hand. "Oh, I won't say a word, but I'll be keeping an eye on *The Telegraph* to see how you use what I told you. Just don't put my name in it."

"Don't worry. Here's my card, Paud, and please call me if you remember anything else or hear anything new."

Paud took the card and stretched out his hand. "It was nice meeting you, Missus Byron. I'll have to wait a few months before I can tell everyone I had such a famous person in here."

"Flattery, Paud," Pauline said, as she turned to leave.

She was at the door when Hughes said, "You can't miss Danny Dowling's house—the auctioneer in Abbeyleix. His house is on the main street, same color as the Bourneville wrapper. You'll see the house before you see his big sheet of brass with his name on it. The man has notions."

"How did you know I was going—?"

"Where else would a reporter go at this point?" Hughes said, his eyes glistening.

Pauline left, but a few seconds later she reappeared in the doorway. "I'm back, Paud." She walked over to the counter. "I wanted to ask you something earlier, but I thought it might be too embarrassing. But now I've decided that if I don't ask you, I'll never know. If the question embarrasses you, I'm sorry."

"I might blush, but I'll do my best to answer you," Hughes said.

"I know you only saw O'Brien's body for a split second. You said he was castrated. Are you a hundred percent sure of that? Is it possible that it was only his penis that had been cut off?"

Paud Hughes's right hand almost got to his crotch before he stopped it. His face turned purple. He looked down at the countertop. "Now that you want me to be specific I can only be less specific," he said. "All I can say is that something had been done to him down there. I have been thinking all along that he was castrated." He stopped talking for a few seconds, stared at the backs of his hands on the counter. "There was a piece of twine there—blue."

"Was the twine attached to anything, Paud?"

Like he was speaking to himself, Paud said, "Yes, there was a piece of blue twine at his crotch."

"Was there much blood near the twine?"

"No blood."

"You said something about the lips, Paud. What was it about the lips that got your attention?"

Hughes lifted his head and looked at Pauline, the color fading from his face. "The instant you said 'lips,' do you know what came into my head? A platypus; you know, that strange animal in Australia. There was something about his lips that reminded me of a platypus." He pushed out his lips and caught them between his thumbs and index fingers. He pulled the lips away from his face. He turned sideways to let Pauline see his silhouette. He turned back. "The lips were shaped like the bill of a platypus and they had marks in them."

"What kind of marks?"

"I don't know," Hughes said. "I can't tell you another thing, Missus. Remember, I only have an impression of the whole thing—I was trying my best to get my eyes off the corpse."

Before she heard the noise behind her, Pauline knew from Hughes's eyes that someone was coming into the shop. She said, "The next time I won't forget the map. Thank you and I'm sorry for taking up your time."

Without missing a beat, Paud said, "You're welcome, Missus. Just stay to your right where the road splits."

Pauline raised her hand to her face and turned to her left, away from the approaching customer. She heard Paud saying, "Another lost tourist, Missus Horan."

"Some of dem are terrible tick, Paud," Missus Horan said. "Was she from America?"

19.

Pauline did not fulfill Paud Hughes's expectations. Instead of going immediately to see Danny Dowling, the auctioneer, she followed Hughes's directions to the house of the late Joe O'Brien, alias Brother John the Baptist.

Two-point-one miles from Hughes Grocery she turned right twice and left once. The turns eventually put her onto a narrow, gravel-surfaced lane whose overhanging leafless bushes and briars scratched at her jeep. The narrowness of the lane left no room for maneuvering around the many potholes, and she bounced and splashed her way to the first of the two red metal gates that Paud Hughes had complained about.

Pauline stopped her jeep, got out and closed the door. She picked her way around the mud to the gate and laid her arms along the top bar, her hands at her chin. Beyond, a narrow lane, with a track of grass running along its middle, made a straight line across a pasture and then turned into a gated opening in thick bushes at the foot of a low hill that could have been a spoil bank.

She could see the roof of the house near the top of the hill. No electricity poles or phone lines were visible. As she gazed at the house in the spaces between the surrounding trees and bushes, she was reminded of a bird's nest built with camouflage and isolation in mind. This house was as solitary as the cottage at Burnt House, with no neighbors to hear or see anything.

Pauline heard a noise to her right and three goats came racing along beside the hedge. Like begging dogs, they jumped up and put their front feet on the gate's third bar.

"Shoo!" Pauline commanded, and she shook the gate. The goats dropped down and looked up at her, their scoop-like ears as attentive as their eyes. She gazed at their faces and realized she was only repulsed by them because they had been demonized in the religious calendars of her childhood. Putting aside her prejudice, she took a fresh look and decided that goats looked intelligent; on the dumb-and-ugly scale they were certainly below sheep.

The goats galloped off, raced each other back to their grazing without the tidbit that would have spiced up their grassy diet.

Pauline returned to the jeep for her winter jacket. She zippered it up to her neck, then tucked the legs of her jeans into her socks. When she lifted the gate's latch and stepped through the opening, she felt disquiet, a physical sensation in her belly that she couldn't identify. It wasn't fear or nervousness. Pauline was rational about visiting the scene of a gruesome crime, knew the killer wouldn't be crouching in the dark waiting to grab his next victim, knew there would be no ghosts nor miasmic mists hovering. The killer had come to this place for a specific purpose. He had done his specific deed and had gone away. He had done the same near Burnt House.

Pauline zigzagged along the wheel tracks, stepping over the grass median whenever she was faced with a muck-filled pothole. Where the narrow lane slipped into the bushes at the bottom of the hill, she opened the second gate. Still the feeling in her stomach had not identified itself to her. Again she put her arms along the top of the gate and gazed back, looked for whatever it was that had loosened the bubble of memory and sent it wobbling to the surface. But she saw nothing, just the goats eating grass.

Her daily jogging made the climb up the circuitous lane easy.

The poor soil of the hill was only capable of supporting furze and dwarfish blackthorns, their attractive purple sloes belying the gum-shrinking tartness within. Clusters of willowy, anemic rowans clung to the thin soil and were bent to accommodate the prevailing southwesterly wind. Along each side of the lane the black, bare pylons of the summer's stinging nettles stood defiantly against intruders. Pauline could see no animal trails or passes through the undergrowth. The two hunters who discovered the dead body in the shed would not have found much to shoot on this barren hill. The poverty of the flora reminded Pauline of the rich grasses, exuberant trees and the fecund berry bushes of Emo Park.

Pauline walked out of the shade of the lane and was confronted by a three-foot, capped, concrete wall, the last vestiges of its pebbled dashing clinging like scabs to its leprous face. Between two five-foot, capped but raveling concrete piers hung a narrow, rusting garden gate that had once been green. Immediately on the far side of the wall, a hedge of boxwood had grown so tall that it had collapsed onto itself and created an impenetrable entanglement of barbed dead branches along the capstone. Pauline was mockingly aware that many Irish homeowners built grand entrances that often belied the grandness of the houses they surrounded. And even up here, a mile from the nearest neighbor, the builder had surrounded his castle with a sturdy wall and a wrought-iron gate.

Pauline strode through the dead weeds and clasped the top bar of the gate. In the garden, the shrubs and flower beds had seen neither shears nor spade in many years, but she could see traces of Victorian edging around what had once been someone's geometric designs. Neglected hedges of dwarf box, thickening the air with their rich,

exotic aroma, marched bedraggedly along each side of
the weedy path to the front door of a three-roomed cottage, its mortar-plastered and capped chimney in the
middle of the rusting tin roof. Pauline knew that thick layers of thatch lay beneath the corrugated metal sheets, the
tin being the owner's solution to the dying-off of skilled
thatchers. Like a skeletal claw of a science-fiction monster, a giant rosebush still clung to the front of the cottage
between the two windows to the left of the door. Some of
its tentacles were still clinging to the eave chute above,
with the wispy remains of a bird's nest still attached to its
thorny foundations.

Pauline wondered how she was going to get into the
garden. Tentatively, she shook the gate and noticed that
the weeds on its far side were flat and broken. When she
pushed down on the curlicued iron hasp she was surprised
at how easily it moved, and she was even more surprised
at how easily the gate swung open.

On the inside of the kitchen window, one end of
the curtain rod had fallen down, and the bottom pane
of glass was dissected by a browned lace curtain. Pauline
put her hand to her face and peered through the glass.
The window panes had a brown hue, as if a sheet of thin
golden plastic had been attached to the inside. Pauline
recognized the sheen, knew it had been created over
many years by drifting turf smoke from the fireplace. As
a child she'd accompanied her father on Sunday visits to
a country cottage in which a solitary and ancient man,
Joe Mack, had lived. Pauline had discovered that everything in Mister Mack's house was laminated with a layer
of damp, black turf soot that would accumulate under the
fingernails no matter what surface was scraped. Even now,
she could recall the smell of the soot on her hands.

Directly across from her a bare window in the back wall
was spotted with dirt. Through it she could see part of the
shed where John the Baptist's body had been found. The

wide windowsill was black. Beneath the window crouched a black table with a mug, a spoon and an empty milk bottle huddled together like three birds of different feathers. At the end of the table a large wooden armchair, the two thin cushions on its seat in disarray, projected the same sense of abandonment as a long-deserted and leaf-filled bird's nest. A person seated in the chair would have been within leaning distance of the open fireplace, which still had ashes in its grate. The entire width of the chimney breast behind the fireplace was coated in soot glistening like wet coal. Anchored in the far hob, a fireplace crane stretched across the grate, a black kettle hanging from a black hook. On the high mantel a few books lay on their sides near a tin box that had once been a tea canister. Pauline made a bet with herself that the canister's sides and lid were decorated with prints of Blarney Castle and the Lakes of Killarney and that it had originally held boiled sweets. Against the wall to Pauline's right an open-shelved, homemade dresser held a cup, a mug, an eggcup and a small blackened saucepan. The floor was a slab of concrete.

In the room to the right of the kitchen Pauline could see a narrow, metal-framed, unmade bed and a straight-backed chair draped with a carelessly thrown soiled white shirt, filthy trousers and a jumper that had once been green. There was no chest of drawers, no freestanding wardrobe. Pauline moved to the window on the other side of the kitchen.

It was obvious from the chaos of this room that the late owner had simply opened the door and flung in whatever he didn't need. Two broken bentwood chairs were bowing toward each other. A heavy Raleigh bicycle, lying on its side, claimed the center of the floor. It was almost hidden under a raveling sweater, a potato sack and what could have been a waterproof cape, its waterproofing cracked along its folds. What appeared to be a bundle of dead potato stalks had collapsed on itself in the far left corner. Glimpses of a mattress were visible under toppled flower-pots and long-handled gardening tools: rake, spade, four-grained fork, hoe. The blades of a hedge clipper were the open jaws of a metal scream. An accordion clothes rack had slipped one of its nails and hung down on the wall, a jacket with rips still attached to one of its pegs. A noseless and handless statue of the Child of Prague lay beside a scabbed enamel chamber pot. Plastic grocery bags dotted the entire tableau. At each window abandoned cobwebs clung to their main suspension cables.

Pauline turned away from the depressive chaos of the room and as she gazed across the abandoned flower beds and untended shrubs, she recognized the feeling that had slipped into her innards at the first red gate: her child-hood reaction to the loneliness of Sister Claire.

When Pauline was twelve, her favorite teacher, her favorite nun, her favorite adult had collapsed and died in her classroom in front of the children. At the red gate, it had been the loneliness of the place Pauline was looking at, that had dislodged the remembrance.

On the evening of the day after Sister Claire's funeral, Pauline had been sent up to Paddy Conroy's on her bike to collect two hundred cabbage plants for her father. Even before she wheeled her bike out onto the road, she had decided to visit Sister Claire in the cemetery. To keep her mother from knowing what she was doing, Pauline sped up to Mister Conroy's house, her head down at the handlebar and her bottom off the saddle. After Mister Conroy placed the plants in the handlebar basket and told her to mind herself, she sped off, pumping all the way to the cemetery. She left the bike propped against the cemetery wall because, at this time of evening, the only way in was through the kissing gate. Along the gravel path through the forest of headstones on either side, she ran flat out until she came to the nuns' plot with its two lines of matching iron crosses. The end of the nearest line was the fresh heap of earth on Sister Claire's grave. There were no flowers in the nuns' Spartan plot of graveyard.

It was only when Pauline walked over to the grave that she became aware she was alone. There were no starlings hopping through the grass, no birds singing. There was no sound of playing children, no lowing of distant cattle, no cackling of hens. There were no breezes, either, in the nearby yew trees. The lack of sound, the absence of breezes and people, had created the feeling of absolute loneliness. Sister Claire, young, vivacious, idolized, smiling, ever encouraging, was imprisoned in loneliness and soundlessness. Pauline thought of her down there, on her back in her coffin with her hands joined at her chest, lying in the black dark forever. The child Pauline had dropped to her knees, put her face in her hands and leaned over till the backs of her hands were on the cool clay of the grave. Then she cried for the young woman she had loved with the fierce bewildering love of a young adolescent girl.

Now, the older Pauline knew that Sister Claire had been dead to the loneliness of the cemetery, but Pauline also knew that Joe O'Brien had been alive to his solitary confinement in this desolate place.

O'Brien had certainly made no effort to make his house comfortable or to keep it clean and neat. He could have occupied himself with the garden. He could have tended the roses, shaped the hedges. But Pauline suspected that the derangement of the garden reflected the mind of the murdered man. And, she thought, the cottage near Burnt House was as neglected on the outside as this one.

The gruesome deaths inflicted on the brothers had to have been punishment for some evil behavior on their part. The interference with the genitals...religious brothers...isolated lives...sexual something...sexual what?...

rape...heterosexual or homosexual...pedophilia...Dach-
adoo Industrial School had been closed "forthwith" in
response to the recommendation of the Kennedy Report
in 1970. The more egregious offenders against children
had been allowed to remove themselves quietly from the
public eye because the church still had some grip on the
government strings that didn't break when pulled. This
man and the man at Burnt House must have had a lot in
common in life because they had a lot in common in the
way they were killed.

Pauline reclaimed her free-associating brain and
walked around to the back of the house to look at the shed,
where according to Jack Rafferty's anonymous caller, John
the Baptist had been nailed to the floor. The shed stood
up the hill, about seven long steps from the house. The
wooden structure, wrapped in three strands of blue and
white crime-scene tape, reminded Pauline of a Christmas
present. Twelve by ten feet, the shed was made of rough
planks that, according to their stains and other embel-
lishments, had come off a building site. Because it was
situated on a sloping hill, concrete blocks had been used
on the down-side to make the structure level. The door
had been built into the side away from the house to allow
for entry without steps. A narrow, paned window ran the
length of the rear wall near the roof. There were no other
windows, but two holes, one in each end of the shed—
each about eighteen inches long and eight inches wide—
were covered with small-meshed chicken wire. Each hole
had been made burglar-proof with a perpendicular iron
bar down the middle. The door was sealed and a notice in
a plastic envelope warned against its breaking.

Pauline pulled a loose block out from under the shed
and placed it under one of the air holes. She stepped up,
tested the shakiness of the block, put her nose against the
chicken wire and surrounded her face with her hands.
Patiently, she stood there and waited for her eyes to adjust

to the weak light inside. She detected the faint whiff of dead flesh, a smell that she might not have noticed if she hadn't known about the body.

The first thing to emerge from the murkiness was the small bench inside the door, the bench on which Paud Hughes had exchanged his weekly deliveries for the money in the tin box. But the tin box was not there, had probably been taken away by the forensic people in hopes it would reveal something. Otherwise, the shed was empty except for a bale of peat briquettes in the far left corner secure in its two narrow strands of yellow binding. But still, Pauline stood there peering, hoping to find some evidence of the horror that had been inflicted on Brother John the Baptist. There was no sign of a struggle because there was nothing in the shed that could have been disturbed during a fight. She concentrated on the floor inside the door. If the body had been rotting when it was found, it had probably stained the floor. She moved her eyes toward the middle of the shed, let them rest unfocused. All she would need was a starting point, something she could be sure of.

And then she knew. The first thing a body does when it dies is relax. So where on the floor were the stains left by the victim when his sphincters opened for the last time? Pauline placed the man's arse more or less in the middle of the floor and she immediately saw an irregular stain. And from that one stain she began to imagine an outline. The remembrance of a photo of the Shroud of Turin came to her mind.

The legs were pointing away from her in the shape of a narrow V. Because she knew that nails had been used on the body, the notion of crucifixion was in her head, and she looked for the arms to be stretched out at right angles to the shoulders. But she was wrong. Eventually she discerned the marks the arms had left. Both lay as close to the trunk as the arms of a man with a heavy bucket dangling out of each hand. She wasn't sure if she could make out the image of the head or if she was just seeing a shadow in the floor where the head should be.

She rested her eyes, allowed them to lose their focus, and as they were about to drift off to infinity, they picked up small spots around the rim of the outline—irregularly spaced darker spots, black spots—coalescing into the shape of the dead man. Pauline pulled her eyes back into focus and the spots were no longer visible. She stared at the floor until her eyes wandered off again. She quickly counted ten spots: two near the feet, two between the feet and knees, two between the knees and crotch, two at the hands or wrists and two at each side of the space where the head would have been. These last two didn't make sense and she let her eyes go out of focus again and, yes, there was a nail hole each side of the head. No explanation for these marks came to her. But Pauline knew that if she were on her hands and knees on the floor, she would see a nail hole in the center of each black spot; that blood or some other bodily fluid would have trickled down the nails and stained the wood around them. If these were the only bloodstains on the floor, the victim had not bled to death.

Pauline's eyes swept the shed one last time and then she stepped down off the building block. She rested a hand against the shed and looked down at the ground at her feet. Her realization that a prolonged and tortuous death had been inflicted on Brother John the Baptist sent a whirling mixture of fragmented thoughts flashing around her brain, leaving behind feelings of anger and sadness.

Without replacing the cinderblock, Pauline turned and walked back to the front of the house, followed the weedy path to the garden wall, pulled the gate behind her and made sure the hasp clicked down into its groove. In a pensive mood, she sauntered down the lane through the furze and sloe bushes until she came to the first gate. She crossed the pasture and didn't even shoo the goats away when they galloped up to her, stared and bleated. She unhasped the gate and went out to her jeep.

Without bending down, she pulled her trouser legs out of her socks and threw her jacket into the backseat. With hands together at the top of the wheel, she looked back to the place she had come from.

"You poor bastard," she said aloud. She turned the ignition key.

On the drive back to Daingean, Pauline stopped in Abbeyleix to see Danny Dowling, the auctioneer. While standing in the doorway of his deep-red house she learned that the house on the hill in Carrowreagh was owned by the Religious Order of Saint Kieran, the same order that had once administered Dachadoo Industrial School six miles outside Daingean. Pauline loved the feeling she got when something fell into place effortlessly. It was similar to—and as rare as—the feeling of knowing that the first dress put on in a fitting room is exactly the right one.

She called Jack Rafferty while standing at her jeep.

"Pauline, I was just reaching for the phone to call you," Rafferty said. "The dead brother on the Daingean road was a Daniel Geoghan, and he has a blood brother living in a place called Ballyglass not far from Daingean. Name is Frank Geoghan."

"I'm in Abbeyleix and I'll go—"

Rafferty interrupted. "What did you find out in Carrowreagh?"

Pauline took a deep breath. "The victim belonged to the Order of Saint Kieran, the ones in Dachadoo. Ten nails were used to pin him to the floor of his shed. Something was done to his gen—"

Again, Rafferty interrupted, and Pauline suppressed the urge to yell at him. "We know his name. Our garda mole has given us the names and addresses of all the

pedophiles in Laois and Offaly on the official list. The
Diggers are now weeding out the ecclesiastical buggers
from the lay buggers and then they'll find the buggers
who were attached to Dachadoo. They'll have their stuff
soon, but in the meantime you should go to Ballyglass,
wherever the hell that is, and—"

"That's what I told you I was about to do, Jack."
Pauline's satisfaction was short-lived because Rafferty
hung up. "You son of a bitch!" she seethed into the phone.
"You fucking rude bastard!" Then she glanced around to
see if anyone had heard her.

As she closed her phone and turned to open the jeep
door, she looked up at a passing car. From the passenger
seat Detective Inspector Tom Breen was gawking directly
at her. The car was gone past before they could acknowledge each other. Pauline sat into her jeep and leaned
back into the seat, tensed her leg muscles against each
other. Through the windscreen, her eyes rested on the
outsized brass plaque of a law office with its engraving of
DOWLING, DOWLING AND DOWLING, VALUERS AND AUCTIONEERS.
She decided not to follow Breen out to Carrowreagh—
she was certain that was where he was headed. She might
antagonize him by crowding him. She would wait for his
promised phone call at four o'clock.

Pauline looked at her watch—3:07. If she pushed it,
she would get to Ballyglass and Daniel Geoghan's brother
around four.

20.

When Tom Breen and Jimmy Gorman stood up off the hay bales, they shook hands with Frank Geoghan and said, "I'm sorry for your troubles, Frank."

Geoghan walked them to their car. "It doesn't matter now if the missus knows you're here. Maybe if she sees you it'll give me an opening to tell her about Dan. Jesus! I hate the thoughts of facing her."

Jimmy Gorman put his hand on Geoghan's shoulder. "Frank, I've often found that when I expect the worst to happen it seldom does. Maybe your wife will tell you she has known about Dan all along."

"She couldn't have found out."

"She mightn't know all the details, but I think she'll surprise you," Gorman said.

While the two policemen belted themselves in, the farmer stood with one hand on the roof. "Detective Breen," he said. "I want to thank you for trying to keep this out of the papers."

"We'll keep doing our best, Frank," Breen said.

Geoghan cocked his ear toward Daingean. "There's the Angelus ringing in the town. Twelve already. Thanks, lads."

As they drove away, Frank Geoghan raised his hand in farewell and turned back to his house and his wife.

"Your man's waistcoat," Gorman said, "it reminded me of the teacher who asked a pupil—"

"Whose waistcoat, Jimmy? God, you come out of nowhere betimes and expect me to know what you're talking about."

"Your man, Frank there..he was wearing a waistcoat."

"And?"

"Well, that's what I'm telling you. A teacher asked a little boy to put the word 'fascinate' into a sentence and the child replied, 'My grandfather wears a waistcoat with twelve buttons, but he's so fat he can only fasten eight.'"

Breen looked at Gorman as if gazing at a crossword clue that made no sense. "There's times I worry about you, Gorman. Fasten eight! That's a child's joke," he said.

"So, a child's joke can be funny, too," Gorman said. "For instance, why did the chicken cross the road?"

"Jeese, Jimmy. To get to the other side."

"No," Gorman said.

"Well, why?" Breen asked.

"It was nailed to the duck's back and the duck crossed the road."

Breen did not smile, but as he did his best to hide his amusement, his body began to shake. Eventually the two detectives were laughing out loud.

"Gorman, you're fucking nuts." Breen whacked Gorman on the shoulder.

The two of them fell into a silence that lasted most of the way from Ballyglass back into Daingean.

Breen phoned superintendent Donovan. The superintendent was back at Brother Boniface's house overseeing the Slashhook Brigade, alias the Hands and Knees—the garda who searched an area on all fours. Breen reported on the visit to Frank Geoghan, and explained the food-delivery arrangements. "There's a key under a stone three feet out from the front door. If it's still there it might be worth checking for prints."

The superintendent told Breen that the Technical Bureau, alias the Brains, had arrived from Dublin. T-Bone, alias the medical examiner, was on his way. "I was thinking, Tom," Donovan continued, "you and Jimmy should drive over to Croghan Hill to talk to the sinners there.

Everything's quiet out there except that both went for a walk together, all dressed up to the nines. Maybe they know something." Donovan hung up.

Breen closed his phone.

"Being overly secretive causes many problems," Gorman said.

"You're at it again, Jimmy," Breen said. "You're being obtuse."

"Nice word, Tom…obtuse. I was thinking about secrecy; secrecy leads to stinking thinking, leads to intellectual inbreeding, physical inbreeding, social inbreeding, behavioral inbreeding, all kinds of inbreeding. Look at all the secrets kept behind the walls of places like Dachadoo or Letterfrack or Baltimore or a dozen other industrial schools. Look at the secrets Frank Geoghan's been hiding for years and now they've turned into one big pile of shite for him."

"Skeletons in the cupboard," Breen mused. "Every family has secrets."

"It's alright to have secrets," Gorman said, "but when the whole family is suffering from secret bad behavior it's not alright—the secrets should be exposed."

"That's easier said than done, Jimmy. Look at your man McColgan in Sligo. He was at his own children for seventeen years, raped his daughter when she was six, and the wife even knew and she was afraid to speak."

"I can understand the fear, Tom," Gorman said. "I had something happen to me years ago—"

"Stop, Jimmy." Breen held up his hand. "Are you going to tell me something I don't want to hear?"

"In the scheme of things this is very low on the abuse pole."

"I'm not a shrink, Jimmy."

"This is not shrinkable stuff, Tom—just a story of something that happened to me."

"Alright, then." Breen gave Gorman a raised-eyebrow warning not to ambush him with something raw.

"When I was in boarding school, the rector brought me up to his private room one night, told me to lie across a chair and then he whacked the arse off me with a leather strap."

Breen waited for more. He looked at Gorman. "Is that it?"

"That's it."

"Did he make you lower your trousers?"

"No...I was fifteen at the time and I never told anyone about it till now, not even Beatrice."

"Why not? It happened over thirty years ago, when children were still being whacked all over the place."

"But this is not about the whacking—it's only in the last few years I've wondered if the rector was getting his rocks off, and I've wondered if he whacked other lads, too. But that's not the point here. The rector told me not to tell anyone what he'd done or I'd be expelled, and to be expelled from boarding school was worse than having a troop of hooded monks push you up against a wall and beat the shite out of you. But even if he'd not warned me not to tell anyone, I wouldn't have. I was so ashamed of myself."

"Ashamed of what you'd done to deserve the whacking?"

"No! I don't even remember why he whacked me. No, it was the shame of having been so humiliated, so debased, of having my arse sticking up in the air like that for him to do what he wanted, to look into my hole even if my trousers were still on. Of course I still believe I must have brought the whacking on myself even if I can't remember what I did to deserve it."

"Jimmy, what are you now, nearly fifty? You've gone through being—and not being—a priest; you've worked your way up through the ranks; you got yourself married to the best woman in Offaly; you have children—"

"And your question is why do I dwell on having the arse whacked off me thirty-four years ago, at ten past eight in a private room on Friday the eighteenth of February, nineteen seventy-three?"

Breen fell silent, gazed out at the road speeding under the front of the car. His eyes lost their focus. "This is about *why* people keep secrets, Jimmy."

"Yes, it's about how difficult it is for people to talk about secrets. My little secret is nothing compared to Frank Geoghan's. The shame of having a pedophile brother— it's no wonder he couldn't even tell his wife. Imagine the children and wife of your man McColgan; they were too afraid to run away. I saw the results of sick living in the rectory in London, but I was fortunate that I was able to escape, that I had a place to go to without anyone coming after me with hard fists and boots."

"Yes, Jimmy, and you were a grown man," Breen said.

"McColgan's wife was a grown woman, only she hadn't a place to run to. Many times, children in abusive families don't even know they're in a sick situation; they think their lives are normal; they've never known any different. And even if they did know, they're too frightened to do anything, too scared to even talk about it. The Ferns Report is full of children who were afraid to talk about the priests who stuck their hands down their trousers, who did things to them that we don't even want to think about. There was one old goat—"

Gorman sped around a corner and jammed on his brakes.

"Christ!" Breen said.

In front of them, a farmer's slurry spreader was taking up more than half the width of the narrow road. "We're having the day of the bad smells...first Brother Boniface and now ten tons of liquid cow shite," Gorman said.

"If you're going to stay behind him," Breen said, "then drop back a bit. God! Don't farmers have a sense of smell? That stink could make a fellow's lungs collapse."

"Careful, there, brother," Gorman said, and he allowed the spreader to pull away. "I'm a farmer, or at least a farmer's son, and as well as that I can always tell when you've eaten eggs."

"Don't get onto that subject because you know damn well you haven't a leg to stand on, Gorman. I'm not the one who farted *on* his wife."

Gorman glanced at the detective sergeant. "I should never have told you about that, Tom."

"I only use it as a weapon of last resort, like Cú Chullain's *gae bolg*," Breen said.

The two of them laughed.

Gorman allowed the slurry spreader to pull far ahead.

"By the way, Jimmy," Breen said, "when I used your phone in Geoghan's shed—"

"Yes, Tom…I knew there was something I wanted to ask you."

"When I called Pauline Byron I didn't want to give away my mobile number—"

"So you used my phone," Gorman said. "And now she has my number. Jaze, Tom, don't do me any more favors today. You even agreed with Frank Geoghan when he more or less called me a dwarf."

Breen smiled. "Anything for an oul laugh, Jimmy. I knew you were sizzling. I could see the steam rising out of your hair." He took a card from his pocket. "Byron's number ends in 312, so when she calls, you can pretend she has reached an artificial insemination station or Ten Downing Street. She'll give up after four or five efforts and in the meantime you can have some fun with her."

"That's why you used my phone, so I could have some fun with her?"

"You'll love it, Jimmy."

21.

The slurry spreader slowed down and pulled into a field. Gorman sped up.

"So what did you think of Frank Geoghan?" Breen asked.

Without hesitation Gorman reeled off his observations. "Frank's crippled with shame on account of his brother, mainly because he kept it all to himself, coddled a secret for years. He still had some feeling for Boniface, but he only brought him food because of a promise to one of his parents. He didn't kill Boniface. Frank should not be dragged into this at all; he's had enough purgatory at his brother's expense, even if most of it was created by himself."

"I agree. Frank had nothing to do with his brother's death," Breen said. He flipped to the tiny calendar in the front of his notebook. "We went out to warn Boniface on November sixth. Frank made the delivery on Thursday, November ninth, and November...wait!" He turned back through the pages. "The date of the last newspaper in the box was November eight."

"Jaze, now you're threshing, Tom," Gorman said. "If Frank brought the food out at eight o'clock every Thursday and if Boniface was an alcoholic, you can be sure that he would have been waiting anxiously for the box."

"And Nailer knew the routine," Breen surmised. "Nailer was waiting for the delivery on November ninth, and the minute Frank drove off, he got the box and somehow persuaded Boniface to open the door; maybe waited for him to come out for his whiskey and food and then pushed his way in."

"Maybe Nailer saw someone getting the key from under the flat stone," Gorman said.

"I doubt it. Who'd have had to use the key? Frank never went into the house. If Boniface brought the food in, the whiskey bottle would have been opened." Breen slapped the calendar with the back of his hand. "If that happened, Boniface was killed just after Frank's delivery on the ninth and when he made the next delivery on the sixteenth Brother Boniface was dead inside. But what happened to that delivery?"

"Nailer took it, only he didn't bring it in; he took it away. Maybe he brought it home and ate it—why waste good food and a bottle of whiskey, even if it's cheap stuff? But to keep anyone from knowing Boniface was dead, Nailer had to risk coming back one week after the killing to take that delivery of food."

"But why was it important to delay the discovery of the body, if that's what he was doing?"

"Well, it would allow for deterioration of any over-looked evidence; one more precaution taken. Or maybe he wanted the body to be in a state of rottenness like the one in Carrowreagh when it was found. Maybe that's another part of his statement."

Breen said, "Then he had spent a lot of time watching Boniface's house, and noting the traffic pattern on the Daingean road. Not that there's much traffic."

"Which means he did a lot of watching at the house in Carrowreagh, too, if he killed there," Gorman said. "And how could he do so much watching without being noticed? A stranger hanging out near the house on the Daingean road would have been seen by the people who travel that road regularly."

"Carrowreagh!" Breen said. "We'll have to go to Carrowreagh. We'll have to take a look at the setup there, see how the killer could have kept himself hidden while he watched, look for similarities with Burnt House."

"And don't forget, the watching may have taken place months before the killings. Nailer not only prepared well; he was also very patient."

Tom Breen phoned Superintendent Donovan and asked if he and Gorman could postpone the visit to Croghan Hill. "We should be eyeball-certain that it was the same killer at both scenes."

"You're right, Tom. Better not let the politicians have a ball-kicking party at our expense. The Portlaoise folder on Carrowreagh is in my safe."

"Also, sir, the lads checking the Daingean road traffic should ask if anyone was seen hanging around Brother Boniface's house as far back as three or four months ago."

"Janey, Tom! People's memories," Donovan said. "That's a long shot."

"It's a very long one, sir, but it's possible the killer staked out the house months ago."

"I'll pass the word. And Tom, you asked me about the floors in Carrowreagh. The Portlaoise super couldn't remember, so check them out while you're there."

22.

Breen collected the Carrowreagh murder file from Donovan's office safe. Before Gorman had driven out of the
car park at the back of the garda station, Breen was turning pages looking for the directions to the house where
Brother John the Baptist had died. Then he called the
Portlaoise garda station to let it be known they would be
visiting in the district. Ten miles later the two detectives
passed the fingerpost pointing to Clonaghadoo.

"Pricks!" Gorman said. "We've been talking about
pricks all day: cut-off pricks, pricks in mouths, pricks up
the arse—and all the time in my head a limerick has been
dying to be told. I heard it when I was a priest in that fucking parish in London. We had a professor in Carlow who
was the only layman on the staff—"

"Wait, Gorman…I'm lost," Breen said. "How did you
get from London to Carlow?"

"Background is necessary for the recitation of the
limerick, Tom. The background adds depth, atmosphere
and color; pathos too." Gorman gave Breen a toothy
grin. "This professor in Saint Patrick's Seminary in Carlow, who taught us Gregorian chant, had been around
priests and clerical students long enough to have a very
jaundiced opinion of them. He was a Fleming or a Wal-
loon—an organist, he was, by profession—and he'd lost
his cathedral job in Belgium because he once played
the wrong national anthem at the end of a mass. When
the archbishop fired him, he told the organist that he'd
never get a job in Belgium again. So, he ended up in
Carlow."

"Are you going to recite the limerick or give the history of Belgium?" Breen asked.

"Patience, Tom...This background is essential. There's a place in the gospels where Christ says—"

"Now we're in the gospels."

Gorman glanced at his partner. "Christ says something like 'Where two or three of you are gathered in my name, there am I in your midst.' But according to this cynical professor what Christ meant was, Where two or three of you—meaning priests—are gathered in my name, there are dirty stories being told."

"Priests and dirty stories don't go together, Jimmy."

"Yes, they do...They go together like dirty stories and adolescent boys, Tom; a lot of priests are adolescents till the day they die."

"Are you going to tell me the limerick?"

"Not yet. *Where* it was told is important."

"I hate it when you take on your professorial tone, Gorman."

"You have to imagine a room in a cellar with small windows at the top of the walls at the level of the street outside. The windows are filthy on the inside and the outside; very little light getting in. There's a dim light in the ceiling because the parish priest is in a constant state of economizing. The corners of the room are dark. Clouds of old cobwebs are clinging to the First World War chandelier. Cobwebs are hanging across the windows and draped over the furniture along the walls."

"You're exaggerating."

"Of course I am, but it's only for effect. The story is still true. Four priests are sitting at a dining room table with dusty and ancient cobwebs hanging from their skeletal faces and hands and elbows. There's a thick layer of dust on their shoulders. Their skin is as heavily wrinkled as a freshly ploughed field and it hangs in yellow, leprous folds from their bones."

"You should have been a poet."

"Arbuttnot, the pastor—the boss—is at the head of
the table. His glasses and ears are covered in cobwebs;
old, collapsed cobwebs cover his clothes. He's a canon of
the church and is wearing his canonical rabbit skins and
his dash of purple. He wears his clerical beret everywhere
now, because it has a purple tassel. He even wears it to
bed. He insists on being addressed as Canon. The second-
ranking diocesan official, the vicar general, sits at the foot
of the table. He is sporting the gules that proclaim his
rank on his row of buttons. He insists on being addressed
as Vicar General.

"I am at one side of the table, and a nervous wreck of a
lad by the name of Joe Perry is sitting across from me. Perry's hands tremble like a newborn, hairless mouse waiting
for its mother to come home to keep him warm. Perry's
face and neck are full of tics. He's terrified of the canon,
hates him. When the conversation lags, Canon Arbuttnot
announces, 'Gentlemen, I have a limerick for you.' And
then he says,

On the bridge stood the bishop of Buckingham
With his thumbs in his mouth and he sucking 'em;
Watching the stunts
Of the cunts in the punts
And the tricks of the pricks that were fucking 'em.

Breen's laughless snort was so violent that the folder
fell off his lap and he splattered the windscreen with spit.
"Gorman, that is the crudest limerick I've ever heard," he
said.

"Only because of who told it and where it was told,"
Gorman said. "It's a limerick that only a celibate could
have composed. I think the crudeness of a joke is in direct
proportion to the teller's lack of sexual experience."

For a moment Breen the bachelor reflected on Gorman's statement. "I'm not sure about your logic, Jimmy. But why did you describe the room that way—cobwebs and dark and dirt and semi-skeletons—a chamber of horrors?"

"For me, the priesthood was a chamber of horrors from beginning to end, all six months of it. It was dreadful—and I mean full of dread. I was living with the living dead. Now, I'm sorry I brought up the subject. Let's talk about the weather."

"You can't just push the topic aside like that."

"I just did. I keep my short-lived priesthood deeply buried because thinking about it depresses me. But sometimes it floats to the top, like just now."

"Wouldn't the shrinks say you should dig it up and deal with it?" Breen asked.

"I do deal with it. Whenever it comes to mind I bury it beneath a virginal young woman lying naked on her back, the sight of my feathered glory loosening her thighs."

Breen persisted. "If the priesthood is buried in there, then isn't it possible you could act off it someday?"

"What do you mean?"

"Well, if you look at me someday and I remind you of that old Canon Arbuttnot, isn't it possible you could whack me before you could stop yourself because of what's inside you?"

"You must be reading psychology again, Tom. And are you telling me that you have nothing buried inside you, nothing at all, not even a little bit of guilt for something mean or cruel you did when you were young—pulling the wings off a fly, killing a swallow with a catapult?"

Tom Breen looked out through the side window. After a while he said, "Yes, I suppose I do have some things in there."

On each side of them, they could see that the land and hedges were settling into their winter sleep. The bushes and trees were bare and the weedy growth of summer had shrunk to leave the tall, woody stems of cow parsley standing like destroyed trees in a blasted landscape. Crows in flocks waddled through wheaten stubbles like miniature nuns of a bygone day. Lines of starlings sat on sagging telephone lines. All the cattle had been brought in for winter housing and feeding, and the pastures were empty except for an occasional horse standing or grazing with its rear end to the breeze.

"Maybe Nailer once lived in a chamber of horrors," Breen said after a long silence. "Maybe he was contaminated, brutalized, robbed of something essential." He was still gazing out the side window as he spoke. "Maybe he's some poor fucker gone mad thinking about the things that were done to him. Maybe he kept everything buried and now it's all exploding out of him."

They drove into Abbeyleix. *Failte Go Mainistir Laoise. Traffic Calming Ahead.*

"Why does he have to be mad, Tom?" Gorman asked. "Why can't he be driven by revenge? Pure, cold, sterile, clinical revenge and nothing else. I think this fellow is far from mad. He's calculating. He's cool. He's ice."

They drove along the main street. "Lunatics can be as calculating as—" Breen let the thought go. "Did you see her?"

"Who?"

"Pauline Byron. She saw me, too. Our eyes met."

"Where?"

"Back there, beside her jeep. What the hell is she doing down here in Abbeyleix? I wonder has she been out in Carrowreagh sniffing around. Or maybe she's on her way there. Keep an eye on your mirror."

"It's a free country, Tom."

"Pauline Byron makes me uneasy. She can open doors and files and mouths that we can't. People like to see what they said printed in the paper even if their names

aren't mentioned. Wouldn't we be desperate eegits if she
printed the name of the killer in *The Telegraph* before we
even know who he is?...Fuck! Where did I put that ord-
nance map?"

Within a mile of Carrowreagh, Gorman's phone
played its merry tune. He looked at the screen. "Three-
one-two... Isn't that Byron's number?"

"Tis."

Gorman put the phone to his ear. "Incontinence Hotline...please hold," he said, in a busy voice. He waited.
"She hung up."

"She'll phone again. I was supposed to call her twenty
minutes ago."

As Gorman was parking the car outside Hughes Grocery the phone rang. "She's back." As he pressed the
speaker button, Pauline Byron's voice came out loud and
clear. "I am using a public phone. I am not calling on
behalf of a loose sphincter. A deal was made this morning. I am about to tell you the number of a public phone
in Emo. Ring me at eight o'clock tonight." She paused as
if giving time for a pen and pencil to be produced; then
she said the number and hung up.

"She's pissed," Gorman said.

"Worse," Breen said. "She's a woman who's feeling
scorned."

"From a furious woman, Lord, please protect me,"
Gorman said.

"Eight o'clock! I'll have to talk to her from the public
phone at the ball alley in Killeigh," Breen said.

"Jesus, Tom! You're covering your arse with four
inches of steel. You'd think you were James Bond. Do you
really think the supe's going to dig around for an inside
leaker, dig into people's phone records?"

"I do. He's very annoyed about Pauline Byron turning
up at Boniface's place right after he did. I'm not going
to do anything to attract the Internals to my name. And

Pauline Byron is going out of her way to be cagey, too, by not having us call on her mobile."

"And shite, Tom, my phone is now connected to her if the supe's poking around and gets that far."

"Relax, Gorman. I'll go on the record as the one who used your phone to contact Byron. As well as that you didn't know anything about Geoghan until you came out to his house around nine o'clock."

"But you don't have to call Byron at all, Tom. She—"

"I told her I'd phone her—a kind of payoff for her promise to keep the Geoghan name out of *The Telegraph*."

They got out of the Vauxhall and went into Hughes Grocery.

23.

By the time Pauline Byron reached the first traffic circle in Portlaoise on her way back from Carrowreagh, she had once again disentangled Jack Rafferty the editor from Jack Rafferty the insecure male, had once more satisfied herself that most rudeness in men toward women is a defense against being found wanting. The insecurity of the world's Jack Raffertys must be constantly challenged; otherwise it would find its basest expressions in the dark dungeon of the burka. What the liberating foremothers had achieved must be protected and advanced to the benefit of all women and all men, even if some of them were bastards.

But as she took the second exit of the roundabout in Portlaoise, Pauline Byron was still pissed off at Jack Rafferty.

When she was entering the first roundabout at the end of Tullamore from Killeigh, Pauline's phone rang. She glanced at the number, then pulled over in front of an arched gate with a notice in large red lettering promising the siccing of guards and solicitors on blockers of the driveway. At the bottom of the notice, the owner of the driveway had signed his name in bold, fighting letters: *Seamus Cooper.*

Pauline pressed the redial button on her phone and Jack Rafferty was immediately in her ear. "I just called you."

"I know. I was having a fight with an arsehole—male, of course."

Rafferty steamrolled on. "There were nine religious pedophiles on the official list: four former priests and five former brothers. Two of the brothers have been recently dispatched in a most satisfying fashion by our serial killer, one is in the geriatric ward in the loony bin—Saint Fintan's Hospital in Portlaoise—and the remaining two are living in a house in a place called Croghan Hill. God only knows what they do to amuse each other. No names there as yet...one of the Diggers will text you directions to the Croghan Hill house in a minute...maybe they're near Ballyglass where Frank Geoghan lives—kill two birds, or three, with the one stone." Rafferty hung up and the phone rang in Pauline's hand to announce the arrival of the directions.

Pauline stared sightlessly at the phone's screen. Maybe it was just a case of business being business for Jack Rafferty; maybe his mother never kissed him; maybe he was still mourning his brother's rocket-scattered bits in Baghdad; maybe he was a genius who could only concentrate on one thing at a time. Or maybe he was just a garden-variety scutterbrain.

A loud thump on the roof of her jeep jerked her back to herself, and as Pauline's heart took off at a frightened gallop, the red face of a bald man descended into her window like a scarlet moon falling out of the sky. He was shouting, pointing to the sign on his gateway. Pauline lowered the window and the last of the man's words screamed into the jeep: "...I ask you, are you blind or what?"

In the instant it took him to recharge his lungs, Pauline clasped her belly. "Mister Cooper...Thank God you came out. I'm having my baby. Please call an ambulance for me."

"Holy Mother of Christ," Mister Cooper said through clenched teeth. "Why the fuck does this shite always happen to me?" As he hurried back into his off-license, his red apron blowing back between his legs, Pauline drove

off, but she wasn't quick enough. Cooper ran back onto
the footpath, banged the moving jeep and shouted with
his hands cupped around his mouth, "You lying bitch! I
hope you have fucking triplets!"

Eighteen miles later, with Croghan Hill looming
ahead, Pauline pulled into a parking space in front of an
isolated country shop. For a moment she sat there looking and remembering. CROGHAN STORES was still done out
in green lettering on the white wall above the door and
the two wide windows. The building in its gleaming whiteness and gleaming green doors still looked as if it had
been painted yesterday. The two old petrol pumps had
been reshaped and computerized. As if flipping through
an old album, Pauline saw two adults and two children
leaning against a black Austin A40, all licking ice cream
cones in the sunshine. They had often come to Croghan
Hill on fine Sundays when she was a child, had trudged
up one of the several steep lanes and through the butter-
cupped and daisied grass of the sloping pastures that led
up the hill. Of those Sunday outings, Pauline cherished
the memory of the climb as much as the ice cream bought
in Croghan Stores after the descent. The woman behind
the counter always wore a navy blue apron printed with
small posies, the strings in a bow at her belly and the bulge
of a crumpled handkerchief in the side pocket.

Pauline looked at her watch. Detective Sergeant Thomas Breen had said he would call her by four. He was
twenty-five minutes late. She got out of the jeep, strode
over to the public phone at the front of the building
and tapped in Breen's number. The coins dropped and
some lunatic told her she had reached the Incontinence
Hotline.

She hung up and returned slowly to the jeep. Leaning her bottom against the front mudguard, she scrolled
down through the numbers in her mobile again, looked
at the number Breen had called from in the morning.

And as she gazed she remembered the words Breen had used: "If you do uncover the name of the man who was found murdered in the house…" She *had* uncovered the name, or at least the Diggers had, and they had also discovered that Brother Boniface had a blood brother, Frank, in Ballyglass. Surely it was Frank Geoghan who had asked Breen to keep the family name out of the paper, and surely Breen had called Pauline immediately to reassure Frank. And Breen, who had refused to give her his phone number out at Burnt House, had not used his own mobile to call her. Maybe he had used his partner's phone.

Pauline walked back to the public phone. Before the sidekick could answer with more bullshit, she silenced him with a few verbal slaps and gave him the number of the phone box outside the Emo Post Office. Then she got into her jeep and turned right at the T-junction beneath the lowering hill. Slowly, she drove until she came to the third lane—narrow, graveled, potholed, steep and bushy. According to the texted instructions, the two pedophile members of the Order of Saint Kieran lived up there in the first house on the left. Pauline decided to walk up the lane and parked the jeep in a pasture gateway.

Still fidgeting with the zipper of her winter jacket, Pauline rounded the first bend on the ascending lane. As she pulled her gloves out of her pockets she looked up and saw a man coming out of a field twenty yards away. He turned his back on her to re-hasp the gate, then stepped out into the lane. Thirtyish, he was wearing a heavy garda-issued overcoat; a white, green and gold scarf; leather gloves; a paddycap; and walking boots. He was too clean and neat for a man of the soil, she thought. Casually, he came toward her, swept his eyes from her boots to her head. "Good afternoon," he said. A tic in his eye persuaded Pauline he had recognized her.

She raised a hand in greeting and said, "Up Offaly," acknowledging the colors of his scarf. Pauline stopped, turned, and looked after him; the man might as well have had a piece of paper pinned to his back with PLAINCLOTHES GARDA on it. He'd probably had her in his sights since she'd stopped her jeep at the bottom of the hill, had probably left his crow's nest to check her out, make sure she wasn't a killer dressed in woman's clothing. So Jack Rafferty was not the only one who believed a serial killer was lurking. Superintendent Donovan was taking care of his chickens even if the chickens were outcasts.

As he was about to disappear around the bend, the guard stopped and looked back at Pauline. For a moment their eyes met and then the guard turned away, knowing he had been uncovered.

Pauline knew that policemen working static protection always worked in pairs. As she continued up the hill she casually cast her eyes around for the guard's other half, but before she could locate him the cottage came into view.

Because she was expecting a dump similar to the Carrowreagh and Burnt House cottages, Pauline was taken aback. This slated house with its front garden of tended rosebushes had been copied off a postcard intended for wistful Irish-Americans whose knowledge of the homeland had been handed down through the misty, alcoholic eyes of a forebear. The garden had been lately tended; beds had been edged and turned, the roses cut back and tucked in for the approaching winter. The trim on the windows matched the red of the front door, which in turn matched the color of the gate set in the three-foot whitewashed wall in front of the house. Tieback white lace curtains created inverted V's in the four windows. Each interior windowsill presented a porcelain bird or animal—a hen with chicks, an alert greyhound, a well-balled bull, a proud stallion—three-dimensional replicas of the fauna that had once, in bas relief, adorned the Irish farthing, halfpenny, penny, three-penny bit, sixpence, shilling, florin and half crown. A pillar of blue turf smoke—Ireland's national wind sock—stood on top of the one chimney in the middle of the roof.

Pauline was halfway along the short garden path when the front door opened. Standing there was a man of about seventy and over six feet tall, straight as a soldier on parade. The top of his head was as bald as a bar of soap, but the trimmed grey hair at the sides was plentiful. His face was tanned, longish, pleasant and inviting, the skin as clear and soft-looking as a child's and showing no signs of daily razor scraping. In his soft shoes, grey slacks, bluish jacket, and open-necked khaki shirt, he was dressed like a man in an upscale Dublin suburb on his way out to take his constitutional.

The man's eyes were the dominant feature, engaging Pauline and soothing her before he spoke. "Good afternoon, Miss," he said in a cultured voice, tinged with an ever-so-slight trace of bog.

"Were you just about to step out?" Pauline asked.

"No. I saw you coming through the gate. I was reading in the window." With a sideward nod, the man indicated the window on his left—the one with the greyhound.

Pauline was now standing directly in front of the man. Despite his inviting face, the position of his body in the doorway indicated he was guarding his castle.

"My name is Pauline Byron," the reporter said, but she was too unsure of the situation to extend her hand. "I'm a reporter for *The Telegraph*."

"I have been expecting a reporter to show up sooner rather than later, Miss Byron. But I didn't think the heavy guns would be sent in. I'm a fan, and I admire your objectivity. Our country is better off without Francis X. Culliton plundering it, and I thank you for helping to get rid of him." There was a certain formality in the way he spoke; he might have held sway over a lecture hall once upon a time.

"Power corrupts," Pauline said.

"Indeed it does, and lack of power corrupts the human spirit, too."

They looked at each other for an instant, each waiting for the other to take the next step. Finally Pauline said, "I'm afraid you have me at a disadvantage; I don't know your name."

"Patrick Bennet."

Pauline knew she was losing ground here. What was it about the man? Then it dawned on her: he was not fitting her preconceived notion of what a pedophile should look like, should speak like, should act like. Sternly, she took control of her whirling brain, reminded herself that pedophiles come in the guise of cardinals, kings, priests, fathers, national heroes, hill bachelors and nuns. She knew that no one strata of society produced more pedophiles than any other.

"Mister Bennet, I know that you—"

"Miss Byron, if you do not know my name, then you know very little about me, and what you think you know is wrong. It is odd that you would come to our house and not even know my name."

Pauline began again. "All I know about you—"

Patrick Bennet interrupted her again. "Miss Byron, it is only your reputation and the fact that I admire your work that persuades me not to ask you to leave immediately. Even so, I will not invite you into my house— you would have certain advantages; be able to deduce things by looking around. There is a picnic table at the back of the house, and if you wish, I will speak with you out there."

"Thank you, Mister Bennet. I would like that."

"Follow this path around to the back and I will join you when I put on something warm."

As Patrick Bennet closed the door, Pauline's eyes flashed across a framed picture on the wall behind him—a large splash of red on top of a long gash of white parallel to a large yellow splash on top of a long stroke of black.

As she turned away, she glanced at the texted directions on her mobile for reassurance.

As Pauline followed the path around the house she smelled boxwood. Again the isolated house at Carrowreagh and the insanity-inducing loneliness of that place rippled across her memory. She remembered, too, Brother Boniface's house in its weedy yard, surrounded by ugly hedges gone wild. But here on Croghan Hill, the back garden of the two pedophiles was an oasis of manicured shrubs surrounding an outdoor table on a slate patio. Instead of grass, the weedless ground was covered in white flint chippings. A right-angled extension, which Pauline had not seen from the front, was identical to the house facing the road except it had no garden wall; it even had its own front door and smoky wind sock. The interior windowsills displayed the remainder of Ireland's original numismatic fauna: a littered sow, a sitting hare, a diving kingfisher and a leaping salmon. The door and trim were painted a deep blue, but Pauline suspected the paint had a more sophisticated name—"Tuscan Vineyard" maybe or "Grape Hyacinth."

The path from the back door of the original cottage to the table was lined with bushy lavender, and Pauline bent down, caressed a stem and brought her fingers to her nose.

"Have you read *The Crimson Petal and the White?*" Patrick Bennet asked from the back door.

Pauline turned around. "No, I haven't," she said. Bennet had put on a black, calf-length camel-hair overcoat and a red scarf. A black woolen ski cap hung from his fingers.

"Lavender is a backdrop to the plot, a lot of lavender." Then he pointed to the blue door, to a man emerging. "This is my brother Cyril."

"Your brother? Your religious brother?"

"My former religious brother and my blood brother."

Cyril Bennet was the same shape and size as his brother, but there was no further family resemblance. The full head of silver hair was swept back from the forehead, the round face dominated by trimmed, severe eyebrows, either of which might unsettle an upstart by the slightest arching. His nose was a good architectural fit for the rest of his face. The lapels of a yellow shirt were visible at the neck of his calf-length, fawn, camel-hair overcoat. He held a fawn headband in his hand.

The hairy head of one and the bald head of the other made it difficult to guess who was older.

Cyril strode along the narrow, cedar-mulched path, held his hand out to Pauline and said, "It's a pleasure to meet you, Miss Byron. I admire your work and your writing style." He put on his headband, trapping his ears under the wool.

"Thank you, Mister Bennet, and I am pleased to meet you, too."

"Did I hear a hesitation in your expression of pleasure, Miss Byron?" Patrick Bennet asked. "Not many people are pleased to meet a pedophile. And to interview a pedophile is surely what has brought you here, especially after the dramatic headline in *The Telegraph* on the sixth of November."

A crow in the Scotch pine at the end of the garden ripped the air apart with one abrasive caw, momentarily holding the three people in their positions between the rows of lavender at the intersection of the garden paths.

Pauline knew she had to come clean with the two men; otherwise she was not going to get anywhere with them. She looked from one to the other. "I have come to your house knowing nothing about you. It is true I did not even know your names. I have allowed myself to get caught up in a race with the Garda Síochána and the

result, as far as you are concerned, has been gross rudeness on my part. I was told by our 'intelligence people'"—
Pauline made quotation signs with her fingers—"that you
both belonged to the Order of Saint Kieran and that you
worked at the Dachadoo Industrial School. And yes, I was
told that you are both pedophiles. Our intelligence people had not yet uncovered your names. As far as I know,
I have never encountered a pedophile before, much less
spoken to one about his being a pedophile. I am at a great
loss here." She paused. "But I hope you can forgive me my
brashness and that we can talk; perhaps you can give me
information for a report I will be writing when I have all
the facts in a row."

Cyril said, "Facts, Miss Byron. Truth, Miss Byron. Are
facts and the truth the same thing?" Cyril's accent was as
refined as his brother's, and the whisperings of the wind
in the bog heather could still be heard.

24.

Exactly one hour and twenty-one minutes after Pauline Byron walked out of his shop, Paud Hughes looked across his counter at the identification card in the hand of Detective Sergeant Breen.

"And this is Detective Gorman," Breen said, pointing a thumb over his shoulder in Gorman's direction.

Paud blushed so violently that a bucket of fresh cow's blood might have just splashed onto his face. The moisture in his throat disappeared with the speed of a fleck of newspaper consumed in a flame. His restless leg took off at a gallop, and the palms of his hands on the counter went wet. He passed a tiny puff of gas. His hemorrhoids glowed red hot.

"I'm sorry to surprise you like this, Mister Hughes," said Detective Breen. "Some people get nervous when they're approached by members of the Garda Síochána."

Paud lifted his hand in silent absolution to the penitent policeman and at the same time tried to direct a squirt of saliva onto his vocal cords. He squashed his posterior cheeks together. "You're right, sir," he squeaked. In a lightning-quick succession of moves he cleared his throat, rammed the seam of his trousers into his arse crack with his fingertips and stepped on the foot of the restless leg. And while subconsciously coordinating those easements, Paud very consciously decided that the best way to deal with the detectives was by not speaking until spoken to.

"We're from the Tullamore Garda Station," Breen said. "We're looking into the death of the man who was murdered here in Carrowreagh on October the twenty-fifth, the one you supplied with groceries. We know the Portlaoise guards have already spoken to you, but we have some questions too."

While Detective Breen was talking, Paud realized the guards weren't there on account of Pauline Byron's recent visit, so he changed his plan of defense into one of offense. His voice was contorted when he said, "The guards from Portlaoise told me not to talk to anyone about that."

Breen and Gorman looked at each other and in their glance each told the other to say something. Breen won.

"But *we* are the guards, Mister Hughes," Gorman said. "It's just that we're stationed in Tullamore."

"The guards from Portlaoise told me not to talk to anyone about that," Paud repeated.

"What they meant was that you shouldn't talk to anyone *besides* the guards," Breen said, "that you shouldn't gossip about it or talk to reporters about the murder."

"Well, that's just it, isn't it?" Paud said, and as he spoke he decided to take a daring gamble. Without pausing, he said, "An hour ago a woman was in here asking questions and it turned out she was a reporter. How do I know that you're—?"

"We know you had a reporter in here, Mister Hughes," Breen bluffed. "Pauline Byron from *The Telegraph*. What did she ask you?"

"The same thing you're asking me."

"And what did you tell her?"

"The same thing I'm telling you."

"And that is?" Breen asked.

"The guards from Portlaoise told me not to talk to anyone about that."

"But we *are* the guards," Gorman said again, his two hands splayed out near his sides like the hands of a saintly statue proclaiming the triumph of virtue.

"Anyone can say they're guards. You could be reporters. Maybe you're guards trying to trick me into talking so
you can arrest me."

"I showed you my identification card," Breen said.

"I never saw a guard's identification card before. You
could be showing me a bull's license."

Gorman glanced at Breen and Breen knew his partner
was having an oul laugh, lads.

"Here, Mister Hughes, I'll let you examine it." Breen
held the card across the counter. "A bull's license has the
head of a bull on it."

"I never saw a bull's license either," Paud said, not even
looking at Breen's I.D. card. "Reporters can make up any
kind of identification to help them get information."

"But we're not reporters."

"That's what you say."

Breen gave Gorman a look that said, Do something.
Gorman took out his phone and pressed a number.
"Here, Mister Hughes. That's the garda station in Tullam-
ore ringing. You can ask them about us; he's Tom Breen,
I'm Jimmy Gorman."

Paud did not look at the mobile. "Put your phone away,
Mister; for all I know you could be ringing your newspaper office. Just because you're reporters from Dublin you
think you can come out here to trick the country pump-
kins. From the minute you two walked in here I knew you
were up to no good. Now, I'm telling you to leave my shop
unless you want to buy something."

Detective Breen held up a hand. "Mister Hughes—"

"I'm here to sell stuff. I am not an information bureau.
Please leave my shop and do not come back. I'm tired of
all these fecking games people are playing with me."

"Mister Hughes—"

"Leave my shop and don't come back."

"Mister—"

Paud turned his back on Detective Sergeant Breen and began needlessly rearranging chocolate bars on a shelf.

"I'd like to buy a bar of Cadbury's Flake, Mister Hughes," Gorman said.

Paud put the chocolate on the counter. "That'll be one euro."

As the coin and the chocolate were exchanged, Gorman tried again to wiggle in under Paud's defenses. "When she left here, did Miss Byron go out to the house where your man died?"

"That's my favorite, too," Paud said, nodding to the Cadbury Flake in Gorman's hand. He dropped the coin into its compartment and closed the drawer with a nudge from his belly.

Gorman glanced at Breen and saw that Breen was enjoying an oul laugh of his own, lads.

"I'll be seeing you, Mister Hughes," Gorman said in defeat. He walked out, followed by Breen.

25.

"Will you put that chocolate bar in as an expense?" Breen asked when they got to the car.

"Feck off," Gorman said, and he threw the chocolate onto the backseat. "The fingers that gave me that had just poked Paud's piles."

As they strapped themselves into the battered Vauxhall, Breen asked, "Did you see the way he turned into a lump of Chivers jelly the minute I showed him the I.D.?"

"I did—it was like he was instantly afraid we had something on him."

Breen flipped through the folder on his lap. "Here's the map to O'Brien's house," he said. "Turn around and go right at the T-junction."

Gorman put the car in gear and moved away from the front of HUGHES GROCERY. "Did you see his face, red as a turkey cock, and the way he stuck his fingers up his hole? God! I hate seeing someone doing that; it's worse than a woman looking at her dog shiting as if the shite was a Valentine card. When he took his hands off the counter he left two puddles of sweat behind. And I think he made a silent fart—unless it was you stinking up the place."

"It wasn't me."

"For a minute he was like someone tied to a chair with us coming at him with a blowlamp. When he tried to talk he sounded like a brain-damaged hen squawking out the side of her—"

"No, no! Go right," Breen interrupted. "Can't you drive and be pissed off at the same time? There's another right about two miles down the road."

"When you told him what we were after, he got himself together as quick as he'd fallen apart."

"You're becoming a real detective, Jimmy. You must be doing some self-improvement in the behavioral psychology department."

"The son of a bitch," Gorman said with an air of discovery. "That country pumpkin just pulled a quick one on us. Pauline Byron! That's what he thought we were there for. Just before we got there he'd spilled his guts to Pauline and when he saw us he thought we knew what he'd done."

"Slow down…there's the lane on…you missed it. Go back."

Gorman put the car in reverse, threw his left arm across the back of Breen's seat, twisted around in his own seat and kept talking. "That's why he went like jelly and then he made an instant recovery when he—"

"Will you slow down, for Christ's sake? You nearly had us in the ditch."

"When you didn't mention Pauline Byron he recovered. Think about it, Tom. It was an amazing performance—a quick-change artist changing right before our eyes and we missed it."

"You didn't miss it, obviously…Stop! We'll be back at Paud's shop if you go any further. Go into that lane there. And then there's a left turn after half a mile. Do you want me to drive?"

"He was the one who brought up Pauline Byron, and his whole performance was to remove himself as far as possible from her; the son of a bitch."

"Maybe you're right."

"Maybe, my arse! On our way back I'm calling in to see Hughes and I'll give him a good kick in his fucking pumpkin."

"Your pride is hurt."

"Bloody sure, it's hurt. I hate being took; I was took once by the Catholic Church and I'm highly allergic to being took by anyone ever since. It makes me fucking insane."

"Maybe it's better to let him go on thinking he took us."

"Why? He has no bearing on the case now; everything he knows the Portlaoise lads know—and Pauline Byron. I just want him to stew in his own juices for a while. I'll drop the idea in his lap that he may be prosecuted for obstructing a murder investigation by talking to a reporter."

"You've no proof that he did."

"The smell of his own frightened fart is all the proof I need."

Tom Breen's phone rang. It was Superintendent Donovan.

"Tom," Donovan said. "Nothing so far from the traffic lads on the Daingean road. What do you think about tomorrow? It's Saturday. Should we keep them out there?"

"I think we should keep them there through all shifts till at least Monday night; that would likely net anyone who saw anything."

"Overtime, Tom. Dublin will be screaming."

"Dublin will be happy with your diligence, sir."

"Diligence...Janey, Tom, you have a nice way of saying things. Alright, I'll take care of that. I think the posts should stay on Croghan Hill till we get something going on the killer. By the way, did you and Jimmy give the killer a name yet?"

"Jimmy baptized him Nailer."

"Nailer...That's a good one. Are you and Jimmy going to Croghan Hill today?"

"No. We're still here in Carrowreagh and it'll be after six by the time we get back. I think the two brothers will be safe with the posts till Monday."

"You and Jimmy can work tomorrow if you want."

"Jimmy has a family trip to Ballysteen planned for early in the morning; he won't be back till Sunday. And I'm going fishing."

"Tom, if you do as much fishing as you claim, I don't know how there's any fish left to catch."

"I don't catch many, sir; the fish are too clever. Still, the flowing water is a drug, and there's always the chance of catching Finn McCool's salmon."

"You're late on that one by a few thousand years. Is there anything I should do besides trying to find the fecker who's talking to the famous Ms. Byron?"

"Yes. Your rank opens doors quicker than mine. Would you arrange with Saint Fintan's Psychiatric for Jimmy and myself to talk to Brother Beatus on Monday?"

"I will. And I have a few bits for you to think about while you're watching Finn's fish eating his hazelnuts. The Slashhook Brigade finished and they found nothing except one enamel piss pot with a hole in it and the handle missing. T-Bone agreed that Brother Boniface was nailed to the floor on that Thursday, like you and Jimmy figured out. It may have taken him two days to die…renal failure."

"Hold on, sir…It's this turn, Jimmy." Breen pointed. "Sorry, sir. You were saying?"

"The Reverend Brother Boniface didn't bleed much; he did have his wanker in his mouth; it had been cooked; crotch scalded like Jack the Bap's; had two mashed big toes; the toenails were in the floor-sweepings in the hallway. The mark on his forehead was similar to Jack the Bap's. We'll have to wait to find out if the grease at the crotch was Dairygold. T-Bone says the whole thing is a match with Carrowreagh. The inside of the nose was burned, too; probably more smelling salts."

"It's looking like we might be using the serial word—"

"Hold on, Tom. Someone's asking me something." Breen heard muffled voices. Then the superintendent was back. "The posts on Croghan Hill just called. A woman they think is Pauline Byron has parked her jeep at the foot of the hill; they want to know if they should stop her if she goes up to see the pedophiles. What do you think, Tom?"

"Jakers. She keeps turning up like a bad penny, sir; she was down here in Carrowreagh just before we got here. But I don't think there's any grounds for stopping her, and if you do stop her she's going to start singing freedom of the press and drawing more attention to—"

"Shite," Donovan said. Then to someone else he called, "Tell them to leave her alone and keep out of sight; she shouldn't even suspect that we're watching the house… Tom, are you still there?"

Gorman had stopped the car in front of a red gate.

"Yes, sir. I'm here."

"Tom, between you and me, do you have any idea how Pauline Byron got on the scent so quick?"

"By the time she got to Geoghan's house this morning, only a few people knew about Brother Boniface. We could work backward from the time she appeared in her jeep to the call to the station by your man with the dog, Deegan. But with today's electronics, sir, maybe it wasn't necessary for anyone to call *The Telegraph*. Who knows who's listening to whom these days?"

"Whom? I get suspicious of anyone who uses 'whom.' But I'm going to do what you said—figure out who knew about Boniface before Miss Byron arrived on the scene."

"Yourself and myself will be on the list, sir. If you don't suspect me I won't suspect you."

"That's a bargain, Tom."

"Sir, would you ask Portlaoise to send us all the notes the lads took when they were sussing out Carrowreagh? Typed, please. They write like lame spiders over there."

"I'll do that, Tom, and I'll see you and Jimmy on Monday."

26.

Breen closed his phone. "Did you hear everything the supe said?"

"I heard it," Gorman said. "I wonder will T-Bone come up with anything more when he excavates The Reverend Boniface."

"Excavates?"

"The body's so rotten he could use a child's plastic shovel."

"I think it's Paud Hughes *you* would like to be excavating with a plastic shovel. Why are we stopped here?"

"Didn't you notice? There's a gate across the road in front of us. A red gate."

"And?"

"And the passenger always opens the gate. When we were children going across the fields in the horse and cart, the driver never got down to—"

"Spare me, Gorman," Breen said, and he undid the seat belt. "If you don't wear me down with your logic you'll wear me down with your verbal diarrhea."

As Breen got out, Gorman said, "Look out for the goats."

"What goats?"

Gorman pointed. "There's three goats over there to the right. Don't let them out through the gate or you'll be chasing them all day to get them back."

"There's tyre tracks out here," Breen said.

"I noticed. Probably Pauline Byron's."

"They stop right here this side of the gate. And there's her boot prints."

"She had no one to open the gate for her, so she walked the rest of the way."

Before Breen got to the gate the three goats came galloping and put their front feet on the third bar. Breen looked back at Gorman. "What am I supposed to do?"

Gorman stuck his head out of the car. "Shake the gate and yell at them to fuck off."

Tom Breen followed Gorman's instructions and the goats ran back to their grass grazing. "God! I'm a goatherd," he called to Gorman. He unhasped the gate and as Breen swung it open Gorman stuck out his head and yodeled. He drove the car out through the gateway.

"You're giddy, Gorman," Breen said when he got back in.

"We're away from rotten bodies, disgraced brothers, raped children, suffering families, severed dicks, the smell of death; I'm looking forward to kicking Paud Hughes in his pumpkin; and Friday is almost over. Tomorrow I shall return with my relatively happy family to the place of my ancestors for two days. I shall renew myself by wallowing in the soil and maybe my sister will recite 'The Lady of Shallot' for all of us."

"And you can recite 'Leda and the Swan.'"

"Not in front of my mother or the girls, or my sister for that matter. There's still a bit of modesty and decorum left in Limerick County in spite of the city."

"Before we get sidetracked…the goats reminded me…"

Gorman put the car in gear and slowly bounded through the potholes that Pauline Byron had recently stepped around.

"When you were talking about the Ferns Report this morning you started to tell me about an old goat."

"That lecherous old bastard!" Gorman spat. "He was worse than any goat. An old parish priest he was, who'd sit on a chair in the sanctuary while a child stood in front of

him to confess sins. Behind him in the church a classful
of children waited their turn. Whenever a young girl presented herself, the priest made her stand very close and,
as she confessed, he'd pull up her dress, put his hand
down into her knickers."

"For fuck sake, Gorman; you made up that one."

"No one could make it up, Tom. It's in the Ferns
Report in black and white."

"That fucker should have been strung up by the balls
from the sanctuary lamp."

"Of course he should, but he wasn't. He didn't even
go to jail."

"The fucker!" Breen said. "I hate hearing about bastards like that, especially when they get away with it."

"Calm down, Tom. It's Friday and here's another red
gate for you to open. Keep your eye out for the goats."

They spent an hour poking around the hilltop where
Brother John the Baptist had lived. Both men grew less
talkative as they walked around contemplating the last
years of the pedophilic outcast. Each went his own way,
rambling around the ruined garden, looking pensively
at the deserted house, kicking at things as they stepped
bent-necked and shoulder-hunched through the dead
and dying grass. Each man looked through all the windows again, stood with his forehead against the glass,
hands surrounding his face. Together they broke the seal
and entered the shed where Brother John the Baptist
had spent the last few days of his life in solitary agony
and madness. When Gorman sat up on the bench where
money and food had once been exchanged, Breen wandered off by himself again.

When they got back into the car they were silent. Gorman drove through the red gates, turned right, left and
left again, and through the one-streeted village of Carrowreagh.

"What about Paud's pumpkin?" Breen asked.

"It's insignificant now, isn't it, Tom? Next to the destruction and the anger and the hurt and the revenge that we're seeing, getting my little bit of revenge on Paud is insignificant. It would only add to the pile of bitter shite. And I think before this investigation is over, a lot of shite, besides Paud's lies, is going to float to the top."

They traveled another two miles before Tom Breen spoke. "I asked someone once why so many politicians become corrupt, and he said, 'Shite floats.'"

They were almost in Abbeyleix when Breen asked, "What did we find out in Carrowreagh?"

"We could make a copy of the Portlaoise file and exchange O'Brien and Geoghan and no one would know the difference. Nailer might as well have left an essay in his handwriting at both places."

"What's he saying in the essay?"

"It's Friday, Tom. My brain is in weekend mode already. On Monday morning I'll give you a copy of Nailer's essay in my own handwriting."

27.

"Come and sit at the table, Miss Byron." Patrick Bennet said. He led the way.

The table was oblong, made of oak, was weather-proofed with many coats of polyurethane, had a hole in the center for the pole of an umbrella and was surrounded by eight outdoor wooden chairs.

Patrick pulled out a chair for Pauline and then joined his brother on the other side.

"The only reason we are talking to you at all, Miss Byron," Cyril said, "is because of your reputation for integrity. Before we begin, we will establish the ground rules—Patrick and I, not you."

"In other words, Miss Byron, it will be Cyril and I who will conduct an interview first, and if we are satisfied we will allow you to interview us within certain parameters. Nothing we say will be recorded or reported by you unless we say so. Is that agreed?"

"Alright."

"Alright? Or yes, Miss Byron?"

"Yes, I agree."

"Why have you come to us at this time looking for information?"

"You already know that a former member of the Order of Saint Kieran was murdered about a month ago. This morning another former member was discovered murdered. The two dead men were on the official garda list of pedophiles. Both of you are on the same list. Two plain-clothes gardai have your house under surveillance."

The brothers looked at each other.

"We didn't know that...about the surveillance," Patrick said. "The guards did tell us this morning that another former brother had been killed."

"The two men were apparently killed by the same person. It would seem that the killer is on a spree of revenge—"

"You could hardly call two incidents a spree, Miss Byron," Patrick said.

"If I were the second victim, I would call it a spree, and in neither case would I call my death an incident. I would call it my exceedingly painful, torturous and horror-filled murder, Mister Bennet. And to answer your question, my purpose in coming here is to ask if either of you can remember an incident in Dachadoo involving the two victims which would, years later, cause someone to torture and mutilate them and then leave them to die over a period of days."

Again the brothers looked steadily at each other for a moment. Then Cyril said, "It sounds like you *are* in a race with the guards...doing police work yourself, Miss Byron."

"The guards will find the killer. They will discover the facts—"

"And you will discover the truth?"

"That is my job. That is what I do for a living. I write about people and the behavior of people. And if I may say so, I find your reaction to what I am telling you rather curious."

"Curious in what way, Miss Byron?" Cyril asked.

"Neither of you have shown any reaction to what I said about the murders; you haven't shown any alarm that you might be on the killer's list."

"As Patrick told you," Cyril said, "we have already been informed about today's discovery on the Daingean Road, and we were also told about Carrowreagh when the body was discovered there on November fifth. As to being

fearful that we might be on the killer's list, the answer is
we have no reason to be fearful. And may I ask you—are
you not afraid that *you* might be on the list, Miss Byron?"

"Me! Of course I'm not. Why would I be?"

"Most likely because you are not a pedophile who gave
the killer cause in the past to torture and kill you in the
present."

The crow in the Scotch pine let loose with an aria of tri-
umphant cawing. Pauline glanced from one brother to the
other and each looked steadily, unblinking, back at her.

"Miss Byron," Cyril said, "like everyone else, you have
come to our home expecting to find the product of your
own imaginings. It is not your fault. I, as does Patrick,
have revulsion for pedophilia. I would have anxieties if I
had to interview a pedophile; I too would bring certain
expectations with me."

"We are pedophiles only by accusation, Miss Byron,"
Patrick said. "The fact is that once an accusation of pedophilia is made, the accused is ruined. Our religious order
demanded that we 'step aside '"—Patrick inscribed quotation marks in the air—"until there was an investigation,
but like many other accused clergymen we have been
abandoned by our order, by the church, by the state, and
by the community in general. We are labeled pedophiles
because we were unable to prove that we aren't; we were
never given the opportunity to prove our innocence
because that would have meant keeping clerical pedophilia in the headlines. It is better that the accused be
rendered invisible than that the stupidity and ineptness
and outright corruption of some members of the church's
hierarchy be exposed. As well as that, Miss Byron, every
pedophile who protests his innocence is perceived to protest too loudly, and he simply draws more negative attention to himself."

Even though she suspected that Patrick had given this
speech before, had dwelt on the subject a thousand times,

Pauline heard only matter-of-factness in his recitation, no bitterness. She looked beyond the two men, put her elbows on the table and a hand to each side of her face. The brothers Bennet waited in silence.

"Who accused you?" Pauline asked.

Neither brother responded. Pauline gazed out at the evergreens until individual shrubs became two in her unfocused eyes. With a blink and a tiny shake of her head, she brought her focus back to the surface of the table, saw how the rim of the umbrella hole had been sanded to remove the sharp edge.

She glanced at one face, then the other. "You will not allow me to interview you unless I am convinced that neither of you is a pedophile?"

"Unless you *believe* us, Miss Byron, that we are not pedophiles. That's what we ask—it's what we demand— that you believe us."

"You are named on two official lists as pedophiles— church and state. Few pedophiles admit to pedophilia. You both say you are not pedophiles. What am I to believe?"

"If you don't trust us, how can you believe anything we say in answer to other questions?"

Pauline's eyes went from the blue of the lavender to the blue of the door and back again to Patrick's blue eyes. "The fact you are listed as known pedophiles is in here in my head." Pauline raised her hand to her forehead.

"As I told you, Miss Byron, the accusation of pedophilia has more clinging power than the burr of a burdock."

"Of course you are torn between getting what you are looking for and the leap of faith you must take in order to get it," Cyril said. "You could easily say you believe us and have your information. But I believe in your integrity, Miss Byron. May *I* ask *you* a question?"

"Of course."

"Have *you* ever abused a child for sexual purposes?"

"No, I have not."

"I believe you, Miss Byron. Now ask Patrick and me if we are pedophiles."

Pauline looked from face to face and neither face was revealing anything. Again, her eyes sank into the lavender, caressed the slightly sticky foliage. She thought about what the brothers Bennet had told her, remembered how a priest in a parish near Emo had once thrown his arms around a gaggle of altar servers and, four years later, was still dwelling in limbo. "This is a facet of pedophilia that I have not thought about before," she said, "guilt by accusation. I did come here blinded by my own expectations. I believe neither of you is a pedophile."

They sat there looking at each other across the table.

Patrick Bennet stood up from the oak table and said, "I'm going to make a pot of tea before we get down to business." He removed his cap and overcoat and put them on his chair. "Are you warm enough, Miss Byron? We have some extra overcoats."

"I'm comfortable. Thank you, Mister Bennet."

As Patrick walked to his house, Cyril said, "You must call us by our first names, Miss Byron; otherwise we won't know to whom you are speaking."

"And you may call me Pauline."

"Thanks, but no, Miss Byron. A certain formality must still be maintained, a certain distance. Your use of our first names is merely a matter of utility, not familiarity."

Silence broke out.

"Who's the gardener?" Pauline asked.

"I pretend to be Gertrude Jekyll and we both share the labor. As you can see, this area only needs a bit of trimming during the year. Are you a gardener yourself?"

"Not yet, beyond a few weedy beds with some busy lizzies and daisies growing willy-nilly. I live near Emo Park, and there's a rumor that a master gardener is about to be hired. I intend getting friendly with him."

"We've been to Emo Park several times...beautiful grounds, beautiful house, but very few flowers."

Patrick approached with a laden tray. "Krups kettles are the best invention since sliced bread," he said.

"Miss Byron lives near Emo Park," Cyril said.

"Lucky Miss Byron. Do you go there often?" Patrick put on his overcoat and cap again.

"Weather permitting, and many times not permitting, I jog in the grounds almost every morning."

"If we allowed the weather to control us we would get little done in these British Isles. We have learned to live in rain like the Inuits have learned to live in snow."

Over more small talk, the tea was poured, the milk and sugar and the plain digestive biscuits passed around.

Patrick put down his cup. "We agree to be interviewed, Miss Byron, with the understanding that our identities will not even be hinted at. Also, we may answer some questions for clarification purposes but may demand that those particular answers be off the record. Are these conditions agreeable to you?"

"Yes, they are."

"Do you have anything to say, Cyril?"

"I believe everything has been said."

Pauline knew she had to take back some of the power she had just given away. "You have obviously prepared yourselves for an interview like this," she said.

"Of course," Patrick said. "Shortly after we were accused of pedophilia, we realized we had to take charge of our lives, something new for us because we had depended on the comfortable supply lines of our religious order for many years. We are unable to do anything about the accusation of pedophilia, nor about being ostracized, but we are determined that neither will destroy us. We are not going to rot away in silent poverty."

"You're not taking notes, Miss Byron," Cyril said. "Are you using a tape recorder?"

"No, Cyril, I'm not. I think each of us has a different agenda here. I'm looking for information that will lead back to the past; the two of you are looking for a platform from which to proclaim an injustice. I—"

Cyril held up his hand. "Stop there, Miss Byron. *We* do not have any agenda. We did not ask for this interview. We do not need a platform. We are not looking for justice because we can never get justice. *You* are the one who came to us. We have simply agreed to answer some questions that may lead to the arrest of a murderer. On our part there is no expectation of a quid pro quo."

Pauline held out her hands, the palms toward the brothers. "I wish I could begin this meeting all over again. I wish I had known—"

Cyril interrupted her again. "Beyond *knowing* we were pedophiles, you could not have known anything about us, Miss Byron, because we go out of our way to be unknown. The label of pedophile has a more deleterious effect than any scarlet letter. All connections to a person come to an immediate stop when the label pedophile is attached to him. You didn't even know our names when you came here; you only *knew* we were pedophiles. The pedophile is an outcast to be avoided and suspected at every turn. He's a snake, vermin. He's someone people don't want to think about, because to do so is to think about what he has done to earn his title."

Another long silence descended on the oak table. In her head, Pauline preened her feathers back into place, then began again from a different angle. "Today I was at the houses where the two former brothers of Saint Kieran were murdered—the places where they'd lived. I didn't see much of the first house, but I saw enough to draw some conclusions. I saw far more of the second house. Those two men lived in squalor. The O'Brien man in Carrowreagh had certainly isolated himself from the world, and judging by the state of his house, he may have developed some kind of psychosis over the years. And unless the Geoghan man near Daingean had some involvement with his brother Frank, he too must have been insane. I confess that I came here expecting to find similar squalor and similar isolation and similar insanity—"

"And similar pedophilia," Cyril threw in.

"Yes...but not even one of my ducks was in a row."

"Miss Byron, you are not the first to come to our home laden with prejudices, but you are one of the few to admit to them."

Silence descended until Pauline finally spoke. "The two men who were murdered—Joe O'Brien and Daniel Geoghan—what were their religious names?"

"O'Brien was John the Baptist and Geoghan was Boniface," Patrick said.

Pauline hesitated, as if making a mental recording. "The Order of Saint Kieran owns the cottage in Carrowreagh where Brother John the Baptist lived and died. I suspect the Order owns Geoghan's house, too. It would seem that the Order made some effort to support its disgraced members. But you said, Cyril, that your order abandoned you. Why did it take care of O'Brien and most likely Geoghan but not you?"

"About a year after we were asked to 'step aside,' the Order did offer to find us a place to live—that was in 1971," Cyril said. "By that time Patrick and I had grown sour, to put it mildly, on the Order and on the church, and we severed all relations with both. As well as that, the Order had been temporarily banned by the government from taking care of children. Our older brother gave us shelter and support until we got on our feet. He even gave us these coats." Cyril tugged the sleeve of his fawn camel hair. "After that initial assistance, Patrick and I rebuilt our lives by ourselves. Financially, we are self-supporting.

Socially and family-wise, we have a sufficient circle of friends and colleagues."

"How do you support yourselves?"

"This is off the record, Miss Byron," Cyril said. "We became devious in order to reclaim our lives to the extent that we have. Under noms des plumes I review books for several top papers and magazines, and Patrick writes a syndicated column on European politics for the international business community. Patrick was professor of political science at UCG and I taught French, Latin and German in our secondary school in County Waterford, so we were able to use our education to survive."

The crow in the Scotch pine sang out its tuneless song. Then Patrick began talking and Pauline held up her hand. "Wait a minute. I have another confession," she said. "When I came here I expected to find two loutish, uneducated—"

"Calibans?" Cyril suggested.

"Yes, Calibans," Pauline said. She dropped her open arms onto the table.

"From what you read in the papers and saw on television and heard on the radio, Miss Byron, your expectations are not a surprise," Patrick said. "The pedophiles within the Order were seen as Calibans; the public perception is that Cyril and I are pedophiles; therefore both of us are Calibans, too."

28.

At last Pauline felt she had dumped overboard the baggage she had brought with her to Croghan Hill. Inwardly, she gave a deep sigh of relief. "How many years did you spend in Dachadoo with Brother Boniface and Brother John the Baptist?" she asked.

Patrick replied. "Neither of us spent *years* with them—we spent a part of each summer in Dachadoo."

"In what capacity?"

"We were volunteers," Patrick said. "We worked with the boys; counseled them in very informal settings, tried to give them some love and respect; that's why we entered the Order in the first place. Full of idealism, we joined up to serve 'the least of these, my brethren.' Our first vocation was to take care of children in need, but obedience was demanded and we were given university educations. Then we were put out into academia to give an intellectual patina to the Order of Saint Kieran, as well as to earn some hard cash. Working in Dachadoo during the summers also gave us the opportunity to spend time together."

"How many summers did you spend at Dachadoo?"

"Sixteen, until it shut down in 1971," Cyril Bennet said.

"During the time you were there, did either of you see anything, or hear of any occurrence that might inspire a former child of Dachadoo to get revenge all these years later?"

The brothers looked at each other. "No, nothing," Patrick said.

"I didn't either," Cyril said, and both men saw a questioning shadow flash across Pauline's face.

Cyril continued, "To understand our answers, Miss Byron, you have to consider several things. There were certain fissures within the Order of Saint Kieran, a pecking order. Lay brothers were basically the skivvies and that's not meant to sound demeaning—they were the muscle, the ones in charge of the boys at the most inconvenient times—mealtime, bedtime, playtime. Then there were the teachers, the ones who were supposed to have educated the children in Dachadoo; there were the administrators at the local level and at the Mother House; and finally, there were about fifteen of us who were considered the cream of the crop, the ones who leant the Order its veneer of intellectual prowess. Each stratum resented the one above it, just like in the civil service, and so the stratum that Patrick and I were in was resented the most. During our summers at Dachadoo we were treated as outside do-gooders by the administrators; we were the long-haired liberals threatening the status quo. Even though we lightened the load of the lower strata, as they saw themselves, to them we were like the visiting uncles who rile up the children and then go home, leaving the parents to restore the established order. We were excluded from the brotherly gossip—and we were excluded from the diseased culture that had grown over the Order's original ideals like the bog that covers the Ceide Fields."

"Did no child ever complain to you?"

"No. The children could never complain to adults about adults. If a child did, the punishment was instant and severe. Several children simply said, 'I'll get punished,' when we probed, and so to protect the children we didn't press them. It was a curious and painful situation to be in; we knew some children wanted to talk to a trusted adult, but we couldn't encourage it. Several times we saw the evidence of physical abuse—welts on the backs of legs, black eyes, split lips—and we did protest to the man in charge, Brother Lazarian. We knew Lazarian resented our interference because he very bluntly told us so. He insisted that the injured children were the victims of accidents or had been hurt by other children. When we spoke to the superior of the Order, he expressed support and confidence in Brother Lazarian. The superior belonged to the administrative stratum. In the end, when the first government enquiry was being conducted and three brothers were accused of pedophilia, two of those brothers *and* Brother Lazarian turned around and accused us of the same thing."

"Why?"

"We believe it was purely a class thing. They were being thrown to the wolves and they would take some of the elite with them. Lazarian's behavior was especially disappointing, but he did have an enormous chip on his shoulder—owed us some payback for talking to the superior about his fitness to run Dachadoo. And of course he was bitterly disappointed that he did not belong to the top tier in the Order."

"Is Brother Lazarian still alive?"

"Indeed he is—he's retired and living in a small place called Cloonagh in the north of Tipperary not far from Roscrea—nothing more than a rural crossroad."

"In a rundown shack?"

"Anything but! He came from a wealthy family."

"Was Brother Lazarian a pedophile too?"

"No. But it was discovered that he knew what the other two were doing and he tolerated it—he called his toleration the lesser of two evils—he limited the pedophiles to certain children."

"God!" Pauline exclaimed. She took a deep breath and the sound of a sigh could be heard on its exhalation.

"There was a third pedophile that Lazarian did not tolerate: Brother Beatus."

"Is he alive?"

"Yes, he is. Brother Beatus still wears his black soutane and Roman collar. He is a resident of the geriatric ward— Saint Martha's Ward it's called—in Saint Fintan's Psychiatric Hospital in Portlaoise. I doubt he is in any danger from your killer."

"What do you know about Brother Beatus? Why wasn't he tolerated like the other two?"

"You're coming on fast and furious, Miss Byron," Cyril said, and glancing at Patrick, he asked him with his hands if he wanted to talk about Brother Beatus.

"You go ahead, Cyril," Patrick said.

"We didn't know Beatus well at all. I only recall seeing him at a distance."

"It was the same with me," Patrick said. "I never spoke to him. Beatus was in Dachadoo one summer when we were there, but only for a few days."

Cyril looked back to Pauline. "A handful of the brothers in the Order were known as Pilgrims, and Beatus was one of them. The Pilgrims were extraordinarily difficult men, brothers who would have been in psychiatric hospitals or in prison if they weren't in religious life. They were constantly on the move from one religious house to another. Within the Order, Brother Lazarian had some clout and he was able to keep his contact with Pilgrims to a minimum; still, occasionally, he had to take in one for the sake of peace within the Order. Beatus was foisted on him."

"But he only lasted a short time," Patrick said. "Lazarian got rid of him after less than five weeks. We were in Dachadoo only a few days that summer when Beatus was admitted to Saint Fintan's."

"Straight from Dachadoo to Saint Fintan's?" Pauline asked.

"Yes. And for those few days we were in Dachadoo with him he was confined to the farmyard, so we only saw him in the distance. Lazarian sentenced 'disobedient' brothers to work in the farmyard—barefooted. Beatus was one of those unfortunate men who had lived in an institution all his life; he was left outside an orphanage as a newborn; when he was eight he graduated to a school for junior boys, probably in Kilkenny; then he was sent to Dachadoo, and under normal circumstances he would have been kept there until he was sixteen. However, at some point he let it be known that he had a vocation to the Order of Saint Kieran and he was accepted into our junior novitiate in Dublin. The master of novices was not one to question the will of God, not even in the face of the obvious psychological ill health of a candidate. You can imagine, Miss Byron, the social skills, the psychological health and the sexual development of Brother Beatus. I don't know what his sexual orientation was, but we know he at least *tried* to rape some boys while he was in Dachadoo for those few weeks in...What year was that, Patrick?"

"Moishe Dyan...Six Day War...Nineteen sixty-seven."

"It came to light during the investigations that Beatus competed for boys with John the Baptist and Boniface. At least once, he was severely beaten by the other two when he tried to partake of their boys. It was even suggested that he might have suffered a concussion at the hands of the two brothers."

"Holy...," Pauline exclaimed.

"*Un*holy, Miss Byron," Cyril said.

"The children...," Patrick said.

"Neither of you knew about the pedophilia before the government inquiry?" Pauline finally asked.

"We never even suspected it. We were as shocked as anyone else."

A momentary break in the clouds of November created shadows and weak wintry warmth was felt. But the sun quickly hid again and an edgy air breezed in to replace the rising heat in the garden. Patrick adjusted his scarf.

"Do either of you feel any guilt about what went on in Dachadoo?"

"There is sadness more than guilt," Patrick said. "Sadness for the children who were raped in body and soul; sadness that the good idea—the noble idea—of caring for lost children was turned inside out by deviants; sadness for the innocent brothers who were tarnished. Besides the rapists there were sadists, who also corrupted the noble idea and destroyed children rather than saved them. Cyril and I have talked about our own feelings of guilt and even though we can plead innocent of wrongdoing, we still feel guilty—and we feel embarrassed for having joined the Order in the first place."

Cyril wrestled with his chair and stood up. "This wading around in such horror drags a person down. But even so, the focus must be kept on those destroyed children. I'll be back in a second." He went to his own front door.

"It is a very painful thing to remember their betrayal— the children of Dachadoo," Patrick said. "The pain comes out in sighs and tears and wall-pounding."

Pauline acknowledged the man's grief and remained silent for some seconds. Then she said, "Regret—the 'if only' syndrome—it has driven many a person mad, even to suicide."

"Over the years, Cyril and I have visited the sites of Ireland's industrial schools and four reformatories, both boys' and girls'. It doesn't do the children any good, but even so, we do acknowledge to the ones who were hurt that they were grievously wronged."

Both looked over to the noise of Cyril pulling his door shut; a bottle and three glasses balanced on the tray he was carrying. "Harvey's Bristol Cream," he said, as he put the tray on the table. He sat down and held up the bottle. "Miss Byron?" he asked. The glasses were Waterford in the Lismore pattern.

"To the lost children of Ireland," Cyril toasted. "Supposedly saved from the proselytizing Protestants only to be destroyed by the Catholic Church that would have saved them."

They sipped the Bristol Cream, and the three of them shuddered as the sweet Spanish sunshine trickled down their throats, spread warmth and reminded them of the November chill in their bodies. In contemplative silence they savored the break from the depressing subject like sweaty, muddy and thirsty players at the end of a tough rugby match.

The chilling breeze announced it was time to leave the patio.

"Thank you both for your patience with me, for educating me. I will not apologize again for my—"

Cyril held up his hand. "Miss Byron...Pauline. On the first Saturday of every month we have a *soirée*, to give our get-together a grand name—about twenty of us. We meet at four for a buffet dinner. You and your husband are welcome to join us whenever you wish. Call the day before so we can tell the caterer how many will be attending."

"Thank you, Cyril. I am honored."

"If you wish you can bring a bottle of wine, but nothing else—it will only be wasted."

Both men walked Pauline down to her jeep at the bottom of the hill. Even though the three of them made a bet of five pennies on who would be the first to see the garda protection, none of them won.

When Pauline was sitting behind the wheel, Patrick asked her through the window, "Have you heard the name Alger Hiss, Pauline?"

"Yes, the American spy."

"The *accused* American spy. It was from his continuous protestations of innocence we learned our lesson of forbearance."

"It is difficult to endure a false reputation."

"It was at first, but we have learned that it's less nerve-racking and humiliating than fighting it."

The brothers raised their hands in farewell and as Pauline drove away she sifted and filed what she had found out. It wasn't until she reached Tess Westman's Tea Rooms in Daingean that she realized she had stumbled across converging timelines establishing the summer of 1967 as the beginning of events that had their ending in Carrowreagh and Burnt House in 2007. She slapped the steering wheel. Then she called Jack Rafferty to tell him what she needed by Monday morning.

SATURDAY

NOVEMBER 23, 2007

29.

On the morning after the cadaver dog Bink had discovered the body of Brother Boniface, Mick McGovern tossed a copy of *The Telegraph* on his desk, threw his overcoat on top of a file cabinet and pulled his chair in against the backs of his legs. The man's height and thinness militated against suavity and he was not blessed with bodily grace. In the act of sitting down, Mick McGovern looked like a child-built Meccano bird whose nuts-and-bolts have all loosened at the same instant. And yet, not one pappus of his dandelion coif was knocked out of place by jolt of arse meeting chair seat.

McGovern picked up the newspaper. Under the headline "Bink the Wonder Dog," a four-column, six-inch color photograph in the top left corner showed Bink and Brian Deegan posed in a patch of cow-grazed grass, replete with cow plops. Deegan was on one knee, his face turned toward Bink, right hand about to caress the top of the dog's head. In the distant background, like a halo, a semicircle of guards and onlookers was focused on the heroic pair.

McGovern took off his wire-rimmed glasses.

Checking for typos and editorial tweakings, he read the article he had written about Bink, Brian Deegan, Missus Daly and the finding of the male corpse at Burnt House. Satisfied that a well-written report free of errors had appeared under his byline, except for the hyphenation of *De-egan* at the end of a line, McGovern scanned the remainder of the front page. Under a two-column headline on the bottom right-hand corner, Jack Rafferty,

alias Staff Writer, had laid claim to the murder near Burnt
House for *The Telegraph*. Even though the statement issued
by the Tullamore Garda Station merely said that a body
had been found in a house on the Daingean/Tullamore
road, Rafferty had given the corpse the name of Brother
Boniface and reported that the body had been mutilated
and was in a state of putrefaction. Rafferty had connected
Brother Boniface to the recently murdered Brother John
the Baptist in Carrowreagh by way of their membership
in the Order of Saint Kieran and their residency together
in Dachadoo Industrial School. Referring to an unnamed
source, Rafferty had noted the similarities of the modus
operandi used in both killings. Without revealing much
to the competition, he had restrained from using the
words "serial killer," but any reader with the intelligence
of a periwinkle could read between the lines. At the end
of the article, Rafferty had given credit to Pauline Byron
and Michael McGovern for their reporting on the story.

McGovern rolled the newspaper into a baton and
threw it at the trash can as if he were spearing a shark. He
missed.

From the array of compulsively arranged knick-knacks
on his desk McGovern picked out the remote mouse for
his computer.

It was Pauline Byron who had insisted that he be given
access to Jack Rafferty's holy of holies, Pauline who had
insisted in a conference call last evening that McGovern
familiarize himself with the file before setting out on
today's quest.

"For Chrissakes, Jack," she had demanded of Rafferty,
"how is Mick going to know if he's hearing something
worth hearing if he doesn't read the file first?" Mick had
held the phone away from his ear during this exchange.

McGovern took out his notebook and followed the
secret steps into the Asparagus file. He noted the "Cay-

enne" warning at the top of the page, and wondered if Jack had read all the Biggles books when he was a lad.

Under the heading Needed, he was amazed at the tone of Pauline's request—demand—that the formidable Jack have information from the Diggers at her home in Emo by nine o'clock on Monday morning. He read the file twice before retreating from Jack Rafferty's inner cyber sanctum.

McGovern used the desk phone to call down to the carpool. "McGovern...Lucan," he said and hung up. Then, engaging all his joints at more or less the same time, he stood heron-like, precariously balanced his various bits on top of each other and looked around. He dragged his London Fog trench coat off the file cabinet and threw it over his shoulder like a farm laborer walking home from the fields in the 1950s.

Despite the thirty people working in the newsroom there was little noise—just hushed phone conversations and the almost silent dackedy-dackedy of computer keys. As he walked past the raised assignment desk, McGovern lifted a hand shoulder-high and said, "Henry." Henry returned the greeting with a nod. "Nice story, Mick."

"Thanks, Henry." He passed the glassed-in research room where two men and three women—boy and girl whiz kids, to McGovern's forty-two-year-old mind—conjured incredibly obscure information out of cyberspace.

Then without knocking, because he knew it was empty, Mick went into Jack Rafferty's office and closed the door. Mockingly, he tugged on a forelock and kowtowed to the empty executive chair. With a key in his leather key case he unlocked the second drawer on the right-hand side of the knee hole. Removing a fat envelope, he put it on the desk and relocked the drawer.

McGovern took out the wad of notes and counted them twice. Two thousand euros.

30.

With the envelope in his inside breast pocket, Mick McGovern stepped out onto the sidewalk and put on his overcoat. Before he had tied the belt, a black Volvo 200 with tinted windows floated to a stop at the kerb.

He got into the car and buckled up. "Two thirty-seven Harbour Street, Lucan," he said.

"You've still got that yoke? That coat was popular in the seventies of the last century," Liam Williams, the driver, said.

"I bought it in the seventies of the last century."

"With that cape thingy you look like a stagecoach driver on a Charles Dickens Christmas card. All you need is a tall hat and a long whip."

There were times when it seemed Williams was a voracious reader—and times when he seemed to have the brain of a snail. Either because he was unable to decipher hints and body language, or because he had made Mick McGovern his clam-to-be-opened project before he retired, Williams was as annoying as a cloud of midges on a summer's evening on the Grand Canal.

"Saturday morning, Mick," the driver said. "No traffic. Isn't it grand, lads? Ten miles...I bet you ten euros I'll get you there in nineteen minutes or less."

"I still don't bet, Liam."

"How about five?" Liam persisted.

"Liam, clean out your ears."

Then assuming that Mick McGovern gave a shit— assuming that his passenger was a big ear—Liam monologued his speedy and reckless way west. McGovern distracted himself by looking at his feet and thinking about the two clergymen nailed to their floors like mounted butterfly specimens.

Williams was still talking about the County Meath football team when he parked across the street from a pair of high wooden doors in a wide archway, which in turn was set in a twelve-foot wall. "Nineteen minutes, Mick," Liam said, tapping the clock in the dashboard. "Ida wun."

"Ya wooda. Wait a few minutes till I find out what's happening."

As McGovern strode across the street, the fortress-like building ahead of him weakened his confidence with every step. As if further protection from the world was necessary, the brass plaque on the wicket door was the size of a stepped-on cigarette. Pushing his wire-rimmed glasses up off his eyes, Mick read: SAINT KIERAN.

A doorbell push, as discreet as the plaque, was the same color as the brown jamb that held it. McGovern, who counted things when he had to wait, looked at his watch as he rang the bell. It took seventeen seconds for a voice to sound in a box which McGovern could not see.

"May I help you?" the deep voice asked, and McGovern imagined a tall, big-muscled bodyguard with a red face and hands bigger than frying pans.

"I have a delivery."

"We are not expecting a delivery."

"Are you the person in charge?"

Four seconds. "Yes, I am. My name is Brother Fidelis."

In his mind, McGovern was hearing a Knight Hospitaller standing guard against the Saracens threatening Jerusalem, sword at the ready, morning star lurking in the folds of his tunic. "Brother Fidelis, my name is Michael McGovern. I would like to donate a gift to the Brothers of Saint Kieran."

It was eleven seconds before Brother Fidelis asked, "In what form is your gift, Mister McGovern?"

"It's in the form of euros, Brother Fidelis."

"Please wait, Mister McGovern."

Forty-four seconds went by. "Are you a former student of any of our institutions, Mister McGovern?"

"No, I'm not, Brother Fidelis," McGovern said.

"Look up at the security camera to your right."

Twenty-one seconds later the lock in the wicket door made a nerve-gnawing electrical squeal.

When McGovern stepped through the high wall he knew he wasn't in Kansas anymore; the enclosed grassy four acres were as silent as an empty theater; within his immediate sight were ornamental shrubs, espaliered fruit trees attached to the inside of the surrounding wall; monkey puzzles, wooden benches, clayey and empty flower beds; white wooden lawn geese bringing out the greenness of the green grass. Somewhere there lurked, McGovern suspected, a gardener intent on gilding lilies. Macadamized paths wound their way through the lawns in fanciful patterns.

The driveway, which snaked in from the street under the two arched gates, swung gracefully to the right toward the front door of what was once the family home of very wealthy gentry of a bygone age. A slated, vaulted overhang, anchored in the wall above the front door, stretched out from the building and rested on two ornamental pillars for the protection of passengers alighting from carriages on inclement days of yore. The walls of the house were built with white cut stone with slightly darker quoins at corners, windows and doorway. The house had three stories, many chimneys and many arched windows, beneath which large stone urns held sculptured boxwood. An apron of flagstones, the same color as the building's quoins and as smooth and tight-fitting as the wood in a ballroom floor, surrounded the front door. McGovern suspected that the symmetry of the entire place had been established long before it had passed into the ownership of the Order of Saint Kieran.

As McGovern reached out to lift the ring in the brass leonine nose, the door was opened by a tall man wearing a Roman collar and a cassock. The whiteness of the hair on the elderly head was as bright as a neon halo on a dark-niched statue. His facial skin had the pallor of a sixty-a-day smoker—or a week-old corpse—and his eyes were large and sunken. But despite the nicotine-stained fingers of his right hand, he was sparkling clean and might have just stepped away from the shaving mirror. In his spotless and perfectly creased cassock, the brother unabashedly gaped at Mick's hair.

"Brother Fidelis?" McGovern asked.

"Yes, Mister McGovern. May I see some identification?"

Mick fingered his way through his wallet, trying to hide his press credentials and at the same time find his driver's license. Brother Fidelis opened the license, looked at the photo and looked at the reporter. "Please come in," he said.

Less than twenty minutes later Liam Williams was shocked out of his sleep by McGovern's urgent rapping on the glass beside him. He lowered the window. "Here," Mick said, and he handed Liam a fifty-euro note. "There's a hardware shop a quarter of a mile down the road on the left. Buy the cheapest hand-truck they have and get a receipt. Get back here as quick as you can and blow the horn when you pull into the gateway." Mick flung his thumb over his shoulder. "I'll open the gates for you. Drive on up to the front door when you come in. This is urgent."

"The union doesn't—"

"Fuck the union. No one will know and I'll give you twenty."

"Fifty."

"Fuck off." McGovern slapped the roof of the car and strode back across the road like a hungry cassowary after spotting a frog. As he approached the wicket gate, it opened in front of him as if someone was watching for his return. He ducked, went in and looked at his watch.

31.

Like a long-stepping don proctoring in a large examination hall, McGovern strode along the footpaths nearest the arched gateway, his hands resting on his buttocks under the tails of his unbelted overcoat. If he'd been a nail biter, he would have had blood on all ten stumps. With every twenty steps, his arms swung out of hiding, and he uncovered his wristwatch with a flick of his left hand. It wasn't the waiting for the Volvo as much as his anxiety about Brother Fidelis that was knotting his entrails; he was afraid that while Liam was gone the brother might change his mind. McGovern swiped a hand across his inside breast pocket and felt that the envelope was still there. If he needed to, he still had eighteen hundred euros left to work on the venal brother.

A horn honked at the gate and Mick stumbled as he turned and loped at the same time. He lifted and pulled several black iron bolts and swung the gates open. As the car slipped through, he told the driver to take out the hand-truck when he got to the door.

"You owe me nearly twenty euros," Williams said. He held up a receipt.

"You'll get it," McGovern said impatiently. Then, obeying Brother Fidelis's command, he closed and locked the gates. He ran across the grass to the front door.

Liam Williams was about to pull down the hatch of the Volvo. "Leave it open and come with me," McGovern told him.

"Union rules...I stay with the car."

"Twenty euros," McGovern said, as he grabbed one handle of the hand-truck and pulled it after him to the front door.

"Fifty."

"Fuck off!" McGovern kept going. The door swung open as he raised his hand to knock.

McGovern strode in and Brother Fidelis was standing there like Lon Chaney pretending to be a butler.

Williams came rushing in after Mick. "Is this man with you?" the brother asked.

"Yes, he's with me," McGovern said.

Brother Fidelis closed the door. "Mister McGovern, please don't run or walk across the lawn again," he said.

Four minutes later the three men were back at the open front door. McGovern, with the hand-truck tilted toward him, was balancing the weight of a blue, four-drawer file cabinet on the wheels. Brother Fidelis put his hand on the reporter's shoulder. "Four things, Mister McGovern: leave the main gate as you found it; when you close the wicket door, push it to make sure it is latched; you must be back here with that file cabinet by five o'clock; and do not walk on the grass."

On the road back to Dublin in the speeding Volvo, McGovern handed eighteen euro and twenty-four cents to the driver.

"The extra for the hand-truck."

"Jazus, Mick! Couldn't you have given me twenty even?"

"I could have rounded it out and given you eighteen even."

"But it's company money."

"It is, but there's change and receipts to be handed in. If I rounded it out to twenty, it would have cost me one euro fifty-three and I don't spend any of my own funds on behalf of my employer. Now...I have to make a call."

"Don't forget you owe me forty more."

"How could I?"

Williams listened to Mick's side of the phone conversation.

"McGovern...The whole lot...*Parietes habent aures*... One four-drawer filing cabinet...They kept very few... Two hundred...Cigarettes, I'd say...It has to be back by five...Yes, today...Four copiers...Three to a copier; two to organize out-and-in, and one to copy. Twelve...Henry."

McGovern folded up his phone.

"You think I don't know you were talking to Rafferty? And you think I don't know the walls have ears? Anyone doing crossword puzzles knows *parietes habent aures* like they know *veni vidi vici* or *amo amas amat* or *mensa mensa mensam* or *Dies irae dies illa*. I hate it when people think I'm thick just because I drive a car for a living."

McGovern didn't answer.

Williams was silent until the wall of Phoenix Park started running along the road. "What's in the yoke?" he asked, glancing over his shoulder toward the file cabinet.

"For everyone's sake it's better you don't know."

"You mean for the sake of *The Telegraph* it's better no one knows."

McGovern didn't respond.

When they pulled into the loading bay behind the Telegraph Building, Liam said, "You'll have to get maintenance to help you with that in the back—too many union eyes around this place."

"Even for another twenty?"

"No."

"Forty?"

"Not fifty nor a hundred. I'd get Jim Larkin if I were you. He's not into union costiveness and he'll get the yoke upstairs for you before next week. His mental acuity is dull and he can't remember his own name most of the time."

"Costiveness," McGovern said. "Is that another crossword word?"

"No. I came across it in Ian McEwan's *Enduring Love*."
Williams leaned across and opened the glove box, revealing a dictionary, pens, index cards and a copy of *On Chesil Beach*. "I don't spend all my waiting time asleep."

McGovern took out fifty euros and handed them over. "For helping in Lucan. Get your wife a bunch of roses with the extra ten."

"Are you buying forgiveness for back there with the Latin, Mick?"

McGovern reached out to take back the money. Williams turned away and stuffed the note into his pocket. "Feck off," he said.

As McGovern climbed the steps to the top of the ramp, Williams shouted, "I don't know what my wife would do with roses."

"Buy her some and see."

✝

SUNDAY

NOVEMBER 24, 2007

32.

"The November light was fading at half-past four when the old man, Mister Turley, passed our house." That's what Nicholas Cahill's widow will tell the guards the next day, and even though she didn't see him she knows it was half-past four because that's the time Mister Turley passed her house every day after his walk to the Roscrea road.

"As regular as a well-fed duck, Nicholas used to say," is what she will say.

He stands at the main road for a while watching the traffic, and the passing drivers lift their pointing finger off the steering wheel in salutation of the solitary, tall, thin figure—the Offaly Salute they call it. He never waves back.

"Nicholas always said the Offalies are a crowd of sleazy hures—sloping in here to Tipperary and lifting their fingers like that and you not knowing if they're telling you hello or telling you to go fuck yourself. Excuse me, Guard—you're young enough to be my own son. Nicholas was a terrible man with the language, God rest him.

"Hail, rain, frost or snow, Mister Turley goes for his walk as long as the rain isn't blowing." That's what she and Nicholas had noticed over the years. "Of course he's right, too. Nicholas always said there's no way to keep yourself dry when the rain's blowing; it's down the back of your neck one minute and up your hole the next. He was terrible vulgar at times, even to a priest; he didn't give a shite what anyone thought.

"After looking at the motors and lorries and tractors on the road for a while he heads back to Cloonagh, one

mile exactly to the crossroads and then turns left for
another half mile to his own house. A very private man.
Only for Murt Kirwin the postman no one would even
know his name. And Murt thought he might have been a
teacher one time. Murt's dead, may the Lord have mercy
on him."

The widow, Missus Cahill, would dare to say that
every boy Mister Turley ever taught—that's if Murt was
right about him being a teacher—sat up straight at his
school desk; he looks like a man who wouldn't tolerate
any slouching nor dragging of feet.

"Not by the way he walks himself! Nicholas said Mister Turley has the handle of a pitchfork up in his arse.
Nicholas hated feet-draggers, wearing out the leather of
the soles like that."

The widow Cahill will not be able to say if Mister Turley ever has visitors, because after all, Mister Turley lives
around the corner at the crossroads and many things go
on beyond the crossroads that Missus Cahill doesn't know
about.

"Jer Dunne's wife might be the one to ask, though.
She'd be nearer to Mister Turley's house than me. He has
a car, Mister Turley, and he still drives; goes to Roscrea
every Tuesday morning for his messages and never offers
anyone a lift. If there's a hiker he drives right past like
there's no one there, even if it's pouring cats and dogs;
he gets his messages at the Spar and comes home again."

Beyond that, Missus Cahill won't be able to say anything about the man, except that he got the house done
up before he moved in, got central heating and new
wooden floors downstairs.

"The man had notions! Why a single man would need
a two-storied house is beyond me, and he had the upstairs
rooms all done up, too, plastered and painted, and new
furniture. And good furniture, too; none of the shite
them fucking tinkers try to sell you. Got the stairs done,

too, with a new banister and nice molded yokes...the little posts that hold up the banister...What are they called, at all? The memory, Guard...He bought everything in Lowry's in Kilkenny, and they sent their own men to do the floors and stairs. He must have money is what Nicholas used to say. Nicholas would go in and have a gawk when the workmen were in there. Nicholas was a curious man. He knew the names of the moons of Saturn and he could rattle off the names of the first forty-one popes just to show priests how uneducated they were—the priests, not the popes...Spindles is what they're called—the thingies for the stairs.

"Twelve years ago it was, he moved in—July 1995— because that same day our last lad got married.

"Forty-four and everyone had given up all hope. The wife is a Laois woman, but beggars can't be choosers; bit of a bogger, but nice for all that, not too many notions about herself. There's nothing worse than a bogger with notions...you know how some of those Laoisies can be. But even so, she whelped six whippersnappers in six years, all boys. And the very next day after the wedding, Mister Turley was out walking to the Roscrea road, always with a walking stick and a black hat with a brim, the same as the ones priests used to wear back when priests wore hats. He looked like Eamon de Valera the first time he walked by—that straight back and he thin and tall.

"No, he doesn't talk to anyone," Missus Cahill will say, "not even in the Spar when he meets some of the locals. He ignores us all. Nicholas said he's quare as a coot or else stuck up—one of them who thinks their own farts don't smell...And why are you asking all the questions about Mister Turley, Guard?"

Missus Cahill will bless herself and say, "May the Lord have mercy on him. I hope I didn't say anything bad about him. And what happened to him, Guard?"

33.

As usual, Mister Turley already had his key out when he reached his front door after his walk. He wouldn't have locked the place at all except that the travelers, formerly known as the tinkers, would steal anything that wasn't nailed down. The name change meant nothing to Mister Turley; a tinker was a tinker the same as a cripple was a cripple, and changing the animal's name didn't change the nature of the animal. In a few years "traveler" would be as offensive as "tinker" because the underlying person would still be as offensive as he was when he made the word "tinker" offensive in the first place.

Mister Turley didn't switch on any lights when he entered. Inside the door in the near darkness, as obsessively as a cat burying his scat, he cleaned his boots on the sisal mat. Then he took a long step onto the deep-red runner to avoid putting a damp footprint on the oak floor. After running its brim through his fingers he placed his hat on the shelf in the press under the stairs. He placed his overcoat on its hanger, brushed its shoulders with a coat brush and hung it on the pole. He unlaced his walking boots and put them on their cut-to-size piece of carpet on the floor of the cupboard. Then, as he pushed his feet into his slippers he became aware that someone was in his house; it must have been an unfamiliar smell that alerted him, a smell of newness, something like the smell of a new book.

Eighty-two-year-old Mister Turley was not afraid. He had never met a man he couldn't overpower physically or psychologically. Still, before he closed the press door, he leaned down and took out a two-foot-long shillelagh with a fist-sized knot at one end. He had inherited the shillelagh when his father's house was cleaned out for selling. His younger brother, Edward, the monsignor, had referred to it as Idi Amin's genitalia, and he and Edward had giggled in the manner of celibates hearing a reference to the sexual. Mister Turley felt the heft of the cudgel in his right hand, then quietly stepped into the room he called the study, the shillelagh balanced for a lightning strike to face, testicles or knees. But the quickness of his old body wasn't quick enough.

Mister Turley found himself slammed into the wall immediately inside the study door. Idi Amin's genitalia were wrenched from his grasp. A hand at his throat lifted him onto his toes and squeezed his windpipe. He saw red, he saw brown, he saw black and then he passed out.

It was the two red-hot spikes searing the brown-yellow mucus membrane in the upper reaches of his nostrils that brought Mister Turley back. He jerked his head away from the pain, but there was no relief. He lifted his head and slapped at the torturous instrument but there was nothing to slap. He sat up, and the room wobbled around him. He was sitting in the chair at his desk.

Vigorously he rubbed his nose; urgently, he extracted a handkerchief from his trouser pocket and blew; he snorted; he sneezed. He wiped the tears from his eyes, fussily rubbed his nose again, pinched it repeatedly to ease the inner burning. He held the damp handkerchief over his nostrils in a useless effort to ease the discomfort. Maybe he'd had a stroke. The room spun to the right again and he thought about eddies and whirlpools spinning to the right in...Mister Turley couldn't remember if it was night or morning, could not recall what had happened to him.

When the walls finally stopped moving, he noticed the apparition on the other side of his desk. It was a face in a rock, a face a sculptor had carved, while leaving the rest of the body trapped in the marble. Then he saw the face had a moustache, thought it was a man's face inserted into a hole in one of those things at carnivals for funny photographs—your own face on the painted body of a donkey or in the place of Mona Lisa's smile. The eyes in the face were looking at him, unblinking, unmoving, just looking.

The apparition stayed where it was. The burning in Mister Turley's nose eased slightly. Then he remembered—it was ammonium hydroxide and alcohol—smelling salts. He must have passed out. Smelling salts had been held under his nose. The apparition became an ambulance man dressed in surgical scrubs, a shower cap on his head, with nothing only his face showing. No ears. He was sitting in the Queen Anne chair that Turley's grandfather had bought eighty years ago in Mallet's in New Bond Street.

Mister Turley blew his nose, rubbed it energetically, then covered his mouth and nose again with the soppy handkerchief. He waited to be told something, because he knew he had missed the passing of some time. He didn't know how he'd got into his chair, he didn't remember switching on the ceiling light. Fearful that he might sound like a stroke victim, all flapping lips and drooling spit, he sat there looking at the ambulance man, his elbows on his gleaming, bare desk, his handkerchief still clamped against his face.

The ambulance man spoke. "You have a scar on your left thumb."

Because he had been expecting a diagnosis of his predicament, it took a few moments for Mister Turley's brain to process the unexpected observation. Then, like a body on the verge of sleep inexplicably jerking itself wide awake, Mister Turley snapped, "Eh?"

The man across the desk didn't answer. Mister Turley said, "What did...what did you say?" He ran the handkerchief around his face. "What happened to me?"

The ambulance man sat silent.

"My left thumb...," Mister Turley said, "that was years ago." He held his two hands away from his face and stuck out his thumbs. He looked at them for a while, then said, "This one...the left one. A dog bit me. But the bite couldn't have given me a turn, made me pass out." He continued to peer at the scar as if he were stuck in the moment of terror when the wound was inflicted.

"You're a liar, Brother Lazarian."

Mister Turley gaped across at the ambulance man. "Mister Turley...Mister Turley is my name."

"You're a liar, Brother Lazarian."

"Who are you?"

"James O'Malley. Twenty-nine Sixty-seven." O'Malley hesitated, allowed the name and number to sink in. "There was no dog, Brother Lazarian. When you were beating my brother, Michael, Twenty-eight Sixty-seven, in Dachadoo, I bit your thumb."

Mister Turley ferociously rubbed his nose in his handkerchief. "I have always considered the animal who bit me a dog...What happened to me? Did I fall?"

For a long time the two men looked at each other, neither blinking.

"Are you speaking from hubris or stupidity, Brother Lazarian?" O'Malley asked.

"Hubris? That's a big word for a former inmate of Dachadoo, for an ambulance man. I'm not stupid, Twenty-nine Sixty-seven. And get out of that chair. Nobody has sat in it since my father died."

James O'Malley ignored the command. "Do you remember *my* father?" he asked. "He came to Dachadoo the—"

"And then he went off and drowned himself—opted out of all responsibility after deserting his two whelps. Is this part of your examination—checking my memory? Now do your job, O'Malley, and tell me what happened to me. I told you to get out of that chair."

Within his protective clothing James O'Malley's body began to heat up.

"How do the smelling salts feel, Brother Lazarian?"

"My name is Mister Turley. Get out of that chair."

"The question is, How does it feel?"

"It's torturous. It's like two…Why did you have to—"

"It's like two *what*, Brother Lazarian?"

"Two hot needles," Turley said. Then he did something he had never done in the presence of another human being—he stuck a pinky finger up his left nostril and swiveled it in great agitation.

"How many boys did you revive with smelling salts in Dachadoo, Brother Lazarian?" O'Malley asked.

"My name is Mister Turley."

Idi Amin's testicles slammed explosively onto the desktop beside Turley's hand. He jumped in fright and fell against the back of his chair. His heart took off at a fast gallop.

"My desk! That's a seventeen-twenty piece of—you great ignoramus."

James O'Malley was now standing, looming over the desk, looking down on the former brother. "The condition of the desk is the least of your worries," he said calmly. He turned his back and with the knob of the cudgel smashed the arms of the Queen Anne chair at their delicate elbows.

"Stop! Stop!"

O'Malley turned back and saw the distress on Turley's face. "How many times did you burn the insides of children's noses with smelling salts in Dachadoo, Brother Lazarian?"

Mister Turley inserted a pinky into his other nostril and rotated as much as physiology allowed. He held the handkerchief to his face with his right hand and placed the other hand on the edge of the desk. "You are a philistine, O'Malley, but what's to be expected from a—"

The balls of Idi Amin smashed down so close to his fingers that Turley felt the rush of the disturbed air and heard the loud bang before he saw what had happened. Instinctively, his body propelled itself backward and he grasped the arm supports on each side of his chair. He shouted, "What's the matter with...That desk was bought by my—"

He was silenced by another loud thump of the shillelagh on the desk. "I asked you a question, Brother Lazarian. How many times did you burn the insides of children's noses with smelling salts?"

"Who the hell do you think—?"

The balled end of Idi Amin's swollen apparatus again whacked into the surface of the James I walnut desk. "Your hubris, Brother Lazarian—it's not allowing you to see who's in charge here," James O'Malley said. "I will ask you the question again. If you do not answer I will break one of your bones." Without a sound, the huge black scrotum rose off the desktop. "How many times did you burn—?"

"You can go to hell, Mister." Turley began to rise from his chair, but before the old man had straightened his knees, James O'Malley had slipped around the desk. A violent push in the face with the flat of O'Malley's hand reseated him. The moment his rear end hit the seat of the chair, his left upper arm exploded in exquisite, excruciating pain. O'Malley grasped Turley's hand and yanked it over his head, and Turley screamed primally as shattered pieces of broken bone grated against each other inside his flesh. O'Malley threw the arm down and the scream that followed was the scream of a scalded pig.

O'Malley sat on the edge of the desk facing Turley, the narrow end of the shillelagh in his gloved right hand, the huge blackthorn knot in the other.

Turley seemed to have aged in the last few minutes, had slumped to one side in the chair, his right hand grasping his broken arm. His face was grey. Eventually in a weakened voice he said, "I don't know how many...I don't know how many times I used the smelling salts on the...on the inmates in Dachadoo...You are supposed to be taking care of me, O'Malley."

"Rephrase that, Brother Lazarian," O'Malley said.

"What? Rephrase what?"

"On whom did you use the smelling salts, Brother Lazarian?"

"On *whom*! My God! On the inmates...I said on the inmates. My arm is broken."

"But that's not the correct word, Brother Lazarian."

Turley stared back at O'Malley. "I'm not a mind reader, O'Malley. You tell me the correct word."

"You haven't grasped the situation here yet, Brother Lazarian. I will explain it to you more fully. When the district nurse comes here in the morning, she will find you dead, hanging from the banister of your stairs. Your swollen tongue will be hanging out of your purple face. Shit and piss will be running down your legs and the nurse will slam her hands over her face to keep out your stink. As it stands at this moment, the coroner will note that you died from asphyxiation; that the back of your head showed signs of slight impact pre-mortem; that fingers had squeezed your windpipe pre-mortem and that the upper left humerus had been broken with a blunt instrument, also pre-mortem. It's up to you whether the autopsy report of your injuries will end there."

Mister Turley stared unblinkingly at O'Malley, like an animal who has never known defeat, who has never contemplated limitations to its own capabilities.

"For purposes of reality your name for the evening is Brother Lazarian. Every time you use the name Turley you will be punished—and the autopsy report will get longer." The balled end of the shillelagh swung up into view. "I am not an ambulance attendant. I am not here to help you. I am here to kill you. I already know the answers to all the questions I will ask you. Every time you balk at giving the truthful answer, I will break at least one of your bones. Sometimes it's difficult to break one bone without breaking others. For instance, each wrist has eight bones."

O'Malley paused and drilled his eyes into Brother Lazarian's. "On whom did you use the smelling salts in Dachadoo, Brother Lazarian?"

Brother Lazarian's momentary silence sounded like defiance. "I used the smelling salts on the destitutes who were incarcerated in Dachadoo."

The shillelagh shattered some of the fingers of the right hand being used to suppress the pain of the broken humerus. The uncontrolled scream of a rat impaled on a crowbar came out of Brother Lazarian.

A few minutes later O'Malley asked, "On whom did you use the smelling salts in Dachadoo, Brother Lazarian?"

Lazarian did not hesitate. "I used the smelling salts on some of the boys who had been committed to Dachadoo."

"Why did the boys need to be resuscitated, Brother Lazarian?"

"To make them come around—to restore them to consciousness."

"How had they become unconscious, Brother Lazarian?"

"They had passed out, fainted."

"Did you ever knock a child unconscious, Brother Lazarian?"

"Yes."

"How many, Brother Lazarian?"

"I don't recall."

The knob of the shillelagh floated up to O'Malley's chest.

"Maybe ten."

The black knob struck again and Brother Lazarian roared like a jackass in the night.

"That's two more bones for the coroner to comment on—ulna and radius. How many young boys did you knock unconscious while you were the superior in Dachadoo, Brother Lazarian?"

"About fifty."

"How many boys did you revive with smelling salts in Dachadoo, Brother Lazarian?"

"About fifty."

"I have told you my name, Brother Lazarian, but you may not have—"

"I heard you…O'Malley, Twenty-nine Sixty-eight."

"I don't believe you heard it properly, Brother Lazarian."

Lazarian tempted the fates with a long hesitation, then said, "James O'Malley—unless you'd prefer *Mister* O'Malley."

O'Malley ignored the sneer in the voice. "Are you a pedophile?" he asked.

Brother Lazarian looked contemptuously at O'Malley. He did not answer. He saw the shillelagh moving but he was unable to escape it. The cap of his right knee shattered and the Reverend Brother's eyes rolled around in their sockets. He groaned. He moaned. He became silent.

"Brother Lazarian, are you a pedophile?" O'Malley asked.

"No." Brother Lazarian's voice had weakened.

"Was Brother Boniface a pedophile?"

"Yes."

"Was Brother John the Baptist a pedophile?"

"Yes."

"Was Brother Beatus a pedophile?"

"Yes."

"Did Boniface, John the Baptist and Beatus rape little boys in Dachadoo?"

"Yes."

"Did they rape little boys in Dachadoo while you were their superior?"

"I was not their spiritual superior. I was in charge of the school—in charge of the boys...My arm is in great pain."

"They worked in the school under your direction?"

"Beatus was there only—"

"These three brothers—you were their superior in the school. Is that right?"

"Yes."

"When you found out they were raping little boys under your care, what did you do to protect the children?"

"I didn't *find out*. I was told before I took the position at Dachadoo that Boniface and John the Baptist were pedophiles. They were practicing pedophiles in Dachadoo before I got there. Beatus came and went within a few weeks."

"Who told you about Boniface and John the Baptist?"

"The brother in charge of our order—the superior general."

"Did he tell you to get rid of them?"

"My arm is hurting."

The knob of the shillelagh smashed the inner side of Brother Lazarian's left knee. His eyes rolled again, his head rolled on his shoulders again. He closed his eyes and lay against the back of the chair as if taking a rest. James O'Malley poked his victim in the chest with the shooting end of Idi Amin's hanging gardens.

"Should I use the smelling salts to revive you, Brother Lazarian?"

Lazarian held up a shaking finger as if asking for time.

"What did your superior tell you to do about the pedophiles in Dachadoo?"

"To keep an eye on them—try to control their activities."

"How did you do that?"

"There wasn't much...I could do. Dachadoo was a big place. I couldn't be in the corner of every shed...and building at once...I need water."

"Did you know the names of the children who were being raped?"

"Yes...That was the only way I could have some...control over the pedophiles."

"What do you mean?"

"I told them who they were...limited to."

Pellets of molten sweat erupted all over his skin and James O'Malley felt as if he were blistering at every pore in his body. His heart began to pound. He swallowed hard, he took deep breaths. The two men eyeballed each other. Neither flinched. The balls of Idi Amin ascended like a black moon rising between them.

"Who were they limited to—the pedophiles?"

Brother Lazarian did not blink, did not look away. "The boys who deserved it," he said, defiant as a prisoner looking his hangman in the eye.

James O'Malley felt the vapors of emotion steaming in among the swirls of wiring in his brain, felt the wires sagging and stretching under the heat. His breathing sped up.

"How did you decide which...why did you pick...what boys were chosen to be raped?"

"I am in pain...I need water."

Suddenly Idi Amin's balls were trembling within an inch of Brother Lazarian's nose.

"Which boys did you pick?"

"The badly behaved ones...the ones who...deserved it."

"You used rape as a punishment?"

"I killed two birds with one stone, O'Malley—controlled the pedophiles and punished the boys who needed punishing."

James O'Malley gripped on the edge of the desk with his free hand.

"Michael O'Malley...Do you remember him? Boniface and John the Baptist...Do you remember Michael O'Malley?"

"I asked you for water, O'Malley."

"If a son shall ask bread of any of you that is a father, will you give him a stone?" James O'Malley said. He didn't know where the words came tumbling from. He thrust the smelling salts under Brother Lazarian's nose, held the back of the old man's head with his other hand.

For ten minutes Lazarian coughed and sneezed and snotted and teared and drooled and moaned and tried to wipe his face on his own shoulders.

"I need water," Lazarian then demanded loudly, as if his loudness could recapture a power he once wielded or as if egging the hangman to get on with it.

"Why did you choose Michael O'Malley for those animals?" James O'Malley hissed, and as he pushed himself off the edge of the desk he felt the clanging collapse of his own steely nerves.

"Nobody bites me like a dog...nobody!" Lazarian shouted. "Nobody touches my body...nobody! You, *Mister* O'Malley, were nothing...but scum. Your brother was...nothing but scum. The whole lot of you were scum. All of you... should have been scraped up off the land like...dog dung and sent out of sight to Australia. And now...here's something you don't know: I gave your brother to...Boniface and John the Baptist to punish...you. I knew it would be worse...for you that way. And you know...and I know...how well I succeeded."

James O'Malley's self-control collapsed and he came charging out of his civilizing restraints, Idi Amin's solid scrotum leading the way.

†

MONDAY

NOVEMBER 25, 2007

34.

The Cathy Carman bronze sculpture floating eleven feet in the air in front of the Tullamore Garda Station was titled *Free Spirit*. Fans of the Tullamore Harriers Athletic Club, believing the sculpture to be a reflection of their particular obsession, called it the Harrier. The town's cornerboys nicknamed it "De Burd," which prompted them to call the garda station the Burd House and its occupants the Blue Burds.

It was beside *Free Spirit* that Tom Breen and Superintendent Donovan met on Monday morning at ten minutes to eight. The superintendent's body language was imitative of a cat with canary feathers in its teeth. The two walked slowly around the building toward the rear entrance.

"Any fish, Tom?"

"Twelve throwbacks," Breen said.

"No sign of Finn's salmon? Someday you're going to come in and surprise everyone with a fish story." The superintendent opened his arms wide.

Breen knew Donovan was sitting on new-found information that he would reveal in a fluttering of yellow feathers at the appropriate time. "Last week I caught a five-pound trout," he said.

"Why didn't you tell us?"

"No one asked."

"And they might think you were bragging if you told without being asked? There's times you're too Irish altogether, Tom. I took my missus to the Riverbank in Birr

on Saturday night. Very posh, and I'm not bragging, just
thinking of the cost."

"How was the wine?"

"I might have whiffed a blackberry in the bouquet, but
I'm not sure," Donovan said, giving Breen a wry smile.
They stepped into the building. "When Jimmy comes in,
the two of you come up and we'll see what we have on the
Most Reverend Pedophilic Brothers of the Order of Saint
Kieran." The detective wondered what his boss could have
discovered over the weekend.

Breen was ordering his thoughts on a foolscap pad
when Gorman knocked on the door at two minutes to
eight and came in without invitation. He placed some
handwritten sheets on the desk and began to speak as if
he were already in the middle of a conversation. "Here's
Nailer's essay writ in ten-penny nails, severed and boiled
pizzles, smelling salts, sewn lips and broken bones."

"How was Ballysteen? Any sign of Tennyson compos-
ing in the hedge of the Big Field?"

"He'd have been decomposing in the hedge if I'd a
seen him. Get it?"

"Jakers, Jimmy, it's only Monday morning and you're
at it already."

"Ballysteen was fine. I got my sister to recite a few stanzas
of Missus Shallot, my mother didn't tell me to get a haircut,
Beatrice and myself went for a long walk by ourselves, and
the adolescents were tolerable—they have amazing personality changes the minute they see Granny. We all went to a
fish-and-chip shop in Pallaskenry and got heartburn, but
my mother fixed us with a dose of bread soda. And here I
am ready to take on the world. Didja ketch any fish?"

"Throwbacks."

"Did you go to see the pater?"

"He was asking for you. He still thinks you're a pleasant lunatic, but he can't understand what Beatrice sees in
you."

"I know you're trying to get my day off to a good start, Tom, and don't think I'm not appreciative. Anything happening with the smelly brothers?"

Breen stood up with his papers in his hand. "Not that I know of. *The Telegraph* has another front-page piece, but there's nothing in it we don't already know. Bring the essay with you. The supe has summoned us and he's floating with excitement. He must have something to tell us."

"You mean he's got a gobful of canary feathers?" Gorman asked.

"He ate at least half a dozen of the little birds."

"He's that excited?"

On the stairs Gorman asked, "Any luck with Pauline Byron on Friday evening?"

"When I heard her voice on the phone I got an attack of nerves about being in touch with her, about the consequences if it was ever found out. She said she understood, but told me she was pissed off about the shenanigans with the phone and the incontinence line."

Breen knocked and they went into Donovan's office.

"Any stabbings in the home county this weekend, Jimmy?" he asked,

"An oul Alzheimer's nun stabbed herself in the leg with a knitting needle, sir, and she started screaming she'd been attacked by a hooligan from Offaly, a bogger with such a flat accent you could skim stones across—"

"Shut up, Jimmy," the superintendent said, in his own Offaly flatness. "I should have known not to ask." He picked a newspaper off his desk and dropped it again. "*The Telegraph*," he said. "'The Devils of Dachadoo,' and on the front page again. It's like they're keeping the story ticking over just in case, or in the hope Nailer will kill again. Some hure's feeding them information, and you may be sure with that one's name—Byron…Pauline— attached to the article they're getting ready to do a big story. Every one of us has to make sure we keep our arses clean on this one." He dropped the newspaper into the trash can. "Now, there's nothing from the traffic lads on the Daingean road." He pointed at a thin sheaf of stapled pages. "That's the medical examiner's report on the Very Reverend Brother Boniface. If you put it side by side with the report on the Very Reverend Brother Jack the Bap, the only difference is the address and the names of the broken bones. And I nearly forgot…There is another difference: the grease used to scald Brother Boniface's pubic area was goose grease, and his dangler had been sautéed in it before being shoved into his mouth."

"Jesus!" Breen said. "Fried dick first thing on a Monday morning."

"*Sautéed*, Tom," the superintendent said. "You'll never get anywhere in a restaurant if you don't know the difference between sautéed dick and fried."

"The English have a dessert called spotted dick," Gorman said. The other two looked at him as if he'd made a loud fart.

Donovan said, "Okay, Tom, you go first and tell us what you think."

"First, I have to compliment Jimmy, sir."

Gorman looked at Breen like a man expecting a sharp stick in the eye.

"On Friday when we were coming back from Carrowreagh, Jimmy said we could exchange the name O'Brien with Geoghan and everything would still be the same."

"Good one, Jimmy…Astute thinking…You'll soon be as good as me." The superintendent smiled, and with the back of his hand waved the conversation over to Breen.

Gorman looked at Breen with "God bless you, my son," written all over his face.

Breen laid the yellow notepad on the thigh of his crossed leg. He didn't look at it as he spoke. "I think the quickest way to find Nailer is to find out everything we can about the two victims, especially what they had in common. We might figure out who his next victim is—if there's going to be another—"

"So far, Tom," Donovan interrupted, "his victims have not been found until two weeks after their deaths. Maybe Boniface is his second victim and the third or fourth has yet to be found."

"I agree with you there, sir," Breen said, and he glanced at his notepad. "I think that the motive behind the killings of the brothers will be found in Dachadoo because I think Nailer was once an inmate there. Dachadoo closed in 1971, thirty-six years ago. That may have been the last time the two dead brothers were together in the same place. So we may have a date to begin with, 1971. We must find out how long they were together in Dachadoo. That will give us another date. The Phoenix Park Collators can bring those dates closer together by figuring out Nailer's age and the years he spent in Dachadoo."

"This sounds good," Gorman said.

"In the past," Breen continued, "when industrial schools were certified by the Department of Education, the schools were obliged to keep certain records. One of the records…"—Breen slipped a sheet of paper out of the pad and read from it—"*was a journal or diary of everything important or exceptional that passes in the school. All admissions, discharges, licenses and escapes shall be recorded therein, and all record books shall be laid before the Inspector when he visits the school. Visits of the Medical Officer will be recorded— admissions to the infirmary shall be kept, giving information as to ailment, treatment, and dates of admission and discharge in each case.*"

Breen moved his finger to the top of the page. "*The Manager or his Deputy shall be authorized to punish the children detained in the School in case of misconduct. All serious misconduct, and the punishment inflicted for it, shall be entered in a book to be kept for that purpose, which shall be laid before the Inspector when he visits.*"

Breen looked up at the superintendent. "If we can only get our hands on those files we might be able to figure out who Nailer is."

The superintendent had been supporting his chin on his knuckles as Breen read. Now he let his arms fall across the desk in a gesture of helplessness. "Tom, I think we spoke about this on Friday, about how no one has ever seen the files of the industrial schools—not even the Department of Education that was financing them. Someone tried to get that very report you mentioned—the record of punishment of the children—from the brothers who ran Letterfrack, but it's"—Donovan made little marks in the air with his fingers—"'missing.' I doubt if the bad behavior of Boniface and Jack the Bap inside the walls of Dachadoo was ever written down. But I agree that we will only find Nailer by digging in the past. Even though I will pull all the strings I can to make the Saint Kieran lads cough up their files, I think our only way to pinpoint a significant event in Dachadoo is to establish precisely the dates you mentioned, Tom, and then work on the surviving Dachadoo pedophiles. We know there's at least three in our district." Superintendent Donovan wrote on the pad beside his hand. "By the way, Tom, where did you get all that stuff about certification?"

"It's in the back of the Kennedy Report on Reformatory and Industrial Schools."

"Good work, Tom. I should look at it so I know what I'm talking about when I'm going after the Dachadoo records."

Breen leaned forward with several pages of print. "I made a copy of the rules and regulations."

"I'm surrounded by competence," the superintendent said. "Thanks, Tom. Now, what do you have, Jimmy?"

"I tried to figure out what's behind the things Nailer does to his victims." Gorman took his folded pages out of his inside pocket, which he glanced at now and then. "Nailer is making very dramatic statements, almost writing the headlines for the press. You yourself, sir, believe that someone called *The Telegraph*. I think it's Nailer who called, that he's manipulating *The Telegraph*. For all we know he may have demanded the involvement of Pauline Byron in exchange for information about the murders. Pauline Byron is the hottest thing in the newspaper business right now. Nailer may be manipulating her into investigating something he wants investigated; something that happened in Dachadoo years ago. Nailer wants everyone to know *why* his victims are being punished.

"Why he has waited until now is not easy to explain, except that both victims were getting on in age and Nailer may have been fearful they would die before they were punished. There is one small coincidence: the Ferns Report was presented to the Minister for Health and Children in October 2005, and Brother John the Baptist was murdered exactly two years later. Before anyone asks; I've had a copy of the report hanging around the house since it came out, and the date is on the cover." Gorman looked up from his notes. "I have read the Ferns Report several times to reassure myself that absconding from the priesthood was the best thing I ever did."

Donovan and Breen glanced at each other.

Gorman looked down at his notes. "This part may be a bit fanciful, but I'll throw it out anyhow: the Ferns Report deals with pedophilia among some of the priests in the diocese of Ferns and how the bishops mishandled it, especially Brendan Comiskey, the bishop who vacationed in Thailand. Some clerical sexual behavior described in the report is criminal, but only a few of the perpetrators have been prosecuted."

Gorman flipped some pages. "The Ferns Report in one place said, *It is noteworthy that only two of the cases that have come to the attention of this enquiry have resulted in a criminal conviction.*" Gorman looked up from his notes. "For example, Comiskey, the bishop, may have walked away from the whole Ferns thing in disgrace, but many people think that wasn't enough, that he deserved prison time for being an accessory by not reporting the criminals in his charge to the authorities." Gorman reined himself in, but not before his ears had turned red. "Maybe Nailer has waited two years to see if the Ferns Report would initiate a hunt that would roust every ecclesiastical pedophile in the country, and since nothing like that has happened, maybe he's trying to resurrect interest in the clerical abusers of children by his dramatic murderous statements. That's the end of the fanciful part." Gorman checked his notes.

"Nailer is very precise," Gorman continued. "You said, sir, that Brother Boniface's whanger was sautéed in goose grease and his crotch scalded with it, and we know that butter was used in Carrowreagh. This is no accident. Nothing is accidental here. Everything is planned to the last detail; smelling salts may have been used on Nailer when he was a child in Dachadoo."

Gorman read again from his notes. "*The number of nails and their size are significant to Nailer, but their placement in the victim's body is purely utilitarian—to keep the brother painfully and bloodlessly pinned to the floor, the nail across the gullet to keep the penis from choking the victim, the ones in the ears to keep him from moving his head. The source of the nails will be impossible to trace. The thread in the lips is of no significance—just practical—keeps the dick in the mouth; it's ordinary thread, impossible to trace. The blueness of the twine tying off the whanger's stump is not significant; that kind of twine can be picked out of any hedge or off any road in a farming community; it's also impossible to trace.*"

Gorman looked up. "One of the outstanding characteristics of pedophiles is their capacity to rationalize and normalize their sexual fantasies and activities. Nailer probably made his victims own up to their crimes before he nailed them down, encouraged them to confess by breaking their bones."

He glanced at his notes. "Another piece of fanciful reconstruction: the two brothers raped Nailer when he was a child, or else they raped someone very close to him. I'm inclined to believe he saw someone close to him being assaulted, or at least knew about it and was helpless to prevent it. He was powerless. But in the killing of the brothers he is the one in complete control, the one with all the power. He is administering punishment in a very slow, very precise and very painful manner of his choosing. The cutting off of the dangler is the violent removal of the enemy's wielded weapon; placing it in the enemy's mouth is the hoisting of the enemy on his own petard." Gorman paused. "And one last bit of surmising; the goose grease and butter are probably the precise lubricants that each brother used. That's all folks—this stuff makes me want to vomit."

"Good...good, Jimmy," Donovan said, "especially that part about the killer calling *The Telegraph,* alerting the press very shortly after the bodies were found. Did you do any thinking about that—about how he knew so quickly the victims had been discovered?"

"Nailer knew the bodies would be discovered; it's precisely what he wanted. The slightest garda activity in the vicinity of either house could have alerted him. He could have picked up the garda activity on a scanner—there's so much electronic gadgetry out there these days. Yesterday morning at Brother Boniface's place I suspected Nailer had to be someone in the guards because the scene was so clean; then the quick call to the paper reinforced my suspicion. But now I'm not happy with that; I think Nailer could be trying to point us up a dead end."

"You think he's that clever?"

"Yes, and for years he's brooded on what was done to him, sir; he has hated for years; he has planned for years; he has worked on every detail for years."

The superintendent rested his chin on his knuckles and looked down at the surface of his desk. Finally he said, "I see no reason to disagree with anything you said, Jimmy. You put a lot of thought into it, and as a matter of interest we should go back over your report when we catch Nailer to see how good you were. What do you think, Tom?"

"I agree with you, sir. It wouldn't surprise me if Jimmy is very close to the mark."

And then the bird feathers moved brightly in the superintendent's teeth and both detectives braced themselves for some good news.

"On Saturday, I had one of the bans—Sheila Feeney—spend the day doing some research, kill two birds with one stone—cool her heels and find out something for me. Young and overenthusiastic guards give me the heebies. Feeney's like a jackass with a bunch of stinging nettles up its arse, shouting at Seamus Cooper for calling us every time someone parks in his bloody gateway. She should know by now that Cooper's a lunatic."

The superintendent's use of digression when he had good news to impart was well known. Jimmy Gorman once became so impatient with the tactic that he had blurted out, "For fuck's sake...," before he was winded by Breen's sharp elbow.

"Beginning with 1972, Bangarda Feeney went through the ledgers back to 1954 looking for crimes and detentions relating to Dachadoo. There were only two Dachadoo entries and each was in 1967."

Donovan picked up a piece of paper and read aloud. "*June the twentieth, 1967; Peter Gilligan, Ballyfin; detained after complaint from Brother Lazarian, Dachadoo; detainee suffering from kidney damage; attended by Dr. McNulty. Entered by Guards Terry Kelly, Peter Fenlon.*" Donovan looked up. "It says down lower that Gilligan was released the next day. Then, on the fourth of July, two weeks after Gilligan was picked up, another man was detained." He put his finger on the paper and read: "*Patrick O'Malley, Mountmellick; detained on complaint by Brother Lazarian, Dachadoo; attended by Dr. McNulty; detainee suffering from kidney damage. Entered by Guards Terry Kelly, Peter Fenlon.*"

Donovan looked up to check on the attention of his audience. "Bangarda Feeney was sharp enough to notice the next entry: *The fifth of July, 1967; Patrick O'Malley, Mountmellick, pulled from Grand Canal at 8:50 a.m. Apparent suicide. Coroner advised. Entered by Guards Terry Kelly, Peter Fenlon.*"

Donovan indicated a folder on his desk. "Terry Kelly opened a file on the suicide of Paddy O'Malley. There's nothing in it beyond the few facts of where O'Malley drowned himself and where he got the wherewithal to put around his neck." Christy Donovan flipped open the file. He slipped an index card from beneath the paper clip holding it to the cover. The superintendent flashed the card at the two detectives. "This is dated the thirty-first of December, 1993, twenty-six years after Paddy O'Malley drowned himself. It's signed by Terry Kelly."

The three men looked at each other, acknowledged that Terry Kelly's signature on something like this was an attention grabber.

Donovan held his reading glasses up to his face. "It says, *If there is ever an investigation into the death of Paddy O'Malley on the fifth of July, 1967, I have peripheral information that may help. If I am dead, my solicitor has an envelope addressed to the Tullamore superintendent. Featherstone, Esq., Edenderry.*"

"Jesus!" Gorman said. "We have a date—July 5, 1967—and Terry Kelly's alive and well and living near Bantry."

"That's some work you did, sir," Tom Breen said. He waved a congratulatory hand at Donovan's desk with its bits and pieces of paper. "We can now go to the other pedophiles and work off that date."

Donovan held up his superintendent's hand. "Tom, it's Terry Kelly we should—"

"But sir," Breen interrupted, "we have Brother Beatus in Saint Fintan's in Portlaoise, and no matter what Terry Kelly knows, he can't know what Beatus—"

"But Tom," Gorman said, "Terry obviously—"

"Tom," Donovan said, "why are you so determined to talk to Beatus when you have the other two pedophiles on Croghan Hill, and as far as we know they're not mad? The nurse supervisor I spoke to on Friday in Saint Fintan's said Brother Beatus is more than mad, is drifting in and out of Alzheimer's."

"That's the point. I did some reading at the weekend. It's his madness and Alzheimer's that might make him leak all over the place. The other two on Croghan Hill might be so interested in protecting themselves that they won't speak as freely as Beatus—if we can get him going. Let's try Beatus first; he's failing and the other two aren't going anywhere."

The decision was reached just after 10 a.m. that Brother Beatus would be spoken to first; Portlaoise was only twenty miles away, and in the meantime, Donovan would call Terry Kelly in Bantry.

As the two detectives stood to leave, Donovan leafed back through his notebook. "It's all set up in Fintan's for ten. Ask at reception for Saint Martha's Ward and then a Nurse Grimes, Ceil—C-e-i-l—will take care of you."

The bells in the superintendent's phone chimed as Jimmy Gorman pulled the door after him.

"Come on," Breen said. "We're off to see Beatus."

"The wonderful brother of Alz," Gorman said, and attempted some fancy footwork. He almost fell.

The station orderly had the phone to his ear as the detectives were passing the front desk. Each gave him a wave of the hand. The orderly shot his right hand in the air and with his index finger signaled to them to wait.

"They're right here, sir," he said into the phone. He hung up and said, "Lads, the supe wants you back in his office. He sounds like he's choking."

35.

Although the near-empty country roads had removed the traffic-related stress from her life, Geraldine Farrell still missed the city. She missed the endorphing busyness of her work as a public health nurse in Dublin; she missed the large staff; missed the dramatic telling of adventures, love stories, sexual safaris; missed the camaraderie, the tears and laughter, the support, even the frustration. She missed, too, the "characters" tucked away in their invisible, slum-lived lives whose tenacity and black humor she had learned to live with without judgment.

Geraldine reminded herself that it was only two months since she had come back to the boggy doorstep of her childhood. She knew she would eventually adjust to the three-woman office, the lighter workload, the quietness of the countryside, the pungent odor of freshly spread slurry thickening the air in the early morning, the breath-taking smell of silage enclouding every farmyard she passed, the meandering lines of ploppy cow shite spluttered during careless ambulations along the blacktop of every byroad. In a few more months she would have adapted to her new position—and to the shite splatters all over her car. But she hadn't—she had to admit it—she hadn't foreseen the scale of the changes in her life. And on top of everything, at thirty-one, she was growing weary of listening to the echoes of her ticking biological clock, a sound her mother and sisters and friends could hear booming loudly out there in the universe.

Behind the wheel of her new, black Skoda Octavia TDI, Geraldine Farrell shivered herself out of her pensive mood and brought a container of hot, sweetened tea to her lips. Rationally, she knew her feelings of loss would lessen in proportion to the number of friends she would inevitably make, in the reassurance she would be seeing in the eyes of her housebound patients, in the cups of tea at their kitchen tables. She would be comforted in seeing the seasons changing up-close in the ditches and fields and trees, in the birds and wildflowers. And most importantly, here in the countryside she would have the opportunity to meet an eligible farmer every day of the week instead of being limited to weekends while based in her mother's house in County Offaly.

Geraldine loved the farming life. She wanted to bring up her children on a farm, far away from city life.

Slowly, she approached a bend in the high-hedged road, aware that the coating of white frost could send her new car into the roadside ditch. It was fifteen minutes to nine o'clock on another Monday morning and she was making her first call of the day in Cloonagh in the northern corner of Tipperary. In this particular part of the country it was difficult to know where the boundaries of Laois, Offaly and Tipperary touched each other. But Geraldine Farrell had a satnav attached to her windscreen and she had no fear of getting lost in the spiderweb of narrow roads and lanes.

This morning she was determined to break through the bitter armor of Mister Turley, a recently diagnosed diabetic and first-class, class-conscious crank. Even though Turley spoke in a refined and affected accent, Geraldine believed he had originated in the bog.

She had prepared her questions: Had he any visitors over the weekend? Had he nieces and nephews? Where had he worked before retirement? But she knew the answer to the last one; according to the C.F.A. form, Turley was a retired religious brother, and his contact person was his younger brother, Edward, a monsignor somewhere in the diocese of Ferns in County Wexford.

The last time she had seen Turley, Geraldine had wondered if the old celibate was repulsed by the proximity of
her female body. Whatever his relational problems, in the
end she had classified him in public-nursing shorthand as
a Cob—Contrary Old Bollicks.

When she stepped out of her Skoda in front of Mister Turley's house, Geraldine Farrell would have been
revealed to any spying young farmer as an attractive
woman—a moderately well stacked, five-foot eight-inch,
clear-skinned brunette, nicely meated, pleasantly faced
potential bearer of children, and a healthy farm assistant.
However, if the spying farmer ever verbalized these observations to Geraldine, he would have quickly received the
equivalent of a sharp, verbal, backhanded uppercut to his
testicles.

Dressed in black trousers, red shirt and V-necked
red jumper under a black anorak, Geraldine walked up
the short pebbly path to Mister Turley's front door. She
tapped the brass knocker on its brass striker button. This
was the second of her once-a-week visits since the patient
had begun administering his own insulin shots.

She knocked again. Then she knocked harder.

Turley usually answered right away. Geraldine went
down on her hunkers and pushed in the spring-loaded
flap of the brass letterbox in the door.

"Mister Turley," she called. "It's the public health
nurse." The faint smell of feces wafted through the letterbox. Geraldine looked through the opening, but all
she could see was the empty hallway and the red runner;
there were no lights on. She turned her ear to the slot but
heard nothing.

She stood up and knocked again, then walked back to
her car. In the ever-locked boot she kept a small wooden
box containing the front-door keys of the houses with solitary occupants. In her bag she located her notebook and
opened it to the page of key codes—another precaution

in case the keys were stolen. She located the "Diabetic
T" key, closed the boot and returned to Turley's front
door. She knocked once more before inserting the key
in the brass keyhole. When she pushed in the door her
left hand flew to her face in reaction to the strong smell.
It wasn't just feces. She dropped her bag on the doorstep
and pulled out a medical mask, sprayed it with eucalyptus
and tied it on. She cleaned her shoes on the sisal mat and
walked down the red runner toward the kitchen and the
study.

In childhood Geraldine Farrell had been curious. On
her hunkers she picked up and examined worms and
creepy crawly things that most young girls screech at. Hairless baby mice and blind newborn kittens were trophies to
be galloped into the kitchen for displaying in the palm of
her hand to her mother. It was something dead and full of
squirming maggots that had flung her hysterical mother
into a corner of the kitchen and which brought about the
enactment of the rule that nothing dead was to cross the
threshold of the house ever again.

"But, Mammy...the maggots are alive."

Geraldine the child had never hesitated to stick her
hand under a laying hen to collect the eggs already in
the nest. When her boy cousins from Portlaoise came to
visit on Sundays, she hid in the farmyard's darkest corners
where the very darkness scared off the bravest seekers.
She had watched entranced as her father and the helping
men pulled up the just-slaughtered pig, hind legs first,
by way of rope and pulley attached to the Boiler House
rafters; watched unblinkingly as Siddy Carter severed the
head with knife and saw; watched as her father, holding
it by the ears, carried away the head; watched enthralled
as Siddy slit the belly from groin to neck and used his
knife to nick the fleshy cables anchoring the intestines to
the carcass; stared as the glistening purplish, bluish intestines slid down into the large galvanized basin; watched

wide-eyed as the steam arose out of the basin and sent the sickly, fresh smell of exposed guts into her nose. By the time she was ten, Geraldine had persuaded her father to let her search through the entrails for the porcine heart and kidneys, the liver and the bladder, too; oh, the feel of the warm, slithery stuff, and she up to her elbows in it.

Even though Geraldine's natural curiosity easily overcame the fear and disgust that lesser mortals felt in the presence of things repugnant, she was still a cautious person. It was this caution which reminded her to leave Mister Turley's front door open, despite her expectation that she was about to discover that Mister Turley had released his lifetime grip on his various sphincters.

She stopped in the hallway between the facing doors of kitchen and study. The kitchen was bright with morning's light. The study was dark and she could see the lines of light around the edges of the heavy drapes. Smells were already seeping through her mask. She stepped into the doorway and felt for the light switch with her right hand.

She was instantly amazed. It was as if she had illuminated a ridiculously overdone Hollywood movie set; as if a giant meat grinder had been opened while still grinding and had spewed its partially ground contents over the walls, the ceiling, the floor, the drapes, the furniture. Her nose, after all, had not been mistaken at the front door—it had, indeed, correctly recognized the odor of exposed guts.

She blinked away the overall picture and began focusing on the individual props. The largest chunk was an eviscerated torso lying on its back on the floor beyond the desk, in front of the fireplace. Carefully, she picked her way through the smaller bits and pieces of bone and flesh on the carpet. She noticed that the penis and scrotum were the only intact appendages on the torso. The flesh-flap that had once contained the belly had been sliced at the groin and the sides, then pulled up over the chest, revealing an empty cavity and the backbone within. The legs had been hacked off above the knees; the arms had been hacked off between the shoulders and the elbows. There was no head, just a stump of bone. On the floor near the torso lay the poker from the andirons and half-way down its shaft was the heart, impaled.

Geraldine knew she should not be in the room and that the guards would shout at her. So she just stood where she was and looked around for the head. But she couldn't find it. It could have been under one of the shreds of bloody clothing lying around the room. She gawked at the places where globs of bloody tissue had been thrown against the walls and had slithered down; a kidney was still attached to the wall beneath the picture of a ship burning in the sunset. Instinctually, she searched for the second kidney and discovered instead what reminded her of an upside-down Portuguese man-o'-war but which, in fact, was the liver streaming various bits of anatomical attach-ments. The liver had come to a stop at the wainscoting as if it had run out of momentum or slitheriness after its long slide down the wall from where it had begun its journey near the ceiling; on its journey it had slipped past a still-life painting with a duck's head hanging over the edge of a table, the eye of the duck closed purplishly in death. What appeared to be the lungs had snailed down the mir-ror onto the mantel above the fireplace. Individual strings and clumped handfuls of grey guts had been flung willy-nilly and had come to rest on the bookcase shelves, on the computer and its printer, on the back of the straight chair at the computer desk, in the cold fireplace, on the compact disc player and its various speakers. Lengths of intestine were hanging from the curtain rails and entan-gled in the chandelier. Legs and arms lay on the floor under the splotchy splashes of blood they had made when they had hit the walls. She saw the remains of a hand with stumps where the fingers had been, but with the thumb still whole. The ceiling was splotched with blood. What looked like a freestanding, erect blackthorn penis with an enormous scrotum attached, was lying beside the torso, pieces of meat attached.

Geraldine looked around one more time for the head. When she turned to leave she saw a Chinese chef's knife embedded by its forward point in the top of the desk. But there was far more besides the knife on the desk. She resisted the temptation to poke through the mess. Mixed into strands of stringy grey hair, there was blood, there was brain matter, there was flesh, there were shards of skull bone, there was one still-whole eye, there were teeth, there was a fragment of a dental bridge, pieces of fingers. To Geraldine it looked as if the head had been beaten off the body, smashed and smashed and smashed again.

But not only had the head been obliterated on the desktop, the desk had been used as a chopping block. Blood-filled, deep gouges showed where the heavy Chinese chopper had hacked through its targets and sunk deeply into the wood. The carpet on the knee-hole side of the desk was blood soaked, still sopping.

Careful of where she was stepping, Geraldine tiptoed to the door of the study, wiped her shoes on the carpet. She turned to look back.

"If that's you, Mister Turley, someone was really pissed at you," she said aloud.

Meditatively, she stepped outside and stood on the pebbly path, took out her mobile and scrolled down to the number of the Templemore Garda Station.

36.

The yellow DHL van left at a quarter to eight, and within seconds Mick McGovern's brown 1967 Volkswagen Beetle pulled into Pauline Byron's driveway. Pauline placed the second DHL package on the hallway table and went out to greet the City Mouse. She was wearing black sneakers, black jeans, black polo-neck pullover. Like water finding its own level, her crop of hair found its own shape every time she moved her head. She had jogged, she had showered, she was makeup-free, she looked clean, she felt great.

In the moments before opening the car door, McGovern, with his hirsute halo and wire-rimmed glasses, was framed in the side window of the Beetle, and it was this view of driver and vehicle that presented Pauline a nostalgic reminder of the carefree and slightly wacky days of youth. She thought of the old joke, How do you fit five elephants in a Volkswagen Bug? God! That had been very funny when it was told in a cloud of university cannabis smoke.

The days of yore fell apart when Mick McGovern began the process of extricating himself from his confinement. To Pauline he seemed to have too many feet and knees and elbows.

"Welcome to the country, Mick," Pauline said. "You didn't get lost?"

"Good morning, Pauline. Satnav is the greatest invention since the star of Bethlehem...Jeese! What's that?"

"What?"

"That smell."

"Oh, Mick, that's not a *smell*. You're too long in city pent, as Keats said. What you are smelling is the aroma of the heartland. In a few hours you'll detect the earth, trees, silage, flowers, animals, freshly harvested crops, slurry, apples and other wafts in the aroma. It only takes a few hours for new arrivals to appreciate the fresh air, to tease the components out of the bouquet."

McGovern looked at Pauline. "I'm sorry I asked."

Pauline wasn't finished. "In a couple of hours you won't miss Dublin's diesel fumes and the Liffey at low tide with the Poddle River, from its sluice in the quay wall, hanging out its tongue of liquid sewage. You'll be going home this evening with an ear catching the notes of Philomel, an eye catching the sailing cloudlet's bright career."

"You sound like a born-again Christian."

"Did you bring anything?" Pauline asked.

"Nothing. I brought nothing." Mick bent back into his car and came out with his satnav. "The DHL chap brought the lot—all the files are in the boxes; two copies of everything." He shut the car door as if he were a newly ordained priest closing the tabernacle for the first time.

In his pink shirt and green tie, in his spotless suit of grey, in his scintillating black shoes, Mick turned around and saw Pauline staring at him as if he were an exotic bird that had been blown off course. Mick always felt a stirring when he looked into Pauline's eyes; no other woman in his circle had that ocular quality that sent ripples along the wiring to his lower body. But Mick knew that if he was foolish enough to act or speak off those tiny electrical pulses, he would be treated like a biting gnat.

Pauline pointed to the satnav. "You're in the country now, Mick. You could have left that in the Bug."

"Every night I lock this into a drawer in the bedroom."

"It's as precious as that?"

"I was born with a piece of navigational equipment missing from my brain." McGovern held up the receiver.

"This is the piece that's missing." He slipped the receiver into his jacket pocket.

Together, they walked toward the front door. "That was a great coup with the Lucan files, Mick. Congratulations," Pauline said. "Playing on a chain smoker's addiction! We're such a venal lot, we humans; we'd sell our own grannies in a crunch."

"He'd have sold me the whole place for a promise of fags till the day he died, which shouldn't be too far off."

"Jack should be happy you got the lot for two hundred."

"Jack needs this story so badly he'd sell his granny into sex slavery to the Brothers of Saint Kieran for the files."

"Jesus, Mick! That's an image—the brothers lining up for their turn with Rafferty's granny." Pauline snorted.

She had never heard McGovern being so voluble; the country air, perhaps. As she stood aside to allow McGovern in, Pauline sniffed a heavy presence of silage in the rural bouquet.

When he stepped inside, McGovern smelled frying bacon. Pauline's husband, Raymond, came out of the kitchen wearing a fawn apron embellished with a large, displaying, red and black cockerel. Raymond held out his right hand in greeting, a metal spatula in his left.

When they sat down to breakfast, Raymond removed his apron and, red-faced, held it up. "I'm sorry about this Mick. T'was the first apron I grabbed."

"Raymond bought it as a present for himself, Mick," Pauline said.

Mick dipped his toast in his egg, did not even try to think of something to add to the repartee.

At ten past nine Raymond had long gone to work and Pauline and Mick had opened the two boxes of copied files. Whoever had done the copying and the collating had done an excellent job. Each bundle, even if it consisted of only one page, had a cover sheet. The pages within each bundle were numbered. The position of the original file in the cabinet was noted—they might as well have had the Lucan originals on the dining room table.

"It's hard to believe that an institution that catered for a hundred and twenty boys per diem for so many years generated only two boxes of records," Pauline said.

"No, it's not hard to believe that," Mick said. "One of the revealing things in the Ferns Report was Bishop Brendan Comiskey saying the entire personnel records of the diocese wouldn't have filled half a shoebox. By comparison"—he waved his hand at the table—"this is record-keeping by an obsessive-compulsive Hittite."

"I imagine the death certificates are complete because of the law, but the rest has to be woefully inadequate."

"It's got to be woefully *selective*," Mick said. "I don't imagine they put anything in here that would hang them…What exactly are we looking for?"

"I don't know. Like the fellow said about pornography, I can't tell you what it is, but I'll know it when I see it." Pauline thought for a minute. "We're in a hurry, so there's no time for browsing. I have the names of six men and I want to find out if they were together in Dachadoo in July 1967. Then we'll try to discover if anything unusual happened at that time."

McGovern sat down, pen and paper at the ready.

"They're all religious brothers: Lazarian, Beatus, John the Baptist and Boniface. I have two Bennets, but I don't know their religious names."

One file on the table stood out because the pages were A3, longer than standard-size copying paper. Mick picked it up, shoved his glasses onto his forehead and read aloud off the cover sheet, "*Manager's Journal. Brother Lazarian, OSK. Dachadoo, 1957-19*—. A journal would be the place to find…" He flipped through the pages and Pauline picked up her copy. Before she could open it, McGovern said quietly, "Eureka. Page seventy-eight. The entry for the fourth of July 1967 has three of the names, and since Lazarian was the scribe he's there, too."

Pauline turned to the page. She ran her finger down the ruled and dated entries. "Look at this shit! God, Mick, when you say, 'Eureka,' you're supposed to shout it," she exclaimed. "And will you look at this? *B Beatus (o), out* on the eighteenth of July...Does it say when he came to Dachadoo?"

"*B Beatus (o), in. Gate* on June eighteen; go back a page," McGovern said.

"Look!" Pauline said. "Whole weeks go by without an entry, but from the time Beatus came and left there's... what?" She counted. "Thirteen entries in one month and three days, counting the palimpsest on July the fourth."

"Palimp what?"

"Palimp*sest*...original entry erased and written on again. I think we've struck the mother lode. All we have to do is interpret it." Pauline scrutinized the entries. McGovern moved his finger slowly down the list.

- *June 18: B. Beatus (o), in. Gate*
- *June 19: McNulty M.D. Annual*
- *June 20: B. Beatus (o). Fyard*
- *July 1: B. Beatus (o). Gate*
- *July 4: W. Rackert. 2*
- *July 4: Michael O'Malley (i), in. 8. 2867*
- *July 4: Error (Br. L.)*
- *July 4: B. Beatus (o). Fyard*
- *July 5: B. Boniface. Rep*
- *July 5: B. John the Baptist (o). Rep*
- *July 16: Michael O'Malley 2867. RIP pneu*
- *July 17: Big shots here to save the world*
- *July 18: B. Beatus (o), out*

"The *B* before a name obviously stands for Brother," Pauline said. "The *(o)* at Beatus and Baptist...what does that mean? The *(i)* after O'Malley might mean inmate, the *8* could be his age, but what's the *2867?*"

"Maybe he was the twenty-eighth child to be admitted in 1967," McGovern offered.

"Good one, Mick. We have to find out about the non-brothers in the same period to see if there was..." Her voice trailed off. "You take these non-brother names and"— Pauline looked at her watch—"contact the Diggers. Tell them this takes precedence, and if that's a problem tell them to talk to Rafferty. McNulty M.D., W. Rackert and Michael O'Malley—everything they can find. Also, Mick, the entry for the sixteenth of July—while the Diggers are digging, look through the death certificates for Michael O'Malley." She swept her hand across the dining room table. "The phone and computer are through the door in the kitchen—the one that says Abandon All Hope. Teen-age daughters! I'll work on interpreting these entries... And I know who can help—the Bennets; they're probably Lazarian's big shots." She picked up her mobile.

McGovern took the bundle of death certificates and went into the office. He typed in his requests to the Diggers, and while he waited for their reply, he examined the death records. Pauline walked in, and even as she inserted a sheet of paper in the fax machine and tapped in a number, Mick gave no sign that he knew she was in the room. Pauline waited for the machine to grind its gears and begin dragging the paper into its innards. She left the room without speaking.

In the kitchen Pauline went through the motions of preparing the coffeepot but her mind wasn't on the job. She was putting a new filter in the basket when her mobile rang.

"Pauline?" It was Patrick Bennet. "The fax is on its way back to you with the answers filled in. Cyril and I are here till noon if you need us. We have an appointment in Naas later on."

When Pauline returned to the office, Mick McGovern was standing and leaning over the printer, a patient hand held out to the emerging page. "I think we've got some goodies," he said.

Pauline held her impatient fingers out for the paper creeping out of the fax machine.

McGovern followed her back to the dining room.

"You go first, Mick."

"Okay...Doctor Alexander McNulty is alive and lives in Tullamore. For many years he was the medical officer of Dachadoo. I have his address and phone number. His signature is on nineteen death certificates"—he indicated a bundle of papers—"including Michael O'Malley's. On all the certificates he signed, the children died of pneumonia or diarrhea."

"No T.B., no appendix, no flu, no—?"

"Just diarrhea and pneumonia."

"How many certificates altogether?"

"Seventy-three."

"What was the cause of death on the remaining certificates?"

McGovern looked at his notebook. "Scarlet fever, flu, measles, whooping cough, diphtheria, ruptured appendix, epilepsy, diarrhea, anemia, general delicacy, and strangulation—suicide by hanging. There were three of those."

"Oh, Jesus! Child suicides." With mouth ajar, Pauline moved her head from side to side. "Holy God," she whispered, "Holy God." She put her arms on the table and hung her head. "Jesus. This is too much."

37.

As Pauline pulled herself back together, McGovern said, "Child suicide speaks of the total failure of adults."

"The feelings of total abandonment don't bear imagining," Pauline said. She sighed. "What else did you find out?"

"The Diggers found W. Rackert—'W' for William. He died on the fourth of July, 1980."

"July fourth?"

"Yes. He once worked for the Society for the Prevention of Cruelty to Children; lived in Mountmellick."

"He was in Dachadoo the same day the O'Malley child was signed in. Can we assume that Rackert brought him there?"

McGovern held up his hand. "Listen to this: Rackert, aged sixty-five, was murdered and no one was arrested for the crime."

Pauline could not contain herself. "How was he murdered?"

"He was found tied to a tree—"

"Shit! Not nailed?"

"—in a field between Mountmellick and Portarlington; place called the Lime Tree. M.E. said death could have been due to several factors, including possible heart attack brought on by struggle against the restraints. Guards treated his death as murder. Sergeant Tony Lynch on the scene said, 'This is the cruelest death I have ever seen.'"

Pauline remembered an old IRA atrocity. "Were there calves in the field?"

"Yes. The farmer who found the body was out in the early morning checking his cows and suckling calves."

"Where's that information from?"

"*The Leinster Express.*"

Pauline's words tripped over themselves as they spilled out. "*The Leinster* is a local family paper and it couldn't say how Rackert was killed, but it gave a broad hint—the calves. About forty years ago the IRA sent a message to all would-be traitors; the traitor in their hands was tied naked with his back to a tree in a field where there were sucking calves. He was doused in milk. The calves came galloping and what do you think they sucked?"

"Jeese." McGovern's hand fell into his crotch.

"You're a city mouse, Mick; you probably never watched a calf sucking its mother's teats; we say sucking, not suckling. A cow can control the flow of milk, and when she cuts off the supply, the calf gives her a header into the belly to tell her he wants more. If the calf is big enough it can stagger the mother. Sometimes the suffering cow gives her own child a kick in the head, tells it to feck off."

"So if a calf wasn't getting any milk out of the guy's willie, the calf—"

"—or *all* the calves had a go at him, head-butting him so much that Rackert's stomach was like a sackful of sausages getting whacked against a rock. You have never felt the inside of a calf's mouth while it's sucking, Mick. The rough tongue pushes your fingers up against the ridged roof of the mouth and at the same time pulls and squeezes like it's going to force the blood out through your fingertips. The calves would have pulled Rackert's entire genitalia out of him."

McGovern held up a hand. "That will do, Miss Byron," he said. "I can see the picture you're so vividly painting." He moved his arse around on the seat of his chair, would have checked his family jewels if Pauline hadn't been there. He went back to *The Leinster Express* report.

"There's an item further down that's significant: Mister Rackert was tied to the tree with baling twine."

"That's him...that's our killer!" Pauline stood up, unable to take any more while sitting. "Baling twine...terror...torture...July the fourth."

"A lot of things happened at Dachadoo on July the fourth. Why is that so—?"

"In 1967 Michael O'Malley was admitted to Dachadoo on July the fourth." Pauline picked up the fax from Patrick Bennet. "William Rackert of the SPCC was in Dachadoo on July the fourth and Brother Beatus was confined to working in the farmyard on the same day."

"And listen to this," Mick said. "Another item from *The Leinster Express* that the Diggers found...There was no mention of a *Michael* O'Malley. This is an article about a *Paddy* O'Malley committing suicide in the Grand Canal in Tullamore on July the *fifth*, 1967."

"Aw, Jesus." Pauline sat down and put her elbows on the table's edge. "This is dreadful."

"O'Malley was from Mountmellick and had come home from England for his wife's funeral. But that's not everything. The story says O'Malley was despondent. His wife had died on July second and she'd been buried on the fourth. And I'll bet my sixty-seven Bug that he was also despondent because his child had been taken from him the day of the funeral. He was a widower and in many instances that was sufficient reason to remove children and place them in the care of the state, enough reason for the likes of William Rackert to make some easy money."

"Sometimes I wonder why we insist that God is good when all the evidence points to the opposite." There were tears on Pauline's face.

McGovern never knew what to say to a weepy woman. "I'm going to put on that coffee," he said. He stood up and strode out in the posture of a man expecting an arrow in the back, shoulder blades almost touching.

He was pouring the water into the reservoir when Pauline ambled in and leaned against the jamb of the kitchen door. Sheets of paper dangled from her fingertips. "This is Patrick Bennet's interpretation of the journal entries between June eighteen and July eighteen: Brother Beatus arrived in Dachadoo on June the eighteenth and was given the job of gatekeeper the same day."

"Open and close the gate...low brain-power job."

Pauline looked up. "The Bennets...they told me Brother Beatus was not the brightest bulb." She shook a crease out of the paper and read. "The *(o)* after Beatus and John the Baptist indicates that both were orphans who had come up through institutions until they were accepted into the Order of Saint Kieran. *McNulty M.D., Annual* means the doctor examined all the children on June nineteen."

"One hundred and twenty examinations in one day?"

"*B. Beatus (o). Fyard* on June the twentieth means Brother Beatus had done something that was punishable by having to work in the farmyard—barefooted, Patrick Bennet adds."

"His third day and he's in trouble?"

"According to the Bennets, within the Order of Saint Kieran, Beatus was classified as a Pilgrim—a man so difficult to have around that he was shifted from place to place," Pauline said.

"Hmm...sounds exactly like the bishops moving pedophile priests around so their sins wouldn't catch up with them."

"What a way to deal with problem people—foist them onto someone else. *B. Beatus (o). Gate* on July the first means Brother Beatus was restored to his gate-keeping job. Next, *W. Rackert.* The notation '2' after his name probably means Rackert got two pounds for Michael O'Malley. Rackert would have been one of the Crueltymen, representatives of the Society for the Prevention of Cruelty to

Children. Some were bribed to bring children into a particular industrial school to keep its numbers up and thus keep the government payments up.

"*Michael O'Malley (i), in. 8. 2867* means eight-year-old Michael was admitted as an inmate to Dachadoo on July fourth, 1967, and given the number 28—you got that right. The children were seldom called by their names."

"Jeese! Were they tattooed on their arms as well?"

"That would have been the last straw, Mick. *B. Beatus (o). Fyard* on July the fourth means Brother Beatus screwed up again."

"How do you screw up when all you do is open and close a gate?"

"Maybe he kept out someone he shouldn't have, let in someone he shouldn't have. Patrick and Cyril had difficulties with *B Boniface. Rep* and *B. John the Baptist (o). Rep* on July the fifth. The Bennets' interpretation here is a bit too stretched to my liking. They knew there was some trouble between Brother Beatus and these two, Boniface and Bapper Jack. Beatus was sent to the farmyard on the fourth, and the following day, the Bennets surmise, Boniface and Baptist were reprimanded."

"If that's what *rep* means, then maybe there was trouble among these three when the O'Malley child arrived in Dachadoo. The Bennets told you that Beatus tried to move in on the pedophilic territory of the other two."

"And that Boniface and Bapper may have concussed Beatus," Pauline added. She stared at the steady flow of the coffee into the Pyrex pot. The pot was almost full and the falling drips made no noise. "Are you saying they had a fight over Michael O'Malley on the day he arrived?" she asked.

"Maybe it's coincidence. But is there such a thing as a coincidence?"

Pauline dragged her eyes off the coffee pot. She looked at her papers. "*Michael O'Malley 2867. RIP pneu* on July the sixteenth means the child died of pneumonia two weeks after going to Dachadoo. *Big shots here to save the world* on July the seventeenth means Patrick and Cyril arrived for their ten weeks as volunteers. Lazarian was so pissed at the Bennets that he wouldn't even inscribe their names. *B. Beatus (o), out* on July the eighteenth means what it says only up to a point. The Bennets said Beatus went straight from Dachadoo to Saint Fintan's in Portlaoise."

"That could mean Beatus had done some something really egregious...something the Order couldn't handle," McGovern said.

"That's good, Mick...very good." Pauline shuffled her papers. "Between the Diggers, the Bennets and Lazarian's journal I think the following narrative can be built: Paddy O'Malley from Mountmellick buried his wife on July the fourth; William Rackert from Mountmellick removed the O'Malley boy from his home and brought him to Dachadoo on July the fourth. That same day Beatus was punished. The next day Boniface and John the Baptist were reprimanded and the O'Malley boy's father killed himself; twelve days later his son, Michael, died of pneumonia. The next day the Bennet brothers arrived and the following day Beatus was removed to Saint Fintan's because of something he'd done, something that if ever discovered could be explained away as the work of a lunatic."

"And would show the Order had acted responsibly by committing the lunatic to Saint Fintan's."

"Acted responsibly, my eye. It was an arse-covering maneuver."

38.

The coffeemaker, hissing out its last drops in steam, filled the silence. Pauline shuddered and shook the pages in her hand. "We know for certain that five people in the July 1967 entries are still alive: Brother Beatus, Doctor McNulty, the two Bennets and Brother Lazarian, who wrote the list. You know from Asparagus what I found out about the Bennets: Beatus is a patient in Portlaoise and a reporter is never going to get to him. Doctor McNulty and Brother Lazarian are the only ones available to us…What do you think of this plan? It's what time?…Half-past ten already? According to the Bennets, Brother Lazarian lives in north Tipperary near Roscrea. You call the Diggers for his address and while they're looking you can get started on your way; squeeze what you can out of Lazarian—he may be a bit of an old curmudgeon and he may be tough. On your way back, go to the garda station in Portlaoise and check the 1980 file on the William Rackert killing."

Pauline waved a dismissive hand as if she expected McGovern to protest. "Keep saying 'freedom of informa- tion.' I'll go to Doctor McNulty and try to get something out of him; then I'll go to the Tullamore guards and get the report of the Paddy O'Malley suicide. What do you think of that?"

"Sounds good to me."

Pauline stretched up for two mugs in the overhead cupboard and filled them with coffee. "Would you like a sandwich before you take off?"

"No thanks. The coffee is enough. But before I go, tell me how you know about the inside of a calf's mouth."

Pauline looked at McGovern. For a moment she seemed to be processing what Mick had just said, looked as if she'd been so far out in space that the radio message from Houston was still coming through.

"A calf's mouth. Our uncle had a farm in Clonaslee, up on Slieve Bloom. My sister and I spent two weeks there every summer and got to do all the farmyard things that were new and exciting: gather the eggs, feed the calves, feed the pigs, bring in the turf, all that kind of stuff. If a farmer doesn't want a cow to suckle her calf—wants to keep that particular cow's milk for himself—the calf must be trained to drink out of a bucket. To train the calf, you quarter-fill a bucket with milk; you stick your fingers in the calf's mouth—it will begin to suck, go into a kind of feeding trance—and while it's sucking you lower your hand into the milk bucket with your fingers still in the calf's mouth. The calf will keep sucking your fingers and at the same time suck up the milk. When you do this four or five times the calf will stick its head in the bucket and drink by itself.

"We loved training a calf to drink out of a bucket; it was our equivalent of the circus man putting his head in the lion's mouth. The feel of the rough tongue and the ridged roof of the mouth and the strength of the calf's suck—there was the childish fear that you'd get sucked right into the calf and down into its belly; there was an element of safe danger attached to it—like being on a roller coaster."

Pauline's phone rang. She looked at the screen and said, "Rafferty." She put the phone to her ear. "Jack?" she said. "We expected that...Holy Jesus...Shit!...It doesn't fit in with the other two...Anything about the penis?...Mick was just on his way out to talk to him."

Pauline pantomimed "write" to McGovern. "Say her name again." She pointed at McGovern. "Geraldine Farrell, Roscrea."

"Jack, let us do the planning here. We have stuff that you don't know about yet...As soon as possible, Jack...This afternoon...We can't, Jack, and if you knew what we know, you would fuck off and leave it to us." Pauline hung up.

"Brother Lazarian's dead," she said to McGovern. "The caller told Jack that Lazarian's in bits—literally in bits. Jack says it was the same voice as before. Also, the caller said, 'Don't be fooled by the modus operandi.' And Jack's garda mole told him it was the public health nurse working out of Roscrea— that name, Geraldine Farrell— who called in the news about Lazarian."

Pauline placed her coffee mug in the sink. With one arm across her belly, elbow in her hand, her chin in her fingers, she stared at the floor. McGovern sipped his coffee and waited. Suddenly Pauline swiped her phone off the counter. "The Bennets," she said and dialed the brothers' number. "It's Pauline Byron again. Patrick?... Cyril, I have some bad news for you and Patrick. Brother Lazarian has been murdered in Cloonagh in Tipperary." She paused to allow Cyril Bennet to absorb the distressing news.

"No, I'm afraid this is worse than Boniface and Bapp... John the Baptist."

She paused again, and Mick McGovern knew that Cyril Bennet was trying to imagine what could be worse than having yourself nailed to a floor, your own willie in your mouth and your lips sewn together.

"It's the same killer but I don't know the details yet. I'm sorry about this. I'll call back as soon as I know. Give Patrick my regards. Oh, Cyril, by the way...did you know a Doctor McNulty who was associated with Dachadoo?"

Pauline looked at McGovern and shrugged her shoulders. "That's alright, Cyril." She hung up. "He only knew McNulty by name. And I didn't tell you...Rafferty told me what we already suspected—the Order of Saint Kieran owns the house where Daniel Geoghan—Brother

Boniface—lived. What do you think we should do, Mick, now that Snipper—?"

"What does it say about him that he used the word 'modus'?" McGovern asked.

"That he's a fan of American cop shows?"

"Or that he's a cop himself?"

"Make a note of that. When he's caught we'll see if it meant anything."

"What should we do now?" McGovern asked. "How about this nurse—Geraldine Farrell?"

"Rafferty wanted us to go after her, but all she can tell us is what the crime scene looked like. That can wait. Rafferty just wanted some gutsy details for tomorrow's headline. I think I should go to see McNulty."

"Yes, and now you have *two* reasons why you should go. Find out if he knows anything about Dachadoo in 1967 *and* warn him that his name is on a rapidly shrinking list. In the Manager's Journal between June eighteenth and July eighteenth there are eight names altogether, plus Lazarian, the scribe. Out of the nine, five are dead—William Rackert, the O'Malley child, Bapper John, Boniface and Lazarian; Beatus is in Saint Fintan's, the Bennets are on Croghan Hill and McNulty lives in Tullamore."

"What are you going to do while I'm with the doctor?"

"I'll get the Diggers onto Terry Kelly—the guard in *The Leinster Express* story about William Rackert. I'll also get the address of Nurse Geraldine Farrell for future reference. I'll have time now to go to the two garda stations, Portlaoise and Tullamore. Then we can regroup. If I'm finished ahead of you I could update the Asparagus file for Jack's sake."

"That sounds good. I'll show you where we hide the key just in case you have to come back here without me. The alarm code is *KCAJ Off*—Jack backwards. Number one disarms; number two arms it."

39.

Their trip to interview Brother Beatus in the psychiatric hospital interrupted before they got out of the garda station, Breen and Gorman strode back to the superintendent's office, wondering aloud to each other what Donovan had forgotten to tell them.

And as Superintendent Donovan relayed what the district nurse told the Templemore guards about what she'd found in the house of Brother Lazarian, Tom Breen and Jimmy Gorman sat transfixed. When Donovan finished speaking there was a prolonged silence as each man let the reality of the butchery sink in.

"This can't be Nailer," Breen said quietly.

"What's that, Tom?" Donovan asked.

Breen cleared his throat and sat up straight. "I said this can't be Nailer. It's too different."

"Maybe you don't want it to be Nailer, Tom," Donovan said. "Up to now he's been a craftsman of sorts. The way this man was killed has changed your opinion of him. But even though the modus is so different, the victim is still a member of the league of gentlemen from Dachadoo. He was the headman there from 1959 until it was closed down."

"I think it's Nailer, too," Gorman said. "With Boniface and Jack the Bap, Nailer was steely cool, steely calm, steely deliberate. But underneath the calmness there must be a boiling volcano that could blow itself apart at any minute. Maybe that's what happened here. If this is Nailer, he may have gone to Lazarian to do what he did to Boniface and Jack the Bap, but the anger or madness or whatever's driving him got the upper hand and he simply tore Lazarian apart, couldn't control himself enough to inflict the maximum pain. On the other hand, sir, you said Brother Lazarian was not on the pedophile list. As a non-pedophile—in Nailer's mind—he wouldn't be entitled to the same death as the other two. One way or the other, even though he seems to have been savaged, Brother Lazarian may only have suffered the pain of one knockout blow. He may have been lucky in comparison to the other two."

"I don't know about the lucky part, Jimmy," Donovan said. "Maybe Lazarian was alive while he was having his legs and arms chopped off, his belly sliced open and his guts pulled out like Oliver Plunkett. But if this is Nailer, in his fit of madness he may have left some clues about himself."

Donovan's phone rang, sounding like pan pipes in a distant dell. Breen and Gorman waited while the superintendent listened. "Thanks, David, and before you go... would you keep an eye out for Pauline Byron...yes, *The Telegraph*...make a note of the time she arrives at Cloonagh? She turned up suspiciously early at the scene here on Friday. And David, do you know if the victim's boner is still in its rightful place?"

Breen and Gorman glanced at each other.

"That was David Stewart," Donovan said, naming the Templemore superintendent. "Boner and balls only things left attached to the torso. A piece of blue baler twine was attached to an upstairs newel post. It was hanging down into the ground floor and ended in a loop made with a running knot."

"Jakers, Jimmy, you're getting psychic," Tom Breen blurted out. He turned in his chair and gave Gorman a gentle punch on the upper arm. "Nailer had prepared for something else but he never got to do it."

"And he purposefully left the noose," Gorman said. "The baler twine is a deliberate piece of Nailer's handwriting, left behind to make sure we know he did it to Lazarian, even if he made a mess of it. I'd like to see that mess before it's tidied up."

"I wouldn't and I won't," Donovan said. "David Stewart said the first five lads came back out to get sick, one vomited on the evidence and another became hysterical… How about you, Tom? Would you like to see the place?"

"I'd give it a go," Breen said. "But if the mess is as bad as you say, they won't be cleaning up for hours yet. We'd only be adding to the feet ploughing through the place if we went to Cloonagh now. I think we should go ahead and see what we can get out of Brother Beatus."

Donovan stood up. "Alright, it's Beatus like we planned. We'll talk later about Croghan Hill and going to see Lazarian's bits."

Breen and Gorman walked out of the station into a dour day. They drove the five miles to Killeigh village before either spoke. Tom Breen said, "If what you said about Nailer in the supe's office is right—that he may be a boiling volcano—how is he able to function without drawing attention to himself? Wouldn't he be on the boil the whole time, exploding over small things?"

As they passed the Welcome to County Laois/*Failte Go Contae Laois* sign, Gorman replied, "Most of us can compartmentalize, store stuff away in pigeonholes in our brains; if we couldn't, we wouldn't be able to get on with the job of living. Look at the people who can't get over the death of someone close, always talking about it, driving the relatives mad, always grieving until they die themselves. Some people compartmentalize so efficiently they can seal off one area of their lives to the extent that it doesn't exist at all in the present. Remember Bill Clinton the time 'that woman' was grooming his feathered glory in the Oval Office? Instead of throwing an overcoat over his head and slinking off into the shadows of shame—like most of us would have done—Clinton went on national

TV, world TV for Christ's sake, and argued a fine point of language—the definition of 'is.' And he's still out there in public as if the whole world had never heard about the kneeling woman kneading his projection. The woman was wearing a thong—I love that part."

"Take your mind out of the thong, Gorman, and answer the question. If Nailer is volcanic shouldn't he explode at the least provocation?"

"Yes, but he would have to be provoked when that pigeonhole in his brain is unsealed—when he's killing or planning the killings. But he has kept the lid from blowing off completely on two occasions. Maybe Lazarian provoked him, poked him into an insane eruption, levered off his controlling lid the way you'd snap the lid off a paint can with a screwdriver." Gorman hesitated. "But, Tom, am *I* a shrink? What the hell do I know? I'm just imagining. But I would love if there was a video of his performance with Lazarian. The blind fury of nature is frightening and fascinating at the same time—raging water, destructive winds. Nailer must have been like a tiger ripping and tearing apart a hyena that has just devoured the tiger cubs."

"You're in your professorial mode, Jimmy."

"In my head, I'm skirting around what I imagine happened in Lazarian's house—I want to look and at the same time I don't. At this point I'm standing at the door with my fingers over my face and I'm slowly uncovering my eyes. I want to look at nature's destruction and at the same time I'm terrified of what I know I'll see. When I see too much, my brain takes flight and I begin talking about tigers and hyenas and anything that will cover my eyes again."

"I think you got sunstroke in Ballysteen this weekend."

"In the annals of Ballysteen, many people have been rainsoaked, some have been dickstroked, but no one has ever been sunstroked."

40.

"Pull in at the Mountmellick Development Association," Breen said. "I want to get coffee."

"What, do they have a restaurant in there?"

"The Old Mill Restaurant…a place for fishermen to swap got-away stories. There's a car park the far side."

As Breen undid his seatbelt he asked, "Do you want anything?"

"Yes. Coffee with the usual. Large. Thanks." Gorman waved to his left. "What's the name of the river?"

"The Owenass."

When Tom Breen returned with the coffee, Gorman was standing on the riverbank gazing down into the peaty water swirling under the bridge. Breen handed Gorman his drink.

"This isn't a river," Gorman said. "It's a wide drain."

"If you don't live near the Shannon or the Amazon, then this is a river."

"Do you ever fish in it?"

"No, this flows into the Barrow about three miles away. All my fishing is in the Barrow."

As they sipped their coffee, the two men stared at the river. Cars came and went over the flat bridge beside them.

"Flowing water relaxes my brain," Breen said.

"There's something primal about flowing and burbling water," Gorman said. "It reminds us of the noises in our mothers' bellies while we waited to get out. It's the same as the attraction of a flickering fireplace or TV screen; the light dimming and beaming through our mothers' skin as they moved around."

Small eddies formed and crashed into each other like colliding black holes. Pieces of broken straw and drowned leaves sailed by.

"Jimmy, do you read that stuff or do you make it up as you go along?"

"I don't know. Maybe someone told me, maybe I read it, maybe I made it up. It makes sense to me."

The long-dead weeds of spring which had grown too close to the river had collapsed into the current but were still attached to their anchoring roots. In the rushing water, the bushy, undulating stems were the tresses of drowned mermaids. A short, stout piece of water-logged fencing-post floated past, bobbing low in the chocolate surface.

"When you were inside," Gorman said, "I was thinking...the files of the industrial schools...how to get our hands on them. Some law agencies in America have people who do dirty jobs for them, like gather information while making the break-in look like an ordinary burglary. Do we...do the guards have any outfit like that?"

"Jesus, Jimmy, you're not thinking of—"

"Not me myself, Tom. I'd be too frightened to do anything like that. But is there a secret outfit, a sort of black arts outfit that the government uses when there's nothing else left? How many U.S. presidents have tried to take a whack at Fidel Castro, given the go-ahead to some secret group within the government, maybe outsourced the job in such a way that it couldn't be traced back to the White House, or even to America?"

"If it couldn't be traced back to the White House, how do you know orders like that ever came from there? And how come Fidel is still giving the finger to the U.S.? Get back in the car and stop dreaming. And don't throw your empty cup in the river either. It's bad for the fish."

"God has his revenge in the form of history," Gorman said, as they walked to the car.

"Who are you quoting now?"

"Someone. I don't know—probably a historian. Maybe I made it up."

"What does it mean?"

"You know...these religious brothers...the whole Catholic priest abuse thing. They got away with it for a while but their place in history is stinking. Many a man has gone to the grave shrouded in his own self-cultivated image only to have the shroud yanked off years later. The English dug up Oliver Cromwell and hanged him years after his death."

"Jimmy the iconoclast," Breen said. "You never pass up an opportunity to take a kick at the Holy Roman Catholic Church."

"It's myself I'm kicking, Tom. Such an eegit I was."

When they were passing the fairy rath on the Bog Road to Portlaoise, Gorman asked, "How are we going to approach this Brother Beatus?"

"Besides fishing and checking up on the pater on the weekend," Breen said, "I read up on Alzheimer's on the Internet. Therapists have devised all kinds of tricks to help victims keep a grip on themselves—puzzles, cross-words, jigsaws, bingo—anything to keep them in touch with their memory. In the last few years reminiscing has become the exercise du jour."

"Exercise du jour! Classy, Tom!"

Breen ignored Gorman. "The therapist begins the reminiscing in a very casual way. The hope is the patient will hear something that jump-starts his memory and start talking."

"As in 'association of ideas,'" Gorman threw in.

"Yes, association of memories. I think we might give it a try with Brother Beatus. Of course it depends on how

far he's gone. If he still spends some time in the present
we might get some information out of him."

Off the old Dublin Road, they entered the Saint Fintan's driveway across the street from the prison. Tom Breen
remembered when Saint Fintan's Lunatic Asylum was as
fortified as the prison, with high walls, high gates. But a
more enlightened age had lowered the walls and opened
the gates. In recent decades, the patients of Saint Fintan's
Psychiatric Hospital had been allowed to gaze out on the
world, and the public had been educated about mental
illness. And a still more enlightened age had emptied the
forbidding grey stone buildings and placed the patients
in community residences in Laois and Offaly. It had been
a long, painful, unenlightened and cruel six-hundred-
year journey since the founding of Saint Mary Bethlehem
in London to the discoveries of psychopharmacology and
the creation of family units for mentally ill people.

Jimmy Gorman drove slowly along the driveway. "I was
in a mental hospital a few times in England—visiting a
nun," he said. "She'd been a neighbor in Ballysteen. She
was a patient but she still dressed in her old-time nun's
habit. I was always reminded of Napoleon when I'd see
her sticking out like a sore thumb in the huge common
room that seemed to have a hundred patients in various
stages of chemical befoggery."

"Napoleon, as in delusion?"

"Yes. She looked like a freak. She looked like the mad-
dest person in the whole place. I hated going to see her.
She died young."

Gorman parked the car in the shadow of a three-
storied, big-windowed, cut-stone building that loudly
roared of British Empire institutional architecture.

"Have you the recorder?" Breen asked.

"I do."

41.

Side by side, Breen and Gorman went up the five lime-stone steps to the unlocked glass doors. They walked into a lobby that had undergone many reconfigurations since the British had departed the country after their long and unwelcome stay. The ceiling was twenty feet high. On their left was a twelve-foot white wooden wall with four closed service windows. Through the hammered, translucent glass there was no sign of movement, but a bell-push was indicated in large red lettering. While they waited for the gentle *ding-ding* to be answered, they strolled around, their hands behind their backs. Six straight-backed institutional wooden chairs were lined up against the wall facing the service windows across the lobby.

"A lot of purple," Jimmy Gorman said, and with a movement of his feet and shoulders he indicated the walls and the carpet.

"That's not purple," Breen said. "It's a light orchid."

"Well, excuse me, Picasso," Gorman said.

"I bought a purple shirt a few weeks ago and the sales-girl took pernicious pleasure telling me my shirt was light orchid. It's the same color as the carpet and walls."

"It's a good thing you're not wearing the shirt or I might lose you."

A noise at the service window behind them drew Breen's attention. Through the hammered glass he saw the shape of a hand unlatching the sash and then disappearing. The bottom sash rattled up in its grooves.

"May I help you?" A distracted woman, fiftyish, continued to sort papers while she waited for a reply. She was smartly dressed and smartly coiffed—and spare on the makeup. Tom Breen waited until she looked up again.

"Yes?" she said.

"Good morning, ma'am. We're detectives from Tullamore. Nurse Grimes is expecting us."

She put down her papers. "Identification, please."

Breen showed his I.D. card. "May I have it, please?" She took the card. "And yours, sir?" She held out her hand to Gorman. No nail polish. "Please wait," she said, then pulled down the window and secured the hasp. The detectives looked at each other.

"Fort Knox," Gorman said.

Mumbles came through the glass-and-wood partition and then the flash of a copying machine bounced off the ceiling. The sash went up and the woman placed a sign-in book on the counter. "Name, date and time," she said. "Both of you. Don't sign for each other."

When both men had signed in, the woman spun the book around. She checked the signatures on the page against the ones on the detectives' identification cards. Satisfied, she handed back the cards. "For security purposes your I.D. cards were copied and will be put on file. I called the Tullamore Garda Station and Superintendent Donovan vouched for you. Saint Martha's Ward is where you're going. I'll buzz you through that door over there." She placed her index finger on the buzzer-button on her side of the window. "Once inside, go to your left. Keep walking. I'll tell Nurse Grimes you're on the way and she'll meet you. Please speak softly. You must sign out here before you leave the building."

As the two men approached the door they heard a sound like a sigh and the oiled sliding of a bolt. They pushed, they went through, they turned left. They were in a long corridor.

"Security is necessary but I hate being subjected to it," Breen said quietly. "It's humiliating—the attitudes. I wanted to say something like, Would you please look at me when you speak to me, treat me like a human being and not like one more fucking llama in a long queue at the airport?"

"I thought we were going to be more Yeatsian in our speech, Tom."

"I'll bet Yeats found himself in situations where he couldn't have improved on 'fuck,'" Breen said.

"Like when Maud Gonne told him to keep his feathered glory in his trousers."

"Your nervousness is showing, Gorman. Shut up. And don't mention anyone's feathered glory again."

"Okay, I'll use the vernacular and non-Yeatsian 'boner'."

Doors were set into the walls on each side of the corridor at regular intervals. They were all closed. The lintels were low like the doorways in castles built in days when men and women were short.

"Were you ever in Kilmainham Jail?" Gorman asked. "There's corridors like this with cell doors like these."

"Maybe there wasn't much difference between jails and asylums in the good old days."

Down the brightly lit and brightly painted corridor the two men walked. "Did you ever hear such silence?" Gorman asked.

"What were you expecting? Maniacal screeching and laughing like in *Jane Eyre*?"

"I was expecting *some* noise."

"There's only a few patients left."

They crossed a narrow intersecting corridor. Suddenly there were high windows on their right and a blank wall on their left. Gorman stopped and went over to a window. "Look at this, Tom. The sill is sloped and what is it...?" He leaned his chest into the sill. "It's five feet off the floor."

On silent shoes a woman had walked up behind them. She startled both men when she said, "In bygone days the

windows were built that way to keep the patients from
climbing up and jumping head-first down onto the floor...
You must be the detectives, Breen and Gorman. I'm Ceil
Grimes."

"I'm Tom Breen; he's Jimmy Gorman."

Nurse Grimes shook the men's hands. "You're welcome to Saint Martha's Ward. But I must see your I.D.
before we go any further."

While Ceil Grimes examined their cards the detectives
looked at each other with raised, disbelieving eyebrows.

Afterward, Jimmy Gorman would tell Tom Breen that
he'd been expecting Nurse Grimes to be a short, frumpy
woman with a severe hairdo and thick hairy legs, baggy
hose, a wrinkled face and liver spots.

Ceil Grimes was thirtyish, taller than Gorman, with
a postcard Irish face set in a halo of red hair. She had
the skin tone that comes with red hair and a figure that
induced instant sexual salivation in the average and
healthy males who met her, all the more so because she
carried her beauty as unselfconsciously as a camel carrying its hump. Ceil was wearing a flowered top, blue scrubs
and white running shoes.

Nurse Grimes handed back the I.D. cards and strolled
over to the window. "This stretch of the corridor is connecting two buildings."

Ceil Grimes was no bogwoman; she spoke in a melodi-
ous, almost north-of-Ireland accent. "We're looking out
on what used to be called an airing court for the patients.
That door over there in the wall on the left opens out of
Saint Martha's Ward and some of the patients still use the
area."

The airing court, surrounded by high grey buildings,
was almost a square, each side fifty yards long. Around the
edges of the trimmed lawn the soil of the flower beds had
been turned for the winter, their shapes and sizes mindful
of freshly closed graves. Along the three sides visible to

the visitors, trestles were attached to the walls between the windows supporting the bare limbs of climbing tea roses and the thin tendrils of clematis. The espaliered arms of pear and apple and plum clung to their supports in skeletal crucifixions. Dozens of hanging flower baskets, deep into winter's sleep, would be replanted next spring in the small glasshouse in the far left corner.

"In the spring and summer this courtyard is very pretty," Ceil Grimes said. "The patients work in there under the supervision of Joe Gardener Lalor—we have a Joe Maintenance Lalor and a Joe Nurse Lalor. You can't see him from here, but Brother Beatus is in his chair on the far side of that big tree—our Atlantic cedar."

"You know your trees, Ceil," Gorman said, making a flirtatious foray. He cleared his froggy throat.

"I don't, Jimmy. But so many people asked me about the tree that I got Joe Gardener to find the name for me."

With Ceil Grimes in the middle they walked slowly toward Saint Martha's Ward. "There are only twenty-one patients left in the entire hospital; all the others have been moved out to group homes in the service area—Laois and Offaly. All the patients here are in some stage of Alzheimer's. Relatives and registered friends can visit the ward twenty-four hours a day."

"Unrestricted visiting hours!" Gorman said. "That must create problems for the staff—having visitors pop in at any hour."

"Actually the staff is very happy to see visitors. There is a noticeable difference between patients who have visitors and those who don't."

"We were impressed with the security procedures on the way in," Tom Breen said. "What's the procedure for late-night visitors?"

"We have always been careful, even before your superintendent spoke to us about the safety of Brother Beatus. When the front-office people go home, a phone is placed outside the service windows. Visitors dial seven and a staff member from Saint Martha's Ward will go up to the lobby office. The night visitors are treated exactly as you were before you were buzzed in, even if the visitor is a regular."

"Then it seems that Brother Beatus and everyone else are very safe in Saint Martha's Ward," Gorman said.

"The safety of the patients and the safety of the staff is our first concern. And talking about Brother Beatus... he hasn't had a visitor since he came in here except from local social and religious groups. He has always ignored their efforts. These days, he seldom comes back to the present, but if you happen to press the right button he will go on about the past, even if most times he makes no sense, at least not to us. If it's not raining he sits under the Atlantic cedar all day, summer and winter.

"The best way to get Brother Beatus talking is to sit near him and begin to reminisce, talk to yourself or to each other about something you know from his past. We know he was reared in an orphanage and an industrial school—Dachadoo in Offaly. He loves to be called Brother Beatus. Billy Walsh is the name on all his papers."

Nurse Grimes touched the two men's elbows and began walking again.

"He's a committal, brought here against his will forty years ago; committed by the superior of his religious order."

"Forty!" Gorman echoed. "And no visitors in all that time?"

"Not one. He was in here before I was born. He's seventy-nine, so he was thirty-nine when he came. Privacy laws don't allow me to say much about his stay here. In very general terms, he was obstreperous for a very long time."

"If we told you we are interviewing him as part of a murder investigation, would that allow you to tell us more?" Gorman asked.

"Someone higher up the ladder would make that decision, Jimmy. I can only tell you the grounds for his admission: he suffered from a violent sexual dysfunction disorder. One of the symptoms of that disorder is that the patient, as the textbook says, may force the sexual participation of unwilling people."

"Is that a dressed-up way of saying he was—is—a rapist?" Jimmy asked.

"Yes, it is."

"Female or male unwilling people?"

"Can be either or both. And that's all I'm allowed to tell you about his condition."

"Children?" Gorman pushed.

"Children are people, Jimmy."

42.

Ceil Grimes opened the door at the end of the corridor and the detectives walked through. To Gorman's surprise, they were in an open male ward with all the privacy curtains bundled to the end of their overhead rails. A few of the twelve beds were occupied by sleeping, open-mouthed and drooling old men, some with heads turned aside on their pillows, others facing the ceiling. Most were toothless. Several men sat in chairs beside their beds, motionless, like birds glued to their perches, their eyes snagged on whatever their focus had lit on. All the patients were clean-shaven and recently bathed and their scarce hairs were neatly combed. A patient in a chair at the far side of the ward held out his hand and said, "Hello, lads. I'm Lar Curry from Garryhinch and I made skibs from scollops."

Gorman went over and took the old gnarled hand. "Hello, Lar. I'm Jimmy. How are you doing?"

"Hello, lads. I'm Lar Curry from Garryhinch and I made skibs from scollops."

Gorman looked back to Ceil Grimes for help. She called him away with a move of her head. "Good man, Lar," Gorman said.

When Gorman rejoined them, Tom Breen and Ceil Grimes were standing beside a life-sized, blue-caped statue of Mary, the mother of Jesus. Hands in prayerful pose between virginal breasts, eyes stuck on a spot on the ceiling, she was standing barefoot on a snake, keeping it from wriggling out among the defenseless patients. Two blue, silk roses were attached to her hands with a piece of thin wire.

Ceil Grimes touched the detectives on the arms, nodded at Lar Curry, and pointed at her eyes. "But he can hear the grass grow," she said. She may as well have lowered the stylus onto a spinning record. Lar Curry began singing in a soft voice:

The grass it grows green around Ballyjamesduff
And the blue sky hangs over it all;
And tones that are tender and tones that are gruff
Come whispering over the sea,
Come back, Paddy Reilly, to Ballyjamesduff,
Come home, Paddy Reilly, to me.

When Lar fell silent, the two visitors continued to look at him with fixed grins on their faces.

"Reminiscence at work…this way, gentlemen," Nurse Grimes said, and she opened the door to the garden that had once been the airing court. She stepped aside and said, "He's all yours." As she closed the door she added, "Maybe one of you could put his cap on."

"How's his hearing?" Gorman asked.

"He can hear the grass grow, too," she said, and again Lar Curry began crooning about the green grass of Ballyjamesduff.

"Jaze, I'd hate to be around when they all reminisce at the same time," Gorman said.

The detectives stood side by side on the metal ramp outside the door, hands clasping the cold, top metal bar like the claws of roosting birds. Brother Beatus was visible from this angle—a small, bald-pated man with white hair on the sides and back of his head. He was faced away from them, sitting in a wooden garden chair, swaddled in a blanket of faded tartan, heather purple the dominant color. A red ski cap lay on the ground beside his chair. Close by were two wooden garden benches.

"What are you thinking, Tom?" Gorman said. "You're too quiet and you look like you ate a bad egg this morning."

"No eggs, Jimmy, but I do feel a bit slurry in the gut. You have a go at Brother Beatus first and I'll listen in the background just in case he talks."

"Alright," Gorman said, "but I'm very skeptical I'll get anything out of him."

"I think you'll do a better job than me, Jimmy. For one thing, you're a better bullshitter."

"I'm taking that as a vote of confidence, and I'll expect you'll put it in my next evaluation. You look like shite, Tom."

"I have a twisted fart that doesn't know which end to come out. Don't forget to turn on the recorder."

They walked across the lawn together. Breen sat behind Beatus, and Gorman continued on. He picked up the red ski cap and stood in front of the brother. He was taken aback by the small size of the man; he could have been a dwarf.

"Your cap, Brother Beatus," Gorman said. Gently, he pulled the woolen cap down and covered the old, skinny, hair-rimmed ears. Beatus's face wasn't easy to gaze at; where it wasn't red it was purple, and the small nose was almost lost among the interlocking fleshy moguls all over his face. His eyes were abnormally close to each other. Gorman tucked in the blanket where it had fallen away from the neck and from the thin, short-fingered, red hands in the lap.

Brother Beatus gave no indication that he was aware of another presence.

Gorman placed an upturned flowerpot in the grass in front of the brother and settled the tape recorder on top. He pulled over the wooden garden bench and sat into one of its corners, his elbow on the armrest. He was within touching distance and facing Brother Beatus.

Gorman glanced around the airing court with the same boyhood wariness he felt when he was about to duck behind a bush to lower his trousers. He felt so foolish about what he was going to do that he would have preferred Tom Breen not to be within hearing distance.

After staring at Brother Beatus's face for several minutes, Gorman realized that a tune was humming inside his own head, then wondered how long it had been annoying him. It was the song Lar Curry had been singing in Saint Martha's Ward. As the tune came around again, Gorman's brain ran ahead looking for rhyming words and he sang quietly.

> *Oh, the school that was Dachadoo vanished they say,*
> *But Beatus knows where it is still;*
> *Just go to the farmyard and sleep in the hay*
> *And feed all the piggies their swill.*
> *In Dachadoo Boniface and Jackie the Bap,*
> *And Lazarian who is very thin.*
> *I wish little boys would sit on my lap,*
> *To play with the hair on my chin.*

Gorman sat up straight and looked around. Tom Breen held his hand up to his ear to indicate he hadn't heard anything. Then he moved his hand in a winding motion to encourage Gorman to get a move on. Gorman made a winding motion back and pointed to Breen. Breen held out his hands to show he had nothing to offer.

"The hures," Beatus said.

"The hures," Gorman said, and as he verbally took off he felt as if he were fumbling in pitchblack darkness. "Dachadoo...Dachadoo...Rhymes with Timbuktu. Hures they were. Timbuktu in Mali in Africa. Dachadoo in Offaly in Ireland...Dachadoo, Dachadoo, the place of the black fog...The dirty hures. Hures, hures, hures." Gorman's voice dropped down into a lullaby croon. "Dachadoo,

where lived the children, where lived the boys. Dachadoo
where the boys ran and laughed and played and Brother
Beatus ran with them and played with them too, in Dachadoo. Hures. In Timbuktu and in Dachadoo, too, Brother
Beatus made a stew. Brother Beatus was the very best, and
made the small boy a little red vest. The hures."

Gorman paused, wondered where such rubbish was
coming from, wondered, too, why he was using the same
voice he had used long ago when he was reading his girls
to sleep. He looked over at Tom Breen, and Breen pantomimed applause and nodded his head in encouragement.

Gorman began again, tried to sound like a doctor
speaking to a patient who has just regained consciousness. "Brother Beatus, you worked in Dachadoo Industrial
School with Brother Lazarian and Brother Boniface and
Brother John the Baptist. Brother Boniface and Brother
John the Baptist and Brother Beatus—you all had a great
time with the young boys. Don't you remember the good
times, Brother Beatus? The excitement of the boys in the
hay and your...the hures."

Gorman hesitated as his conscience shouted for attention.

"O Holy Christ, Beatus." Gorman changed into a co-
conspirator. "They were the best days of our lives; they
were the good old days, you and me and Bony out in the
hay shed together, swapping the boys around. You'd say
to me, Bappy John...you'd say, Bappy John, aren't these
the best times we ever had, Bappy John? All these little
boys, one after the other, and they're ours. Two holding a
boy while the other greased his gauntlet. You needed the
most greasing, Beatus, as big as a donkey you were. Was it
you or Bony who liked the goose grease? Was it Bony or
Beatus? Bappy John you'd call me and I'd call you Beauty
Boy and we'd call Boniface Bony. The way Bony used to
roar, and we'd roar along with him and laugh. Don't you

remember, Beauty Boy? Wolves baying at the moon. Oh, God! They were the best days. The hures."

"I got my own back on them hures! I got my own back. I got the hures, I got the hures," Beatus said, sounding as if his vocal cords were caked in rust.

Gorman was startled by these more-or-less complete sentences from the small wrapped figure. He glanced over at Breen. Breen was standing, was energetically winding up the air with his hand. Gorman fumbled in his coat for his notebook. He flipped it open, scribbled and talked at the same time.

"Of course you got your own back and I never saw a better way to get your own back. Hures is what they were alright—real hures. It was the best bit of getting back I ever saw. That was the best I ever heard of, the best way to get back at them, the hures. They were the worst hures ever. Who could have thought you would get away with it? Who could have thought it? Bony and Bappy didn't think you were smart like them. But they didn't know how smart Beauty Boy was. And Lazarian, too, he thought you were dumb as a box of rocks and stupid as a chicken. Nobody would have thought you'd get your own back on them hures. And the way you did it. That was—"

Beatus croaked, "No blood, not one drop, and the nail in him and he didn't even wake...just the heel of my hand, not a sound...I gave him a good feel and he couldn't stir...dead as a doornail, I got the last feel of him when he was still warm...the hures...my face in his fork." The sound of a giggle came from the multicolored blanket. "I liked the feel of him dead and warm; he couldn't wiggle like a fish."

Gorman glanced at Breen again. Breen was still standing, his hands hanging, his mouth open. Gorman scribbled, waited a few seconds for Brother Beatus to continue. Then, afraid the brother might slip back into the river of forgetfulness, Gorman began speaking again.

"The nail was the best. Who would have thought of a nail and they all thought you were not as clever as—"

"Biggest nail in the box in the sawshop like a dagger straight in with a push from the heel of the hand...dead as a doornail when they found him...the yellow curls." While he was babbling Brother Beatus did not look around, did not move any part of his body except his lips. Gorman waited again but feared that Brother Beatus was limping back into his darkness.

"I remember him, the yellow curls, the eyes blue—"

"If I couldn't have him, they couldn't have him, the hures...I got my own back...they nearly murdered me... the next time, cut the balls off me, they said. I got the hures, I got them, and they never knew...in goes the nail so easy...no hammer and there's no blood...hures...their best prize I took off them, the hures."

Gorman wrote and spoke. "The yellow curls of him. He was the most beautiful one you ever had, the little lad with the yellow curls. The face of him, the lovely face of him; and his name was as nice as his body. Every time you said his name you thought of the yellow curls, the body of African ivory. His name was as beautiful as the yellow curls; his name was as beautiful as his body. You thought of the lovely body when you thought of the name; a warm alabaster body, your hand between his legs, and he couldn't wiggle away and he still so warm. That was the best. The lovely name for a lovely body, the silken body. Every time I hear the name I see the lovely face and the lovely yellow curls and the lovely body like ivory, like alabaster. His name—"

"Michael, oh yellow curls on Michael oh, and his lovely Michael oh." Brother Beatus opened his blanket and he pushed his hands into his crotch. He sought out his antique penis. "The curls, the curls Michael, oh...legs on my face. The smooth...the smooth."

Gorman expected that every time Beatus said, "oh," that the oh would be followed by another word—"Michael oh *so beautiful*, Michael oh *such skin.*" Then Gorman said aloud, "Michael O," and the flash almost melted all his axon terminals. "Michael O'Somebody," he hissed. He stood up and said, "Michael O'Reilly, O'Neill, O'Byrne, O'Malley, O...O...O'Shea..."

Brother Beatus was now rocking back and forth in his chair, the hands at his crotch trying to entice life into his lifeless bit.

"O'Casey. O'Boyle, O'Bannon." Gorman's brain seized up again and he sat down, tried to relax. He waited for the old man to forget what he was trying to do with his hands. Gorman glanced over at Breen, but Breen was gone, had vanished without a sound.

"O'Reilly," Gorman said. He went over to Brother Beatus and took the forgotten hands out of the forgotten crotch, laid the hands on the thighs and tucked the brother into his blanket. And as he did it, he softly said, "How about Brother Lazarian...Brother Lazarian... Brother Lazarian."

Gorman went back to his perch on the garden bench and repeated the name. Lazarian, Lazarian. On and on Gorman went—tempting, cajoling, whispering, pleading, groveling. But Brother Beatus had slipped back under the waters of Lethe.

Gorman slouched forward on the bench, rested his elbows on his knees, put his head in his hands. He felt as if he'd been playing for hours in the unrelenting waves at an ocean beach, only noticing the exhaustion when he'd stopped.

He didn't know that Ceil Grimes was present until she put her hand on his shoulder. He wondered if he'd fallen asleep.

43.

Doctor Alexander McNulty was still able to take care of himself—but just barely. His eighty-nine-year-old body had shrunk. The five-foot ten-inch frame of his youth was now bent at the shoulders and twisted slightly to his right side. The skin on the front of his skull was so wrinkled, his wattles so long and flappy, the backs of his hands so mottled with liver spots that middle-aged people turned away from the reminders of what was in store for them.

Because his eyesight was failing he was unable to see the results of his grooming in the mirror, and wisps of silver hair stuck out willy-nilly like straw from a scarecrow's hat. But his shoes were always polished to a brilliant shine. Generations of Tullamore's corner boys had referred to him as Shiny Shoes.

Every morning, with the assistance of a walking stick, the retired doctor shuffled down Store Street and up the steps of the Church of the Assumption of our Blessed Lady. Dressed in a dark blue suit, white shirt, blue tie, black-banded trilby and an overcoat if necessary, he purposefully arrived fifteen minutes before the eleven o'clock mass began. During that waiting time he prayed for the peaceful repose of the soul of his dear Elizabeth, for the well-being of his children and grandchildren. He then proceeded to bore the brains out of God by begging forgiveness all over again for his sins. He asked for divine mercy for his sins of commission and omission and he named every sin he remembered committing. Every sin he had committed since reaching the age of reason on his seventh birthday was dug up and basted with guilt; sins of greed every time he took the thicker slice of bread, the biggest potato, the biggest spoon of cabbage. He mentioned the lies he had told, the cheating during childhood games, the childish fights out of which he always emerged battered and bleeding. He repented again for the violent imaginings he had entertained against the bullies in his life. And then there was the disobedience to his teachers and parents; the urinating over the wall of the lavatories in the Boys' School—hump on back, pelvis thrust out, penis aimed like a fireman's hose; the saying of his prayers under the bedclothes instead of kneeling on the cold floor beside his bed; the omission of grace before or after meals. He repented again for the smashing, with well-aimed stones, of the ceramic cups on telephone poles along the railway track; the sneaking into Missus Piggot's garden and the spoliation of her bush of ripe raspberries after ripping off the protecting lace curtain. And then the rueful Doctor McNulty entered into the domain of the black sins against the sixth commandment that he'd committed when he'd masturbated with the wantonness of an adolescent monkey before he discovered such acts were mortal sins; he begged forgiveness for the improper use of prayer when he'd asked God for an abundance of nocturnal emissions to relieve the pressure that his wanton simian behavior had once taken care of; he drew God's attention to the sin he had committed against the sixth commandment in medical school while massaging a young woman's clitoris in a doorway as she'd brought him to an in-trouser orgasm. There were the sins of impatience against his patients, especially the hypochondriacal nuns and the fat, nervous, unwashed women who presented themselves for vaginal examinations. He had violated the ninth commandment in his later years when he'd imagined he was screwing the Princess Diana while he was humping toward climax on top of his withered Elizabeth. He had committed sins against the

commandment to love one's neighbor when he snapped
at his sixty-one-year-old daughter for nagging him to
move into a nursing home near where she lived in Navan
in County Meath: "That's only for *your* bloody conven-
ience. No one's asking you to come to see me. I can take
care of myself." Half kneeling and half sitting, he ended
his pre-mass pleadings by knocking on heaven's door to
remind them up there that it wouldn't be long before he
arrived, and to humbly pray that he would receive a cor-
dial welcome.

When the sanctuary bell sounded to announce
the arrival of the priest on the altar, Doctor Alexander
McNulty struggled to his feet with the grace of a cow
hoisting herself onto her hooves after a three-hour cud-
chewing session. Even though he could not make out the
features of the priest, the moment the clergyman opened
his mouth the doctor knew it was Father O'Shea. "Dis
mass will be offered for deh repose of deh soul of Pádraig Turley who was known as Brodder Lazarian. Brodder
Lazarian was deh superior in Dachadoo Industrial School
for meny years and was known to meny people in dis parish. Brodder Lazarian was a man who dedicated his life to
deh welfare and education of unfortunate byes. Defi-*nite*-
ly, deh man was a saint. May his sowl and the sowls of all
the fateful deparded rest in peace."

Doctor Alexander McNulty remembered Brother
Lazarian, one of the most dedicated, the most kind, the
most thoughtful men he had ever known; a man who lived
every syllable of his religious vows to the fullest; a true
servant of the poor and the abandoned; a loving, protecting father of hundreds of undeserving boys. If Brother
Lazarian hadn't the qualities of sainthood, then nobody
had. If only the world had a hundred like him!

When mass was over, Doctor McNulty remained
in the church, and for a few moments he labored over
a conundrum: should he pray *to* Brother Lazarian as a

saint already in heaven like Father O'Shea said, or *for* the man of God? In the end he prayed to Brother Lazarian because to do the other would be to suggest the man had not been perfect.

As he shuffled home after his morning worship, Doctor McNulty always felt good. To himself, but to no one else lest he sound like he was playing touch-and-go with blasphemy, he would compare this feeling to the satisfaction of body when a visit to the lavatory has resulted in success. The doctor knew he had righted things between himself and God. Once again, he was prepared for death, his soul was clean and shiny and he looked forward to his release from his ancient and aching body. Like all the old people he had known in the days of his doctoring, he hoped, too, that he would go to sleep one night and not wake up—that he would regain consciousness as his soul was already winging its way into the face of God.

As he crossed a side street, Doctor McNulty wondered why the parish priest, Father O'Loughlin, had never spoken to Father O'Shea about "defi-*nite*-ly." Surely that pronunciation was the boggiest of all bogger pronunciations. No wonder the Laois people raised their eyebrows at the way the Offalies spoke. Laois people laughing at us, for God's sake, and they all speaking like they'd never heard of half the alphabet.

Homeward, the old man limped and short-stepped and stumbled along Church Road enjoying the respectful greetings and forelocking of those he met. Even after twelve years of retirement, Doctor McNulty remained an integral part of the fabric of Tullamore. For fifty-two years he had healed and calmed, scolded and praised, lanced and sewn, birthed and buried and become comfortably well-off taking care of the sick men, women and children of Tullamore.

He turned off Church Road into his own tree-lined cul-de-sac. The farther his feet shuffled along the sidewalk the higher grew the walls surrounding the houses. Doubled, black-and-gold, wrought-iron gates allowed views of the short, curved avenues leading to the secluded dwellings which were within a few rooms of being mansions. Through the gates could be seen, too, the manicured gardens, the exotic shrubs, the ancient cedars, the copper beeches and oaks and chestnuts, the autumn leaves of the English ivy fastidiously trimmed to expose the window quoins and the arched, keystoned doorways. Several gardens were hosts to the monkey puzzle tree, that symbol of money, of gentility, of difference.

Doctor McNulty pushed open one half of his own high, iron gate, and he heard the familiar, comforting protest of the pivot-hinge grinding in its shallow hole in the block of buried granite. Gently he closed the gate behind him and listened for the sound of the latch falling into place. He opened the back of the long letter box he had designed forty-one years ago; Hugh Nolan, the blacksmith in Mountmellick, had made it, Hugh in his leather apron and bare, glistening arms. McNulty took out *The Telegraph.*

The avenue to the doctor's front door was just long enough to indulge one bend allowing for the camouflaging of the front of the house with a strategically planted blue spruce. Along the golden flint chippings the old man noisily tottered, the grass of the lawns still white with hoarfrost. When he reached the spot that permitted the viewing of the house and the garden at once, he stopped and cast a long lingering look behind. Every day since Elizabeth's death, he had stood at this spot and looked longingly for the last time, just in case God called him home before tomorrow.

In a gardening magazine the doctor's grounds would have been described as bordering on the formal, but it would have noted that the plethora of annual beds had introduced an uneasy feng shui. Elizabeth McNulty had been a fanatical gardener, a woman who wrestled with the tail end of winter every year, shooing it away and dragging in the reluctant spring with her early plantings of pansies and her forcing of the daffodils with coverings of warm horse manure.

In an architectural digest, the doctor's house would have been described as a nineteenth-century classical farmhouse—hipped, slate-roofed, a segmented fanlight above the front door, the upstairs and downstairs windows and the chimneys perfectly symmetrical. Boston ivy, now gold and orange and red and brown, bearded the front of the house. As he stood there casting his lingering look, Doctor McNulty imagined Timmy Dalton's hearse slowly purring up the driveway followed by a group of elderly, black-dressed, shuffling, hunchbacked mourners. In the coffin were his own mortal remains already uncoiling themselves back to their clayey state. The doctor was pleasantly warmed by his imaginings. As he turned to go into the house, he rummaged fussily in a trouser pocket and pulled out a folded handkerchief to wipe a cold November drop off his nose.

The exterior of Doctor McNulty's house was the beautiful wrapping of a very comfortable home. The wide interior windowsills in the thick nineteenth-century walls had been cleverly incorporated into the twenty-first century appointments. On the ground floor, besides the kitchen and the full-sized bathroom, was a formal dining room, a sitting room and an office. The office had been converted into a bedroom for the ailing Elizabeth, and when she had died the previous year the doctor had moved into her bed to save himself the agony of the stairs. The big surprise of the house could be seen from the dining room through the French doors in the rear exterior wall of the original building—a conservatory, three-quarters the width of the house with a cathedral ceiling and six skylights.

As he did every morning when he returned from mass, Doctor McNulty tottered into the conservatory to commune with Elizabeth by watering her hanging plants or hoovering the detritus that had fallen since the day before. Even though the care of the plants had become an ordeal for him, the doctor knew his Lizzie would be pleased with his dedication to her. He feared, too, that if he stopped performing the ritual he would break another connection with his very adoring and supportive wife. Not once had he referred to her as "my wife"; she was always Elizabeth—except in the bedroom, where she was Lizzie.

When the conservatory was new, every visitor asked the same questions about the plants and the two lofty, fire-scarred beams from which they hung. "How do you water them?" and "What happened to the beams?" Elizabeth, with the glee of a young girl showing off a new summer frock, would press a button beside the light switch. The visitors never failed to smile in admiration as the eight hanging plants descended slowly and silently to belly level. Doctor McNulty's unbearably loudmouthed sister had clapped her hands the first time she saw the magic show, and said at their Christmas party for everyone to hear, "Oh, it's just like the chandelier at curtain time in the Metropolitan Opera House in New York."

"The beams came from a Protestant church in County Meath that burned down in the late fifties," Elizabeth would reply to the second question, as the plants sailed up again to their set height. "The parishioners held a fun-draising auction and Alexander insisted on buying the beams. As usual he had a plan in the back of his head, even though a conservatory hadn't even been discussed yet."

When he had finished his chores, Doctor McNulty returned the watering can and hoover to the press in the kitchen. He came back into the conservatory with *The Telegraph*. At the light switch, he pressed two buttons and the shades in the skylights silently slid open. Then into his ancient, baggy, reclining chair he lowered himself and, with a sigh, lay back into the enfolding fat arms. Elizabeth had wanted to get rid of the chair years ago, but he had insisted it was too comfortable. In his aging male world comfort came before appearance.

The old doctor used the lever on the right side of the recliner to raise his feet. He opened the paper and turned to the death notices. Brother Lazarian wasn't in there yet.

Doctor McNulty was sleeping in this chair just after noon when the front doorbell wakened him. For several moments he didn't know where he was—in his bed, in hospital, on the floor, dead? Was it morning or night? The newspaper had fallen over him like a sheet. The doorbell rang again.

"Death is come," the doctor whispered.

Like a fly struggling to get out of a cobweb, McNulty wrestled the paper off to one side. He lowered the foot-rest. Arthritic bones in his shoulders, arms, back, knees and ankles slowed down his effort to extricate himself from the chair; even his hands had gone numb from the narrowing of his carpal tunnels. He shook the pins and needles out of his fingers. When he finally stood up, he waited until all his bits and pieces assumed their proper places.

Across the conservatory he shuffled, and he saw a new frond had floated down from one of Elizabeth's ferns. Maybe it was a sign from her—a "Hello Alexander" from heaven. He flicked his eyes upward and said, "Hello, my dear." The doorbell rang again.

"Impatient death."

He fumbled his way out through the French doors and then around the end of the long dining-room table with its ten chairs. Out into the slate-floored hallway he dragged his feet noisily, each loose slipper-heel following like a whisper.

Widely he opened the front door and there he saw an angel dressed in black, a bright halo around his head.

"Death. Death, you are welcome. Blessed be the holy will of God. I've been waiting for you."

"Doctor McNulty," the angel said in response. "My name is Pauline Byron. I am an investigative reporter for *The Telegraph*. I want to ask you about some death certificates you signed while you were the medical officer in Dachadoo Industrial School."

"What did you say?" Doctor McNulty asked.

44.

When Jimmy Gorman looked up in response to the squeezing hand on his shoulder, Nurse Ceil Grimes's face was there. Gorman wished he was twenty-two again.

"Did you find out anything?" Ceil asked.

"I did, but Brother Beatus slipped away before I got the final bit. Thanks for the reminiscing tip—it worked, but I feel guilty about the raunchy stuff I was feeding him. I gave him enough impure thoughts to keep him entertained for a year."

"Go to confession." Ceil Grimes smiled, and she pulled Brother Beatus's ski cap down over his ears, tucked his blanket inside the loose Roman collar, all the while clucking softly like a mother hen beaking her chicks into her warm belly feathers.

"When I'm old like that," Gorman said, "I hope I have someone like you to mind me." He stood up. "Could you find out for me the exact date Brother Beatus was admitted?"

Ceil Grimes held Brother Beatus's face between her hands like a farmer's wife shaping butter into an ingot between two wooden paddles. "Where are you, Brother?" she said, a mother playful with her child.

The nurse joined Gorman and they walked across the grass toward Saint Martha's Ward. "Alzheimer's is the cruelest disease—more for the relatives than the patient. Eventually there's nothing to visit but a shell."

"Like visiting an old snakeskin," Gorman said. He opened the door and stood aside. "As a nurse, is it easy to slip into familiarity and boredom with Alzheimer's patients?"

"If there is proper management and the minders are not stressed, familiarity and boredom never enter in. Minders establish close relationships with their...I was going to say babies because, for a woman at least, taking care of five or six Alzheimer's patients is like taking care of the dolls of childhood, cleaning and grooming and cooing and dressing and positioning them. And the dolls just look back at you, but you believe that inside the empty heads and behind the eyes they are grateful. We are always sad when a patient dies."

Nurse Grimes led the way to the glass-walled office in the far side of Saint Martha's Ward. She waved a hand toward a chair, told Gorman to sit. "Don't poke around, Detective," she said, "not even with your eyes."

It took only seconds to locate Brother Beatus's file. Nurse Grimes placed the folder on top of the cabinet, moved her body between the cabinet and Gorman. "Brother Beatus, alias Billy Walsh, was admitted to Saint Fintan's on July the eighteenth, 1967."

Gorman scribbled while the nurse filed Brother Beatus back into his drawer.

"Does that help you at all—the date?" Ceil asked, as she walked Gorman back across the tiled floor of the ward.

"It's one more piece in a large puzzle," he said, "but I think it's a very important piece." Gorman raised his hand in greeting to any patient who looked at him.

"Hello, lads. I'm Lar Curry from..." boomed through the ward.

"Will I be reading about this case in the papers?" Ceil asked.

"It's been in *The Telegraph* three times so far—Saturday, Sunday and today. Beyond that I can only be official...

Did you happen to see where Tom Breen went? He wasn't feeling too well this morning."

"He asked me to tell you he'd meet you at your car. He looked a bit ashy, had to stand for a while holding on to the foot of a bed, just staring." Nurse Grimes held out her hand. "This is as far as I go, Jimmy."

"Thanks, Ceil. Maybe someday you'll read *The Telegraph* and realize how helpful you've been. Of course, neither your name nor the hospital's will be mentioned... You know who Pauline Byron is? She's investigating this story for *The Telegraph*."

"It must be serious if Pauline Byron is on it. I'd hate to have that one's teeth in me."

"Me too."

When Jimmy Gorman came out through the glass doors, Tom Breen was leaning against the car. With his hands in his trouser pockets, his face bent to the ground, Breen was a study in depression. He lifted his head to the sound of Gorman's footsteps. Gorman walked around to the driver's side and when he clicked the door open, Breen turned around and rested his arms and elbows on the roof of the car.

"I feel like a real rat shit for doing what I just did," Gorman said.

"You'll get over it. Did you find out anything?" Breen asked.

Gorman held up the tape recorder. "The batteries kept going," he said. "How are you feeling? You're face looks like white pudden, uncooked."

Tom Breen waved an impatient hand. "I'm fine, Jimmy. You saw me that day we went to warn Brother Boniface; I don't do well with pedophiles...What did you find out?"

"Let's talk about it on the way to Croghan Hill, Tom," Gorman said, and without waiting for his senior partner's approval, he sat into the car.

On the Mountmellick road as they approached the entrance to the dump at Kyletalesha, Gorman glanced at his notebook. "This is what Beatus said...," and he glanced from notebook to road as he read. *"Not one drop of blood, not one drop, and the nail in him. And he didn't even wake; just the heel of my hand. Not a sound. I gave him a good feel and he couldn't stir; dead as a doornail. I got the last feel of him when he was still warm; the hures. Face in his fork, the whole thing in my mouth. I like the feel of them dead and warm; can't wiggle like a fish."*

"Stop the car!" Tom Breen slapped his hand over his mouth.

Gorman braked and pulled into the grass verge. Before the car had stopped, Breen opened the door and hung out his head. The sounds of painful regurgitation filled the car and Gorman placed a hand on his partner's back.

"Move up a few feet," Breen gasped, and he undid his seat belt. He got out onto the grassy verge and bent over, his hands on his knees, his arse resting against the side of the car. Gorman went to the back of the car and removed a reflecting orange triangle from the boot. He trotted back fifty yards and placed the warning sign on the busy road.

Breen was standing straight, but holding on to the car door when Gorman returned.

"I must have a bug."

"You look like shite, Tom. I'll take you home."

Breen flung out a hand. "No, Jimmy. This is nothing a swig of Phillips' milk of magnesia won't fix. I'll get some in Mountmellick."

"Tom, as your partner and your friend I'm supposed to tell you when the arse is out of your trousers; you look like a dog after swallowing a fish backward. Next thing, you'll be doing the Cadbury squirts all over the car. Go home till you get this out of your system."

"That's what you're worried about, the squirts?"

"Damn right, Tom. God knows, your farts are bad enough."

"Don't kick a man when he's down, Jimmy. I'll be alright in a minute with this fresh bog air."

"Fresh air, my arse! That's the Kyletalesha dump you're breathing in. People get cancer from this air. I'm taking you home."

"No, you're not."

"Shite, Tom."

"Shite, Jimmy. I'm still senior to you."

"You're pulling rank."

"I am. Get back in the car...and the next stop is the chemist at Church Open in Mountmellick."

Cars had begun to queue up behind the detectives' Vauxhall, waiting for the oncoming traffic to pass on the two-laned road. Impatient horns began to blow. "You're not thinking straight, Tom."

As Gorman trotted back for the reflecting triangle a young man asked from an open window, "Wha's goen ahn up dare?"

"Breakdown," Gorman said. "We'll be moving in a minute."

The orange triangle was under the back wheel of one of the waiting cars. Gorman turned around and cantered back empty-handed.

"Are y'out for a walk or wha?" a man in a plumber's van barked after him.

"Are y'out taken a piss or wha?" a speckled teenage boy demanded.

"Would you get yer yoke off the fucking road?" a red-faced drunk shouted.

"Did you lose your dangler in the bushes?" a young woman screeched, then rolled up her window while she and her female passenger fell into paroxysms.

"Will yah move dah piece ah yella shite!" a man with a tiny trailer attached to his car commanded.

Gorman smiled to himself at the creativity of his fellows but ignored them all. With a sigh of relief he slammed the engine into gear and sped off.

In front of the National Bank near Smith's Corner in Mountmellick, Jimmy Gorman watched Tom Breen coming down the steps from the chemist across the street. When he plonked into the car, Breen shook the blue bottle, unscrewed the lid and drank.

"Jesus, Tom. Go easy on that or you'll surely get the trots."

"I don't care what I get as long as it settles my guts."

"There'll be nothing left in your guts to settle."

"Stop being my mother, Gorman." Breen was screwing the top back on when his phone rang. He found a level place for the bottle on the dashboard, wiped the white residue off his lips with a folded handkerchief and flipped his phone open. "Yes, sir."

"Where are you, Tom? I have some info for you."

"We're on the way back from Saint Fintan's, heading to Croghan Hill to see the other two pedophiles. Can I put you on speaker, sir, so Jimmy can hear?"

"Sure. Hello, Jimmy."

"Sir."

"You'll have to interview the two fellows on Croghan Hill another time. I just got word that they went by taxi to Portarlington station and bought tickets to Naas. The Plainers got on the train with them. I'm going to tell them to come back. What do you think, Tom?"

"I agree, sir. I don't believe Nailer kills without preparation, so even if he knows where these two are, I doubt he'll venture into unfamiliar territory."

Gorman nodded in agreement.

"Right, Tom. I'll bring them home. Next thing... there's no way we can get the Saint Kieran files. The Department of Education has tried before, even asked the Health people to help out…so, no luck there. Those lads must have an awful lot to hide. Next thing you know, we'll hear all the files got destroyed in a fire."

"That wouldn't surprise me," Gorman said. "I've often wondered why the Orders didn't burn them when they had to give up their schools."

"Next thing," Donovan said. "A reporter from *The Telegraph*, a fellow named McGovern—Mick McGovern—was in Portlaoise Garda Station a few hours ago and asked to see a case from 1980. I asked Portlaoise to send me the file just in case *The Telegraph* is onto something we don't know about. The file's about a fellow named Rackert; he was tied naked to a tree for calves to suck the entire bollicks out of him—and they did, too."

"Jesus!" Tom Breen moaned.

Gorman paled, then groaned and winced, and his two hands went to his crotch. "Fuck!" he said.

"It turns out that this lad Rackert worked for the Society for the Prevention of Cruelty to Children."

"The Crueltyman," Tom Breen said.

"Yes. Rackert was associated with Dachadoo and he lived in Mountmellick."

"Holy shit!" Gorman said.

"He was gagged with the arse of his own trousers; tied to the tree with baler twine and found on the morning of July fourth, 1980."

"Nailer!" Breen and Gorman said together.

"I didn't tell you the good part yet, Gorman. Rackert was also nailed to the tree with eight ten-penny nails."

"*Te Deum laudamus!*" Gorman almost shouted. He slapped the steering wheel. "Nailer's been doing his stuff for what?…twenty-seven years? He's been out there all that time and we only noticed him a few weeks ago when Jack the Bap was found. Who else has he killed?"

"Calm down, Gorman, for Christ's sake," Donovan said. "You're beginning to sound like an opera singer."

"How did *The Telegraph* get onto this lad Rackert, sir?" Breen asked.

But it was the excited Gorman who answered. "Because Rackert would have been mentioned in the Dachadoo files and *The Telegraph* has managed to get the files."

"Balderdash, Jimmy," the superintendent said. "The fecking Minister for Justice can't get those files, the Minister for Health can't get those files, the Minister for Education can't get those files. How the hell's *The Telegraph* going to get them?"

"They bought them, sir," Breen said. "There's always that weak link in the chain. All they had to do was find it."

"But how so quickly?"

"Maybe there are many rats in the ranks of the Brothers of Saint Kieran," Gorman said. "It *is* a sinking ship, sir."

Everyone went silent. Behind the Vauxhall, an articulated lorry built for autobahns began the laborious turn out of Church Open into Patrick Street. There was much shunting, grinding of gears and bursts of diesel smoke before the monster snarled itself around all obstacles and set off toward Tullamore.

"I have more," Superintendent Donovan said. "This reporter—McGovern—came in here to Tullamore too, just a few minutes ago. As thin as a fishing pole and hair like a thistle gone to seed; Dubliner and as rude as one, too; accent like a fruit seller in Moore Street, and he dressed like he was going for an interview with the archbishop of Dublin...pink shirt and green tie, creased suit of grey and his shoes like two suns."

"Get to the fecking point, Chris," Gorman muttered through his teeth.

"He was looking for the file on Paddy O'Malley from 1967—"

"O'Malley. Beatus. Michael O," Gorman yelped.

"—the very one I was reading from this morning. I told him it was an active file and not available; he kept talking about freedom of information. And now that I think about it, you're right, Jimmy. How could *The Telegraph* know about William Rackert and Paddy O'Malley unless they have the Dachadoo files? Those files are the only place where the two names could be in the same place."

"This McGovern, sir," Gorman said. "He's surely in this with Pauline Byron. If *The Telegraph* has the Dachadoo files, then they're ahead of us on this. They're going to name Nailer before we do." Gorman could not suppress the urgency in his voice. "Do you think we should—?"

Breen slapped Gorman on the thigh and cut him off, put his fingers across his lips like a nun telling a child to stop talking. "The one thing they don't have, sir, is Terry Kelly," Breen said.

"They do have Terry, Tom. Terry Kelly's name is in the *Leinster Express* report about Paddy O'Malley's suicide, Tom, and I phoned Terry an hour ago. *The Telegraph* had called him five minutes before I did. But he's not at home. His youngest daughter is house-sitting and Terry and the missus are in Zanzibar."

"Zanzibar? Where the fuck's Zanzibar?"

"Somewhere near Lake Tanganyika, where there are no telephone masts. He'll be there for another three weeks."

"At least that means *The Telegraph* won't be able to get to him either," Breen said.

"But if *The Telegraph* can get their hands on the Dachadoo files, would it be surprising if they found Terry through some newspaper office out there? Shite!" The two detectives heard the anxiety in the superintendent's voice. "If the fecking *Telegraph* names Nailer before we get the bastard, we'll all be arsed off to Wexford to watch over priests' zippers. In the meantime, are you and Jimmy going to the place where Brother Lazarian was gutted?"

Gorman looked at Breen, mouthed "gutted" and made a swimming fish with his hand. "Sir, if it's alright with you, I think Jimmy has an idea, at least he's behaving like he does or else he has to go to the jacks badly."

"Sir," Jimmy said, "your man, Paddy O'Malley—he killed himself on July the fifth, 1967. Brother Beatus was put into Saint Fintan's on July the eighteenth. We believe Brother Beatus just told us that he killed a boy in Dachadoo and that the boy's name was Michael O'Something. We think there might be a connection between Beatus's committal to Saint Fintan's, the death of Michael O'Something and the suicide of Paddy O'Malley."

"Jimmy, you *think* that the boy's name is O'Malley, but even if it is, what advantage over *The Telegraph* does that give us?"

"I don't know, sir. We have a load of things happening to people who were in contact with Dachadoo at the same time in July 1967: Paddy O'Malley's death; Brother Beatus's committal to Saint Fintan's; Boniface and Jack the Bap and Lazarian have suddenly turned up dead, and they were in Dachadoo in 1967. You have just connected this murdered William Rackert who worked for the SPCC to Dachadoo. Brother Beatus may have been hidden away in Saint Fintan's after killing a child whose name may have been Michael O'Malley, which could mean that he had killed the boy in July."

"Wouldn't his committal papers say he had murdered someone?"

"We were told he was diagnosed with a 'violent sexual dysfunction disorder,'" Breen said. "The brothers in Dachadoo were not going to tell anyone if he did indeed kill a child; they didn't want anyone poking around and finding out more than they were looking for."

"What about the child's death certificate?"

"I doubt the death certificate is going to give murder as the cause of death, sir," Breen said.

"Sir," Gorman said, "I think we have to look at the Order of Saint Kieran through new eyes. We have to look at it as an isolated group of maladjusted men who functioned in their own limited and self-made reality. And that reality is revealing itself to us as...as corrupt as the leadership of—"

"What are you getting at, Jimmy? You sound like a fecking professor. Spit it out!"

Gorman said quickly, "I believe the brothers would have had no problem disposing of a murdered child."

"Jesus, Jimmy! That's too much."

"Don't think of them as clergy, sir; think of them as a collection of institutionalized, emotionally underdeveloped men. Think of them as xenophobes who knew their sick system of living would wither under an outside spotlight. Think of Jim Jones in Guyana, sir."

For several seconds nobody spoke. Gorman suspected that Donovan's unexamined Catholic beliefs were under stress.

"What was that word, Jimmy? The one beginning with zed?" Donovan asked.

"Xenophobia, sir—fear of outsiders; Greek word; begins with an 'x.'" Gorman suspected that Donovan wasn't thinking about xenophobia.

"Alright, Jimmy, from now on I'll try to think of them as a crowd of weirdos. Still, I have to ask you: what if you do find out that this murdered child's name was O'Malley? How will it help us?"

"I'd like to answer that one, sir," Breen said. "If we can establish who the boy was, then we can find out if he had any siblings. He might even have had a sibling in Dachadoo. Paddy O'Malley was from Mountmellick. We're in

Mountmellick now and it'll only take a few minutes to
check the baptismal and burial records a few years each
side of July 1967."

"Alright lads, give it a try. Don't bother asking the parish priest. Talk to the nuns who work as the sacristans;
nuns know more about what goes on than anyone else,
keep tabs on the town by getting the children to write
compositions like 'What I Did during the Summer Holidays.' When you finish with the church records go down
to Tipperary for a look because they'll surely be sweeping
up Brother Lazarian before the day is out."

As they pulled away from the National Bank, Gorman
said, "We wrote the same compositions for the nuns in
Ballysteen. I think it was their way of trying to have some
normalcy in their miserable lives."

"Miserable?"

"Nuns," Gorman said. "Talk about repression! James
Joyce said that barbed wire was invented by a nun. And
why did you give me a whack when I was talking to the
supe?"

"I thought you were going to say we should speak to
Pauline Byron, ask *The Telegraph* to help us," Breen said.

"I was. How did you know?"

"I was thinking the same thing, especially after chatting to Pauline on Friday evening. She sounded like she
would be willing to help us without making a story of it for
The Telegraph. But if we do take her up on her offer and
it does turn into a mess, we don't want to have the supe
involved."

"Mess? How would it get messy just talking to her?"

"Gorman, sometimes your belief in human nature
needs a good sprinkling of reality, skepticism. *The Telegraph* and the Garda Síochána are in two different busi-
nesses; if it is advantageous to Pauline Byron's career and
the circulation of her paper, *The Telegraph* would knife the
gardai through the eye in two shakes of a drake's tail. If

we do talk to Pauline Byron we will have to be very careful."

Gorman pulled into the car park in front of the convent. "We'll lay down some ground rules with her...with Pauline Byron."

"Even so," Breen said, "we have to *know* that we can trust her. If she's going to give us something we'll have to give her something in return. But we have to be convinced that she won't run off waving her knickers around her head at our expense in *The Telegraph*."

Breen opened the car door and looked at the convent. "Let's see what we find out in here and then we'll talk about Pauline Byron. Maybe she really does have the Dachadoo files."

"Wanna bet?"

"How many times have I told you I don't bet?"

They walked up to the imposing, honey-colored front door and Gorman rang the bell. "How's your guts?" he asked.

"Much better, but I need a jacks. Do they have toilets in convents?"

"Of course not."

45.

"I'm a reporter from *The Telegraph*," Pauline Byron repeated loudly at Doctor Alexander McNulty's front door.

"My obituary? *The Telegraph* has...Did I—?" The old man's hands were shaking, and his entire lower jaw was trembling like a leaf caught in a breeze at the corner of a wall.

"I'm sorry if I'm bothering you, Doctor McNulty," Pauline said. "It's important that I speak to you."

The doctor held up a quivering handful of gnarled fingers. "No, no. Hold on a minute. I'm confused. I fell asleep under the paper and sometimes I feel dis...dis...disconnected when I wake up. My wife is dead...deceased."

"I'm sorry if I'm intruding. I didn't know you were in mourning."

"No...Not dead...deceased right now. She died some time ago, last year. Who are you?"

"Pauline Byron. I'm a reporter for *The Telegraph*."

"I know you, Miss Byron. I was just...did I just see your name on something in the paper? Terrible thing about those two brothers, and Brother Lazarian was just prayed for at mass, the holy sacrifice. I thought he was younger than me. I knew the others as well."

"May I come in for a few minutes?"

Crookedly, twisted slightly to his right side, the doctor led the way into the kitchen. Behind him the reporter's eyes registered the money and good taste that had been expended on the interior of the McNulty house. Across the dining room table she saw one of the French doors ajar, got an impression of a large and bright conservatory and its floating flowerpots.

The kitchen wasn't anything to write home about; everything about it, except for the ill-fitting, protruding refrigerator was from the nineteen fifties. But it was spacious, with a plain wooden table and four bentwood chairs under the window in the far wall.

The doctor stopped in front of the high, black Aga cooker, large enough to intimidate the most ambitious housewife. The wrinkled and wattled old man raised a mottled hand as if he was about to swear to tell the truth. "Tea?" he asked.

Afraid that any distraction might take the man's mind to the outer reaches of sensibility, Pauline turned down the offer.

For a moment the doctor stood there refocusing his thoughts. "Was it about the obituary?...I will sit over here at the table." Raspily, he dragged his loose slippers across the stone floor. "Elizabeth liked to look out at her nasturtiums from here. I made that fence for her—American. Abraham Lincoln used to split rails for a living and that's where she got the idea. Terrible job, splitting a long piece of..." The doctor dragged a chair from under the table. "*Naris* and *torquere*; nose twister; nasturtium; great smellers. She'd stand here kneading dough with the window open, mixing the fragrance into the flour. She'd say, 'Flower into flour.' She had all the colors: cream and crimson, orange and gold and red. Nothing left now only the haulms and I can't see them. The eyes. *Naris* and *torquere*; 'immersed in the bleak rigidities of the ancient tongues,' someone said. I always loved languages; they were not bleak to me."

Pauline, without invitation, pulled out a chair across from Alexander McNulty.

"You said you knew Brother Lazarian."

"And Brother John the Baptist. He died weeks ago. I saw that in the *Offaly Independent*. My obituary will be in it…I saw it. The editor let me read it. Two pages with—"

"Did you know a Brother Boniface?"

"Yes, big man with big hands. Dug up out of the bog fully formed, that lad; heather for eyebrows, bits of bog deal sticking out of his frontal lobes. West Offaly like your man at mass today. Lazarian and myself used to chuckle. Defi-*nite*-ly."

"Brother Boniface was found dead last Friday. Three brothers have died in about three weeks."

"Isn't that a coincidence!"

"No coincidence, Doctor McNulty. Did you know William Rackert?"

"William Rackert?" He tasted the words several times. "No. Was he a brother, too?"

"No. Did you know Brother Beatus?"

The doctor flapped his lips around the sounds. "Beatus? No. Why are you asking me about him? Did you come here to tell me Brother Lazarian died? He was prayed for at mass today. The holy sacrifice of the mass will be offered for the repose—isn't it a lovely word, repose, be at—"

"Doctor McNulty, I want you to think about Brother Lazarian, Brother John the Baptist and Brother Boniface. All three of them were assigned to Dachadoo when you were the medical officer there and all three of them have been murdered."

The wattles flapped, the wrinkles moved like wavelets on a pond surfaced with grey algae. "No, you're wrong."

"No, I am right, and they were murdered by the same person."

"No one would murder…kill Brother Lazarian. A saint of a man he—"

"Look at me, Doctor McNulty." Pauline rapped her knuckles on the tabletop. "Look at me. There is no question at all about how these men died; they were tortured and brutally murdered."

"But Brother Lazarian devoted his entire—"

"It doesn't matter what Brother Lazarian did. He was murdered. Boniface and John the Baptist were murdered. I want you to answer a question for me that might help find the killer. Are you listening?" Pauline rapped the table again and McNulty refocused on her face. "Keep looking at my eyes, Doctor, and answer my question. How many boys died in Dachadoo when you were the medical officer there?"

"None. Not one."

Surprised by his immediate response, Pauline believed McNulty was answering some other question he'd heard in his head.

She spoke louder, put force into her voice. "Doctor McNulty, how many boys died while you were the medical officer at Dachadoo?"

"None. I said none." A weak fire glowed in the doctor's eyes. "No boy died when I was the doctor at Dachadoo. Not one. Brother Lazarian was devoted to those boys, took care of them, stayed up at night with the sick ones. He was as good as Father Damien with the lepers. Lepers they were, too. He was a father to all those...those terrible—"

Pauline waited for him to finish. His lower jaw moved up and down as if it were trying to get hold of a word, give shape to a fading thought.

"He was a father to all those terrible...?" Pauline prompted.

"Dung," the doctor said, and fire flared in his eyes. "The dung of society, they were; the scrapings of whores' wombs. But I did my duty for the sake of Christ. And *he* did it, Brother Lazarian, out of pure love, devotion, vocation. He was a father to them. A saint, that man was. *Nous lépreux*. He kissed their hurts and sprains. He wrapped his arms around them in love, but I only took care of them out of duty to Christ—a duty, but I did it; 'as long as you did it to one of these my least brethren, you did it to me.' Brother Lazarian was kind to everyone, to me too. He did everything to keep my visits..." The doctor drifted off.

Pauline waited, hoping he would finish the sentence. She waited in vain.

"Brother Lazarian did everything to keep your visits... to keep your visits what, Doctor McNulty?" she prompted him again. But the doctor had lost that particular train of thought in the gathering fog enclosing his brain.

Pauline summoned McNulty back to the present with another sharp rap on the scrubbed wood. He jerked as if he'd touched a live wire, his wattles shook, the wrinkles lapped against each other, the lower jaw yapped silently.

"How many boys died when you were the medical officer in Dachadoo?"

"I told you that not one boy died when I—"

"Then why is your signature on nineteen death certificates dated during the years you were the medical man there?"

"What are you talking about? Why are you tormenting me? No boy died when I was working in Dachadoo—not one boy." The fire in the eyes burst into flame, and amid a lot of noise and with a lot of effort, the doctor tottered to his feet. His grasping fingers at the table's edge were the claws of a very old turkey. "I am a dying man. My obituary will tell you how I was respected in this town for more than fifty years, how I served those...those...in Dachadoo with no recompense, compensation, payment. Even if I did dislike the place, not one boy died; not one while I was the doctor. Now leave me alone to die in peace. Get out of my house."

Pauline stood up. "Why did you dislike Dachadoo, Doctor McNulty?"

"Because...because..."

Pauline could see the old eyes going away. She tried to haul them back. "Because why? Why did you hate Dach-adoo?"

"Because, because *lasciate ogne speranza, voi ch'intrate.*"

"What does that mean?"

"*Lasciate ogne speranza, voi ch'intrate.*" The doctor limped out through the kitchen door, the heels of the slippers lisping after him.

Pauline caught up with him before he reached the front door. She touched his arm. "Doctor McNulty, before I leave I have to tell you—"

The old man stopped and looked at Pauline. "Before God, before his son Jesus, before Mary his mother," he said, "my life was a life of service."

"I must tell you—"

"I must tell *you* to leave my house. Go away. You are not welcome here." The doctor pointed a shaking hand at the kitchen door. "Leave my house. *Saevitia in una femina et in hominibus sentum aequa est.*"

"There is a list, Doctor McNulty, and your name is on—"

"It's a lie. It's all in the obituary, how I served them. Now go. You are upsetting me." While he groped in the gloom for the knob of the Yale lock, Pauline said, "There is a—"

"Leave my house now."

When the door closed behind her, Pauline took out her pen and wrote *lasciate...speranza* and *in una femina et in hominibus sentum* in her notebook. Without looking back she walked up the pebbled path to the iron gate.

Before unlatching the gate she wrote: *Lazarian did every-thing to keep McNulty's visits...; scrapings of whores' wombs; dung of society.*

Back in her car, Pauline phoned Mick McGovern.

"Where are you, Mick?"

"Car park behind the Tullamore Dew Heritage Centre, using their wireless connection, working on Asparagus."

"Good. Can you Google something for me while I have the sounds in my head? I've just come out of Doctor McNulty's place and he used a phrase that might be significant; I think I got two words. They may be Latin; *l-a-s-c-i-a-t-e*, then *speranza* like Oscar Wilde's mammy without the initial 'e.'"

"Google asks, did you mean *lasciate ogne speranza?*"

"That's the missing word—*ogne.*"

"It's from *The Divine Comedy*; it's what's on the office door in your kitchen. When Dante passes through the gate of hell, on it is inscribed—excuse my Italian—*Lasciate ogne speranza, voi ch'intrate.*"

"Abandon all hope ye who enter here," Pauline said.

"Does that give you something?"

"Confusion is what it gives me. McNulty was all praise for this Brother Lazarian, even canonizing him for his devotion to the children in Dachadoo, but at the same time McNulty saw the place as hell. He even compared it to the leper colony in Hawaii where the Mother Teresa of Molokai—that French priest, Damien—did his thing. Before you get off the Internet...McNulty threw some Latin proverb at me and I only caught some familiar words: *in una femina et in hominibus sentum.*"

"I know that one. *Saevitia in una femina et in hominibus sentum aequa est.* One woman is as cruel as a hundred men."

"Jesus, Mick!" Pauline sounded like she'd been hit in her solar plexus. "I'll admit I was tough on him but...I'll tell you later. Did you get those files on William Rackert and Paddy O'Malley? Wait...don't tell me. Stay where you are. We have to compare notes and plot some plans and we should get something to eat. I'm so hungry I could eat the leg of the Lamb of God."

46.

When Pauline eased into the space beside the brown Volkswagen at the Tullamore Dew Heritage Centre, McGovern was using the roof of his car as a bench while he velcroed his laptop into its case.

Pauline stepped out of her jeep. "Taking precautions against the local kleptos, Mick?" she asked.

"My satnav is in my pocket and if I could, I'd fold up my VW and take it with me, too," McGovern mocked back. "Where in this metropolis do we get a sandwich free of malodorous farmyard garnishes?"

"There's a cafe in the heritage centre. We'll be walking beside the canal for a bit to get to it. I should warn you that a Dublin accent in these parts—not to mention sarcastic comments about the hinterland—could land a fellow in the canal, laptop and all."

"Jealousy," McGovern said. "They'd rather be chic than hick, too."

"You'll have to get out more, Mick, blow the pollution of big-city self-importance out of your brain." Pauline leaned into her jeep and came back with her computer.

"So, you don't trust the natives either?" McGovern said.

Pauline held up the laptop. "I'm not protecting it," she said. "I'm going to use mine in the cafe."

"Great minds think alike," McGovern said.

In the eye-searing, silver winter sunlight, McGovern and Pauline wended their way through parked cars until they emerged onto Bury Quay. The low sun glared its reflected rays out of the canal. With shielding hands to

their foreheads, the two reporters continued their trek
along the narrow footpath beside the buildings as the
side mirrors of passing cars came within inches of their
elbows. Pauline stopped suddenly and held a green, large-
paned door open for McGovern. Inside, they waited for
their eyes to adjust before heading for the food counter
at the back.

"That kind of sunlight makes me nauseous," Pauline
said.

"It's the slurry and the silage make me nauseous,"
McGovern said.

"Jesus, Mick, surely you can't get the rural aroma in
here?"

"You're inured or your nose isn't working," McGovern
said. "I can smell it off people's clothes."

"So it must be on your clothes, too. When you go
home your wife won't let you back in the house. You'll
have to burn everything, bathe in diesel fumes and apply
parfum de Liffé, and scrub the Brown Bug."

They gave their order to the counter worker—a tall,
good-looking and well-spoken young woman. She recognized Pauline and congratulated her on her exposé of
F. X. Culliton.

As the reporters worked their way to the most remote
table, people looked up from their plates, some whispered to each other.

When they sat down, McGovern leaned across the
table and stage-whispered, "You're a personality."

"God between us and all harm, as my mother would
say," Pauline said, then dismissed the flattery by diving
straight into the business at hand. "You go first," she said.
"What did you find out at the garda stations?"

"Tullamore wouldn't let me see the file on Paddy
O'Malley's suicide; they even brought the superintendent
down—Donovan—to persuade me to leave. He said the
file is still active and not available to the press."

"So Donovan and Breen may be trying to connect the O'Malleys, fit them into the picture, with the dead religious brothers," Pauline said.

"Looks like it." McGovern dug his notebook out of his inside pocket. "William Rackert's file in Portlaoise had some interesting items that were not published in *The Leinster Express*. For one thing, as well as baler twine, nails were used to secure him to the tree."

Excitement raised Pauline's voice by an octave. "It's him for sure—Snipper. How many years ago was this?"

"Nineteen-eighty. Twenty-seven years. Snipper was killing twenty-seven years ago, if he *did* kill Rackert."

"Maybe William Rackert was his first and last until your man in Carrowreagh, Bapper John," Pauline said. "If Snipper did kill people between Rackert and Bapper, surely the guards would have noticed a common thread, a common background of the victims. Alright…what's next?"

McGovern looked at his notes. "A sergeant, Tony Lynch, wrote this report about Rackert and I'm quoting: *The hands were pulled around toward the back of the tree and nailed in place through the wrists; the feet were nailed through the arches; each deltoid muscle was nailed through to keep the victim upright. Each quadriceps femoris was nailed.*" McGovern touched his thigh above the knee. "*All the nails were ten-penny. The seat had been cut out of the victim's trousers and pushed into his mouth, held in place with a piece of baler twine that went all the way around the tree to keep the head pulled up as well as to keep the gag in.*" McGovern looked up.

"Was the penis cut off?" Pauline asked.

McGovern looked up from his notes. "If the object of the exercise was to fool the calves into believing they'd get milk from the man's dangling particle, then it was probably left in situ."

"Nice, Mick. Dumb question."

"The report does say that the penis was never found. And before we leave the field of hungry calves…do you want to know the condition of the body when the calves were finished with it?"

"I do and I don't."

"Alright, I'll use some euphemisms. To Sergeant Lynch it seemed the cows with their long horns had joined in the fun...what do you call those things full of goodies that children in Mexico break apart with sticks at parties?"

"Piñatas?"

"Yes, piñatas. Well, William Rackert's body was a piñata to the bovine mothers and children. They had a real party. All the goodies fell out and were trampled into the ground."

"That will do, Mick. It sounds like you're enjoying this."

"I'm not enjoying it. This is the only way to talk about it to a member of the delicate sex."

"Delicate or not, I've heard enough about this particular birthday party."

McGovern turned a page. "This is a direct quote from the file: *The industrial schools needed live bodies to keep their per capita income coming in from the government. It is known that William Rackert of the Society for the Prevention of Cruelty to Children was paid by Dachadoo School to keep them supplied with replacements.*"

"*What?* Did they put in an order with Rackert for a child the way a shopkeeper puts in an order for sausages?"

"The government payment to the school stopped on the boys' sixteenth birthdays, and ready or not, the boys were released into the wild. Still quoting from the file: *William Rackert was a pub poker-player and a braggart. He created his own onerous reputation by removing children from their families on the slightest pretext. Most of his victims came from poor and uneducated households. One account related to this officer had William Rackert driving his car onto the bog on his way to the judge in Portlaoise. In the car he had three brothers who were ten, nine and six years old. Rackert put the boys out of the car and made them change into tattered clothing he'd brought along. He threatened to abandon the boys on the bog unless they daubed their faces and arms and legs with bog dirt, wet their hair with boghole water and stand in bog water until it seeped into their boots. It could be concluded that one of William Rackert's victims caught up with him."*

McGovern looked up. "This copper does not write like your average copper and, you're right, this William Rackert was a child dealer. Also, he was not a nice human being."

But Pauline didn't hear the last remark. She was staring at something twelve miles off over McGovern's shoulder. "If my girls were taken when they were chil..."

With a gentle "ahem," McGovern got Pauline's attention and closed the notebook. "Sergeant Lynch tried to get at the files of Dachadoo School but of course he failed. When I was leaving the Portlaoise Garda Station I got chatting with the desk sergeant, an old man with a withered arm. He told me Tony Lynch spent a lot of his own time tracing men who'd been sent to Dachadoo during William Rackert's years with the SPCC, but he never found anyone to fit the time frame. Emigration to England was at full flood in the sixties and seventies when Rackert was prowling the countryside. Sergeant Lynch surmised the killer could have been someone who came home for a few days just to get Rackert, might even have been one of the boys he'd forced to dress down."

"I'm wrestling with the urge to sympathize with Snipper," Pauline said. "William Rackert deserved what he got."

"If you don't mind me saying so, you wouldn't say that if you owned a penis and some testicles."

Pauline raised her eyes to the ceiling and then continued. "If Bapper John and Boniface and Lazarian were as guilty as William Rackert in the eyes of Snipper, then they deserved what they got, too."

"People have different reactions to a serial killer in their midst. Yours is one of them—sympathy," McGovern said.

"But is Snipper a serial killer at all? A serial killer has no motive that a sane person can understand, which implies serial killers are mad. But Snipper's victims, as far as we can tell, were all involved in *some one thing* that he has decided requires retribution. Maybe he was waiting for someone else to do the retribution but acted when he feared his victims would soon die off. Three of his victims were old, each with one foot in the grave. Or maybe he had a different motive for going after Rackert—maybe he just couldn't wait to get his hands on him. I think when he has killed a specific number of people, he will stop. Maybe he's stopped already."

"There's still four names left on that Dachadoo list—the two Bennets, Beatus and Doctor McNulty."

"He has no reason to go after the Bennets; they're among the good guys—unless of course Snipper has decided that they stood around with their hands in their pockets while their fellow brothers wreaked havoc on young lives. Beatus might as well be in prison as in Saint Fintan's; McNulty is holding on to the perch with one toe." Pauline continued, "As far as our list is concerned, Snipper is finished. He's punished people that the state has failed to pursue and punish. Except for Rackert, his victims were clergymen. The clergy may have been the only educated people in Irish society in the time of the English, but now they're quickly slipping down the rungs of the power ladder. When the English left in 1922, the country's politicians were in thrall to the clergy. We have all remained in thrall to them far too long. But their time is past. Most bishops and archbishops are self-deluded princes, costumed martinets, living in their palaces with their housekeepers and drivers and secretaries and hangers-on. Remember the Ferns Report? Bishops don't even have a job description. They do next to nothing. And they are all so isolated that when the clerical sex-abuse epidemic surfaced, their first and only consideration was the safety and welfare of the institutional church's arse; they didn't give one flying fuck about the abused children. They're nothing but a plague on the land. It's time the lot of them were told to fuck off."

McGovern glanced around the other tables to see if any ears were leaning in their direction. When Pauline paused in her speech, he said, "I have a feeling the clergy will be offered that advice very soon."

"What do you mean?" she asked.

"You're identifying with Snipper. If you discover he's not a serial killer, just a man who has done what the state, society, failed to do, then the doors are wide open for you to ride in and shine a spotlight on the doings of the church ever since it grabbed political power after the British left. Remember, for decades Dublin was the city in the shadow of the archbishop's house; generations of politicians were cowed by Archbishop John Charles McQuaid—as political an animal as Pius the Twelfth; and there was the clerical ouster of Noel Brown with his Mother and Child Scheme. Even today, many local communities are ruled by latter-day witch doctors."

"That's work for historians, Mick."

"Who reads history books? You have your name. You have the paper. The paper has Rafferty. You could daub some ink on clerical collars."

"That's a huge undertaking, Mick, and come hell or high water, Raymond and I are going to New Zealand early in the New Year." Then Pauline said, "Of course, together, you and I could get the project onto its feet and you could keep it running while I'm away…equal billing."

Pauline watched the blood rise in McGovern's face, saw the tensing of his fingers. "Thanks. That's very generous of you, Ms. Byron and—"

"Oh, for God's sake, Mick, will you call me Pauline?"

"Thanks, Pauline."

"You're an excellent reporter, Mick, and you know it. I'll talk to Jack Rafferty, but you'll have to fight him yourself for a raise." Pauline turned around and wrestled with her jacket hanging on the back of her chair. She returned with her notebook.

"Let me tell you about Doctor McNulty with his languages and his convenient slipping in and out of forgetfulness...and I *wasn't* cruel to him. What did he say? One woman is as cruel as a hundred men? The fecking misogynist. He has burnished his reputation for posterity and he was afraid I'd tarnish it."

47.

In the Tullamore Dew Heritage Centre, Pauline was describing her unceremonious ejection from Doctor McNulty's classical farmhouse when the counter girl arrived with the food. The two reporters moved their laptops onto the spare chairs at their table.

"Are you a local?" Pauline asked the girl.

"As local as local can get, Miss Byron," she replied. "I'm third-generation Tullamore."

"What's your name?"

"Clara. I'm named after Clara Schumann," she said, "*not* after Clara town here in County Offaly."

"My, my," Mick McGovern said, "are we defensive or what?"

"Yes, we are! Most people think it's the town I'm called after but I always *cla*rify—get it? The first time my boyfriend drove through Clara it was a wet day and he reacted by saying"—Clara lowered her voice and bent forward—"'What a fucking dreary amalgamation of shite!'"

The reporters laughed.

"Chicken for you, Miss Byron." She put the plate in front of Pauline and gave McGovern the fish sandwich.

"This is my colleague, Mick McGovern, Clara."

"Hello, Mick."

"Hello, Clara. Are you a student?" McGovern asked.

"Yes. Law in Trinity."

"What's your last name?" Pauline asked,

"McNulty, and yes, I am related to Doctor McNulty, that bastion of something or other who's been in Tullamore since the arrival of the *Tuatha dé Dana,* who lives in the nineteenth-century classical farmhouse. I'm his youngest grandchild and he's my identity."

Pauline had an urgent need to glance at McGovern. "How do you mean? He's your identity?"

"In Tullamore, I'm not Clara McNulty; I'm Doctor McNulty's granddaughter. My father is Doctor McNulty's son; my mother is Doctor McNulty's daughter-in-law. We have this burden to bear—we're saddled with the myth of the great man."

"So, with a name like McNulty you've got to be good," McGovern said.

"Perfection is demanded." Clara grinned. "And with a name like Clara! The burdens our parents place on us when we're born! My children will have ordinary names like Paudie and Brudgie." She laughed. "And I'd better get back to the counter. Excuse me."

As she walked away McGovern's eyes stayed glued to Clara until she disappeared behind the counter. "'A violet by a mossy stone, half hidden from the eye…,'" he said.

"'Fair as a star when only one is shining in the sky,'" Pauline finished. "She is beautiful, Mick, and you're mooning like an adolescent. Maybe your wife should come with you when you're sent out to the boonies, hold your hand."

When the plates were finally pushed aside, Pauline and McGovern wrote up their day's findings and sent them to the Asparagus file.

McGovern logged off first and he stared at the tabletop while he waited for Pauline. When Pauline folded down her screen, he said, "I think we have to tell the guards about McNulty, about his name on that page in Brother Lazarian's journal."

"Yes," Pauline said. "We'd be guilty of something or other if he turns up nailed to his dining room table in the morning. What do you think of having a meeting with Detective Breen and sidekick?"

"You made them that offer on Friday and they turned it down."

"We didn't know then what we know now. They know that we went after the William Rackert and Paddy O'Malley files, and they've probably concluded that the only way we could have connected the names was by reading the Dachadoo files. And even if they haven't figured it out, we can whet their curiosity by telling them we have the files. Then we can bargain with them. We tell them something, they tell us something before the competition gets hold of it."

"Could they arrest us for withholding information in a murder investigation?" McGovern asked.

"I don't know. But I don't think they'll demand to see the Dachadoo files. The way the files were procured in the first place might cause a problem for the Director of Public Prosecutions."

"Then let's give it a go," McGovern said.

"We can phone that mobile number Tom Breen called me from on Friday. I suspect it belongs to his Tonto."

"If we're going to make an unofficial approach—a covert approach—we can't use mobiles; they're worse than Hansel's pebbles."

"We can use a public phone and give him a number to contact us at."

"Good idea...and at the same time we can unload responsibility for McNulty onto them."

"If Tom Breen agrees to a get-together, the actual meeting place is going to be a problem for him. He'll have to keep his garda arse protected. We should have a place in mind that's safe for him so he can't use fear of discovery as an excuse."

"He'd hardly go for a public place or a bar or a restaurant unless it was far from here. What's that place on the Curragh? The Standhouse Hotel?"

"We're in Ireland, Mick. You can't go anywhere without running into someone you know. Breen will have to be *certain* he will not be seen talking to us. I was thinking of some place up on Slieve Bloom, but even on the loneliest road up there you're going to meet walkers." Pauline paused. "Maybe the Rock of Dunamase…but there's no place to hide the cars, and it's too close."

Clara McNulty arrived at the table with an empty tray. "Are you interested in a sweet?" she asked.

"No sweet for me. Just coffee, please…Clara, we're trying to outdo each other here. What is the most godforsaken place in Ireland that you've ever been in? So godforsaken it's almost scary."

"Dachadoo," Clara replied without hesitation. "It was a school for homeless boys. And it's here in County Offaly, out in the middle of the bog. Nothing but curlews. It's all closed up now, all ivy and nettles and briars, but there are a few ways to get in. We—some school friends, five of us— went there on a dare once on Halloween in the daytime. We had to stay for one hour. It's a haunted place."

"Haunted?" McGovern asked.

"Not ghosts or any of that stuff. But it was like the walls were reaching out to touch us like the arms of an octopus. We stood in the one place for the hour holding each other, shivering, afraid to look around. It was the weirdest…It gives me the heebie-jeebies just thinking about it. One girl started saying the rosary out loud and we all joined in, ended up shouting it out at the tops of our voices." Clara shivered a flock of geese away from her grave. "Jesus, I thought I was over that. What about you… what's your most godforsaken place?"

Unprepared for the question, the reporters looked at each other. Pauline spoke first. "You go first, Mick," she said.

"The vaults of Saint Michan's in Dublin with the mummies," McGovern threw out.

"I went there when I was ten and I thought it was great," Clara said. "How about you, Miss Byron?"

"A cemetery for unbaptized babies on Achill Island, the one at the edge of a cliff outside Dugort. As well as being the most godforsaken place, it was the saddest."

Clara McNulty touched Pauline on the upper arm. "I didn't know there were such things—cemeteries for the unbaptized. That's cruel."

"Every bit as cruel and stupid as the Spanish Inquisition or going to hell for eating meat on Fridays, or the perfidious Jews or the Children's Crusade."

For a moment after Pauline's self-revelation there was silence. Then, as if to break a spell that had enveloped the table, Clara said, "Right then...and coffee for you too, Mick?" She went away.

"Dachadoo it is, Pauline. I admire your opportunism."

"You were too busy trying to see through her clothes, Mick. Yes, I think Dachadoo is the place to meet Breen. So, what do you think of this plan: you drive to Mountmellick and find out what you can about Paddy and Michael O'Malley. Try the nuns. They have the longest and most detailed institutional memory in any town. I'll go to Ballyglass to talk to the Geoghan family. They might know something of value."

Pauline's phone rang. She glanced at the screen. "Rafferty," she said. She leaned toward McGovern and held the phone away from her ear.

"I see you've updated Asparagus," Jack Rafferty began, without any pleasantries. "This story is developing greyhounds' legs. Mahoney the archbishop just called to ask us to soften the coverage of the murdered brothers, keep it off the first page."

"I hope you told him to feck off," Pauline said.

"Not precisely...but I did say, 'From the blind and pompous folly of inflated functionaries, deliver me. Go to hell, sir!' Nearly all the big European dailies are in on it,

along with New York's *Daily News* and *Post*, San Francisco's
Chronicle, Canberra's *Times*...We'll be all over the world
tomorrow. People love a serial killer."

"Oh, what a lovely killer...," Pauline tried to sing. "You
sound happy, Jack."

"I feel great, Pauline. Tomorrow 'Serial Killer' will be
in our headlines. Stretching the story back to the grisly
death of William Rackert in 1980 adds a hefty splash of
vindaloo to the stew. The advertising chaps are getting
calls asking about Christmas. What are you and McGovern doing next?"

"Mick is sitting here listening in."

"Hello, Mick," Jack said.

"Hello, Mister Rafferty," Mick said.

"I hope you're not going to discover who Snipper is
for a while yet; give him time for the Christmas advertising."

"Jack, I don't think Snipper is a serial—"

"Every definition of serial killer the Diggers found fits
this fellow. A serial killer is someone who murders three
or more people in three or more separate events over a
period of time for largely psychological gratification."

"If you go back to Asparagus, Jack, you'll see that—"

"I can read, Pauline. I read—"

"Goddammit, Jack. Will you let me finish?" Pauline
snapped, and Mick McGovern looked around at the other
diners. They were all listening.

He touched Pauline's arm. "*Parietes habent aures,*" he
said.

Pauline glanced around. "Hang on a minute, Jack—
and don't hang up before you make a big mistake." She
stood up and walked the gauntlet of staring eyes to the
front door.

"That's Pauline Byron!" someone whispered sufficiently loud to draw attention to himself. Mick McGovern picked up the two laptops, paid the bill, said goodbye

to Clara McNulty and left the heritage centre. When he emerged into the November sunlight he saw Pauline standing beside the canal fifty yards away. She was gesticulating with her free hand. McGovern stepped across the narrow street and stared into the canal's murky waters. He waited.

When Pauline finally joined him she said, "He saw it my way. He's not going to use the nickname Snipper— every time people read 'Snipper' they'll think of a dick being severed. He'll use 'The Avenger.' If it turns out that we do an investigative series, 'The Avenger' will garner more sympathy, will have more appeal as someone who was grievously hurt in the past. He'll be a man that everyone who's ever been hurt can sympathize with."

"That's everyone in the world, Pauline."

"It is indeed."

48.

The old nun who opened the door to Breen and Gorman introduced herself as Sister Assumpta. With the loose habit, the paunch, the grin and the wrinkles, she looked like a female Friar Tuck just after stepping out of the bushes in Sherwood Forest. Her face was encased in an old-fashioned wimple and the beads of an enormous rosary—sufficiently large to brain a sheriff wearing an iron helmet—rattled with each step taken. She fluttered when told she was in the presence of two detectives.

"First thing, sister," Breen said, a fleck of dried milk of magnesia at the corner of his mouth, "may I use a bathroom?"

Sister Assumpta showed Breen to the bathroom, led him in and showed him how everything worked, including how to flush. She waited outside the door until he had finished.

When Gorman asked if she would show them some parish records Sister Assumpta flapped her wings. By the time they reached the church sacristy she was shamelessly bragging. As she unlocked the sacristy door she told the men that she had taught boys who were now guards; one of her students had become a lecturer in Oriental literature in Downing College in Cambridge, and he still sent her a Christmas card each year. Then there were the girls: "One is a barrister—the smartest child I ever taught—and two are doctors...Which do you want first? Marriages or baptisms?" she asked

"Marriages between 1950 and 1960," Gorman said.

Sister Assumpta unlocked a small cabinet door and dragged out a large register with a red and gold marbleized pattern on the cover. "What name?" she asked, as she placed the book on the vesting bench.

"O'Malley, Patrick. We don't know his wife's name."

"If he was called Paddy and drowned himself in the Grand Canal in Tullamore on July the fifth in 1967," Sister Assumpta said, "his wife's name was Maura and their children were James and Michael."

The two detectives glanced at each other, and each saw in the other the sparkling eyes of the hunter who has seen the wild pig stirring in the bushes.

"Fu...for the love of God, Sister," Gorman gasped. And before he could help himself he said, "Michael oh. Beatus. James is the—"

Breen grabbed Gorman's upper arm and squeezed it hard, told him to remember the walls had large nunnish ears.

"How do you know those names, Sister?" Breen asked, his voice higher than usual.

"How do I know? How could I *not* know?" Sister Assumpta paged through the register. She found the year she was looking for and ran her finger down the left-hand column. "Here...Patrick James O'Malley married Maura K. Beglin on May the second, 1954. Do you want best man and bridesmaid?"

"No," Gorman said, his voice a controlled shout. Then, remembering his manners, he said, "No, thank you, Sister. You said, how could you *not* know about the O'Malleys, Sister. What do you mean?"

Sister Assumpta closed the register and rested an elbow on the bench. "The O'Malleys' story is one of the family tragedies that the church and the Irish state created together. How could anyone forget their story, even if was fairly typical except for the father's suicide? Do you want anything else out of this?" She patted the register with a plump hand.

"No, thank you."

"Do you want me to look up the births of the two boys?"

If Gorman had been a small child he would have been holding the front of his trousers and dancing. "Yes, please. But tell us about the O'Malleys, Sister." When the nun turned her back, Gorman mimed a man hand-cranking a Baby Ford into life. Breen heard Jimmy hissing, "For Christ's sake, tell us."

While she spoke, Sister Assumpta stowed away the marriage records and took out a second volume. On the outside it was a twin of the first. "Michael O'Malley was a student in my classroom when the whole thing happened; James was already in the Boys' School—he was never in my class and I didn't know him at all—just saw him in the playground. What happened to the family was a terrible shameful and cruel thing that should never have happened; lives destroyed for a few pounds." She dropped the birth register heavily on the vesting bench. "When it happened, the rest of the children in my classroom—the rest of the children in the whole school—developed a kind of a...a hysterical nervousness, all terrified that the guards would come to take them away...kidnap them."

The nun ran her fingers down the columns. "It was all too dreadful...Here it is, almost nine months to the day. James Thomas O'Malley, born on February the seventh, 1955. James was twelve when he was taken."

As Sister Assumpta flipped forward through the book the sound of the heavy pages slapping onto each other swished through the stale air of the sacristy. Again, the old knuckle-knotted finger ran down the column. Again, Gorman cranked up the Baby Ford behind the nun.

"Without looking at this I can tell you that Michael Francis O'Malley was born on June the sixth, 1959, and was eight when he was taken. Michael was a lovely child in manner and appearance. Yellow hair cut long enough to let the curls spring back into place. He was the spitting image of Rubens's daughter Clara Serena." Sister Assumpta said this as if Peter Paul was living across the street. The two detectives looked at each other.

"Sister Assumpta—" Gorman began, and Breen recognized the edgy tone in his voice. Breen squeezed his partner's arm again and interrupted. "Sister, can you tell us what happened to the O'Malley family?"

"Do you want the story in a nutshell or with all the details?" Sister Assumpta asked. She closed the register, turned and leaned against the vesting bench. Her hands fell down and she held on to her outsized rosary.

"We're in a bit of a hurry," Tom Breen said. "So if you would give us the short version you might let us come back for the details if we need them."

The old nun moved the wimple on her forehead and a thin, red line was left where the headdress had been. Her demeanor in comparison to Jimmy Gorman's was that of a glacier to a frothing mountain torrent.

"Paddy O'Malley was in London, working on the buildings to support his wife and children. Maura developed galloping T.B. and died quickly in July 1967, just before school closed for the summer holidays. Paddy O'Malley, of course, came home for Maura's funeral. Immediately after the burial our SPCC representative, a mean, cruel beast of a man named Rackert, went to Paddy's house with two guards and took the boys away to that terrible place."

Sister Assumpta held out her hands to convey she was indulging in an aside: "Rackert was in the Hill Bar that night playing poker and he bragged about how he had got his forty pieces of silver." The nun lowered her hands back to the beads. "When Rackert took off with the boys toward Tullamore and Daingean—I can't or won't

mention the name of that concentration camp—Paddy
O'Malley went after them in Father Nannery's motor with
Maura's bike in the boot. Father Nannery came home
by himself and the next thing we knew Paddy was found
drowned in the canal in Tullamore. The shock of it! Nothing was ever heard of the two boys again. I wrote to that
place many times, even wrote to the bishop hoping he
could get the brothers to answer my letters. But knowing
what I know now about bishops, I don't believe the letter
was ever read. After all, it was only from some nun."

Achingly, Sister Assumpta pushed herself away from
the vesting bench and stood up straight. "That's it in a
nutshell, gentlemen. I will add something that gives me
pleasure to dwell on and which is a matter of confession for me. Mister Rackert met with a dreadful death.
He was murdered in a way that is embarrassing for me
to describe...in 1980, in a field out near the Lime Tree.
Sometimes God takes his revenge in this life."

Sister Assumpta suggested tea and sweet cake for the
detectives, but Gorman thanked her and turned down
the offer. "But if we are ever coming through Mountmellick, can we take you up on your invitation?" he asked.

"Of course," the nun said, and she smiled with pleasure. She showed them out of the sacristy without bringing
them back through the convent.

Before the sacristy door was completely closed, Gorman gushed, "Tom, we have him and his name is James
O'Malley." He slapped Breen on the shoulder. Each went
to his own side of the Vauxhall. "We have the fucker and
we'll have him by the short hairs before Pauline Byron
and *The Telegraph* know what hit them." He dug for his
mobile in his breast pocket. "I'm going to call the lads in
Phoenix Park and they'll have his address in—"

He was about to flip open the phone when it rang.
He glanced at the screen, did not recognize the number.
"Yes?"

"I am about to give you a phone number," the caller said in a Dublin accent. "Detective Breen should call it within thirty minutes from a phone box. Are you ready for the number?"

"McGovern?" Gorman asked, and he glanced at Breen who had his elbows on the roof of the car, waiting.

The voice paused for a millisecond. "Yes," McGovern said, and he gave a number. Gorman wrote in the dust on the roof of the car with his finger.

"Give me one good reason why Detective Breen should call you."

"We have the Dachadoo files."

Gorman looked as stunned as a man who'd been shit on by a flying cow. "There's a phone box outside the post office in Mountmellick," McGovern continued. "The post office is on the Tullamore side of the Square. It's the only working public phone in the area."

Trying to exude nonchalance, Gorman said, "Thank you. That will save us the trouble of running all over the place like two Keystone Kops with our heads up our arses."

"It will, Tonto," McGovern said.

"Tonto! Who the fuck's Tonto?" Gorman asked, but McGovern had hung up.

Gorman was unable to suppress this added voltage to his excitable self. "Tom, that was McGovern, Pauline Byron's yeoman; they have the Dachadoo files."

Breen suddenly became a man who's stepped on a yellow jacket nest in long grass, afraid to lift his foot because he knows he's going to have his arse stung off. "Shite!" he said. "They have to know what we just found out...James O'Malley. Fuck!" In a rare display of emotion, Breen kicked the door of the Vauxhall. "Fuck!"

"McGovern gave that number." Gorman indicated the writing in the dust. "You're to call it on a public phone within thirty minutes. He said there's a phone box up at the post office here in Mountmellick."

"That was decent of him," Breen said. "How does he know we're in Mountmellick?"

"Maybe he doesn't know. He just said it's the only working public phone in the area. Thirty minutes, and we haven't even had time to—"

"Pauline Byron is calling the shots," Breen said.

"Even if she is, we can't afford a pissing match here, Tom. Remember *we* were thinking of contacting *her*."

"It's not a pissing match at all, Jimmy. I feel I'm on overload. If we *do* talk to her we'll have to play it by ear— figure out as we go along what information we can swap with her. I hate being in that position. Let me think for a minute." Breen turned and walked along the car park toward the entrance to the convent garden.

"I'm calling the Phoenix Park lads," Gorman called after him.

Breen waved a hand in response. When he reached the ornate garden gate he grasped an iron bar with each hand. He let his head fall forward and closed his eyes.

Gorman finished the call and rested his rear end on the bonnet of the car, his hands buried in his trouser pockets. He stared at the toes of his shoes and images floated into his head: William Rackert tied to the tree, silently screaming through the shitty arse of his own trousers as he saw the calves trotting toward him; Jack the Bap and Boniface nailed to the floors, their slow deaths; Lazarian beaten and broken and eviscerated; dreadful retribution for something that happened decades ago. Was Nailer still in such agony that he was driven to deliver equally intense pain after all these years?

Tom Breen's footsteps behind him pulled Gorman out of his reverie. "Well, Tom?" he asked.

"I think we should contact her...Byron. All we need do is agree to meet with her, see what she has to offer, and in the meantime we can try to put what pieces we have together. What do you think?"

"I'm with you, Tom. Do you know someplace where there's no squinting windows?"

"I do. Were you ever in Dachadoo?"

"No, I've only seen it in the distance off the Daingean road."

"It's an isolated place and has only one approach, beside the old railway bed. We would have to stagger our arrivals. That mile from the Daingean road to the school is very visible. If anyone saw a procession of cars, even two, they might think there was a cockfight and call the guards." Breen looked at his watch. "I suppose we'd better find that public phone."

"I know where it is—sticks out like a sore thumb," Gorman said. "It's been there since the year of the flood."

"Something else, Jimmy. The number eight—we've heard it twice in the last hour. Sister Assumpta said Michael O'Malley was eight when he was taken away; Christy Donovan told us there were eight nails holding the SPCC man at the tree. Am I out-Sherlocking myself?"

"Eight in Rackert and eleven each in Boniface and Jack the Bap; the brothers got three extra for some reason," Gorman said. He stopped the car before pulling out of the car park onto the street. A brown Volkswagen came from his right with its left indicator blinking. As Gorman turned right onto the street, the VW turned left into the car park.

"Did you see the hure?" Gorman asked. He was as excited as a dog barking at a cat from a car window.

"Which hure was that, Jimmy?" Breen asked.

"The fucker in the VW—the one who just called us, McGovern with the hair."

"You're seeing things; it could have been anyone."

"He had hair like a thistle gone to seed, just like the supe said."

"If it was McGovern, then we and the reporters are beginning to trip over each other. Drive on, Gorman, calm down and think."

49.

When Tom Breen stepped out of the phone box he looked like a man who had lost his bearings. Absentmindedly, he turned up the collar of his jacket against the edgy breeze speeding through the winter shadow cast by the post office. Across the street, a bunch of uniformed girls squealed in exaggerated adolescent distress as the same bitter breeze blew up their skirts and scalded their bums. Like calves galloping from the summer gadfly, the girls ran as a group into the yard of the Community School and fled screaming and laughing around a corner and out of sight.

A shiver ran across Breen's shoulders and brought his mind back to the matters at hand. Keeping his lapels in place with his hand, he walked over to the Square, spotted the yellow Vauxhall and slid into the warm car as Gorman's phone was ringing.

"This is he," Gorman said, then listened. "Thank you." He snapped his phone shut.

"Fuck and fuck! That was the Boys in the Park. They found James Thomas O'Malley's birth certificate, a record of his attendance at Mountmellick Boys' School until he was twelve, and court records showing he was admitted to Dachadoo Industrial School in 1967. After that he disappeared, no trace. Scuttering shite!" Gorman hit the steering wheel.

"Gorman, if you believe people disappear, you have to believe in fairies," Breen said.

Gorman pulled out of the Square and headed down to Smith's Corner. "But if the Boys in the Park can't find him, we sure as hell can't," he said.

"If the Boys in the Park can't find him," Breen said, "neither can *The Telegraph*. But he didn't just disappear. He's walking around somewhere or he's dead in his grave. He's somewhere. Maybe Pauline Byron has a lead that she doesn't realize is a lead." He leaned forward and cleared a patch of condensation off the windscreen with the back of his fingers. "Tomorrow you and I are meeting her and her sidekick, McGovern, in Dachadoo, in the ruins of the school; tape recorders permitted to both sides. She and McGovern will arrive at half-past ten; we'll get there at eleven. Nothing we say will be published by *The Telegraph* unless we give specific permission."

"She had no problem with Dachadoo for the meeting place?" Gorman asked.

"Actually, it was she who proposed Dachadoo before I got around to it."

"That's curious—she proposing Dachadoo of all places, especially when Dachadoo is at the center of all this. Maybe she's creating a dramatic backdrop for some stunt she's going to pull. Maybe she's sussed out the place already, picked out the best places for hidden cameras, and we'll be all over *The Telegraph* on Wednesday. Can't you see the heading? "Keystone Kops Look for Their Dicks in Ruins of Investigation.""

"She said there wouldn't be tricks. I believe her."

"Remember you gave me a lecture recently about being naive—"

"I did, and I do believe Pauline Byron won't do anything dirty."

In silence, they negotiated Portlaoise's roundabouts and headed onto the Limerick road toward Roscrea. Each comfortably wandered off into himself for many miles until Castletown loomed in the distance off to their left.

"Are you anxious about viewing Brother Lazarian's bits and pieces?" Breen asked.

"Of course I am," Gorman said. "But I've been keeping the viewing at bay."

"How? Naked young woman admiring your feathered glory?"

"Jeeze, Tom, you're showing signs of recovery—the miracle of the milk of magnesia. This morning you banned the use of 'feathered glory' in this old yellow Vauxhall"—Gorman suddenly became a TV preacher from Alabama—"and now, hallelujah, by the power of magnesia's milk you have seen the light of the Lord Jeeesus! Send in money for the Lord Jeeesus!" He turned to Breen and gave a toothy smile. "And no, Tom, it just happens I wasn't thinking about a naked young lady with loosening thighs awaiting my ministrations. I was thinking about my pastor in London—fantasizing about doing to him what was done to Lazarian."

"Why are you still giving that fellow free lodging in your brain, Gorman?" Breen asked. "Are you still trying to justify leaving the priesthood to yourself by taking a kick at priests and the church?"

"It's not the priests or the church I take kicks at—it's myself I'm kicking for allowing myself to get sucked into it in the first place. If I'd been born a Muslim I might have been suckered into being a suicide bomber for Allah, such an eegit I was. The whole fucking experience got so burned into my psyche that I still dream about being a priest, about people trying to pull me back into it. How could I have been so fucking dumb? What a fucking waste of the best years of my life."

"T'wasn't a waste, Gorman. Look what you got out of it."

"Got out of it? Like Brando said, 'You don't understand. I coulda had class, Charley. I coulda been a contender, I coulda been somebody instead of a bum.'"

"What's wrong with being a detective sergeant? What would be so different about your life if you hadn't—?"

"I could have been a contender—"

"Stop saying that...Tell me what you could have become if you hadn't become a priest? What would you have been a contender in?"

"In normal fucking life, Tom; a contender in normal fucking growing up. I spent years going around with a knot on my dick, knots on my personality, knots on every aspect of normal growth. I was stunted, pruned back constantly. I never touched a woman till I was twenty-four. I didn't grow up like a normal human being, and it's this knowledge of growing up stunted that I drag around with me all the time. I'm always wondering if I would be more complete, more whole, a more normal person if I'd been a normal contender in life instead of...Do you know how Chinese girls used to have their feet bound up to keep them from growing? That's what the priesthood did for my soul, for my personality; I spent years bound up in its stupid rules; I didn't grow as a normal human being."

"Oh, for Christ's sake, Gorman, everyone is constricted some way or other when they're growing up," Breen said.

"Nothing could constrict like the fundamentalism of the Catholic Church."

"Maybe it wasn't 'the church,'" Tom Breen said, and he made quotation marks in the air. "Maybe you were reared in a repressive brand of Catholicism."

"Whatever I was reared on, someone fed me a line of bullshite that my young self swallowed hook, line and sinker."

Breen knew it was a waste of time to argue with Gorman when he was up on his high horse spouting about the wasted years of his life. He decided it was time to get back to business.

"We've got to talk about the case, Jimmy. You've said all along that maybe a sibling or a relative of who we now know is Michael O'Malley may have killed the brothers. I think now that you are right. Even though the Boys in the Park could only trace James O'Malley to 1967 doesn't mean he's dead."

"I think if everything goes right tomorrow in Dach-adoo we may know where James O'Malley is—*The Tel-egraph* has been better than us at getting their hands on... and if it was O'Malley who killed Lazarian last night he is still here...somewhere nearby. If he's finished killing—"

"*If* he's finished," Breen repeated. "There's been about two weeks between each killing. If he's got a list of names and if he knows we're sniffing at his heels, he may hurry up, bring his plans forward, even if there's a risk of slipping up. But Nailer doesn't make a move that's not planned to the last detail. I think he's too self-contained to react clumsily, even if he feels he's been pushed in the back."

"I don't agree with you there, Tom. He lost control of his steely nerves when he did away with Brother Lazarian. Maybe he's...maybe he's weakening...maybe the killings are getting to him...maybe inflicting pain is not as easy as he thought it would be. I remember in moral theology in the seminary, a professor saying the pain suffered by an animal is not as evil as what the infliction of the pain does to the inflictor—the act debases the inflictor. He gave the exam-ple of the men working in the Chicago slaughterhouses. Maybe Nailer isn't able to deal with the debasement; maybe he's finding that the difference between the fantasy of kill-ing and the reality is more than he can bear. If he has any-one left to kill, he might just shoot them from a distance instead of dealing out death close up and personal."

"And?" Breen asked.

"And maybe he'll wrap up his campaign quickly, to have it over and done with before he weakens entirely. So maybe we shouldn't wait till tomorrow to find out what's in the Dachadoo files. If Nailer kills someone today or tomorrow, we would find ourselves in the position of 'should have, could have, but didn't.'"

"I don't agree," Breen said. "You're only interpreting Brother Lazarian's killing to support your hypothesis. If Pauline Byron had deduced from the Dachadoo files that someone else is in danger, she would have told me; she knows enough not to withhold information like that, knows she would place herself in legal jeopardy."

Each man indulged his own thoughts for a few miles.

"Do you think Nailer qualifies as a serial killer yet?" Gorman asked.

"No, I don't think Nailer's a serial killer at all. For one thing I can't see any sexual element in the killings."

"How about the dick amputations?"

"I don't think the amputations sexually excite Nailer," Breen said. "You said yourself, the removal of the dicks is part of the message he leaves. I don't think he qualifies as a serial killer as defined in the psych books. Nailer is hurting people who hurt him in the past. I think Nailer is all about payback."

"Not just payback, Tom. I'm beginning to think Nailer is all about a publicity stunt. Like I said in the supe's office, Nailer is writing the headlines for *The Telegraph* in the way he carries out his killings."

The brown "Welcome to Tipperary/*Failte Go Tiobraid Arann*" sign loomed on their left and Gorman pointed to Breen's folder. "Get out those directions. There's more boreens and laneways around here than veins in a drunk's nose."

Breen removed the printout. "It's from Roadwatch." He ran his finger down the page. "Did you see a sign for Cloncourse yet?" he asked.

"There it is."

"We take the sixth right turn after the second Cloncourse sign. Do we count laneways?"

"I'd say we do," Gorman said.

When they turned off the Roscrea road, Roadwatch led them to a crossroads and then left for half a mile, until they saw the official vehicles parked willy-nilly in front of Mister Turley's house. Gorman pulled over and turned off the engine.

The youthful garda at the door gave a perfunctory salute when the two detectives showed their identity cards.

"Did they start cleaning up yet?" Gorman asked.

"No, sir."

"Did you get a look?" Breen asked.

"No, sir...You're going to get the smell when you open the door. I have masks and Vicks here."

"Thank you. We'll take them."

Gorman went into the house first, shouted for permission to enter the abattoir.

"Who is it?" a voice came back.

"Detectives from Tullamore."

"Gorman and Breen?"

"Yes."

"Come to the door and wait. We have to look at your I.D."

A man wearing a white paper suit, booties, gloves, head cover and mask came to the open door. He glanced at the I.D.'s and asked the men to pull down their masks. "Jer Maher, Phoenix Park," he said, and lifted his gloved hand in salute.

"Jimmy Gorman and Tom Breen, Tullamore," Breen said.

"That's Patrick Burns." Maher indicated with a wave of his hand. Burns was kneeling near the far wall. He looked over, waved and replaced a piece of red meat on the floor.

"Keep to the left when you come in," Jer Maher said. "Make yourselves at home." Maher went back into the room, stepped carefully and knelt down near Patrick Burns.

The Tullamore detectives went in. Gorman glanced around without focusing on anything. "Has this man been pronounced dead?" he asked.

"We have a comedian," Burns said.

"This is dreadful," Breen said.

"It's not too bad once you get to concentrating on one little piece at a time," Jer Maher said, as he continued to sift. "If you isolate one square foot you nearly forget the rest of the stuff is there. Do you think you know who did this?"

"If we can eliminate several people whose identity we may know by tomorrow, we *may* be on his trail," Breen said.

"Doesn't leave any trail, does he?" Patrick Burns said. He sat back on his hunkers and looked across the room. "We haven't found one thing that we can say came off the killer. He must've dressed up for the occasion. I'd hate to meet him in the dark."

"If you did he wouldn't touch you, Patrick," Gorman said. "You're not on his hit list."

"Of course *you* don't have the list?"

"No, but the four men he has already killed were all connected in the past," Breen said.

Patrick Burns and Jer Maher had set up a klieg light on its tripod within a foot of the white ceiling; every object in the room was infused with light. As he looked around, Gorman saw the bits and pieces of the brother as separate objects and colors in a Dali dreamscape. But this was the dreamscape of a Dali who had awakened before the shapes and colors had flowed into cohesion.

The smells of the late Lazarian began to penetrate Gorman's mask, shifting the detective's mind away from the unfinished nightmare. He was left standing in a room where a long-buried anger had erupted out of control and had ripped a man to shreds, had shredded him with the ferocious violence of the spinning iron arms of an old mechanical digger tearing a drill of potatoes apart and turning it into a fine cloud of soil.

Tom Breen stood there, too, his hand to his mask, like a man gazing at the aftermath of a frightening act of nature.

The noose made of blue baler twine was still hanging down from the newel on the first floor. On their way out the two detectives looked at it.

"You were right in the supe's office, Jimmy," Breen said. "Nailer hadn't planned to do that to him." He waved at the room where Lazarian had come apart.

50.

When she saw the tall, dandelion-headed figure looking down at her, apprehension flashed across Sister
Assumpta's wimpled face.

"Sweet Jesus tonight! What happened you?" she asked.

Mick McGovern swiveled his head and looked over his
shoulder.

"Hello, Sister. My name is Mick McGovern and I work
with—"

"We're not buying anything, I'm afraid. I would like to
buy something from you—I imagine you have a wife and
children—but we have everything we need. I'm sorry. But
I can give you a sandwich of butter and jam."

"I'm not selling anything, Sister," McGovern said. "I
work with Pauline Byron, the reporter for *The Telegraph.*"

"Pauline Byron!" Sister Assumpta suddenly looked as
if a beam of sunshine had fallen all over her. "Come in…
come in."

McGovern stepped over the threshold, the front door
closed behind him and the old nun waddled her way
across the hallway to a polished brown door. She turned
the bright brass knob and pushed, stood aside and waved
her guest in.

McGovern found himself in a nuns' parlor. He had
heard of such places just as he'd heard about harems and
Ali Baba's cave and hotel rooms in Dubai. As he glanced
around he understood why nuns' parlors might be a
topic of conversation; formality to the extreme of discomfort and sterility and wax polish were the overwhelming
motifs. A glistening wooden table, its carved feet inspired

by the paws of the Sphinx of Giza, stood chairless in the center of the room. Several engravings with religious themes hung at eye level on the walls.

If Sister Assumpta's verbosity could have been alchemized into a physical force, it could be said she slammed McGovern into a straight-backed chair with a punch to his chest. She pulled over a matching chair and sat opposite him like a doctor about to examine his eyes. She let her chubby hands come to rest in her black lap, like two white pigeons snuggling. She smiled contentedly. "Now! Show me your identification card."

She fingered McGovern's I.D. as if it were a first-class relic. "May I keep this?" she asked in a childlike voice, and the card disappeared among the folds of her black habit. "Now," she said, "tell me about Pauline. I think she's a wonderful woman. The way she laid out the story of Francis Xavier was masterful. But do you think she's ever afraid the people she investigates might try to harm her?"

"Pauline is very careful. *The Telegraph* knows exactly where she is at all times when she's on the job. Her driver is always close by, very visible, and always with her when she goes into a building. And I imagine her own house is very secure."

"She's so smart. I couldn't be objective like she is. I'm afraid my anger would come through. She just lays it all out and lets the readers come to their own conclusions. She never sneers, never editorializes, and I like that."

Sister Assumpta sat there as contented as a cat at a saucer of milk, tail in the air. "Well," she said. "What did you say your name is?"

"Mick McGovern."

"I'm Sister Assumpta. I have never been interviewed before. Is that a camera?"

"No, this is a satnav," McGovern said, and the curious nun asked him how it worked. McGovern switched it on and when it determined their location, Sister Assumpta was like a little girl sitting on her hunkers beside a country ditch in springtime watching the wiggling of a million tadpoles in teeming water. "There's so much information on such a small thing!" she said.

"And I'm looking for some information from *you*, Sister," McGovern said. "I'm looking into the history of a family that lived here in Mountmellick about forty years ago."

"The O'Malleys?"

"How did—?"

Sister Assumpta clapped her hands silently. She smiled at her little triumph. "Two detectives just left here. They wanted to know about the O'Malleys, too. If the guards come, can the press be far behind?"

"If winter comes, can spring be far behind?" McGovern said.

"*O wild West Wind, thou breath of autumn's being.* Oh, it's grand to meet someone who knows a bit of Shelley," the nun said. "Grand. I love Shelley, even though I always thought the Bysse part was strange. It's a queer name, Bysse. They say he was mad."

"Were you able to tell the guards anything?"

Sister Assumpta told Mick McGovern exactly what she had told the two detectives. When she mentioned that Michael Francis O'Malley had an older brother named James Thomas, the reporter's heart made a lunge in his chest; he felt the blood surging up past his Adam's apple as if a blockage had suddenly been breached. When he asked about the day the boys were taken away, the nun told him there had been a big fight; Paddy O'Malley had gone mad and one of the guards had run out of the house with a child under each arm while the other guard held Paddy. "There was blood all over the place."

Mick McGovern then asked Sister Assumpta a question that the detectives had not asked. "You wouldn't happen to remember the guards' names, would you, Sister?"

"Indeed and I would," the old nun answered, a touch of pride in her voice. "Guard Donnelly was one; he had a daughter Gwendolyn and she was beautiful, always had her hair in ringlets. You never see them now, ringlets. You're too young to remember Shirley Temple. The other was Guard Pearse. His wife, Patricia, came to me one time to ask me to make a novena to Saint Gerard Majella for her." The nun eyed McGovern like a thrush eyeing a movement in the grass that whispered 'worm!' "You haven't a clue who Saint Gerard Majella is, do you, Mick?"

McGovern shook his head. He had folded his notebook and was in the act of clipping his pen into his inside pocket.

"I thought not. He's the patron saint of pregnant women. If a woman can't get pregnant she prays to Saint Gerard Majella. Patricia Breen was a gentle woman if there ever was a gentle woman. They moved away not long after the—"

"Excuse me, Sister...you said 'Breen.' How did the name Breen get into the story?"

"That was the guard's name—Pearse Breen—only he was called Guard Pearse because people thought that was his last name."

McGovern's heart wobbled. "Tell me about the Breens," he said calmly.

With enthusiasm, Sister Assumpta told McGovern about the Breen family and showed him her Christmas card collection.

Ten minutes later McGovern, his mobile at his face, was sitting in the VW Bug in the convent car park, talking to Pauline Byron in Emo. "There were *two* O'Malley boys taken away to Dachadoo: Michael Francis, the youngest, and James Thomas, aged twelve."

"Lazarian's palimpsest," Pauline whispered, disbelief and relief in her voice.

"William Rackert brought two guards with him in case there was trouble. There *was* trouble. James O'Malley, the elder child, kicked one of the guards in the face and broke his nose. The guard's name was Pearse...Pearse Breen."

"*Breen?*" Pauline said. Then she whispered in McGovern's ear. "Breen! Detective Sergeant Tom Breen! Oh, Jesus, Mick! Jesus, Jesus."

51.

In her kitchen in Emo, with the phone at her ear, Pauline slapped the kitchen countertop. "Jesus, Mick, you're good—first the Dachadoo files and now this. Let me think, put this together. It can't be a coincidence...the name. Breen. James and Michael are brought to Dachadoo. Michael dies. James's name is scratched out. He disappears. The guard with the broken nose...Shit, Mick. Are you thinking what I'm thinking?"

McGovern held the phone away from his head. "Let me tell you more, Pauline. Pearse Breen was married but had no children. His wife asked Sister Assumpta to pray for her to become pregnant."

"Yes."

In the VW bug, Mick McGovern shifted around as he tried to give ease to his long legs. "The Breens left Mountmellick in the October after the O'Malley boys were taken away. Patricia Breen, the wife, told Sister Assumpta that her husband had requested the transfer because some of the townspeople blamed him and Guard Donnelly for helping William Rackert to do his dirty work. The other guard, Donnelly, eventually became a drinker and he—"

"Feck Donnelly. Mick, our meeting with Tom Breen is set up for eleven in the morning in Dachadoo. This changes everything...Hold on one second, Mick..."

"Wait, hold—" McGovern said, but he heard Pauline's phone coming to rest on a hard surface; he heard her take two steps, heard the keys of another phone being punched. Then Pauline was saying, "Jack, don't say anything; just listen. I want you to tell the Diggers they have to work tonight. I'm hanging up now and I'm calling them to tell them what I want. I'll call you back in a few minutes to explain." McGovern heard more tones from the phone keys. "Melissa, it's Pauline here. It's late, I know. Jack is on his way to tell you...I'm sorry, but this is urgent. You have to find me the whereabouts of a Pearse, as in Padraig Pearse...Pearse Breen who was a guard in Mountmellick in 1967...Hold on..."

Suddenly Pauline's voice was in McGovern's ear. "Mick, any idea how old Pearse Breen was when the O'Malley boys were brought to Dachadoo?"

"Only that his wife was young enough to be trying for a baby. And Pauline there's—"

But Pauline had gone back to Melissa. "No age, except that his wife was still of childbearing age...Hold on..."

"Mick, did you say the wife's name is Patricia?"

"Patricia, yes. Pauline—"

But Pauline was gone again. McGovern heard her relaying the wife's name, then saying, "Melissa, book a room for Mick McGovern in the Montague Hotel in Portlaoise. He doesn't know it yet, but he won't be going home tonight."

McGovern heard a phone clunking onto its cradle. "Mick, I'm—"

"Pauline, I have to interrupt you. The nun, Sister Assumpta, has saved every Christmas card she's received since she became a nun. She showed me a card she got from Patricia Breen telling her about how Saint Gerard Majella had—"

"Who the hell is Gerard Majella?

"The patron saint of women who want to get pregnant. The Christmas card said Saint Gerard Majella had answered Sister Assumpta's prayers and the Breens had been blessed with a child named James Thomas. The card was dated Christmas 1968."

"The O'Malley boys went to Dachadoo in July 1967. Are you thinking what I'm thinking, Mick?"

"That Guard Breen and his wife adopted James O'Malley out of Dachadoo."

"I don't know about adopted. If he was adopted why would Brother Lazarian have scratched him out of existence in the journal?"

"It looks like the Breens got James out some way or other, probably illegally. Maybe that's why Lazarian made him disappear."

"So, the Breens got the boy out of Dachadoo. With your success buying the Dachadoo files it wouldn't surprise me if the Breens *bought* James out of the place, paid Lazarian."

"And if that—" McGovern heard a phone ringing in Pauline's house.

"Hold on, Mick." McGovern dropped his hand with the mobile onto the passenger seat and silently snarled, "Fuck." He put the phone back to his ear and heard Pauline: "Yes, I'm on the mobile…Great, Melissa. No, no…call me as you find. Thanks."

McGovern heard the clunk of the wall phone being hung up.

"Mick, that was Melissa with the Diggers. Guard Pearse Breen received a letter on September the seventh, 1967, transferring him to Navan, County Meath. On October thirtieth, he took up residence in garda housing in Navan with his wife and child."

McGovern was unable to stop himself. "The Breens left Mountmellick childless and arrived in Navan with a son."

"We're getting the pieces together, Mick. Change of subject. You heard me telling Melissa to get you a room in the Montague? Call your wife and tell her you won't be home tonight. Of course I'm doing a lot of presuming here, but if we're meeting Detective Sergeant Breen in Dachadoo in the morning, we have to arrive knowing whether or not he's the avenging Snipper."

"Joanne won't mind and I'll be able to have a fried breakfast in the morning."

"Good. Come here to Emo now and have dinner with us. In the meantime I'll call Rafferty so he doesn't wet himself. And by the way, I went to the Geoghans in Bally-glass. Nobody would open the door, but there was smoke in the chimney. I went down into the farmyard but there was no one there. They must have seen me coming and hid."

Mick McGovern tapped 'Emo' into his satnav and stuck it to the windscreen. He dialed his wife's number in Dublin, started the engine and switched on the head-lights. The setting sun and the encroaching darkness had turned all the buildings around the convent into silhou-ettes.

52.

When Pauline opened her front door, the smell of cooking food pierced McGovern's nose and set saliva to dripping off his teeth.

"God, that smells good, whatever it is." He handed Pauline a bottle of wine.

"You didn't have to do that, but thanks. Don't get excited about the food; we're having shop-bought meatballs and sausages with spaghetti. Raymond's the chef." Pauline stood aside and gestured McGovern in out of the November darkness. "How was Joanne about tonight?"

"She was fine, and her mother is there, down for a few days from Armagh."

Pauline pointed to the satnav in McGovern's hand. "Put your star of Bethlehem up on that shelf there." Pauline wasn't able to keep her lid on any longer. "The Diggers called again," she said. "In September 1968 a James Thomas Breen was enrolled in the Boys' National School in Navan."

"September *1968*. The Breens moved to Navan with James in October *1967*. Almost a year before he goes to school. I wonder why they waited that long."

In the kitchen, Raymond Byron was bent over, slicing a long thin loaf like a fishmonger opening the belly of a fish. He looked up and said, "Mick, how are you? Do you like garlic?"

"I do, Raymond, thanks. I see you have a variety of aprons."

Raymond straightened up, loaf and knife in outstretched hands, and looked down at his apron. In bright colors, the map of Ireland was turned north to west; a few deft and unremarkable touches of an artist's hand had turned the map into a dog on all fours. A naked man streaked with sweat, with the unmistakable face of Francis X. Culliton, an erect penis out of all proportion to his body and the testicles of a prize bull, was entering the dog in Waterford Harbor. "This is one of Pauline's," Raymond said.

"Yes, it's mine, but Raymond had it made for me."

"I'm wearing it this evening to encourage her—the two of you—in your quest for dragons."

"Well, Culliton certainly has one hell of a dragon in that picture."

"He was one hell of a fucker; fucked the country blind," Raymond said.

Pauline answered the phone twice during dinner; both calls were from the Diggers. But she refrained from bringing business to the table and after each call she joined in the banter being thrown around by her husband and their guest. When the plates had been wiped clean with wedges of bread, Raymond cleared the table, poured coffee and put an open package of Jacob's chocolate-coated digestive biscuits on the table.

"No crumbs, please," he said. "I'm disappearing to let you two hatch your plots." He picked up his coffee and headed to the office door.

"We're going out in a minute, Raymond." Pauline said. "The directions are on the computer under Clarahill. If we're not back in six hours, send in the marines."

"Look out for men on motorbikes at traffic lights," Raymond said.

"Will you stop saying that!" Pauline was annoyed. "It's like telling me I'm an idiot."

Raymond came back and put his hand on Pauline's shoulder. "I'm only telling you to be careful." He bent down and whispered in her ear, but McGovern heard what he said. "It's because I love you, Paulie."

Pauline pushed him away playfully. Then she said to McGovern, "Do you know what he's talking about, Mick? Motorbikes and traffic lights?"

"Veronica Guerin?" Mick asked.

"Saintly, heroic Veronica," Raymond said. "It's a good job the Polish pope didn't get his hands on her—he would have canonized her." He disappeared into the office and closed the door.

"Where're we going?" McGovern asked.

"The Diggers have found Pearse Breen. He lives by himself in a place called Clarahill between Rosenallis and Clonaslee, which means nothing to you. His wife died last year. Clarahill is seven miles from Killeigh, where Tom Breen lives. Clarahill is twelve miles from here. We're going there now."

"How old is Pearse Breen?"

"Seventy-eight."

McGovern looked at his watch. "I know, Mick," Pauline said. "It's a quarter to seven. It will be almost half-past seven when we get there, and the old man will probably be getting ready for bed or already in it. Bring your coffee and drink it in the car." Pauline stood up and put her face to the office door. "We're off, Raymond."

"Will I bring my satnav, Pauline?" McGovern asked.

"I know the way...first house on the left just over the Clarahill Bridge." As they went out through the laundry room, Pauline took a blockish, yellow flashlamp off a shelf.

"My car or yours?" McGovern asked.

"Mine. You can't find your way around in the daylight. I know these roads."

For the first several miles, the two reporters applied a timeline to everything they knew. In the glow of the passenger's reading light, McGovern wrote and erased and moved facts and events until he and Pauline were satisfied. When McGovern put away his notebook, he asked,

"Do you think Detective Breen has been manipulating *The Telegraph*?"

"I do."

"Does that bother you?"

"No. There's a bit of manipulation in every human transaction. Tom Breen's been manipulating us. In return, we'll manipulate him. He'll get what he wants; we'll get what we want."

"How are you going to handle this interview with old man Breen?" McGovern asked. "Do I keep my mouth shut and let you handle it?"

"Not at all, Mick. You have a good eye for details, like asking Sister Assumpta for the names of the guards at the O'Malley house when Rackert took the boys. Feel free to ask or comment anytime. We're in this together."

"Thanks, but I have to confess I am a little nervous about this."

"Why? Because you're afraid Tom Breen might pay a visit while we're there?"

"It's on your mind, too."

"It is, but I imagine Tom Breen and his adoptive father have prepared for our visit. One thing Snipper has done all along is take care of the details. Tom Breen knew we'd eventually find our way here."

Two low walls, one each side of the road, came into view. "Clarahill Bridge," Pauline said.

"What does it cross?"

"The Glentahan River; it joins the Barrow about half a mile further down the mountain, over there on your right."

"The Barrow, the Nore and the Suir—the Three Sisters," McGovern said.

When the first house on the left lit up in the headlights, they saw a whitewashed cottage set back from the road, black paint at the windows and door, a low white wall around the front garden, a black wrought-iron gate.

The window to the left of the door was dimly lit. Pauline parked the jeep in front of the wall and both reporters took deep breaths as they got out.

Pauline put the beam of the flashlamp on the gate hasp. When McGovern released it, the gate swung in and made a screech like a scalded cat.

"Pearse Breen's alarm system," Pauline said.

McGovern felt it was the manly thing to do, so he led the way. From behind, Pauline illuminated the short path to the door. A bright outside light came on and momentarily blinded them.

Before his raised, knocking hand made contact with the door, a man's muffled voice came through the wood. "Who is it?"

"Two reporters from *The Telegraph*, Mister Breen."

"Who?"

"Two reporters from *The Telegraph*, the newspaper."

"What do you want?"

McGovern glanced around at Pauline. "We're looking for some information, sir."

"Stand in front of the door, one at a time."

The reporters did as told. When the door opened, a tall, slightly stooped, elderly man stood there blocking entry. "Show me some I.D.," he said loudly, the way some deaf people speak. Then satisfied with what he saw, he stood aside and said, "An old person can't take anything for granted in Ireland anymore. Come in."

Mister Breen was dressed in a plaid shirt buttoned to the top, a thick grey cardigan with imitation chestnut buttons, grey corduroy trousers and black running shoes. "As far as I know I've never been asked questions by newspaper people before," he said. "I was a guard and I was usually the one asking the questions...Sit down over there on the couch. That fire would roast you. I'll put on the kettle." He short-stepped out of the room with the caution of a man in fear of falling. "Take off your coats," he called back through the doorway.

"Our arrival didn't seem to surprise him," Pauline said quietly.

Mister Breen was a minimalist when it came to decoration and furniture. A print in an expensive frame hung on the chimney breast two feet above the mantelpiece— from the couch it looked like splashes of red and white and yellow and black. There were no photos on the walls or windowsills. There was no TV. And there were none of the usual religious icons found in the houses of older people—no flickering imitation candle flame beneath the picture of the Sacred Heart, no piece of dried palm from Palm Sunday stuck over a door, no holy water container beside the door, no Brigid's Cross made from rushes.

A brass lamp with a shaded, bright bulb stood on the end table on Pauline's right, beside its base a well-worn volume with a marker sticking out. She picked up the book and glanced at the spine. She poked McGovern and pointed to the title: *The Complete Poems of John Milton.*

McGovern raised his eyebrows and indicated the picture hanging on the chimney breast. "Renoir," he said. *"Danse à Bougival."*

Pauline made a face of mock astonishment. McGovern didn't know if she was reacting to the Renoir or to the fact that he had recognized it.

Pauline stood up and stepped nearer to *Danse à Bougival,* studied the couple moving in close embrace, the woman with a red hat and white dress, the man in a yellow straw hat and blue suit. Friends were drinking in the background. It was a summery, warm-colored picture, one to be cheered by on a winter's day, a winter's night.

Mister Breen arrived back in the sitting room with a laden tray. "Our son, Tom, gave that painting to us, Patricia and me, for our fortieth wedding anniversary. He said

that's how he liked to think of us—when we were young."
He lowered the tray onto the coffee table in front of the
couch.

"I have seen that Renoir recently," Pauline said.
"Maybe it was in a magazine."

The reporters returned to the couch and when Mister
Breen began to drag an armchair to the table, McGovern stood up to help. Before he sat down, Mister Breen
poured, sugared and milked three mugs of tea according
to the tastes of his guests. Carefully, he lowered himself
into his chair, lifted his cup of tea as if for a toast and said,
"You're welcome to my house. What can I do for you?"

"Do you remember July the fourth in 1967?" Pauline
asked.

Without hesitation, as if he knew already what the
question would be, Mister Breen said, "How could I forget
it? That day changed my life. It changed five other lives
as well: Patricia…"—he nodded toward the Renoir—"the
three O'Malleys…Paddy, James and Michael; and Sean
Donnelly, the other guard who was there—he became an
alcoholic and lost his job, died young. The fourth of July,
1967. It was a Tuesday."

53.

It was in the conservatory, in his old chair which the late Elizabeth had tried to replace, that Doctor Alexander McNulty was reclining, lying almost horizontally. In the small circle of light cast by the shaded table lamp beside him, McNulty had been reading a worn, self-annotated copy of Plato's *Republic* in Greek. He knew some of the passages by heart and he was exercising his memory by reciting one of them aloud with his eyes closed, the book and his hands on his stomach.

An unexpected sound over at the French doors gave him pause and he opened his eyes. He saw the streak of light that was reflected in the brass handle move out of the horizontal into the perpendicular, like the finger of God pointing downward. In the ever-present expectation of his own demise, Doctor McNulty was inclined to see many divine signs and wonders.

The old medical man took in a sharp breath and held it. "This time it is surely Death!" he said quietly, and he brought his right hand over his heart.

The white, twenty-paned French door swung open into the conservatory, and standing there was a shrouded corpse. It was wrapped from head to toe; only the face was uncovered. He recognized Elizabeth's features. Until this moment, he had not believed in visitations from the grave.

The door closed silently on its three steeple-tipped, brass hinges. The corpse took one step into the room. The doctor's heart shook on its struts, transferring the vibrations into his entire upper body.

"Doctor Alexander McNulty!" Even though the voice was normal, the name filled the conservatory with a shroud-like miasma and hung there in the deathly silence.

The doctor's mouth was dry. He was so frightened that he was unable to jump-start the muscles that would get his vocal cords to quivering. In the angle of the light hitting his wrinkled face he looked like an old potato studded with protrusions.

"Doctor McNulty, I was once known as Twenty-nine Sixty-seven. That should tell you where I spent some of my childhood."

The corpse floated straight toward him, and as the doctor clutched the upholstery in the recliner's arms, Plato fell on the floor beside him with a loud plop. Unaware that his bladder's sphincter had opened, the doctor did not feel the warm water in his crotch, did not feel it running back under him, soaking his scrotum before it sank into the chair. The corpse floated into the circle of light cast by the table lamp. It sat in Elizabeth's chair and McNulty saw it wasn't a corpse at all, but some chancer with a moustache dressed up for work in an operating room. In one hand he held a brown paper bag, in the other a pen and a sheet of white paper.

When his breathing had returned close to its normal rhythm, when his heart had braked itself back to near normalcy, when he'd sucked enough saliva into the vicinity of his vocal cords, Doctor McNulty asked, "Who are you?...What are you?"

"Twenty-nine Sixty-seven." The voice was gentle yet clear and firm. The intruder put the piece of paper he was carrying on the floor beside his chair. He placed the pen and the brown bag on top of it.

Groping in the fog of his early-stage senility, the doctor looked at the corpse, the mummy, the operating room attendant.

"Are you a Jew?" he asked.

"No, I'm not."

The doctor saw again the sputtering exhaust pipe of the hearse hauling his mortal bits along his own drive-way. He saw Elizabeth lowering the eight hanging ferns, spider plants, wandering Jews and jades from the seared Protestant beams. His saw his sister with her enormous, braying mouth. Doctor McNulty brought his left hand to his face and rubbed his chin like a man in deep thought. He adjusted the recliner and moved himself into a sitting position. "Camps," he said. "Concentration camps used numbers. Pull up your sleeve."

"There were no tattoos, Doctor McNulty."

The doctor looked up to where his wife's plants should be, but it was dark up there. "Turn on the switch at the door," he said.

"We can see each other."

"Why are you dressed like that...like a—?"

"So I'll leave no evidence; not that it matters anymore."

"What evidence?"

"Evidence that I was here."

"Why are you here?"

"I want to talk to you about something and then I am going to execute you."

The confusion in the doctor's brain flowed out over his face. If Doctor McNulty had been examining himself he would have said that he had lost control of his extraocular muscles—his eyeballs were floating freely around in their sockets. But he marshaled the ocular orbs back under his control, stared into the distance for a moment as if he'd just awakened, then looked at the talking mummy. "Take off that ridiculous hat. You look like a fishwife with curlers."

"Are you afraid, Doctor McNulty?"

"I'm confused. I have been thinking about my death... when I saw...I thought you were Death. I was half asleep, reciting Plato to myself, and you were there when I opened my..." The doctor's voice wandered off. Then he suddenly said in a stronger voice, "You broke into my house."

"It's not the first time."

"Why didn't you knock at the front door like a civilized person?" McNulty asked. "Even the reporter had that much manners...she's famous enough to be rude but she rang the bell. I'm going to call the guards." But the doctor made no move toward the portable phone on the lamp table. The two men looked at each other like two bantam cocks giving each other the eye, each on his own side of the chicken-wire fence. Finally, the doctor said, "You wouldn't let me call the guards, would you?"

"No, I wouldn't."

It was several minutes before the intruder spoke again. "My name is James O'Malley. We met once before; you gave me a half-minute physical examination when I was a child. You should have examined my brother when he was murdered, but you didn't."

"Wait a minute—"

"Shut up and listen!" O'Malley's voice was commanding. "You met my father once, too, in the garda station here in Tullamore. You were called by the guards to check him out because the brothers injured him when he tried to rescue my brother and me from Dachadoo Industrial School. That same day he had buried his wife, and his two children had been taken away from him by the man from the Society for the Prevention of Cruelty to Children. The morning after you saw my father he drowned himself in the canal."

"Dachadoo! Brother Lazarian...he died this week... The Reverend Brother Lazarian dead," McNulty said, then nodded as if to convince himself.

"Yes. He died on Sunday night."

"Did you know him?"

"Yes, I knew him. I knew him inside out."

"Brother Lazarian was a saint, a true apostle of Christ."

"No, he wasn't—Brother Lazarian was a bitter, cruel and vindictive man."

"God forgive you for saying such a thing about the dead. Brother Lazarian dedicated his life to the welfare of homeless boys. I told the reporter—"

"Brother Lazarian was a liar and a monster. Brother Lazarian, despite his accent and his manners and mani-cured fingernails, never could escape his own dunghill; the snot-nosed, smelly boys of Dachadoo were a constant, distasteful reminder to him."

"Stop it!" the doctor snapped. "It's sinful to say bad things about the dead."

"May we not say bad things about Josef Stalin? Or Pius the Twelfth? Or about Hitler? Or should we only say that he built the autobahns? When you die, Doctor, people will say bad things about you, too."

"Leave my house," the doctor commanded.

"Whether I leave or not, bad things will still be said about you."

"Stop it!...Stop it!...Leave me alone. That reporter was like you. Get out." The old man lowered the footrest of the big chair, leaned forward like a game cock stretching its fighting head toward a rival, neck feathers bristling, eyes glistening.

"I'm not ready to leave," James O'Malley said in his soft, even voice.

Doctor McNulty glared at him. "*The Telegraph* has already shown me my obituary. The *Offaly Independent* will have a two-page spread with photos. The taoiseach will mention me on the floor of the Dail. I served the people of Tullamore for fifty-two years, and when I die, they will say nothing but good things about me."

"Will the taoiseach mention that you served as the medical officer of Dachadoo Industrial School?"

"Yes, he will, and that's in the obituaries, too...my serv-ice to the poor boys."

"*Poor* boys! They were scum to you when you worked there and they're going to be *poor boys* in your obituary. You were never of service to the *poor* boys of Dachadoo. You were of *dis*service to them." O'Malley's tone was still even.

McNulty put force behind his voice. "*Dis*service! What are you talking about, Mister? I *served* the boys of Dachadoo. I served them and I didn't charge the brothers one halfpenny for that service."

"That's a grand thing to say when you're polishing your own reputation—that you worked pro bono. Like your pal, Lazarian, you are a liar too. You *were* paid by the Department of Education, which controlled the purse strings of all the Dachadoos in Ireland. The brothers were not obliged to pay you."

"No one could ever repay me for all the things I did in Dachadoo," McNulty said firmly.

"That is true, Doctor McNulty; you could never be repaid. And that's why everyone who reads *The Telegraph* and *The Offaly Independent* will discover what you did for the brothers and the church by *not* doing what you should have done in Dachadoo. Your reputation will sink into the ground with you and it will rot along with your rotting corpse."

"Stop it! Stop it!" The doctor glared at O'Malley. "I am a good man...I am a good doctor...I was always a good doctor...I never collected half my...I'll be meeting my God soon and you're saying—"

"God, my arse!" O'Malley said dismissively, a small rise in his voice. "But I *do* wish the Christian hell did exist, Doctor McNulty. You would have an honored place in the section reserved for those who should have but didn't, who could have but wouldn't. It would be called the Cowards Gallery."

"*Stop it!*" the doctor shouted.

"Are you afraid your God will hear me?"

McNulty put his hands over his ears. "Stop it! Stop it!" he called again.

O'Malley waited for the doctor to lower his hands. In the end he went over and pulled the bony hands away from McNulty's head. He put the slightest pressure on the stick-like arms. "If you cover your ears again I will break your wrists," he said, and gently shook the doctor as if waking him from a nap. "Did you hear me, sir?"

"I did."

"What did I tell you?"

"That you'll break my wrists if I—"

"And do you believe me?"

"Yes."

O'Malley freed the doctor's hands and returned to his own chair. He waited until the doctor had reassembled his terrified wits.

"In the Cowards Gallery you can rub elbows with all the civil servants and politicians and priests and brothers who knew what was happening in Dachadoo but who did nothing. There'll be a lot of Germans in there, too, from—"

"I'm not a coward. I did what the brothers—the church—told me to do. I only obeyed the—"

"I only obeyed! I only obeyed!" O'Malley repeated. "The plea to the virtue of obedience—the last refuge of the coward." O'Malley's voice was that of a weary parent reading an oft-told bedtime story. "Were you only obeying, being virtuous, when you wrote the reports dictated to you? Were you only obeying when you ignored the cuts and scars on the boys' bodies, ignored the blatant evidence of caned flesh on backs and backsides? The classless children of Dachadoo didn't deserve your concern, did they, Doctor? Were you only obeying the representatives of your church when you wrote 'accident' for broken bones even though you knew the bones had been broken by adult fists, by slammings against walls and floors, by kicks from hard boots? Were you only obeying when you looked into the boys' mouths and saw rotting teeth and diseased gums, saw the bits of trapped paper and chalk the boys had been eating to keep the unrelenting hunger at bay, and did nothing, said nothing? Were you only obeying when you knew, could plainly see, that the boys were underfed? Were you only being virtuous when you saw the lice and the open sores and the boils on the backs of necks, saw the runny chilblains on the hands and feet and did nothing? Were you only obeying when you said nothing about the boys' thin clothes, about the ruination of their feet in the ill-fitting boots? Were you only obeying when you saw the ripped and bleeding anuses of small boys and said nothing?"

"I didn't know what to do. I was serving the church. I was obeying the representatives of the—"

"Coward!" O'Malley roared. He stood up, moved as if about to step toward the doctor, but he checked himself in mid-stride. "You were a coward! You are still a coward, unable to own up to what you didn't do. How could you, you who knew far more than any of those ignorant, grubby churchmen, you who were far wiser to the ways of the world than any of them, far more aware of the damage being done than anyone else? You, the outsider who could come and go as you pleased, you were the only hope those boys had and you did nothing. Those boys were led to believe they were going to a better place in Dachadoo, only to be met with the cruelty of the brothers as well as your own. You are worse than the worst brother."

"No, don't say that. There were inspectors from the Department of Education. They knew what the conditions—"

"Bullshite...and you know it, Doctor McNulty. Bullshite, because the inspectors always sent notice that they were coming. The brothers in Dachadoo used Potemkin scenery and the inspectors pretended to be fooled—just like you pretended to be blind. You knew exactly what was going on behind the walls of Dachadoo but you were too loyal, too virtuous, to speak up against the clerical ignoramuses, the monsters, the undeveloped people who inhabit religious orders." O'Malley was on the verge of shouting. "What were you afraid of? Were Dachadoo boys not worth saving? Were the boys getting what they deserved? Did you treat the boys as the shite of society because you assumed their parents were the shite of society? Was that it, Doctor? Were they not as deserving of your attention as the lucky children of the lucky parents of Tullamore?"

James O'Malley paused, calmed himself with deep breaths. He turned his back on the doctor, sat down and put his head between his hands. After a long time he spoke again and his voice was back in its bedtime tone. "That's what it's all about, isn't it, Doctor? Luck...it was all a matter of luck. If the parents were lucky, then the children were lucky. If the parents were unlucky, then the children slithered to the bottom of the heap. Look at my brother and me; we were lucky once upon a time. We were loved and we were happy. But our mother died and it didn't matter that we had a good father. It didn't matter because a greedy man was in the pay of your greedy Brother Lazarian to keep Dachadoo's population steady—keep the government funds coming in. You knew the living conditions of the unlucky boys and you did nothing about it because it would have meant scandal for the brothers and bad publicity for your beloved church."

O'Malley leaned forward, put his elbows on his knees. "You may have persuaded yourself, Doctor McNulty, that going along with the wishes of the brothers was more virtuous. You were so virtuous and obedient, that according to the late Brother John the Baptist, you even signed a book of blank death certificates for Lazarian. And now in your old age, when you believe you are about to stand before your God, you are hiding behind the skirts of their deficiencies and corruption and ignorance and stupidity and depravity. If you are as saintly as you think you are, then you must know what your Christ said when someone tried to shoo children out of the way: 'Suffer the little children to come unto me.' And surely you have heard a thousand times what your Christ said about the abusers of those children: 'Whoever scandalizes one of these my least brethren, let a millstone be tied around his neck and let him be drowned in the depths of the sea.' You may *think* you are a holy and virtuous man but from where I am sitting, your God, your Christ, is waiting for you, Doctor McNulty, and he has already put in an order for another millstone, and your Blessed Virgin Mary is crocheting the rope to tie you to it."

When O'Malley stopped talking, the doctor looked across at him for several seconds before he feebly said, "It wasn't like that at all. There was nothing I could do."

James O'Malley ignored the bleating. Patiently and quietly, as if explaining to a small child, he continued. "Do you know *who* those little boys were, Doctor McNulty? Did you ever stop to think of them as individual children who had already suffered terrible losses before they ever reached the walls of Dachadoo? Did you ever think of them as little boys who had no parents to protect them against the cruelty of the brothers? Did you ever think of them as small children looking up at you, wanting you to assure them that you were on their side? Did you ever think how those boys felt when you treated them like shite? Did you ever wonder what went on inside the bellies and the hearts of those small boys when they held out their hands for a piece of assurance and got nothing but a punch in the face for their efforts? Did you ever think of the damage you were doing, that you were scrambling these little boys' heads every bit as much as your wife scrambled eggs for your breakfast; that you smashed those boys so badly that not even your fucking God could put them back together again? What kind of a bollicks were you, what kind of creeps were the religious brothers who slaughtered the boys, not only destroyed them emotionally, but raped their souls as much as they raped their little bodies with their overeager pricks? Don't you remember your own children looking up into your face, looking for assurance that you would protect them from biting dogs and nasty people? Don't you remember that?"

O'Malley was back on the edge of the precipice.

There was no response from Doctor McNulty. He was a man in a trance, a battle-weary soldier lost at his own end of the twelve-mile stare. When O'Malley clapped his hands together, the doctor moved in his chair and whispered, "It wasn't like that at all." He shuddered. He sat up straight. He was a man readjusting his armor after falling off his horse. "I didn't know...I didn't know..."

"If you didn't know it was because you made the decision *not* to know," O'Malley shouted over him. "Do you know about the cemetery at Dachadoo? Or is that something you decided you didn't want to know about either?"

"You're wrong, Mister. There is no cemetery at Dachadoo. Any brother who died in Dachadoo was brought home to the Mother House in Lucan for burial."

"Your speech betrays you, Doctor McNulty," O'Malley shouted, and he jumped up. He kept himself from striking out, remembered how he'd slipped over the edge in Brother Lazarian's study. "When you think of Dachadoo, you only think of the brothers. Dachadoo was for *the boys*, not for the brothers. You know what happened to the brothers who died there. But do you know what happened to the *boys* who died there? Do you think the brothers paid to send them back to their own villages for burial? Do you think the brothers wanted anyone to know that a child in their care had died?"

"Not one boy died at Dachadoo while I was the medical officer there, Mister."

"How do you know that, Doctor McNulty?"

"Because I was the doctor; the doctor is the one who pronounces death. The doctor signs the death certificates."

"Yes, he signs them, but the doctor also completes the certificates after pronouncing death. Did your religious beliefs completely stupefy you, Doctor Alexander McNulty? Did your belief in the goodness of brothers make you so blind?" O'Malley was shouting. "There *is* a cemetery in Dachadoo, Doctor McNulty, and there are seventy-three graves in it. All children—no brothers. Dachadoo was about the *boys*, you dumb fuck. And how many of them died during your time as medical officer at—"

The doctor yelled as loudly as his old body would permit him. "Liar! You are a liar...She was a liar, too. Why are you saying these things? Are you a temptation sent before I die to get me to betray the church, the consecrated brothers, my religion?"

"Fuck you and your fucking church and your fucking consecrated religious brothers! The voodoo woman biting the head off a chicken on a dark beach in Haiti has more religion in her little toe than all the brothers of Dachadoo ever had. I have no need to tempt you to betrayal, Doctor McNulty. You betrayed your Hippocratic Oath a thousand times. You betrayed hundreds of little children to cover up the *criminal* behavior of people you were afraid of."

"Before God, I—"

"I have no interest in what you might have to say before your God. You can talk to your self-made God about all this when you run into him."

O'Malley bent over suddenly and put his hands on his knees. He was breathing hard.

"I didn't know what to do," the doctor said.

Long after his breathing had restored itself, long after the wires in his brain had cooled, O'Malley said, "There was something you could have done; you could have committed suicide and left a message giving your reasons. Your own suicide would not have been less virtuous than what you didn't do."

"Suicide is a sin—"

"Oh, shut up," O'Malley said. He held out a hand, halting the doctor's speech. "Don't talk to me, because I swear if you do I will do to you what I did to Lazarian." He sat down, put his hands on his knees.

Eventually, O'Malley leaned over the arm of his chair and picked up the pen and paper he'd brought with him. He stood up again and went to the doctor. "This is a blank death certificate. You will write what I tell you to write." He placed the certificate and pen on the lamp table.

Doctor McNulty looked up at him and moved his head from side to side. He was almost whispering when he said, "I think you *are* going to kill me. I don't know what your game is but I'm not going to help you out, Mister. I won't bring shame on the church or the brothers or whatever it is you're up to. I will die a martyr."

"Be a martyr if you like, but first you will write what I tell you, Doctor McNulty."

"I'm not writing anything for you, Mister." The doctor lifted the death certificate off the table and tore it into two pieces. He let the pieces float onto the floor and he looked up at O'Malley. "Who do you think you are? Breaking into my house and threatening me and telling me what to do. You're the same as the reporter, only she used her sex; twisting everything I said. I wasn't afraid of her, and I'm not afraid of you either, Mister. If you're going to kill me, go ahead and do it. I'm not afraid."

O'Malley waited for the doctor's words to fade into the furniture. Calmly and softly he said, "If you're not afraid, then why have you pissed yourself? Now, I want you to listen to me carefully, very carefully. When I was finished with Brother Lazarian he was disemboweled, he was decapitated; his arms and legs had been chopped off, his guts were hanging off his chandelier." O'Malley hesitated, let the words sink in. "I am going to get another death certificate off the pad in your office. I will leave you here in your chair. I will leave the phone where it is. When I come back, you will be sitting in your chair. You will not have used the phone. I will give you the new certificate and tell you what to write on it. If you do not do as I tell you, I will force my hand into your mouth, I will twist your lower jaw off its hinges and then pull it off your face." O'Malley paused again. "Repeat back to me, Doctor McNulty, what I will do to you if you do not cooperate."

The doctor muttered, "You will pull off my lower jaw." He touched his hand to his face.

"Do you believe me, Doctor McNulty?"

"I do."

James O'Malley turned and walked out of the solarium. The doctor sat motionless, staring at the open door.

In less than half a minute O'Malley returned and placed the new certificate on the table, handed the pen to McNulty, told him what to write.

The old man didn't understand. "What?" he said.

"The first word is 'I.'"

McNulty wrote in a shaky hand.

"The second word is 'signed.'...'I signed...a book... of blank death certificates...for...Brother Lazarian.' Now sign it and date it the twenty-fifth of November."

When the doctor was finished, O'Malley took the paper and returned to Elizabeth's chair.

"You *do* know the consequences of what you did, Doctor McNulty?" O'Malley asked.

"No, I don't. I was just—"

"You said you have been thinking about your own death, Doctor. You go to mass every day. I imagine you believe the things the catechism says about death—personal judgment immediately and general judgment on the last day. Do you believe all that?"

"I do, yes. I believe all that."

"Then why tell lies when you *know* that you will be dying soon?"

"I haven't told you any lies, Mister."

"Then maybe your intelligence is letting you down, Doctor McNulty, former medical officer of the Dachadoo Industrial School for boys."

The doctor said nothing.

"How about this, Doctor? Blank death certificates and Brother Lazarian."

"I don't know what you're getting at."

"I think you do, only you won't admit it. Did you supply Brother Lazarian, superior at Dachadoo, with blank death certificates?"

For a minute the doctor didn't speak. He scratched the edge of his mouth, felt the stubble on his chin.

"Yes, I remember. I did do that. I told you Brother Lazarian was kind and thoughtful. Brother Lazarian knew I was a busy doctor and a family man. He knew it took time and petrol to get to Dachadoo and back again. He knew the roads were bad and that the potholes shook my car apart. Outside the annual checkups, he only sent for me when I was really needed, if there was an outbreak of measles or something."

"And he asked you for blank death certificates in 1959 to save you the journey to Dachadoo whenever a boy died?"

"I told you, Brother Lazarian was a thoughtful and kind man, and a dead body is dead no matter who says so. I trusted Brother—"

"My brother was murdered in Dachadoo," O'Malley said. "His name was Michael. He was eight years old. But his death certificate says he died of pneumonia. His murder was never investigated because no one outside of Dachadoo knew he was murdered. If you had certified the cause of death, Doctor McNulty, Michael's death would have been investigated and Dachadoo would have been closed down immediately. Fourteen other boys died in Dachadoo after my brother was murdered. How many of those died of natural causes, Doctor?"

"I trusted Brother Lazarian to do the right...I don't believe you..."

"You don't *want* to believe me because if you *do,* all your hopes and plans for your eternity will be all fucked up. Won't they, Doctor? You're already beginning to realize that the path to your heaven is suddenly strewn with small dead bodies." O'Malley picked up the brown paper bag. "I have told you what will happen if you don't do what I tell you; that still holds true."

The old doctor gaped up from his enfolding chair, his tongue showing, like a dog awaiting its master's command.

"You will stand up now."

It took nearly a minute for McNulty to bump his way out of the chair. He looked up at O'Malley.

"Turn around."

The doctor shuffled around without lifting his feet off the carpet.

"Put your hands behind your back."

"What are you going—?"

"Do not speak."

The doctor heard the rustling of the paper bag. Then his hands were tied together. The thin rope cut into his leathery skin. "You're hurting me."

"Offer up the pain to your God for the repose of your soul. Stay here and contemplate the pool of fright on the seat of your chair. Do not look around."

The doctor waited, waited so long that his shoulders began to ache, and his lower back screamed for release from the position he was maintaining to relieve the pain at his wrists. McNulty's lips flapped around for a moment before he brought them under control with the words he prayed but which only he himself could hear: "Hail Holy Queen, mother of mercy! Hail, our life, our sweetness and our hope! To thee do we cry, poor banished children of Eve, to thee do we send up our sighs, mourning and weeping, in this valley of tears..."

When O'Malley touched the doctor on the shoulder, McNulty twitched as if he'd been bitten by a horsefly.

"Turn around."

The old man shuffled in tiny steps. O'Malley took him by the arm and led him along the room until they came to the prepared place. The doctor looked at the moving loop of blue baler twine dangling in front of his face. He did not have to look up to know what it was hanging from. "You're going to murder me, aren't you?"

"You flatter yourself, Doctor McNulty; I'm not about to murder you. When you present your C.V. to God, the word 'executed' under *cause of death* will jump out at him. How will you explain that to him? Stand up on the books at your feet."

The doctor didn't move. "I don't understand why—"

"You can talk to your God about it. Maybe he'll explain it to you. The seventy-three boys buried in Dachadoo can help him out. Now, step up on the books."

54.

While Doctor McNulty struggled to maintain his balance atop two thick medical dictionaries, James O'Malley passed the Church of the Assumption as he walked to his car. If anyone had met him, they would have seen he was wearing a black beret and a knee-length overcoat, would have noted his trim moustache and dark-framed glasses.

While O'Malley was entering the last roundabout at the eastern end of the town, Doctor McNulty bent his knees to ease the pain in his thighs but in so doing he slipped off his scaffold and the noose tightened around his neck. In a panic, he straightened himself and tried to find the dictionaries with his toes. His face turned deep red and he coughed as parts of his throat were squeezed against each other.

James O'Malley stayed at the edge of the speed limit as he drove out of Tullamore to begin the twenty-mile journey to Portlaoise. He adjusted the glasses on his nose and his action conjured up the memory of Brassie Avenue in London with its theatrical supplies shop and the loud, painted and ballistic-breasted woman who'd served him. He'd felt the fresh air on his face when he'd come out of the shop with everything on his list, including the plain-lensed glasses and the fake moustache.

As O'Malley drove out of Killeigh, Doctor McNulty was visited with the false sensation that he was slipping off the books again. In the effort to counteract the alarming feeling, he caused himself to fall forward and the falling instinctively threw the muscles into gear that would have brought his hands to the front to break the fall. But the only thing the muscular reaction achieved was to further bury the baler twine in his wrists behind his back. Immediately, another instinctual instruction forced the doctor's feet to take short and quick steps forward to keep his legs under his body. But his feet tripped over each other and the twine felt the full weight of his body; it stretched by two inches.

As he drove along the deserted streets of Mountmellick, James O'Malley was gratefully aware of his calmness. Any killer on his way from the hanging of one man to the killing of another should at least have been elated by the success of the one or anxiously anticipating the next. But it was all coming to an end for James O'Malley; it didn't matter now when he was uncovered because he was about to finish the whole thing. When this night was over, they would all be dead, all executed and the media attention he had set out to achieve had blossomed far beyond his wildest hopes.

With the stretching of the twine Alexander McNulty's toes had touched the carpet and it was his toes that were now at the mercy of the survival instinct. But his toes could not endure the pain inflicted on them by the weight of the body from above and they gave up quickly. The air in the doctor's windpipe scraped thinly and noisily in and out and he lost consciousness. The baler twine went as taut as a fiddle string; the blood in the face took on a purplish hue; the eyes bulged, saliva drooled out of the mouth, the eyes appeared to send out tears, the upper dentures slipped forward; and the body jerked like a dying fish, finally spasmed itself into quietude and hung as limp as a wet facecloth on a hook. A noise came from the throat. The smell of excrement seeped into the hanging plants on the charred Protestant beams above.

James O'Malley drove into a space in the car park in front of the Midland Regional Hospital in Portlaoise. When he walked out onto the old Dublin Road he turned

left with Alexander McNulty's emergency bag in his hand
and a walking stick in the other. He could have been a
doctor going home after a late night call to the hospital. A quarter of a mile later, just before he turned left
into the grounds of Saint Fintan's Psychiatric Hospital, a
delivery lorry passed him, its clackety diesel engine loud
in the early morning silence, JONAH'S FISH on its side and
back.

Along the edge of the hospital driveway O'Malley
strode. He bore right toward the split-up-the-middle
chapel that made it easy for God to distinguish between
the Protestant and Catholic hymns of praise that caressed
the divine ears on Sundays. Over to his left were the
unlocked glass doors that allowed visitors into the lobby
day and night. As if he did it every day, O'Malley loped up
the five limestone steps and disappeared inside.

O'Malley put his doctor's bag and the walking stick
on the shelf beneath the service windows to his left. He
walked across the lobby, took one of the visitors' wooden
chairs and carried it to the secure door that led into the
hospital. He leaned the chair against the door at such an
angle that when the latch was undone, the chair would fall
through. He brought another chair to the wooden wall
with the windows, picked up the walking stick, stepped
up on the chair, stepped up on the shelf beneath the
windows and held on to the top of the wooden wall with
his left hand. He peered over, stood up on his toes so he
could look straight down. He brought the walking stick
up and held it in his right hand on the other side of the
wall. He moved up on his toes again and he touched the
tip of the stick to the button of the release switch. A short
buzz sounded as the lock was released in the secure door.
The chair leaning against it fell in.

O'Malley returned both chairs to their places, picked
up the doctor's bag and entered the hospital on his silent
shoes. Every other ceiling light was off. He left the stick

and the bag in the first shadow on the long corridor. He moved slowly across the bright spots. Several times, he stood in a dark area to listen and look, and each time the fingers of his left hand caressed the weapon in his pocket.

It was the patch of darkness nearest the door to Saint Martha's Ward that he used as his final base to reconnoiter. The silence rang in his ears. Through the pane of safety glass in the door he saw that the ward was almost in darkness, lit only by some dim light hidden from his view. The shapes of the beds were easily discernible. Across the ward behind the large glass panel, the light in the nurses' office was dim too. O'Malley waited for movement in the nurses' glass wall. It took him almost five minutes to determine that he was seeing the night nurse's head; that the nurse had her elbows on a desk and that her head was resting in her hands. She was either reading or sleeping.

He took two steps and put his hand on the door's handle. Gently, he levered it down, pulled the door open and slipped inside. He closed the door silently, then boldly walked past the first two beds on his left and stepped into the space beside the third bed. Without hesitation he gently lifted the covers and pushed aside Brother Beatus's pajamas. He took out the sharpened, ten-penny nail and placed the point between the second and third ribs, held it in place and put his left hand over the brother's mouth. He gave a quick push with his right hand, felt the nail piercing the flesh, and then he leaned down until the head of the nail would go no further. Brother Beatus tried to take a breath. But as the nail went through the left atrium and came out through his back, his impaled heart came to a sudden stop. O'Malley pulled the covers up to the chin of the corpse. Without turning to look at the nurses' office, he walked out of Saint Martha's Ward and held the door until it silently fitted itself back into its jambs. In a steady, unrushed gait, he moved along the long corridor, retrieved the doctor's bag and the walking stick, let himself back into the purple lobby and out through the glass doors.

On the footpath back to the Midland County Hospital car park, he did not meet man or beast. He drove away, and before he reached Mountmellick, he removed his disguise.

Back in his house in Killeigh, O'Malley closed his front door and walked into his front room. The light on his answering machine was flashing.

He took off his overcoat, hung it on the rack. He pressed the play button.

"Tom, it's Pops. You were right; Ms. Byron came tonight about eight. And she left around half twelve. She had a fellow with her, name of Mick McGovern...Dubliner. They said they were looking for background for a story they're doing on Dachadoo. I told them what you told me to tell them. Tom, I was surprised how bad...how sad I felt when I was talking to them. It made me feel terrible sad all over again, for you and Michael and your father."

Tom Breen played the message again, then erased it.

He sat at his kitchen table and wrote down the names of the people he would call in the morning. He allowed the pen to fall out of his fingers.

He made a pillow of his arms on the kitchen table, put his elbows on the pillow and wept.

TUESDAY
NOVEMBER 26, 2007

55.

4:30 a.m.
"Shit, Paulie. Half-past four?" Raymond grumbled.
"Be nice to me. I have to talk to you."
"It couldn't wait?"
"I've been awake most of the night. I'm in a quandary."
"Alright. Tell me."
"The last line is that the killer of the three pedophile brothers is Detective Sergeant Tom Breen."
"Holy shit!"
"He also killed the Crueltyman in 1980—Rackert, the one with the sucking calves."
"Jesus!" Raymond switched on his bedside light and fell back down on his pillow. "The implications! Jack Rafferty has better headlines than he ever hoped for."
Pauline told her husband what she and Mick McGovern had discovered in the last eighteen hours; told him that she and McGovern were to meet Tom Breen and his partner in the grounds of Dachadoo Industrial School at eleven o'clock.
"Does Breen know that you know he's the killer?"
"He knows we know."
"And you still plan going ahead with the Dachadoo meeting?"
"Yes."
"You're not afraid of him?"
"No. There's nothing to fear. But yesterday, when I was setting up the meeting, I told Tom Breen that Beatus and McNulty were the last two names on the list we had from

the Dachadoo files—that maybe the guards should keep an eye on them; I told the fox to guard the chickens."

"But you didn't know then he was the fox. That's what you're thinking, isn't it...that he killed Beatus and McNulty last night?"

"Yes, that's what I'm afraid of."

Raymond spoke as if he were reading off a list. "Paulie, you have had a few hours of bad sleep in the last twenty-four hours. You're working off the assumption that Beatus and McNulty are on Breen's list; you're attributing powers to Breen he doesn't have. Beatus and McNulty are separated by twenty miles. Beatus might as well be in prison; McNulty, you said yourself, has one foot in the grave and the other on a banana skin. And Breen wouldn't risk killing someone who's going to be dead in a few months."

"But Breen knew we were about to find out he is the killer. He knew that after the meeting today we'll be obliged to turn him in. If McNulty was on his list, then last night was his last chance to kill him."

"There's nothing you can do at this point."

"But this is my dilemma; should I go to Tullamore Garda Station right now and tell what I know?"

"I think your real dilemma is that if you do hand Breen over to Superintendent Donovan right now, you won't get to meet Breen in Dachadoo. And why is it important to meet him at all at this point? It's over."

"But it's not over for Breen. That's why I want to meet him. On our way to see Pearse Breen last night, Mick asked me in a kind of passing way if I thought Breen has been manipulating *The Telegraph* all along. When we got home here, we sat outside for a long time talking—"

"And..."

"We agreed Tom Breen has been manipulating *The Telegraph* and using the garda system to avoid discovery before he finished what he has set out to do," Pauline said.

"You're not thinking Breen joined the guards as part of a long-range plan?"

"I wouldn't go that far, but I do think we can make decisions for reasons that we're not aware of at the time," Pauline said. "Our desires get fed into our brains and over the years the brain subtly suggests a path to follow. We found out last night that Tom Breen earned a degree in psychology before he joined the guards. For all we know, for all *he* knows, maybe the decision to study psychology was part of his preparation for what he's doing now."

"I think that's stretching it a bit, Paulie."

"It is a stretch. More likely, he went into psychology because he spent years getting his mental health back after what happened to him in Dachadoo. Pearse Breen told us Tom went to a shrink for seven years before going to Galway University."

"Seven years!"

"When Guard Pearse Breen was told that Paddy O'Malley had drowned himself in despair, he was so guilt-ridden about his part in the children's abduction that he and his wife went to Dachadoo to try to adopt the boys. But Michael was already dead and James was 'gone into himself,' as Pearse said. In the end they bought James out of Dachadoo for three hundred pounds—in cash, paid to Brother Lazarian. At the same time, Pearse Breen had himself transferred to Navan and he and his wife pulled off the pretense that James was their child. They called him by his middle name."

"What did Pearse Breen have to say about the killings of the brothers and the Crueltyman?"

"Before that even came up, he let us know that he had cut himself off from all the happenings in the world—no radio, TV or newspapers—and that he spends his time reading the books he believes educated people read in order to be educated—the classics—and he did have all the heavy tomes to prove it. But Mick wondered if the adoptive son has taken precautions to protect the adoptive father against the charge of being an accessory."

"Tom Breen has shown what a detail man he is," Raymond said. "He probably took care of that detail, too."

"Probably, and I think it's his intention to bring the first act of his play to an end in Dachadoo today."

"You're convinced he has a second act in mind! For all you know he's going to perform his grand gesture today, maybe blow his brains out in front of you."

"He's not going to do that at all. But I'm convinced there are more acts."

"And they are?"

"I don't know, Raymond. Maybe he's going to stage a spectacular arrest to bring attention to what was done to him as a child."

"You're talking a bad television plot."

"Maybe so, but no graduate of the industrial schools has ever done anything as spectacular as Breen has. He has searched out the people who almost destroyed him, and he has shown how badly he was dealt with by inflicting barbaric deaths on them. He's screaming, *This is what it was like!* The books and the TV shows have not been able to get across the pain of one individual like Breen has done."

"Paulie, you have removed yourself from the horns of the dilemma. If you believe the meeting today is the closing of act one of Breen's story, then you should attend the opening of act two. If you are accused of harboring a murderer, *The Telegraph* has enough money to hire the best to defend you. But tell Jack Rafferty what you're doing, just to spread the responsibility around."

Raymond switched off the light and for a long time he stared at the fire detector's flashing diode in the ceiling. Pauline began to snore.

6:00 a.m.
Jimmy Gorman was in the habit of letting the answering
machine take the phone calls when he was home alone.
Being the only man living in a house with four females,
the chance of a call being for him was about one in six bil-
lion, he once told Tom Breen. But when the phone rang
at 6 a.m. he knew it was probably the garda station calling. He let the machine take it. Standing at the kitchen
counter in his pajamas and slippered feet, he returned
the electric kettle to its base and kept his ear cocked.

His youngest daughter's announcement came on. *This
is the Gorman and Gorwoman residence. Please leave a message
for Theresa. You may also leave a brief message for her sisters, her
mother and the detective sergeant. After the beep, of course. Ciao.*

"Jimmy, pick up. It's Tom."

"Yes, Tom?"

"Jimmy, I know it's early. I tried your mobile. I hope I
didn't wake everyone. Can you come over to my place as
soon as you can? Don't ask any questions."

"I'm on my way in two minutes."

"I'll have some sort of a breakfast for you."

"No eggs, unless you want to be asphyxiated."

Gorman switched off the kettle and took the stairs
back up to the bedroom two steps at a time.

"Piss and shit," he said softly. "Tom's figured it out. I
thought I'd beat him to it."

6:30 a.m.
Of all the things Pauline had heard in Pearse Breen's sitting room, her mind had snagged—was still snagged—on
the image of James O'Malley's head resting on Pearse's
shoulder as he was carried out of Dachadoo, a destroyed
boy. Pauline thought that if the emotional state of the
child could be equated to a physical state, then James

had been castrated and his Achilles tendons severed with
the slashing machetes of Dachadoo. And Dachadoo was
not the school with the worst reputation. That title might
have to be shared by the Letterfrack institution in Galway,
Artane in Dublin and Mount Cashel in Newfoundland,
all three under the auspices of the Irish Christian Brothers. Baltimore, in County Cork, administered by diocesan priests, was in its own special category of cruelty and
abuse.

Pauline looked at her watch. Two hours had passed
since she'd wakened Raymond with her dilemma. She slid
out of the bed, turned off her alarm and silently left the
room. At the laundry door she hit the button on the talking thermometer and was quacked at.

On the smooth, sole-gripping surface of Emo Park's
main avenue she gave her brain free rein, allowed it to
jump head-first into the swirling cauldron of destroyed
children. And the effluvium in that cauldron was a mixture of child suicides, parental deprivation, state imma-
turity, state neglect, political cowardice, plain human
cowardice, church hubris, religion-bred obsessiveness,
religion-bred compulsions, religion-bred insanity, religion-bred sexual repression, religious institution–bred
dementia, clerical betrayal, clerical self-enrichment,
xenophobe-bred societal dysfunction, greed-driven Crueltymen, sexual abuse, sadism, sexual perversion, unrelenting adult-bullying, insatiable emotional and physical
hungers, lies, lice, medical neglect, medical malpractice.
No wonder so many children became the living dead after
passing through that inferno.

Suddenly, Pauline came to a halt, put her hands on
her knees and whispered, "Feck!" She was breathless,
her muscles aching for oxygen, lungs on fire. While the
pot of human failings had been boiling in her brain, she
had not heard the body's warnings. She straightened

up, took deep breaths and began to walk. In the distance she heard the Emo rooks shouting out their battle cries, imagined them playing chicken, swooping toward each other.

She stopped again but her brain continued on its freewheeling spin, and she thought of the emotionally insatiable children put into the care of the emotionally undeveloped adults overseen by an inexperienced government, the system maintained by the church lest the children fall into the hands of Protestant proselytizers, the system maintained by the state because the religious orders were the least expensive contractors on the market.

She began a slow trot. She could see the green copper dome of Emo Court now, and could plainly hear the baggy-trousered rooks battling for its possession.

As she ran through the noisy pebbles in front of the house and waved to the anorexic lions, Pauline forced the past out of her mind and began to ponder how she would handle the meeting in Dachadoo. No matter what scenario she came up with, it fell apart. There were too many unknowns.

She arrived home with her breathing back to normal. While she was taking off her jogging gear in the laundry room, Raymond called from the kitchen, "Detective Breen phoned. You're to bring a photographer with you to Dachadoo."

7:45 a.m.
When Superintendent Donovan said good morning to his secretary Florence, she told him she had just hung up from speaking with Superintendent Cousins in Portlaoise.

"He wants to talk to you the minute you arrive."

"Get him on the line, Florence, please."

As he hung up his coat, his phone whispered for his attention, like bells tickled with feathers; Donovan hated clangy noise. "Good morning, Phil. It's Christy Donovan."

"Hello, Christy. That religious brother what's-his-name in Saint Fintan's Hospital...the pedophile? He was murdered last night."

"Scuttering fuck!"

"A nail through the heart."

"Scutter! That's our lad. The nail's his trademark. How did he get—?"

"So far there's not one sign of anything; so clean it could be an inside job."

"But it wasn't, Phil."

"Dublin's going to have my balls."

"Tisn't your fault, Phil, and I'll vouch for that. I asked Saint Fintan's to vet any visitors the lad might have."

"Thank God. Thanks, Christy."

"I'll be in touch later, Phil." Donovan hung up. He put his head between his hands, stared at his desktop. For a few moments his thoughts were full of darkness. He sat up and reached for the phone.

"Get me Tom Breen, Florence," he said.

7:44 a.m.
As Jack Rafferty placed his fat fundament on his editorial chair, his secretary called.

"The Weird One," she said.

Rafferty loved code names as much as military people did. His heart sent a surge of blood squishing and hissing through his narrowing arteries. He activated the recording device and picked up the phone.

"Yes?"

"Doctor Alexander McNulty, Tullamore, was hanged last night with blue baler twine. There's a second one:

Brother Beatus in Saint Fintan's Hospital, Portlaoise, stabbed in the heart with a ten-penny nail. It's over, Mister Rafferty, at an end. Serial killers can't stop killing." The caller hung up.

7:47 a.m.

Looking like a building left standing after the Nagasaki blast, Tullamore's ugly and ancient water-tower cast its cold, concrete eye on everyone who entered the town on the Mountmellick road. Tom Breen was in the Cyclops's gaze when his mobile rang. He looked at the number. "Yes, sir."

"Tom, that Brother Beatus was murdered in Saint Fintan's last night."

"Fuck!"

"Nail through the heart."

"Fuck! And you'd warned the hospital."

"At least my arse isn't in a sling. Where are you, Tom?"

"The water tower, sir; behind ten cars following a piece of farm machinery. Maybe it'll turn off at the traffic circle."

"Get Gorman in. Come to my office when you land."

7:52 a.m.

Superintendent Donovan's intercom rang. Florence, the secretary, answered. "Anonymous caller on two, sir."

"I told you, Florence—"

"He says he knows where there's a dead body, sir."

The superintendent sighed loudly. "Put him on."

Donovan disconnected and Florence flashed the red button.

"Superintendent—"

"Doctor McNulty was killed last night," a man's voice said, and the connection was broken.

7:52 a.m.

Pauline Byron had showered and dressed for the day, was sipping tea at the kitchen table when Jack Rafferty called. "I just got in," he wheezed, "and I read Asparagus."

Jack was panting so hard that Pauline asked, "Are you alright?"

"Fine...I'm fine. If only I'd read Asparagus before Snipper called—"

"He called again? Is there another killing?"

"Two." Jack sounded like an asthmatic horse.

"Two! Who?" Pauline shouted, but she knew the answer.

"Brother Beatus with a nail in the heart and Doctor Alexander McNulty by way of hanging with baler twine." Jack was gaining control of his diaphragm as he spoke.

"Holy shit," Pauline moaned. "I should have—"

"Don't start beating yourself up, Byron, for Christ's sake," Rafferty said fiercely. "All you're doing is creating drama. Get over it. Beatus and McNulty are dead because Tom Breen killed them. Their deaths had nothing to do with you."

Pauline stood up from the kitchen table and went over to the window. A green linnet and a yellowhammer were at the bird feeder. Slowly, she ran the fingers of her left hand through her hair.

"Are you there?" Rafferty asked.

"I'm here."

"What's wrong with you?"

"There's nothing wrong with me. But I should have remembered to call the Tullamore guards last night when we—"

"Tell it to a priest, Byron. I don't want to hear about it."

Pauline rested her free hand on the window sash and watched the linnet fly onto a branch of the ash tree she and Raymond had planted together before the girls were born.

"Are you there?" Rafferty asked.

"I'm here. What else did Tom Breen tell you?" Pauline strolled out of the kitchen into the living room.

"He said, 'It's over. It's at an end. Serial killers can't stop killing.'" Jack Rafferty paused. "You were right, Pauline. Thanks for persuading me to keep 'serial killer' out of the story." Before she could acknowledge Jack's compliment, he added, "It's a better story this way—the investigator is the killer. There's going to be red faces in the Garda Síochána."

"I wouldn't be so sure about that, Jack. Tom Breen probably took precautions to protect his friends in the Tullamore Garda Station."

"It's a pity the whole thing is over," Jack said. "I was hoping we'd get a fat Christmas of advertising out of this."

"It's not over at all, Jack." Pauline perched on the arm of the sofa. "Tom Breen has brought the whole story this far by himself, and I suspect he's going to hand it over to *The Telegraph* when we meet in Dachadoo today."

"What are you talking about?"

"Tom Breen has been his own publicity agent since this began. He manipulated you and—"

"Manipulated *me*, Pauline? No one manipulates me, not even the presumptuous archbishop of Dublin." Rafferty's voice was heavy with annoyance.

"Jack," Pauline said firmly, "you have a habit of hanging up on people when you're pissed off. Do not hang up on me. Keep reminding yourself how I already saved your oversized arse once. I'm not going to beat around the bush to spare you your image of yourself—you can go to a shrink for that. Tom Breen obviously planned what he has done for a long time. A major part of his plan was publicity. He manipulated you all along."

"If he manipulated me, Pauline, I knew he was manipulating me and therefore there was no manipulation."

Rafferty did not hang up, but he changed the subject. "I'd love to be in Dachadoo for the meeting with Breen. Do you think we should have some muscle down there in case it gets out of hand?"

"No. But you can put a photographer on the road right away. Send him to Daingean; there are dozens of Daingeans so make sure he knows it's the one in County Offaly. When he gets here tell him to call me."

"By the way, did you see the front-page sidebar today?"

"No, I haven't."

"*Telegraph* to Archbishop: Get Lost!"

Jack Rafferty hung up.

7:58 a.m.

In the dining room of the Montague Hotel, as he waited for his breakfast to arrive, the smells from the kitchen primed Mick McGovern's salivary system.

The plates of his customized breakfast order began to arrive by individual delivery with the word *Now!* attached to each one. A pot of tea was carried by a small woman with a limp who had not made financial plans for her old age: "Now!" she said, as if to say, *Ya spiled bollocks.* Slices of brown bread arrived by way of a spotty-faced young man with something black under his fingernails: "Now!" as if to say, *I had to geh up early to puh your bread on yer fucken table.* The butter dish was delivered by a young woman whose clothes were straining to contain her overendowment in the mammary, belly and arse departments: "Now!" as if to say, *Grease yer greedy chops wid dat.* And finally, to the accompaniment of the *Prince of Denmark's March* in McGovern's head, the little limping woman returned with a large plate containing three fried eggs, four fat sausages, six slices of bacon and a large serving of mushrooms: "Now!" as if to say, *Ate dat, ya pig!*

As the plate was lowered onto the table in front of him, McGovern's eyes went down with it and he decided a piece of sausage would be the first thing to ease his gastronomical craving.

He stabbed a sausage with the fork and sliced off an inch and a half. He speared the morsel and his phone rang.

"Mick, it's Pauline. We have to move quickly. Meet me in Tess Westman's Tea Rooms in Daingean in half an hour." She hung up.

"Shit! What...?" McGovern glanced around and put the chunk of sausage in his mouth. He stood up, spread his napkin on the table, scraped the bacon, sausages and mushrooms onto the napkin, folded it and put it into his coat pocket. He left the three eggs.

"There's many a fucking slip twix sausage and gob," he said aloud.

8:10 a.m.

The large farm machine bouncing along the road ten cars ahead of Tom Breen and a lorry the size of a three-bedroom house locked horns on the small Ardan roundabout. The lorry driver had been holding a phone to his ear with one hand when he should have been steering with two. Tom Breen abandoned his car and was within shouting distance of the accident when his phone rang. He saw it was the superintendent again but he did not answer.

"Yah big stupid fucken hure av a fucken lorry driver. Didn't I see yah on de fucken phone meself, you big ignorant fucken cunt of a Dublin hure? Dat's a bran new combine fucken harvester, yah fucken lyin bastard."

Breen ran in between the two men and held up his identity card. "Shut up, the two of you!" he shouted. "There are women and children here. Get over there to your harvester! And you—get back in your lorry!"

The phone was still ringing in his hand when he saw Jimmy Gorman trotting into the roundabout. Gorman had abandoned his car, too. For the last hour and a half he'd listened to his partner's confession. His initial anger had quickly turned to grief and his eyes were still red.

"Jimmy," Tom called, "get these two yokes out of the roundabout." He swept his arm over the lorry and the harvester. "The supe is calling me." Breen put the phone to his ear. "Sorry, sir. There's a holdup—a minor accident at the Ardan rounda—"

"Tom!" the superintendent barked. "We have another dead fucking body. Did you ever hear of a Doctor Alexander McNulty, an old retiree, been in Tullamore since the Flood? He was hung with blue baler twine. It has to be Nailer, but why the fuck would Nailer kill this old geezer and right under our noses? The fucker! Dublin's going to be so far up me hole I'll have a matching pair of shoes hanging out of me arse...What's all that horn blowing about? I can hardly hear you."

"Sir, I'll call you back in a few minutes. Jimmy's here directing traffic and I'm going to help him. Can you send a few uniforms around? The Ardan roundabout."

When he looked up, a red Citroen Berlingo van speedily spun out of the roundabout, the gold lettering on its side boldly proclaiming DEEGAN DOGS.

8:10 a.m.
Pauline Byron called the Bennet house on Croghan Hill. "Good morning. Cyril?"

"Right the first time. Good morning, Pauline. It *is* Pauline?"

"Yes. Were you expecting I'd call you today, Cyril?"

"Is this off the record, Pauline?"

"Yes, it is."

"Are your using a tape recorder?"

"No."

"Yes, Pauline, Patrick and I were expecting you would call."

"Do you know about Brother Beatus and Doctor McNulty?"

"Yes."

"You know it already?" Pauline asked, an indirect prompt.

"Yes."

Pauline hesitated, gave him another opportunity to tell her how he knew. Cyril did not oblige her. "Did you and Patrick know a Michael O'Malley in Dachadoo?"

"No."

"Did you know a James O'Malley in Dachadoo?"

"No."

"Do you know a Tom Breen?"

"Yes."

Pauline paused, decided there was no need to ask if Cyril knew Tom Breen was James O'Malley.

"Do you know about a meeting Tom Breen is having today at eleven?"

"Yes."

"Were you invited to attend?"

"Patrick and I were invited *not* to attend."

"Why was that?"

"Pauline, you probably know the answer to that."

Pauline paused again. Cyril remained silent.

"May I make a wild guess about something?"

"Of course."

"Last Friday when I went to see you and Patrick, I saw a framed painting on the wall inside your front door, *Danse à Bougival*. Did you receive that print as a gift from Tom Breen?"

"Yes."

"So you are well acquainted? He would have known your taste to give you a painting."

"Right again, Pauline."

"That invitation to attend one of your *soirées,* I think you called it—I would like to attend some Saturday and maybe we could discuss the morality of revenge."

"Revenge is an interesting and vexing question, Pauline. But the responsibility of the individual to take action when the state fails in the performance of its duty is also an interesting topic."

"That sounds like a tough position to defend, Cyril."

"The position does not need defending, Pauline. It needs explication by a gifted lawyer."

"And is such a gifted lawyer ever a guest at your *soirées?*"

"Yes."

"Cyril, say hello to Patrick for me."

"I will indeed, Pauline, and you say hello to your husband for us."

"Raymond."

"Yes, Raymond. I imagine you keep him on his toes."

"I do, Cyril. You're not a bad dancer yourself. Goodbye."

56.

At twenty minutes past ten, when Pauline Byron drove off the Daingean road onto the approach to Dachadoo, her jeep bounced in and out of a deep, lane-wide, water-filled pothole. Sheets of muddy water flew up in the air blanking out the windscreen. Pauline braked sharply and the three occupants slid forward against their seat belts.

"Japers!" the young woman in the back hissed. She clutched her camera bag with its precious Nikon 300 tightly to her belly and planted her feet firmly on the floor.

Pauline slowed down to walking speed, switched on the wipers and sprayed the windscreen. "Sorry about that, Kathleen," she said over her shoulder, and she pushed the tape recorder, hanging from her neck on a red and black bootlace, back inside her jacket.

"There's someone gone in ahead of us," Mick McGovern said from the passenger seat. He pointed through the windscreen at the set of fresh tracks connecting the potholes.

"I wonder has Detective Breen changed the rules," Pauline said. "We're supposed to get here first."

"Should I be afraid there's going to be some unpleasantness?" the photographer asked.

Mick McGovern turned around. "You sound like Dorothy Sayers," he said. "And no we do not expect any unpleasantness at all. The only unpleasantness will be mud. I wasn't as far-seeing as you—wearing boots out into the country."

"I'm used to mud, Mister McGovern. I live in Debbicot on the road between Mountmellick and Emo."

"You're surrounded by two country biddies, Mick," Pauline said. "Can't you get the smell of slurry and silage off us?"

Kathleen realized that Pauline was the captain of this ship. "Miss Byron, can you tell me what to expect when we get to wherever we're going?"

"Call me Pauline, Kathleen, and Mick is Mick. We're meeting with two detectives in the ruins of that industrial school over there on the right." Pauline pointed to the high walls.

Then in a few sentences McGovern filled in Kathleen on the goings-on of the past few days without mentioning the gory details. "It's likely that Detective Breen will set up your shots," he said, "and you will only have to choose the best angles. He was the one who asked for a photographer."

"But Kathleen," Pauline said, "I want you to do the usual photographer's thing—be opportunistic. You will have to be in charge of yourself. Don't depend on Mick or me to direct you. And don't give Breen power over you."

The jeep splashed and bumped along and the abandoned buildings grew in size. Pauline tried to keep her wheels in the fresh tracks on the lane in the hope they had been made by someone familiar with the more precipitous potholes. Following the instructions given by Detective Breen, she drove her jeep around the high wall and past the high rusting corrugated gates. She came to a railway bed that had once brought the train to the school with its cargo of third-class meat, coal and sometimes a small boy with his fearful face pressed against the glass of the carriage, a watchful adult behind him.

A yellow Vauxhall Vectra with a slightly buckled hood and a dented front bumper was parked at the overgrown right-of-way.

"That's the car I saw at the convent yesterday—Breen and his sidekick are here," McGovern said.

Pauline pulled on the handbrake and switched off the engine. As if suddenly unsure of themselves, as if stunned by the uncertainty ahead of them, the three passengers sat silently until Pauline took in a loud breath and opened her door. Before she had swung off the seat, before Mick McGovern had opened his door, Tom Breen came around the corner of the wall in his khaki-colored, winter gabardine overcoat, grey scarf, paddycap, red tie, blue denim shirt and green wellington boots. He removed his cap, held the door open and stood aside to allow Pauline to step out. The bare ground had frozen overnight, but the weak morning sun had thawed it again, leaving it a mess of cloying, slippery muck.

"Good morning, Pauline. I'm by myself," Breen said, and held out his hand.

"Good morning, Tom," Pauline said and shook the proffered hand. "You changed the rules."

"Circumstances changed since we spoke yesterday, as you undoubtedly know."

"I know. I'm wearing a tape recorder and it's running." Pauline pulled her jacket apart and put the tape recorder on the outside.

"This is my microphone," Breen said, and he touched the small enamel primrose on his lapel. "Thanks for not turning me in."

"My motive wasn't pure, Tom. I expect to get something out of our meeting," Pauline said. "And you know I will have to turn you in when we're finished."

"You won't have to do that, Pauline. I've arranged to have myself arrested."

"Why am I not surprised to hear that, Tom? You're as fastidious as a clocking hen." Pauline indicated McGovern. "This is my partner, Mick McGovern."

McGovern, pleased to hear "my partner," carefully stepped his way around the front of the car. The men shook hands. "I should have told you to wear boots," Breen said. "There's a few pairs of wellingtons in the Vauxhall."

"And this is Kathleen Hayes, our photographer." Pauline pointed to the car and moved away so Kathleen could get out.

"Good morning, Kathleen," Breen said. He reached in under the driver's seat, moved the lever and slid the seat forward. "Let me take your camera," he said. He held out his free hand and assisted Kathleen out of the jeep.

Kathleen took back her camera, forced out a thank-you and twisted her face into a smile.

"Tom," Pauline said, "Kathleen must be free to take any photograph she wishes."

"That's fine, Pauline." Breen put his cap on. "Are you interested in the boots, Mick? They'll save those shoes."

"Thanks."

When Breen stepped back through the muck from his car, he handed the boots and a pair of socks to McGovern. "If these are too big, the socks will tighten them on your feet."

"Is your partner here, Tom?" McGovern asked as he went back to the passenger side to change his footwear.

"No, he's not."

Kathleen's shutter had already clicked five times.

"If you don't mind, Pauline," Detective Sergeant Breen said, "I would like to be in charge for a while."

"Haven't you been in charge all the time, Tom?" Pauline said. "You've even succeeded in manipulating the fearsome Jack Rafferty. You've manipulated me and Mick here. You've manipulated the Garda Síochána. You manipulated your way into Saint Fintan's in Portlaoise and killed a man in his bed last night. You have unilaterally adjusted the rules of engagement since we spoke yesterday."

"Only slightly...You and Mick put pressure on me to move faster than I'd planned. I'm here by myself because Jimmy Gorman, my partner, is in Tullamore persuading Superintendent Donovan that his rear end—Donovan's—is covered, that he won't be demoted or ridiculed for looking for a murderer who was so close to him he couldn't see him. Jimmy will tell Christy Donovan he doesn't know where I am, but that I will call and tell them where to come to arrest me."

"You should have been a stage manager, Tom," Pauline said. "*Our* camerawoman is one of *your* props?"

"Yes," Breen said. "I would like photos taken today; I'll be in jail tonight."

"Don't you think you might be presuming a bit much, Tom?" McGovern came around the nose of the jeep in his knee-high wellingtons. "How many photos do you hope to get in tomorrow's *Telegraph*?"

"Only the one of my arrest, Mick," Breen said. "I'm counting on Pauline and you, hoping that you will develop what you have found out so far—and what you will dig up in the future—into a front-page, deep-headlined, investigative report beginning in tomorrow's paper and ending the day after my trial ends."

"Now you're really presuming—"

"Mick," Breen said. He held out his hand against McGovern's words. "Please hear me through. I am not being presumptuous, I am being hopeful. I *hope* that I can persuade you and Pauline to take on this story after I walk you around Dachadoo. I am not stage managing anymore. At this point I have lost all control and I hope *The Telegraph* will pick up my quest from here."

"Quest, Tom?" Pauline asked. "Do you see yourself as a knight on a white horse?"

"No...Please, Pauline, I'm not delusional." Again Breen's hands went out, but this time they were supplicants. "Please, I'm not quixotic. 'Quest' is the only word that fits, and I used it to be as precise as possible. All I'm asking is that you walk around the school with me. If you don't come with me, it's all over and I'll just be another whacko."

Pauline and Mick looked at each other.

"We'll go with you," McGovern said.

"I'm in your hands," Breen said.

"Okay," Pauline said. "But before we set out, Tom, and this is purely out of curiosity...did you manipulate Jack Rafferty into putting me on this story?"

"Yes. I told him unless you were put on it there would be no more phone calls."

Pauline looked at the ground and slowly moved her head from side to side.

The Nikon 300 shuttered.

"Alright, Tom," Pauline said. "You're in charge up to a point. But this meeting is not going to be a one-sided affair. We have some questions and we expect answers to them."

"Of course," Breen said. "Ask anything you wish and I will answer if I can."

Again Pauline glanced over at McGovern. He gave her a nod.

"Lay on, Macduff. You're in charge of the tour." Pauline looked back at Kathleen, made eye contact with her.

"Thank you both," Breen said. "Thank you. We'll begin right here."

57.

The little group walked along the old railway bed beside the high wall. Twenty yards to their left a hedgerow had spread itself into an entanglement of glorious confusion, had grown unchecked by tool of man or mouth of beast for more than twenty-five years. Between the visitors and the hedge, the long grass had collapsed like ripe cereal in harvesttime after a hailstorm, but the stalks of last year's dead weeds stood defiantly within the greenness.

Led by Breen, they ascended the slope of the short railway platform. An opening, without its door or frame, led through the eighteen-inch-thick wall on their right. They followed Breen through, and on the other side found themselves standing in a bushy and long-grassed enclosure.

"This was the playing field of Dachadoo." Breen swept his arm around. "That's the rear of the dormitory." He pointed to the two-story building they were facing, every windowpane broken, but with the roof still intact. "Along this wall, over to the left, were the outdoor toilets, the day toilets. Now I'm going to bring you through to the Assembly Yard on the far side of the dormitory and to the main entrance gate. Follow me on the track through the bushes."

He turned to go but Pauline stopped him. "Tom, whatever it was that motivated you to murder six people happened here forty years ago. Why did you wait all this time?"

"I did kill six men," Breen said, "but I didn't murder them, Pauline. I executed them. I waited years for the state to administer justice. Even when I realized that wouldn't happen, I kept putting off the killings because I couldn't bring myself to kill again, not after my up-close-and-personal execution of William Rackert. In the end, it was their old age that got me moving—I was afraid the men would die unpunished and that the opportunity to use them to dig up the past and push it in the country's face would soon be gone. Of course there was always my underlying motive—justice for my brother Michael. And it wasn't just killing that was difficult; it was doing it in such a way that the guards, and the media especially, would see beyond the dead bodies." Pauline glanced at McGovern and nodded.

"Bring us to the main entrance gate, Tom," McGovern said. Kathleen Hayes had become invisible, but her camera was active.

As the guard and the reporters wound their way through the frosty bushes, Kathleen slipped off her jacket and used it to protect her legs and skirt from burrs. Like forest denizens dodging thick undergrowth, they walked around the end of the dormitory and out into the Assembly Yard. The area was as overgrown as the playground. Through haw- and sloe-laden bushes they advanced, the thorny, fingery blackberry briars grabbing at them like street urchins begging for coins.

Breen stopped when he came to the high corrugated gate. "The day my brother and I were brought here the Crueltyman blew the horn outside the gate." Breen lifted the flap of the peephole. "The eyes and eyebrows that appeared in this slot were...At that moment of my life it was the most horri..." Breen looked at the others and gave a wry smile. "Seems stupid now that I talk about it."

Pauline and Mick had nothing to say. Mick picked at the burrs in his trouser legs.

"I'm not looking for sympathy here," Breen continued. "I'm trying to recreate an atmosphere which can't be recreated. For one thing, I was twelve, Michael was eight. That very day, July the fourth, 1967, our mother had been buried. When our father brought us home after the funeral, the Crueltyman arrived almost immediately and took us to a judge in Portlaoise, who committed us to Dachadoo. It was a long journey from Portlaoise to here, and when these buildings began to rise up out of the bog and grew bigger and bigger the closer we got, the more terrified we became. And then when those eyes and eyebrows appeared in the slot in the gate it was like the giant in *Jack and the Beanstalk* had captured us for his sandwich." Breen stopped for a moment, as if he had gone away to someplace else inside his head.

The terror of the O'Malley boys threatened to overrun Pauline's defenses.

Mick McGovern strode over and leaned against the high gate. Kathleen took several shots of the sun glistening in the glass shards on top of the wall.

Breen turned his back to the gate. "That building across the yard was called the Brothers' House," he continued. "That bow window on the first floor to the left of the main entrance was Lazarian's office. That's where we'll go next."

As Breen began to walk away, Kathleen asked, "Can the gate be opened, Mister Breen? I'd like to get a shot of the slot from the other side."

Tom Breen pulled a rusty iron rod out of its socket, twisted another out of its hole in the ground, and slid two wooden beams inside their guides from one side of the door to the other. He pulled the unlocked half against the long grass and the protesting hinges, made a narrow opening.

"Would you look through the slot, Mister Breen, please?" Kathleen asked, and she squeezed through the gap in the gates.

While Kathleen issued instructions from the other
side of the gate, McGovern picked at the annoying burrs.
"How come you didn't get any of these?" he asked.

"I'm from the country."

"What, they don't stick to country people?"

"I know what to look out for. Can you recognize stinging nettles?"

"No."

"You will."

When the photo had been taken and the door
relocked, Breen set out for the Brothers' House. "That
building on the right was called the Factory. That's where
the classrooms and the workshops were."

"What happened to the windows, Tom—the glass?"
Pauline asked.

"Boys, I suppose. Boys will walk miles to break a window."

The reporters followed the policeman through the
grabbing bushes to the limestone-arched entrance. The
door and its frame were gone. Breen held the thorny
branch of a whitethorn aside to allow the others to enter.

Pauline hesitated in the doorway. "Are the floors
sound in here, Tom?"

"Yes, they are. I've been here recently and I know it's
safe."

Breen led the way across the slated, leaf-littered, guano-
strewn floor and up the wide stairs. Weeds had sprouted
and died in the crevasses where the risers met, and paint
had fallen in flakes from the walls onto the steps. Breen
waited on the landing, and when the others caught up, he
strode across the hallway and through a doorway.

58.

Brother Lazarian's old office was bare, cold and damp. The built-in seat beneath the bow window was still in place, its polished surface long faded and bird droppings thick on the grey wood. Stalks of grass had grown, died and collapsed in the tiny crevasses where the seat was attached to the wall. The floor around the seat was grey and spotted with wormholes. Some of the boards were warped.

Breen faced the newspaper people and resumed his role of guide.

"Michael and I were handed over to Brother Lazarian in this spot. Lazarian's big desk was right behind me. The Crueltyman told Lazarian I was a difficult child, that I had been physically violent while being brought here. The moment the Crueltyman left, Lazarian set about establishing his authority. Without warning he banged our heads together and sent us sprawling on our backs. When we didn't get up fast enough, he picked Michael off the floor and began to shake him. Michael screamed and I ran at Lazarian, got his thumb in my teeth, and I bit down hard and I wouldn't let go. Another brother—it turned out to be Boniface—heard Lazarian roaring and ran in here. When I recovered my bearings, Boniface had me pinned to the floor and Lazarian was holding a bottle of smelling salts under my nose.

"All the time, Michael was screaming for our parents... He was only eight, for Christ's sake." Breen hesitated for a moment. "We were made to sit on the bench over at the window while Lazarian dealt with his injured thumb, and then we heard our father calling our names down

in the Assembly Yard. We knelt up on that bench and
began shouting to him through the open window. The
yard was full of boys and our father was running around
calling us and Brother Beatus was running after him. Our
father heard us and saw us, and he ran to the front door.
Brother Boniface closed the window and we were made
to sit down again. We heard a lot of shouting, heard our
father calling our names from the stairs, and then everything went quiet."

Breen walked over and looked out through the broken panes. "Years later, I learned that my father had been
severely injured in the kidneys by the brothers' fists and
boots. He was carried outside the gate and left for the
guards. They took him to the garda station in Tullamore,
the old one, and kept him overnight. When he was let
out the next morning he drowned himself in the canal in
Tullamore...He had tied a twelve-by-nine building block
around his neck with baler twine."

With the fingers of her right hand, Pauline pushed
her cheek into her teeth until it hurt.

Tom Breen turned back to the reporters. "When the
brothers had taken care of my father, Brother Beatus
was brought into this room. Over there, against the wall
beside the door, Brother Lazarian beat Beatus with his
open hands and fists. My father had paid Beatus to open
the gate to let him in. Beatus was beaten until he handed
over the money. Then Lazarian made him take off his
shoes and socks.

"There was dreadful anger in this room when Beatus
was gone. Lazarian's thumb was wrapped in a handkerchief. Brother Boniface was very big." Breen looked up at
Pauline and Mick. "*Achtung*," he said. "That's what he was
to me then, in this room. *Achtung*. He was the big dumb
German soldier in the pictures who always obeyed without hesitation—someone yelled, *Achtung!* and the soldier
jumped. Boniface pulled Michael and me out of here—

dragged us by our clothes, one each side. He brought us down the hallway and threw us into a small room. That's where we'll go next." He turned toward the door.

"Mister Breen," Kathleen said, "I would like to get a shot of you at that window from outside—the one you saw your father through. Is that okay?"

"Yes, of course."

Breen walked back to the window and leaned in over the built-in bench, rested his hands on the windowsill.

When the photos were taken, McGovern asked, "Tom, why did you kill the Crueltyman in 1980? He wasn't so old."

"He had liver cancer and didn't have long to live."

"But that was a reason *not* to kill him. You only cut short his suffering."

"Rackert was the cruelest of them all," Breen said. "He stole children out of their homes and sold them like another man sells pigs. Like the others, it wasn't his death as much as his terror before his death that was the point. Even so, no matter how much terror he endured, it was not enough to balance out the terror he inflicted on the children he kidnapped. Rackert was as monstrous as the man to whom he sold the children."

"And that was Brother Lazarian," McGovern said. "Is that why you obliterated Lazarian?"

"It wasn't my intention to tear Lazarian apart, Mick," Tom Breen said. "I went to Cloonagh with the intention of hanging Lazarian from his staircase. He knew what I was going to do because I told him so, and I also told him it would take him hours to die. But he goaded me into killing him quickly. I became an animal. When he was dead, I realized he'd defeated me again."

Breen took off his cap, looked at it and put it on again. He walked over to a window and gazed out on the Assembly Yard. There, forty years ago, Pearse Breen had carried the distraught James O'Malley out of Dachadoo, his wife

Patricia behind like a cow wanting the farmer to put her calf down off his carrying shoulders so she could lick it clean.

McGovern glanced at Pauline and she nodded encouragement. "What did Lazarian say to set you off?" he asked. "To make you drop your original plan?"

Breen did not turn away from the window.

Pauline glanced around at Kathleen. The photographer wiggled a reassuring finger without taking the camera from her face.

"Before Lazarian died he answered some questions I needed answers to," Breen said, then turned around. "He said that when he was appointed headmaster to this place, Dachadoo, the superior of the Order of Saint Kieran informed him that two of the brothers were pedophiles and that he, Lazarian, was to control them. He told me he controlled them by limiting their sexual activities to certain boys—the ones who needed punishment the most."

"Holy shit!" Mick McGovern said loudly.

Pauline brought her hand to her mouth.

Breen continued. "I told you already that I bit Lazarian's thumb within minutes of getting here. In his house in Cloonagh he told me that he punished me for biting him by consigning Michael to his two animals. That's when I lost it. When I finally calmed down, I was kneeling on the floor with my hands around Lazarian's heart and it impaled on the fireplace poker."

Pauline sucked the flesh of her cheeks into her teeth and bit down. She turned her back and walked over to a window. Her throat constricted as she tried to control herself. She clasped a hand over her mouth but a muffled cry was heard.

For almost a minute the only sound was the clicking of Kathleen's camera.

Pauline pulled a handkerchief out of her jacket pocket and blew noisily and wetly. She faced back to the room. "You were going to take us to a room, Tom."

Breen led the way out of Brother Lazarian's office, turned left and walked down the wide corridor. Open doors on each side were the only source of light. The dried carapaces of insects and shells of nuts crackled beneath the feet of the intruders. A vague white line ran along the floor on each side, four inches from the walls. Tom Breen took out a small flashlamp, aimed the beam at the ceiling and lit up dozens of swallows' nests. "That's where the two white lines on the floor come from," he said.

Breen walked past a narrow stairwell and stopped at the first door on the right. He switched his flashlamp on again, waited for the others to catch up.

"We were thrown in here by Brother Boniface after he dragged us out of Lazarian's office. Everything happened so quickly that we didn't see where we had landed. We ended up flat on the floor." Breen opened the door and stepped back to allow Pauline and Mick to see in. The small room was empty. There was no window.

"I remember the bang of the door and the turning of the key. We were in pitch blackness. We ended up spooning each other on the floor against that wall on the left and we fell asleep. Michael had wet himself in Lazarian's office. At some point we woke up. Brother Beatus was in the room with a flashlamp. He managed to separate us. When Beatus pulled Michael out through the door, I held on to him. Beatus punched me in the chest and I fell back into the room and he locked me inside." Breen stepped in front of the reporters. "If you would stand back against the wall, I will show you something."

He went into the room. "When I close the door you will see a small knothole once I find it with the flashlamp. You may have to bend down a bit to see it."

Pauline and Mick put their hands on their knees. "We see it," Mick said.

Breen rejoined them in the corridor. "When Michael was out here with Beatus, I peeped through that hole. I saw Beatus removing Michael's clothes, I saw Beatus with his trousers at his ankles and I saw him placing Michael on a bench that was over there." Breen pointed. "Michael was screaming and I was screaming and banging the door. At that age I did not know what was going on, but in time I came to realize that Beatus had been raping Michael. Then the other two, John the Baptist and Boniface, came running. They were shouting, 'He's ours! He's ours!' Michael was lying with his face and body pushed into the angle of the wall and the floor. He was naked from the waist and there was blood on him. Boniface and John the Baptist flung Beatus up against the wall and banged the back of his head over and over. At some point, Boniface carried Michael by the clothes back into the cupboard like he was carrying a pup by the scruff of the neck. He left him face down on the floor."

Breen turned off the flashlamp and stood against the wall as if giving the visitors time to absorb what he had told them.

Pauline's instinct was to put her arms around Tom Breen, but she forced herself to act professionally, give the impression of pure objectivity.

"Tom," Mick McGovern said, "I want to play devil's advocate. Do you have any way of proving these things happened?"

Breen touched the primrose on his lapel. "I recorded everything the brothers and the doctor told me. My partner, Jimmy Gorman, recorded what Beatus said in Saint Fintan's. The tapes will back up what I'm telling you."

"What was the significance of the number of nails you used on the victims?" Pauline asked.

"The Crueltyman had eight nails in him," Breen said, "one for each year of Michael's life. Boniface and John the Baptist had the same, plus three for the number of times they each raped Michael."

"You're very precise with the number," McGovern said.

"Each time it happened, Michael came to me with blood running down the backs of his legs...He was in agony, not able to sit down, hardly able to walk. I tried to stay with him all the time, but we were often separated because of our ages...Boniface and John the Baptist confessed to the number of rapes—it's on the tapes."

No one spoke for a long time. It was Kathleen Hayes who broke the spell. "Mister Breen, would you stand in the middle of the corridor and point to where your brother was lying while the two brothers were beating Beatus?"

As Breen obliged, Kathleen clicked several times.

"Where to next, Tom?" Pauline asked.

"There are three more places, Pauline."

59.

Detective Sergeant Breen led the reporters and the photographer back toward Lazarian's office and down the main stairway. They followed him to the left and stood in front of the first doorway. "The doors on this floor were oak. They were all removed with their frames and fittings by an enterprising young carpenter who thinks no one knows he took them. But it's better he took them; they'd only rot here."

He brought them into a long room with another doorway in the far end wall. "This was the visitors' parlor. You can still see it was wallpapered to impress, to allay any suspicion that the children were living in squalor. This is where my adoptive parents saw me for the first time. I wasn't well and I don't remember this room at all—I had found Michael dead in bed the night before. What I am telling you is hearsay from my adoptive mother. That far door up there was the one Lazarian came through, swept through like an actor coming onto a stage to steal all the attention for himself, my mother said. They paid him three hundred pounds for me. My adoptive father carried me out of here in his arms because I couldn't walk."

"Your name was scratched out of Lazarian's journal," McGovern said.

"Yes, Mick. Lazarian told my parents I had no history in Dachadoo, never to come back looking for anything about me because there wouldn't be anything. This way..."

They followed him back out through the arched doorway, and Breen turned right along the front wall of the Brothers' House. When they came to the dormitory building he made a left turn and still remained close to the wall where the bushes were not as thick. Two steps led up to the doorway.

The room was the size of the entire building, a vast spread of floor with no dividing walls, no glass in the windows. For years the weather had blown in through one side and out the other without hindrance. The floor was littered with the collapsed ceiling plaster and the debris of birds' nests fallen from the exposed rafters. A long row of sinks, once attached to the walls to the left and right of the door, had been smashed, pieces of white ceramic still clinging to their bent drainpipes. Small scabs of plaster clung to the walls, but the rest had collapsed, had been washed across the floor to mix with the other debris. Rotting glass cracked underfoot. Birds and bats, disturbed by the intruders, chirped and squeaked in the darkness overhead.

When they were all inside, Tom Breen said, "I'm not sure of the sturdiness of this place."

"I'd like to get to the end wall, Mister Breen," Kathleen said. "If I stay close to the wall will I be okay?"

"I would keep away from the wall—the broken ceramic can be deadly," Breen said. "Check every step before you put your weight down."

Kathleen turned away and began her cautious journey.

"All boys under thirteen slept in this room and the older boys' dormitory was on the floor above us," Breen said. "Down here there were six rows of beds that went from one end of the room to the other. The bigger boys were at this end and the smaller ones up there." He pointed to his left. "A narrow walkway separated the two sections. The tension in here at bedtime was thick. Four brothers roamed the room with their leather straps looking for violations of the rules. The bed-wetters were threatened and the leathers waved in their faces. Some boys wet themselves from anxiety before they even got into bed, and then the humiliation of the turban punishment followed and the mopping-up on hands and knees. Michael slept in the first bed in the row beside the sinks—there on the left. My bed was over toward that corner—the third row over and down near the end wall.

"On the day before my brother was murdered, I saw John the Baptist pulling him out of the playground and through the farmyard gate. I ran after them, saw them going into the hay shed. But I didn't know Boniface was in there, too. Boniface grabbed me and locked me into a wire cage where young chickens were kept. I saw John the Baptist and Boniface greasing each other's penises. The things we remember: Boniface preferred goose grease and John the Baptist liked butter. They laughed about it as they stimulated each other. One held my brother down across a bale of hay while the other raped him."

McGovern looked at Pauline and surreptitiously touched her elbow.

"That night I stayed awake, waited for the monitors to leave so I could get into bed with Michael. That was rule number one in the dormitory—never get into bed with another boy, not even if he is your brother. If boys were caught breaking the rule, the punishment went on for hours—standing in the same spot in the Assembly Yard no matter the weather, the excrement running down the backs of legs."

Pauline made a noise.

"Eventually, I crept through the rows of beds. I climbed in with Michael, and pushed him over to make some room. I wasn't long in the bed when I realized he wasn't breathing and I felt something hard on his chest. I suppose I screamed. When the lights came on, I saw the head of the nail sticking out and Michael's eyes half open, half closed."

Pauline put her hand on Tom Breen's arm. Breen put his hand on top of Pauline's hand.

Kathleen's camera flashed. Birds in the rafters fluttered. Mick McGovern turned away and took off his glasses.

When he regained his composure, McGovern said, "The nails, Tom. That's how you killed Beatus last night in Saint Fintan's—a nail through the heart."

"A *ten-penny* nail thought the heart, Mick," Breen said. "If Beatus couldn't get his share of Michael, no one could. So he murdered him in his bed with a ten-penny nail."

"According to Michael's death certificate he died of pneumonia," Pauline said.

"You visited Doctor McNulty, Pauline," Breen said. "You know he signed blank death certificates and that Lazarian filled in the details. I *saw* my brother lying dead with the head of the nail on his chest."

"I had to ask you about the certificate, Tom," Pauline said.

"I know you did."

Pauline disengaged herself from Tom Breen and stood back.

"I don't remember anything after that," the detective said, "until I wakened in the backseat of the Breens' Morris Minor near Oldcastle in County Meath. There was a dog. We were at my adoptive mother's parents' house."

Neither reporter could find words of consolation. Standing each side of Breen, they were numbed. When Kathleen rejoined them, Breen said, "There's just one more place—the cemetery. That's where Christy Donovan will arrest me. Before we set out, I'll call Jimmy Gorman to tell him to saddle up the posse."

The phone call lasted less than five seconds.

"The cemetery isn't far, but we have to follow an obstacle course to get there. We'll go slow."

Breen led the way. Around the gable end of the Brothers' House he went, keeping to the perimeter of the playground until they came to a wide opening in the wall. The twisted halves of a high galvanized gate still clung to their top hinges.

"Careful here," Breen said, and he stopped. "There are bits of jagged iron lying around." He waited until the others had passed through the gateway.

"It's going to be mucky for a while...This was the farmyard." He pointed to a number of sheds with doors and many roof slates missing. "A local farmer bought the big hay sheds and dismantled them. We're heading for the hedge over to the left." He gestured with a wave of his hand. "Someone has been grazing their cattle in the fields. Watch out for old cow plops; you could slip if you walk on one."

Through wet ankle-high grass he led them to the dense evergreen hedge growing high out of its foundation of a lower, untended barrier of leafless, thorned bushes and briars and furze.

"There's a gate at the end of the evergreens," the detective said, and the two reporters and Kathleen followed his track through the grass.

The space in front of the wooden gate was closed in with a wall of briars, but a neat, narrow pathway had been cut through them. The gate itself had once been tarred to preserve it against the weather. Most of the tar was gone now and most of the gate was rotten, held together with the barbed wire that had been wrapped around it to make it impenetrable, boy-proof. But there were signs that it had been recently opened—drag marks could be seen in the grass, and briars that had wound themselves around the lower bars were chopped. Pauline knew she would only have been filling empty air if she asked Breen had he been there recently with a billhook. But she couldn't let the moment pass.

"You had planned to meet with us here in Dachadoo all along, Tom, hadn't you?" she said, and she pointed to the prepared pathway to the gate, to the chopped bushes.

"Yes, Pauline, but you suggested it."

A car horn sounded twice in the distance. Breen looked back in the direction of the school's ruins. "They're here." He lifted and dragged the gate. He let the others through one at a time while he kept the gate from leaning back into its space.

They had arrived in a small enclosure about fifty feet wide and two hundred feet long.

"This is the cemetery—the boys' cemetery," Breen said. "Any brother who died in the school was buried in the grounds of the Mother House in Lucan."

The cemetery was thickly covered with bushes of varying sizes and types—hawthorns, blackthorns, hazels, osiers, alders and the ubiquitous blackberry briars. Pauline, Mick and Kathleen followed Breen as he walked out into the middle of the plot. "I have looked for a marker of some kind that would say this is a burial ground," he said. "I didn't find one. But I know this is the school cemetery because Brother Boniface told me about it. Seventy-three boys are buried in here. At least one of them was murdered. As you can see from the overgrowth, this would seem to be the final effort by the Order of Saint Kieran to cover up the abuse some of their members inflicted on little boys. If none of the other children here are murder victims, then some of them probably died of disease, malnutrition, neglect, hunger, or even broken hearts—if that's possible. There have been reports from graduates of industrial schools that some children hanged themselves in despair. But that has never been proved."

"According to the death certificates issued before Doctor McNulty gave free rein to Lazarian, three died from strangulation," McGovern said.

Breen raised his eyes to Pauline. "A church-state system that drove children to commit suicide…what a terrible failure." He shuddered. Then marshalling his reserves of strength, he said, "I am going to be arrested now. I would hope that *The Telegraph* will uncover everything it can about what led to these boys being buried here. And you can use the story of Michael and me to personalize the suffering endured by all the children who got entangled in the system created by the hubris of bishops and the weakness of politicians."

"We'll do that, Tom," Pauline said. She put her hand on his arm. Mick McGovern stood on Breen's other side. Kathleen moved away.

From the near distance they heard a voice shouting, "Tom!"

When Breen called back, his voice was surprisingly weak. "Over here, Jimmy. Come down along the evergreen hedge."

Breen looked over to the gate, and the others followed his sight line.

A guard walked into the cemetery followed by Detective Sergeant Jimmy Gorman. Then Superintendent Christy Donovan came in, followed by another man in uniform. As if posing for a photograph, the four of them stood in a line, the gardai on the ends, all with their hands behind their backs. Twenty feet away, the two reporters and Tom Breen stood in a row facing them.

Gorman raised a hand to his shoulder and said, "Tom."

Breen raised a hand to his shoulder and said, "Jimmy."

Kathleen Hayes clicked.

Acknowledgments

My thanks to Superintendent Christy McCarthy, Garda
Síochána (retired), for his patient assistance with garda
protocols and procedures.

Superintendent Denis Bowe graciously gave me permission to visit Tullamore Garda Station, and Detective
John Walsh was my excellent guide. I also appreciate
the assistance of Gerard Lovett, general secretary of the
Garda Retired Members Association.

I am also grateful to Anne-Marie Hourigan, always
patient researcher and cheerleader. Patricia Kavanagh,
Fidelma McEvoy, Larry McGuire and Jim Hourigan
facilitated a tour of Saint Fintan's Psychiatric Hospital,
Portlaoise. Mellissa Brodrick was my guide in the now-
closed Saint Conleth's Reformatory for Boys in Daingean,
County Offaly. Kieran O'Donohue conducted me around
the grounds and buildings of the former Saint Joseph's
Industrial School, Letterfrack, County Galway, and related
stories of times past. Mary McCarthy Hourigan directed
me to the site of the Baltimore Industrial School.

The following people provided valuable information: Cathy Carman, sculptor; Marie Gormley Hourigan,
solicitor; Darren Deegan, wrestler; Theresa Hourigan,
public health nurse; Bernadette Keating, photographer;
Seamus Deegan, linguist; Joan and Seamus Clarke, readers; Chuck Mansfield, Latinist; Annemarie Ní Churreáin,
Gaelic; Claire O'Brien, journalist and former guide at
Emo Court, County Laois; Kate O'Connor of Dingle,
translator; Eileen O'Duill, genealogist; Tina Phelan, Athlone Institute of Technology; Martha Phelan, oenology;

Steven Pinsky, M.D., Joanne Hourigan, Martha Hourigan, Bill Lalor, and Teresa Phelan were also of assistance. Denis Hernandez, computer expert, was very patient.

Marsha Swan's critical eye and helpful suggestions are gratefully acknowledged. Lyn Swierski's reading of the manuscript is very much appreciated.

My thanks to my sons Joseph and Michael for their unflagging encouragement.

I am thankful to the Achill Heinrich Böll Association for awarding me a residency in the Heinrich Böll Cottage, where part of *Nailer* was written.

I am grateful to the Tyrone Guthrie Centre at Annaghmakerrig for a residency during which the *Nailer* manuscript was chiseled, sandpapered, and polished.

I am also grateful to the Christopher Isherwood Foundation for its recognition and generous financial support.

Special thanks to my wife, Patricia, for a first read, numerous edits, and many excellent suggestions and for her unending patience and encouragement.

Glossary

amadán: fool, idiot, eegit.

amen't I?: Am I not?

Artane Industrial School: industrial school in Artane, County Dublin, administered by the Irish Christian Brothers.

aten: eating.

Baltimore Industrial School: in County Cork; administered by diocesan priests; arguably the cruelest of all the industrial schools.

ban, bangharda: female garda. *Ban* is singular of *mná*, a word seen on the door of public toilets in Ireland.

beastings: colostrum; cow's thick, creamy yellow milk produced immediately after she has given birth.

bet: beat. *I bet him with my ashplant.*

betimes: sometimes.

Biggles: nickname of James Bigglesworth, adventurer in boys' books by W. E. Johns.

bog accent: a flat midlands accent with a lack of *t*'s, *th*'s and- *ing*'s and with overall poor enunciation.

bollicks: nasty curmudgeon. A man may be classed a bollicks for a multitude of reasons; not a nice appellation to be saddled with. *He's a pure bollicks.*

Bord na Móna: Bog Board; government department overseeing the harvesting of peat for fuel.

boreen: narrow, unpaved lane.

bot fly: insect that lays its eggs on horses; its larvae bore through horses' hides.

Boys in the Park: the computerized intelligence department of the Gardai Síochána headquartered in the Phoenix Park, Dublin.

Brain Trust, the Brains: the forensic department in the Garda Síochána.

Bulmer's Sedona: nonalcoholic drink.

C.F.A. form: Comprehensive First Assessment form used by the Health Board.

C.I.E. (Coras Iompar Eireann): literally, "travel around Eire"; Ireland's national transportation system.

Cadbury squirts: diarrhea.

Caliban: character in *The Tempest*; a malicious, ignorant and bestial man.

C.V.: curriculum vitae, résumé.

Ceide Fields: ancient settlement in Mayo now overgrown by peat bog.

chancer: someone willing to try anything he might have the slightest chance of getting away with.

codding: kidding; pulling a leg. *I'm only codding you.*

collators: profilers of criminals.

Comiskey, Brendan: Bishop of Ferns in County Wexford, 1984-2002.

cratur: creature; old dear. *The poor oul cratur.*

Crimson Petal and the White, The: a novel by Michel Faber.

Dail: Irish parliament. Pronounced "dawl."

Diggers: the electronic researchers in *The Telegraph* office.

Dorothy L. Sayers novel: *The Unpleasantness at the Bellona Club.* The unpleasantness was the murder of a ninety-year-old general in the genteel Bellona.

doul wan: the old one; the old woman. Used disparagingly.

dry cow: cow that is not being milked because she is very pregnant.

Dublin jackeen: derogatory name for a native of Dublin City.

dunghill: heap of farmyard manure.

dunghill cock: a strutting and showy rooster (or man) that will run away from a fight with a pure-bred cock.

dure: door.

eegit: idiot.

et: ate. *I et the face off him* means *I gave him a severe dressing down.*

fag: cigarette.

fairy rath: fairy fort; circular ruins of an ancient homestead once believed to have belonged to the fairies. Some consider it unlucky to interfere with the trees and other growth in a rath.

Ferns Report: report on sexual abuse by some of the Catholic clergy in the diocese of Ferns in Wexford. This inquiry was chaired by Francis D. Murphy and the report was presented to the Minister for Health and Children in October 2005.

Finn's salmon: legend; whoever tasted this particular salmon first would be given the gift of wisdom. Finn McCool (Fionn mac Cumhaill), as a child, received the gift when he touched the cooked fish, burned his finger, and put his finger in his mouth for relief.

gae bolg: legend; literally, spear of the gut; weapon of last resort used by the mythical Cú Chullain against his friend Fergal; the spear was attached to the foot and flung with unstoppable force against an enemy.

Garda Síochána: literally, the civic guards. Ireland's national police force. Pronounced "GAR-dah shee-a-CAW-na."

garda, guard: policeman.

gardai: plural of **garda.** Pronounced gar-dee.

gas: fun.

gob: mouth.

gobshite: nasal mucus; bollicks; an underhanded person. *He's a real gobshite.*

grain of a dung fork: tine of a fork used in the removal of animal waste. A dung fork has four grains.

grey crow or **hooded crow**: eats carrion, small animals, and chicks of various feather.

Guerin, Veronica: Irish reporter murdered in 1996 while single-handedly investigating drug dealers in Dublin. Despite having been shot in the leg by her enemies and threatened if she continued her work, she dismissed the police protection that had been assigned to her.

Guy Fawkes: a Catholic, he tried to blow up the English parliament and the king in 1605.

hape: heap.

Haughey, Charles: three-time prime minister of Ireland (1979-81, 1982, 1987-92).

hay knife: two-foot blade with a T-handle, used for cutting "benches" in a hay rick; the bench was a manageable "slice" of hay.

hoovering: vacuuming. The Hoover company is an English manufacturer of vacuums.

hoult, holt: restraints. An animal in holt is entangled in painful restraints.

hure: whore. Not necessarily a female. This appellation is often applied to a man who is a real bollicks.

hurler: a man who plays the Irish sport of hurling.

Irish twins: two children born to the same mother in less than twelve months.

Jekyll, Gertrude: English garden designer, writer and artist (1843–1932).

Kennedy Report: 1970 government report on the state of Ireland's industrial schools.

Knock: site of a religious shrine in County Mayo.

lodged: as in *The barley was lodged.* When the straws of the barley were beaten flat to the ground by rain and wind, they were difficult or impossible to harvest.

lorry: truck.

McColgan, Joseph: Sligo man sentenced in 1995 to twelve years in prison for physically and sexually abusing his own children for seventeen years.

Meccano: children's erector set.

messages: groceries. *She's gone to town for the messages.*

morning star: medieval weapon with a metal, spiked ball on the end of a short handle or chain.

nanny: chamber pot.

Nous lépreux ("We lepers"): Father Damien of Molokai reputedly addressed his congregation of lepers this way after he himself was diagnosed with leprosy.

Pádraig: Irish for *Patrick.*

Parietes habent aures: The walls have ears.

Paud: nickname for *Patrick.*

pig ring: open, circular piece of metal painfully squeezed into a pig's nose to keep it from rooting. Pigs dig up the ground with their snouts when they smell truffles beneath.

piñata: a suspended cardboard animal, often filled with candy, broken open by blindfolded children wielding sticks at parties in Latin America.

plainer: a garda working out of uniform.

playing chicken: a foolish "game" in which two drivers race head-on toward each other; whoever veers away at the last second is the chicken.

Plunkett, Oliver: Irish Catholic martyr, hanged, drawn and quartered at Tyburn in London in 1681. Canonized in 1975.

press: built-in or free-standing cupboard for clothes, books, etc.

puhum: put him. *I puhum in his place, the old bollicks.*

Pulse (Police Using Leading Systems Effectively): computer system for national police communication dealing with crimes.

punter: policeman's term for a member of the public.

quare: queer, meaning odd.

reed thatching: thatching with reeds as opposed to straw.

RTE: Radio Telefís Eirean, Radio and Television of Ireland.

Saint Conleth's Reformatory for Boys: school in Daingean, County Offaly, for boys in trouble with the law.

Saint Mary Bethlehem: the first hospital for the insane, opened in Bishopsgate, London, 1403.

scollop: thin, pliable sapling used in thatching.

scutter: watery feces of an animal, bird, or human.

shag: mild form of *fuck*.

shagger: mild form of *fucker*, but without sexual connotations.

Sin a bfuil go fóil, a cairde: "That's all for now, my friends." Pronounced "shin a will go foal a cord-je."

sínte: accent over a vowel in the Irish language.

skib: basket; Danish for *vessel.*

slane: tool for cutting turf; a spade with a wing on it; cuts the turf into the shape and size of a loaf of bread.

Slieve Bloom: mountain range straddling the border of counties Laois and Offaly in Ireland's central plain.

slurry: a mixture of cow dung and urine spread on fields as fertilizer. Can be smelled at long distances. Cures tuberculosis if the lungs do not collapse first.

stook, stookawn: idiot, gullible fool. *He's a ferocious stook.*

Strongbow: nickname of Richard de Clare; representing the English king Henry II, he came to Ireland as an invited guest in 1170.

taoiseach: Irish prime minister. Pronounced "tea-shock."

tay: tea.

Te Deum laudamus: You, God, we praise.

that one: usually applied to a woman whom the speaker dislikes.

thrashing, threshing: producing results; in good health. *How ya doen, Paddy? Thrashin' Mick, sure I'm thrashin'.*

tick: thick, stupid. *He's terrible tick.*

tip: rubbish dump.

Tuatha dé Dana: the people of the goddess Dana, one of the early mythological invaders of Ireland, who arrived on dark clouds.

turban punishment: In some industrial schools a boy who wet the bed was made to wear his wet night attire around his head like a turban.

Valley of the Squinting Windows, The: 1918 novel by Brinsley MacNamara.

wellies, wellington boots: knee-high rubber boots, named after the Irish-born Arthur Wellesley (1769–1852), the duke of Wellington.

white pudden: white pudding, a kind of sausage made with oatmeal and pork.

Ypsilanti: city in Michigan in the United States.

yoke: thing. Can be applied to anything whose name the speaker cannot remember. Also used disparagingly of people: *Isn't that fellow a dreadful yoke?*

your man, yer man: a man whose name the speaker cannot remember.

Select Bibliography

Aalen, F. H. A., Kevin Whelan, and Matthew Stout, eds. *Atlas of the Irish Rural Landscape*. University of Toronto Press, Toronto, 1997.

Arnold, Bruce. *The Irish Gulag: How the State Betrayed Its Innocent Children*. Gill & Macmillan, Dublin, 2009.

Bettelheim, Bruno. *The Uses of Enchantment,* Vintage, 1989.

Doyle, Paddy. *The God Squad.* Corgi Books, London, 1989.

Finklehor, David. *Child Sexual Abuse: New Theory and Research*. Free Press. New York, 1984.

Goulding, June. *A Light in the Window*. Poolbeg Press, 1999.

Harris, Michael. *Unholy Orders: Tragedy at Mount Cashel*. Penguin, 1991.

Kearney, John. *From the Quiet Annals of Daingean*. Daingean, County Offaly, 2006.

McGee, Garavan, de Barra, Byrne, and Conroy. *The SAVI Report: Sexual Abuse and Violence in Ireland*. Liffey Press, 2002.

McKay, Susan. *Sophia's Story*. Gill & Macmillan, Dublin, 1998.

Murphy, Buckley, Joyce. *The Ferns Report*. The Stationery Office, Dublin, 2005.

O'Mahony, Alfie. *Reminiscences of Life in Baltimore Industrial School*. Carraig Print, Carrigtwohill, Co. Cork, Ireland.

O'Malley, Kathleen. *Childhood Interrupted*. Virago, London, 2005.

Reformatory and Industrial Schools Systems Report, 1970 (Kennedy Report). Stationery Office, Dublin, 1970.

Sipe, A. W. Richard. *Preliminary Expert Report*.

Sipe, A. W. Richard. *Sex Priests and Power: Anatomy of a Crisis.* Brunner/Mazel, New York, 1995.

Touher, Patrick. *Fear of the Collar: My Terrifying Childhood in Artane.* O'Brien Press, Dublin, 2001.

Tyrrell, Peter. *Founded on Fear.* Irish Academic Press, Dublin, 2006.

About the Author

Tom Phelan is the author of the novels *The Canal Bridge,* *In the Season of the Daisies, Derrycloney,* and *Iscariot.* Born and raised on a farm in Mountmellick, County Laois, in the Irish midlands, he now makes his home in New York. For additional information, see www.tomphelan.net.

Made in the USA
Charleston, SC
17 July 2011